Magical Girl Raising Project

breakdown

I

Asari Endou

Illustration by

Marui-no

Characters

Miss Marguerite
Can bend straight objects.

Love Me Ren-Ren
Anyone she shoots with her magic bow will fall head over heels in love.

Nephilia
Can hear the voices of dead people.

Dreamy☆Chelsea
Can freely control stars.

Pastel Mary
Can materialize the sheep she draws with her pastels.

MAGICAL GIRLS

Tepsekemei
Can become one with the wind to go anywhere.

7753
Uses magic goggles that tell her all about her targets.

Clantail
Can transform the lower half of her body into different animals.

Clarissa Toothedge
Knows the location of any object she's bitten.

Maiya
Fights with a magic staff that beats liars.

Rareko
Can fix things that are broken.

Mana

John Shepherdspie

Touta Magaoka

Navi Ru

Yol

Ragi Zwe Nento

Agrielreymwaed Quarky

14

Asari Endou

Illustration by Marui-no

NEW YORK

Magical Girl Raising Project, Vol. 14
Asari Endou

Translation by Jennifer Ward
Cover art by Marui-no

MAHO SHOJYO IKUSEI KEIKAKU breakdown (first part) by Asari Endou, Marui-no
Copyright © 2021 Asari Endou, Marui-no
Original Japanese edition published by Takarajimasha, Inc., Tokyo.
English translation rights arranged with Takarajimasha, Inc. through Tuttle-Mori Agency, Inc., Tokyo.

English translation © 2022 by Yen Press, LLC

Yen On
150 West 30th Street, 19th Floor
New York, NY 10001

Visit us at yenpress.com
facebook.com/yenpress
twitter.com/yenpress
yenpress.tumblr.com
instagram.com/yenpress

First Yen On Edition: October 2022
Edited by Carly Smith & Yen On Editorial: Rachel Mimms
Designed by Yen Press Design: Liz Parlett

Yen On is an imprint of Yen Press, LLC.
The Yen On name and logo are trademarks of Yen Press, LLC.

Library of Congress Cataloging-in-Publication Data
Names: Endou, Asari, author. | Marui-no, illustrator. |
Keller-Nelson, Alexander, translator. |
Ward, Jennifer, translator.
Title: Magical girl raising project / Asari Endou ; illustration by
Marui-no ; translation by Alexander Keller-Nelson and Jennifer Ward.
Other titles: Mahâo Shâojo Ikusei Keikaku. English
Description: First Yen On edition. | New York, NY : Yen On, 2017–
Identifiers: LCCN 2017013234 | ISBN 9780316558570 (v1 : pbk) |
ISBN 9780316559911 (v2 : pbk) | ISBN 9780316559966 (v3 : pbk) |
ISBN 9780316559997 (v4 : pbk) | ISBN 9780316560085 (v5 : pbk) |
ISBN 9780316560108 (v6 : pbk) | ISBN 9781975358631 (v7 : pbk) |
ISBN 9781975386603 (v8 : pbk) | ISBN 9781975386627 (v9 : pbk) |
ISBN 9781975386641 (v10 : pbk) | ISBN 9781975386672 (v11 : pbk) |
ISBN 9781975335441 (v12 : pbk) | ISBN 9781975339098 (v13 : pbk) |
ISBN 9781975348014 (v14 : pbk)
Subjects: | CYAC: Magic—Fiction. | Computer games—Fiction. |
Social media—Fiction. | Competition (Psychology)—Fiction.
Classification: LCC PZ7.1.E526 Mag 2017 | DDC [Fic]—dc23
LC record available at https://lccn.loc.gov/2017013234

ISBNs: 978-1-9753-4801-4 (paperback)
978-1-9753-4802-1 (ebook)

1 2022

LSC-C

Printed in the United States of America

Contents

Go ahead!!

A certain distinguished mage lost his life due to an accident during an experiment. This great man had lived a long life, creating countless spells and items, and the people of the Magical Kingdom mourned his loss.

A few months after his death, his representative began sending invitations to his surviving relatives. The invitations instructed people to come to a little uninhabited island the deceased had used as his getaway/laboratory. There were also some conditions written on said invitations.

They read:

Identical letters have been sent to all those with the right of inheritance.
It will be decided at the designated location who will inherit the estate of the deceased.
Those who fail to respond to this invitation will lose the right of inheritance.
Each heir is to bring a maximum of two magical girls to accompany them.

Mana had received a letter as one of these potential heirs, and though she was suspicious about its content, after careful consideration, she contacted two magical girls with whom she was close…

PROLOGUE

If you said the official title of the place, which was prefixed with the name of the founder—"The Pos Rapvu Deim Multipurpose Disaster Management Laboratory"—some mages wouldn't know what you meant, but if you said only, "the Lab," they'd nod, going, *Ah, that place.* Some would be frightened, some would look away, and some would put on polite smiles.

Ever since the age of legend when the first mage had created the Magical Kingdom, as many organizations as there were stars had been created to research the magical craft that was the foundation of the nation itself. And of these organizations, the Lab had the worst reputation.

Rumors said they performed heinous human experiments that ignored laws and ethics, and those rumors were further exaggerated in the telling. The place wasn't actually that awful, and the fear was beyond the reality. But the people at the Lab didn't deny the rumors—in fact, they took advantage of them to establish their image. It was useful to them, and it pushed negotiations to their advantage.

"We're aware of the rumors that we're cruel and inhuman and all that, but do those who lambaste us for emotional reasons understand what's going on at ground zero? We're just highly flexible, making the best choices we can in order to do what needs to be done," the higher-ups at the Lab would say, flattering themselves while they were at it.

They were, in fact, flexible. They could pull off things that other more respectable research organizations wouldn't be able to do, since their pride would get in the way. If it looked like they wouldn't be able to manage something themselves, they would turn right around and go bow their heads elsewhere to seek their aid. Even for major projects that could turn the tides among the factions, they wouldn't fixate on making the product entirely in-house. That was how the Lab operated.

This project had already gone through a mountain of iterations and failures. No matter how they switched up the methods or the equipment, it was clear to everyone that it was far from success—here is where the Lab showed its flexibility. If they couldn't accomplish it themselves, they just had to get help from someplace else.

Chosen from multiple candidates was a mage named Lyr Cuem Sataborn. He was at an age when he would see a mage hailed as an old veteran from the Lab as still a young sprout. However, he was brimming with youthfulness in his own way, and he had inspiration.

Sataborn used the wealth he'd inherited from family generations for hobby experimentation. But despite engaging in experiments and research from such an untroubled and carefree position, he covered all the necessary fields on his own. Such a feat could normally not be accomplished outside of the social framework for it, and without any expertise or anything, you wouldn't be allowed involvement in scholarship. The most you could expect would be to have your master scold you, saying if you did something like that, it would never get properly finished.

But Sataborn had had no master to get angry with him, and formidably enough, his abilities were generally acknowledged.

Ever since his youth, he'd been praised as a mage who could do anything—the sort of genius who hadn't been seen since the dawn of the Magical Kingdom—and when it came to his ability to develop new magical formulas in particular, it was no exaggeration to say his skills were incomparable. And those skills of his never declined even as he got on in years; Sataborn was still actively developing new magical formulas that enlivened the industry.

There was no question of Sataborn's competence, but that wasn't to say there were no issues. Others claimed he was awfully eccentric and pigheaded. If he was completely off the rails and couldn't be controlled at all, there would be no point in hiring him. An intelligence unit under the employ of the Lab set out to investigate Sataborn's character.

Sataborn was satisfied so long as he was doing research. He wouldn't even express anger if his results were stolen from him, moving straight to his next project and astonishing the others around him.

He'd had a lover once, but he wasn't the one who had pursued it out of wanting her. Rather, she'd marched herself in on him before disappearing not long after having a child. Was that because she'd gotten sick of him or because she'd been worried her child might also be used for experiments?

Sataborn would never laugh at anyone's jokes. But then he would sometimes smirk to himself over nothing at all.

Someone could be right there, but if Sataborn wasn't interested in them, he wouldn't notice them. It wasn't that he deliberately ignored people, but he truly didn't realize they were there.

If someone was able to chat with him, that would tell you they were an excellent researcher. They had to be, or the conversation would never happen.

Sataborn had once been so into an experiment that he'd forgotten to eat and had almost died. Then he had developed a spell for nutritional replenishment, eliminating the danger of starvation.

He didn't seem to value his own life, performing dangerous

experiments on himself. When people tried to stop him, he would look at them curiously as if to ask why.

After going a long time without seeing his brother, Sataborn even forgot what he looked like, asking him, "Who are you?"

He'd go so long without bathing that the smell would build up in his room. One time, a maid carelessly opened the door of his research lab and was hit full-on by the stench and passed out.

It was also not uncommon for him to turn his back on ethics. He had once attempted to buy illegal magic items from a suspicious pawnshop, and the authorities were still monitoring him as a result.

The more someone looked into him, the more awful things came up. Everyone asked about him seemed both aggravated and yet also enthused to talk about just what an eccentric Sataborn was.

He wouldn't be easy to deal with—but he was too valuable not to make use of. Maybe one had to use a researcher this extraordinary in order to create something new that had never before existed. Besides, it wasn't a bad thing for him to be the type to be satisfied so long as he had research to do. That was far preferable to an unwisely ambitious mage who would try to get into their business.

The Lab often used the fact that they were feared to make outsourcing requests that amounted to intimidation or blackmail, but such methods probably wouldn't work on Sataborn. It would be a disaster if they were to offend him through such careless means. Nonetheless, bowing their heads deeply and offering a huge stack of cash probably wouldn't make him listen and acquiesce, either.

The faction had many meetings about the matter but never quite came to a conclusion, moving one step forward and two steps back as time passed in vain. Eventually, they even got sick of meetings, and when the chair said, at this point, why not just toss everything off on him, everyone leaped on that idea and decided that for now, they might as well ask what Sataborn's conditions were.

It turned out they were simple and straightforward: arrange

the research facilities to his demands. He would do everything on his own. No interference or complaints.

Not many mages could demand this much from *the* Lab, but this was *the* Lyr Cuem Sataborn. He was the kind of eccentric who might say anything out of the ordinary, so you could even say they were grateful he'd come up with such basic demands.

For the time being, they made it look like they'd left everything to him, kept him under observation as needed, and put him to work. As such, Sataborn received a single island as a research facility.

CHAPTER 1
THOSE GATHERED

The island was blanketed in green. Aside from the rocky area of the cape that jutted out from the north end, the beach that stretched out a long ways on the south side, and the residence in the style of a stone castle situated right in the middle, it was mostly covered in vegetation. A man sighed as he peeled his eyes away from a tapestry depicting a bird's-eye view of the whole island. He appeared to be somewhat over the hill of middle age, but he was plumper than one might expect of a middle-aged man. His belly was portly enough to slow him down a bit, for one thing, but he wasn't sighing over his weight. This room was so messy, it made him want to cover his eyes.

He rolled up the sleeves of his robe and thrust his right hand outside the room, moving his thumb like he was rubbing his index finger between the second joint and the tip. With a weak snapping sound, the chair slid aside, the bed tilted over, and all the empty bottles, metal parts, and balled-up parchment piled atop them fell to the floor. The carpet balled up around it all and swept it into the garbage along with the dust. More dust still hung in the air, but the room was tidy enough.

The room was small: about ten feet to each side—practically a closet. The stone walls were bare and gray. The tapestry hanging there featured an illustration of the whole island. Large, heavily locked glass windows invited the light of the moon and stars into the room. The rough-hewn wooden table and chair were knotty, and atop them had been left a feather pen, stationery, inkwell, and blotting paper, plus herb-scented candles in a candelabra and other necessary writing tools.

The man nodded in satisfaction and inhaled a small breath. He smelled dust.

Standing by the window, he pulled out a key ring and used three keys to open up the lock, struggling with the rusty door. Grumbling to himself about how it needed oiling, he moved to the window and opened it with both hands. There was the forest below, with its green continuing to the edge of the island, and beyond that stretched only the endless dark-blue ocean until the horizon. The sound and smell of the tides breezed into the room, ridding it of the dusty odor, and now it smelled fully of the seashore. The scent of the night wind was even saltier, and it was cold on the skin. Though this island was hot in the afternoon, the evenings were shockingly frigid. The man held his rotund body and shivered a little, but he didn't close the windows.

This room had once belonged to an eccentric researcher who must have thought the scent of the briny ocean, the splashing sound of the waves, the cold of the wind, and everything else were entirely unnecessary distractions. He had certainly seen this room, isolated by magic, as the most comfortable place to spend his time, with no need for meals, sleep, or relieving himself. Immersing himself in research and experiments had been his joy. Anyone who had known the man would agree to that with confidence and say that was exactly so.

The rotund man currently standing in the room was the nephew of that researcher. He was not a researcher himself. He neither immersed himself in independent research like his uncle, nor did he work a steady job. He was a self-styled high-class man of leisure, living his life seeking pleasure and good food. Not all mages were seekers of truth dedicating themselves body and soul to the development of magic. If you were to ask his uncle, who had been single-minded in his research, his nephew was an "ordinary lout who simply used the great works of our ancestors without attempting to move beyond them," but the nephew in question had always declared with arrogant indifference that one who lived as a high-class man of leisure would always suffer harsh criticism.

This man was not a pragmatist, as mages were wont to be. The smallness of the room, the smell of the ocean, the sound of the waves, the cold of the wind, hunger, fatigue—all the unnecessary inconveniences his uncle had eliminated as unpleasant impurities, this man actually thought were elegant. It wasn't bad at all to be forced into inconvenience. Starting a fire with a primitive incendiary device could be more fun than creating a flame with a single command word.

His uncle had said that being able to enjoy inconvenience was the arrogance of the upper classes—that those who were right in the middle of actual misfortune would prefer mages who prioritized efficiency, thereby directing the world toward a better future. There was some truth to that. But if this was arrogance, this man was fine with arrogance. The most important thing was how it felt to him. When it had been his uncle's place, he'd been able to run things how he pleased. There was no need to stick to his uncle's ways now that the man was gone.

Nevertheless, he had to fulfill the directions of his uncle's will, at least. The man sat down in the chair and was about to pick up a pen when there was a knock on the door. He looked up. "Come in."

The door opened with a creak. That would have to be oiled, too.

The magical girl he'd hired the other day bobbed her head in a bow. "The annex...wait, is that what you'd call an annex?"

"Yes, it's an annex."

"Right. I finished cleaning the annex."

Between the woolen dress and woolen hat, her costume was fluffy all over. Long sleeves covered her whole arms, and the voluminous fur went over her wrists, too. She wore tights as well, making for a very modest outfit. The man had an almost superstitious bias that "magical girls generally wear revealing attire," but he also thought that precisely because the majority of them were like that, there was a special value to a modestly dressed magical girl. There was something mysterious about it that was difficult to even verbalize—things like that were just for an aesthetic. Regardless, there was no need to put all that into words. It was a trivial matter that could be written off as "how it was to be a man of taste."

"Thanks," the man replied with a smile as he examined the girl. Her face was beautiful, of course. Her platinum-blond hair was cut short and even, with the unaffected sincerity of practically over fashion. In combination with the connoisseur point of modest dress, her evenly cut hair gave her a dignified air. That was also nice. This was a good kind of magical girl to have in your employ.

The sheep behind her went *baaah*, and she hastily attempted to restrain it as it struggled to escape. The combination of a beautiful girl and an adorable animal was very lovely indeed. He would forgive the animal smell and hoof marks on the carpet. There was nothing to be done about that.

The sheep bleated particularly loudly, shaking off the girl to race to the hallway. The motion flung the girl in a full somersault in the air. She tumbled down the stone corridor before smacking into the wall, and her shoddy attempt to catch herself caused her to crack the back of her head on the floor. The man lifted his large rear from the chair and extended his hand to the girl, who was lying on her back and trembling, with both hands against the back of her head.

"That was quite the ruckus. Are you all right?" the man asked.

The magical girl rose to her knees, then stood and waved her hands with a smile. "I'm okay… I'm actually really okay." That sounded convincing enough, but her eyes were swimming.

"You don't look very okay, though."

"I like drawing, you know."

"Mm-hmm. I hadn't heard that." When he looked to the

hallway, there was a large crack there he didn't think had been there before.

The girl's head was swaying like a pendulum, but for some reason, her words came out steadily. "But, but—! I can't make a living with just that, which is sad, you know?"

"Why are you telling me about this?"

"It's fine, though. I'm not thinking of this as just a part-time job for my free time, I'm really not thinking that, okay, I will work really hard for this job, I'll do my best… Urkkk, I'll do my best."

"Are you really all right? I know magical girls are resilient, but—"

"I'll do my best, do my best, do it do it, do it Mary do it hard you can do it." The girl bowed and closed the door. The sound of her footsteps grew distant.

He very much wanted her to do her best, but he didn't get the sense that everything was okay with her. The man waffled a little but then decided to trust her. She did seem interesting in her own way, and she was rather charming, too. Besides, magical girls were a sturdy bunch.

Well then, I'll write the letters to the heirs while I enjoy the poor thing's company, he thought as he adjusted his seat in his chair, faced the desk, and took up a pen. But before he could even put pen to paper, he noticed an issue. It was too difficult to do any writing with just the available moon and starlight. He wouldn't have enough visibility. The man flicked his index finger, igniting a magical light in hand to drive away the dark. A burst of magical illumination was a mere trifle, but he had no other options right now. He'd have to wait a bit for an alternative. The silver candelabra he'd made detailed orders to a craftsman for would really set this scene. He wanted to arrange the property's interior, exterior, and household items to his own tastes, bit by bit.

While occasionally furrowing his brow at the strange conditions the deceased had listed out—whatever did they have to have magical girls accompany them for?—the man's pen scribbled along.

◇ **Miss Marguerite**

A few winters ago, when the cold winds had been raging, a magical girl named Annamarie had passed away. It had not been an honorable death on the job, and neither had it been an abrupt, accidental death. She had challenged the employee of another department to a duel and been roundly beaten. It was a fairly dishonorable death as a fighter, a professional, and as a magical girl. Her employer, the Inspection Department, had scrambled wildly to clean it up.

While Annamarie had been working as a trainee inspector, she'd been under the guidance of Miss Marguerite, her combat instructor. Plenty of magical girls had trained in karate, judo, kendo, and other martial arts as humans, but combat was neither for sport nor a duel when it came to the Inspection Department. And not just the athletes—even those who had killed before would sometimes think of magical-girl battles as an extension of lethal combat between humans and consequently get themselves hurt. Those like Marguerite, who could train others in the basics of magical-girl combat, were valued wherever they went, and in the Inspection Department, she had a particularly vital role.

Many students had passed before Marguerite. Some of them had come to be called aces, while others followed her recommendation to transfer to office work. Some had fought with villains and died on the job, while others had been dragged into political conflict and mysteriously disappeared. Annamarie, however, had been the only one foolish enough to attack a magical girl from another department, get beaten instead, and lose her life.

Marguerite had gone under only some mild inquiry, purely as a formality, and her responsibility had never been questioned. That was why she had voluntarily written her resignation letter. She was so desperate to get Annamarie out of her head, and if she continued as an instructor, she wouldn't be able to avoid remembering her. Marguerite didn't listen to the superiors or past students who begged her to change her mind, abandoning everything to her successor to quit the department.

She hadn't done anything in particular since then, whittling down her savings to support her lifestyle.

Since quitting the Inspection Department, Marguerite had had more opportunities to eat out, but she'd stopped going to what you'd call high-class restaurants. There was no need to waste money on that if it wasn't for a business dinner with someone important on the department's dime. This particular occasion, however, might count as a business dinner with someone important, in a sense.

Marguerite looked out the window. The drizzle wet the gravel of the playground outside, the rain mild enough that it would be too much trouble to open an umbrella. Just looking made her depressed and fed up; her eyes returned to the room, to the girl there. Her apparent age was around fifteen. You couldn't call that young or old for a magical girl. Her attire was simple: black hair with straight bangs and a plain, long gray skirt, but the white dress shirt she wore was one size too small, restraining breasts that looked like they were about to pop out, and the way she left it open to the second button had punch. Back when Marguerite had first met her at the Inspection Department, as well as when Marguerite had retired from her post and they had regretfully parted ways, she'd always worn shirts of the wrong size. She had rolled the sleeves of this one up to her elbows.

She was gathering up a few strips of beef with one chopstick to pluck it up and stick it in the egg. Stuffing the meat in her mouth with a hearty voracity that belied her sweet and delicate appearance, she chewed slowly, then swallowed.

Marguerite looked away again, eyes shifting to the sliding screen. It was illustrated with a number of variations on a rabbit and frog launching pro-wrestling moves at each other in the style of ukiyo-e. Businesses that could be used openly by magical girls often had strange accents like this.

Marguerite faced forward. The girl stuffing her face with

sukiyaki was in front of her. Marguerite didn't like to remember the past. It always came with pain. This girl had been under her in the Inspection Department, and just seeing her made Marguerite remember the past and brought a steady burning in her heart. Remembering things she didn't want to remember was an unbearable suffering. Even if this girl had no ill will—even though Marguerite knew she wasn't a bad person—that didn't change how much the memories pained her.

"You're not gonna have any meat? It's so good, though," the girl said.

"I'll pass," Marguerite replied.

Someone whose mere sight made her remember unpleasant things was *right there*. Not knowing where to direct her gaze, Marguerite looked down at the hat she'd laid in her lap. The peacock feather decoration and silk veil were too fancy for everyday wear, but they were appropriate for a magical girl. Shifting her gaze slightly over, the rapier she'd left to her right caught her eye. She never, ever left it out of her reach.

"The meat's good, though. And soft," the girl told her.

"So even an old woman can enjoy it?"

"No talking about age."

"It's already too late for you."

"So you're not having any meat?"

Right now, Marguerite didn't have the appetite to put food in her mouth for pleasure. She nodded briefly and indicated her reservation with a raised palm as a way to prompt the girl to hurry up with her business.

The girl closed her eyes, nodded a few times, and blew out a breath in a deliberate fashion. "Ahhh, I'm only ever treated like I'm in the way, at home and at work. Even with you, when we haven't seen each other in so long."

"That's really not true."

"We were partners once. You could be a little more friendly, you know?"

What would she say if Marguerite was to reply that she thought coming all this way to see her fulfilled her obligation? "I've never been a friendly person."

"I know, I know. Well, it's fine. I don't mind brusque types like you."

"I get that often."

"There you go, so shameless about it."

"I get that often, too."

"Uh-huh. Well, I want to ask you a favor. I'll pay you for it, too. It's the type of thing that normally you wouldn't think is dangerous, but I can't promise it's completely safe. That means this job should be left to a veteran who won't be careless or show weakness. Since, unfortunately, someone who's just strong would underestimate the job and think like, *Nothing's gonna happen; this is boring.*"

"I haven't accepted this job."

"So you're planning to stay a hermit until you're dead?"

"I'm thinking once my savings have run out, I'll be forced to work because I want money."

"The heck, that sounds like a motive for a crime!" The girl snorted and then, once she'd soaked it in plenty of egg, bolted down some *shirataki.* "I heard you're still training to keep from getting rusty."

"I don't know who exactly gave you that idea, but even a hermit will get some minimal exercise."

"Well, maybe a magical girl will do that much."

"Yes, a magical girl will do that much."

"And if you're a magical girl, then of course you'll be helping people, too."

Marguerite's arching eyebrows came together in a frown.

That didn't seem to bother the girl, who cut her fried tofu into four equal cubes and proceeded to chew one quietly. "Come on, don't be so suspicious. It's not like I'm gonna ask you to terminate some criminals with extreme prejudice or resolve some dispute that can't be made public or anything like that. I just want you to help out a poor boy who has no one else to turn to. See, this is getting magical-girl-like."

"What are you talking about?"

"You sound eager now."

"I'm not."

"Since you want to hear about it so badly, I'll explain. A mage who's not from the administration has apparently died in an accident during an experiment. So everyone related to this guy who got accidented is gonna be getting together to talk about the inheritance. One of these heirs is a kid—a distant relative. He originally lived an ordinary life away from magic and everything, so that makes it difficult to hire a magical girl to guard him, but he apparently can't go without one."

"You want me to be his bodyguard?"

"All the magical girls of the Schoolroom, myself included, are crazy busy right now. We're all running around trying to manage training some unseasonal new hires. If I'm the only one taking time off work, I'll get stabbed. For real."

"The Schoolroom" was a nickname only used within the Inspection Department for the instruction team. Marguerite even wondered if there was some kind of reason to take on new people in the off-season. She laid her right hand over her lap. This wasn't a matter she should be thinking about.

"...There have to be lots of people outside of the Schoolroom who would want to repay a debt to an old teacher," said Marguerite.

"I don't think I should be sending off magical girls in public office for private business," the girl replied. "Plus, I feel bad standing by and letting capable personnel rot."

"Do you know what the word 'busybody' means?"

"Oh yeah. Maybe you should actually meet him, to see what kind of boy he is."

Marguerite had no time to voice her doubts. The girl cupped her right hand by her mouth and called out loudly toward the sliding screen, "You can come in!" As Marguerite turned around, the screen slid open.

She had sensed his presence and breathing behind the screen, so she'd known someone was there. A ten-year-old boy bowed his head energetically and cried out, "Nice to meet you!"

Formality demanded that Marguerite had to respond in kind, so she said, "Nice to meet you" as well, shooting the girl a mildly accusatory look.

The girl smiled completely shamelessly. "Hey, come join us for some sukiyaki."

"Can I? Phew. I've been smelling it only the whoooole time, y'know. That was so mean, when I'm hungry, geez." The boy shuffled over the tatami on his knees, eyes flicking to the girl's plunging neckline, then to the sukiyaki, then to Marguerite.

"This is the lady who's gonna be going with you," said the girl.

"Whoa-hoa, cool. Is that sword real? You're...a magical girl... right?" He stared at Marguerite's sword before he opened his mouth wide and breathed an *ohhhh*.

"And you're...?" Marguerite trailed off.

"Oh, I'm Touta. Touta Magaoka," the boy answered, puffing out his chest, and then he immediately changed his stance to lean forward with enthusiasm. He grabbed a bowl, and with the large serving of rice that was offered to him in hand as well, he scarfed down the meat, green onions, and Chinese cabbage that were served to him. "So, like. You're sorta like a hero who beats the bad guys. That's so cool."

"Well..."

"Yeah, yeah, this lady is really good at beating bad guys," the girl told him.

"Wow, that's so awesome!" Touta gushed. "So are rangers and riders and stuff real, too? Um, if you don't mind telling me?"

Annamarie had been the most energetic magical girl. No matter what obstacles were in her way or what insurmountable walls she slammed into, she'd never lost natural enthusiasm. Once she had become a member of an investigation team in the Inspection Department, she began researching the incident caused by Cranberry, the Musician of the Forest. She discovered that the death of a friend of hers had been caused by Cranberry's exam. After using the authority of Inspection to look up the magical girl who had murdered her friend in an exam, she'd challenged her to a fight and lost. The incident had been written off as an unjustified attempt at getting revenge for her friend, and Miss Marguerite had gotten sick of remembering it and so had left the department.

That individual had apparently been one of "Cranberry's children," having gone through one of her lethal exams, and she'd also been a part of the violent magical-girl group that was the Archfiend Cram School. Marguerite thought there had to be a way to fight her, but nobody was going to listen to her about that, and it wasn't as if she wanted to tell anyone about it anyway. It was just that thinking about her foolish student made things unbearable.

The boy looked excited. He was grinning from ear to ear as he competed with the girl to scramble for meat. Thinking of the student she'd once had who had been just as energetic as an elementary school boy, Marguerite made a smile that didn't go past her lips.

◇ Ragi Zwe Nento

Ragi had been shoved into the Magical Girl Management Department thanks to an incarnation of one of the Three Sages. Ragi had been against making a magical girl the incarnation and had even loudly criticized the idea.

A magical girl should only ever be an observer rather than in command. Diverting a craft designed purely with strength of the flesh and power of magic as opposed to another purpose was sheer blasphemy and faithlessness. What made a Sage a Sage was esteem for intellect and virtue over trivial attributes that could be expressed in numerical values.

The few comrades who had agreed with him had either given in to bribery or feared retribution; one by one, they were cut from the opposition. When Ragi had discovered that the friend who had sworn with him to fight this until the end had diverted information to the pro side, Ragi had quickly come to the realization he was helpless on his own, and so he had finally given in.

He was removed from the mainstream and distanced from research work. They started giving him a bureaucrat's tasks rather than a researcher's work, following which he received a notice of personnel change. "Your work was so good, we've decided to have you take the position officially," they said, words kind enough on the surface so that he couldn't refuse. This was how he had been driven into the do-nothing job of the head of the Magical Girl Management Department. The die had been cast.

This downward move was basically harassment. It wasn't like Ragi hadn't considered quitting. Even if getting a job with the Puk Faction was out of the question, he knew it would be possible to switch to the Caspar Faction and live more freely—or leave the service of the Magical Kingdom to retire. But both options were irritating in their own ways, essentially acknowledgments of his loss. Maybe it was a fact that he was a loser both objectively and subjectively, but admitting that was a separate issue.

Most of all, despite his fall from grace, Ragi still revered the Sage Chêne Osk Baal Mel. When he had seen Osk as a young mage, the Sage had been a majestic ball of light that warmed body and soul upon approach. And when the chief magician at the time had summoned Osk with her own flesh and blood as catalyst, she had become a Sage in the form of a peaceful, elegant elderly lady who gently guided lost mages and spoke of harmony with the world. But she had been unable to bear such a great and powerful spirit— when her body had faded, she had disintegrated along with it, still smiling.

It was nothing more than a sentimental memory, and that was what made it so irritating. A god who should have been the subject of reverence and awe was now made a toy to fools. Those people would say, "That's not true at all; we're endeavoring to have Master Osk manifest more powerfully," but if you asked Ragi, that didn't even fly as a pretense.

Loving and revering Osk, Ragi mourned the situation of the Sage while being enraged at his own. These negative feelings kept him from ever sitting still, and in his office at the Management

Department, the fires of his anger burned constant as he worked on. He managed the physical register of names of the magical girls, which changed day by day, and when occasionally mages or magical girls visited, he would allow them to peruse it if they had official permission, and he would shoo them away if they didn't. One magical girl coming around had basically been a thief looking to steal personal information. He had immediately reported her to Inspection, but they had never really cleared things up, telling him only that the incident "has been resolved."

Even if that was true, weren't rule breakers deserving of punishment? They said the thief, who was also known as the Magical-Girl Hunter, was still breaking rules to expose criminals. This fact made Ragi's rage burn all the brighter.

The physical names register had become more detailed than ever before after inheriting a vast amount of data, which he was told had been generated by the IT Department. It even kept record of a magical girl's special magic and an evaluation of her abilities. There were any number of ways for those with the inclination to abuse this information. Ragi could come up with ten or twenty in just a moment's consideration. Such information shouldn't even be used freely, let alone be stolen.

As a result, he upped the security in his office at the Management Department. He made it resistant to every kind of magic: teleportation, mind-reading, mind-control, scrying, informational analysis, bending of space, causal manipulation, concept alteration, dimensional leaps, limited-area control—and he drove away every single one of the ill-advised fools who showed up one after another. Since the theft by that Magical-Girl Hunter, he hadn't let even a single piece of information leak. His primary motivation was anger, and so long as he was head of the Magical Girl Management Division, that continued to well up indefinitely.

And so Ragi spent every day in his office at the Management Department, now made an independent space cut away to become an isolated island, surrounded by magical sigils floating in the air as he attempted to make it an indomitable fortress of invincible, absolute defense, continually polishing its security day and night until, one day, a letter came.

In a space with no up or down, surrounded by five formations of magical figures, Ragi picked up a white envelope. It had far too strong an air of "this world" for something used by mages. "What is this?" he demanded.

"I'm told...it's an invitation." The one to have brought this letter was, annoyingly enough, a magical girl. Her warm and fluffy-looking costume got on his nerves for some reason. In his head, he nicknamed her Sheep.

Responding with a snort, Ragi picked up the white, wax-sealed envelope.

Just by touching it, the information flowed into him. Ragi scowled. Scowling made him feel his deep wrinkles, which made his whole body tense up. He forced his stiff expression back to normal. Even just changing his expression was a struggle, compared to when he was young, but he didn't feel like doing something about it with magic.

The one to send this letter—Lyr Cuem Sataborn—was a mage who had lived for his hobbies. At the drop of a hat, he would be neck-deep in nothing but hobby experiments. Experiments upon experiments before all else. They were his number one priority, to the exasperation of everyone around him. He had no family, either. Avoiding association with people of character, among other things, had put him in a similar situation to Ragi, but since Sataborn had inherited family wealth, his fortune had gained him the right to deepen his research as he pleased and do what he wanted, living freely and at his whims without being tied down to organizations and factions like Ragi. Trace his family tree, and it went a ways back, and this meant his family had status. His family was associated with the Osk Faction, formally speaking, but Ragi had never heard of Sataborn working with them for anything. Sataborn's irresponsible lifestyle with no obligations did irritate him, but

Ragi also envied him. Though that envy was directly linked to that irritation.

"So he died... I see," Ragi muttered.

It was *apparently* true that he had died during an accident. Ragi closed his eyes and prayed for Sataborn's peace in the afterlife.

"But why would he leave anything to me?" Ragi wondered.

"I-I'm sorry," Sheep stuttered. "All I've been told is what was in the will..."

Had Sataborn felt sympathy for Ragi, thinking of him as a fellow outsider? It was hard to believe that Sataborn had privately respected him, but was there absolutely no possibility? All Ragi could say was that he didn't understand the mind of that eccentric researcher.

"But this is inscrutable," Ragi said.

"Um, yes?" Sheep answered timidly.

"Why is one of the listed conditions that I bring magical girls?"

"Well, um... I haven't been told the reason for that, either, so... I wonder. Maybe to attend to your personal needs or as a bodyguard...I suppose?"

Ragi scowled again, then tried to relax his expression once more, but it froze up in a slightly disgruntled look. "Wouldn't a homunculus or golem be enough?"

"There are a number of other heirs, and they're apparently going to be bringing magical girls with them... I really don't know about just one person not having them..."

What if only Ragi, who had a tenuous connection to the deceased, had homunculi accompanying him, while the other heirs brought magical girls? Imagining that, it did seem uncomfortable. Ragi struck the floor with his staff, and the cringing sheep girl trembled, gripping the fluffy cuffs of her sleeves.

Before she could say anything, Ragi ground his teeth. This was so vexing—*enraging*. "Just what do they think magical girls are? Items of personal status or accessories? Nonsense—what absolute nonsense for Sataborn to demand..."

Ragi thought it over despite his anger at the situation. He could procure some basic organic bodies. If you added only so much sense and comprehensiveness to remain short of generating an ego, wouldn't you be able to create something that looked sort of close enough? And then if he declared it a magical girl, and he could somehow squeak by...

"Um, you probably shouldn't do anything too strange...," Sheep said.

"What in the blazes?!" Ragi cried. "You scoundrel! Did you just read my mind?! Unbelievable. I need more security."

"No, I didn't read your mind... You were talking out loud."

His teeth grated audibly. It seemed he had to bring one, no matter what.

"I'd be too scared to read your mind now anyway...," Sheep muttered.

"What do you mean?"

"Well, um, I overheard things about that."

"Tell me what."

The sheep scrunched up her face like it was terribly difficult to say, then looked up, then to the side. It looked like she was searching for someone to save her, but there was nobody here but Ragi, and the sheep, and the magical figures. "Um... They're saying the Magical Girl Management Department is hot right now."

"Hot? What's that supposed to mean?"

"They're saying trying to steal trivial information from the Magical Girl Management Department has become a fad with magical girls who are good at these things... It's a competition called 'extreme information theft,' and people are even more excited about it because Magical-Girl Hunter has been the only one to ever succeed..."

Ragi's temperature above the neck shot up, making the sheep girl's face twist up into an even more pathetic display, following which she leaped out of the space a split second before Ragi could yell at her. On her way out, she struck her forehead on part of the barrier and went head over heels, hitting the back of her head, writhing in pain as she crawled the rest of the way.

What an incorrigible lot were these creatures known as magical girls. After chasing out the sheep, Ragi activated a searching spell. He was no longer thinking it absurd to bring a magical girl for private business, but it was still out of the question to misuse his authority as department head to order one to accompany him. So that meant hiring a freelancer, but Ragi had no such connections. There had been just one freelancer with a debt to him—her name had been Tot Pop—but she'd apparently joined an antiestablishment faction and had caused a prison break incident, during which she had died.

Ragi's thoughts began to get off track, wondering why she would do something foolish like that, and he cleared his throat loudly.

So then some other magical girl he knew personally. Not long ago, that number had been zero, but during the incident the other day at an event called "The Great Magical Girl Athletic Meet: Beef Broth–Flavored Rice Balls Included," he had become acquainted with a few. Of course, they were neither friends nor associates, and it would even be presumptuous to call them acquaintances, but it would be better than making a request of someone he didn't know at all.

Minus fifteen seconds later, which he could sense accurately via magical means, he discovered where all those magical girls were right now via the search spell. One of them was looking for a partner to compete in a ramen tag battle. Another was riding a lawn mower on a journey through a parallel world. And the others also seemed busy with jobs or missions and such, but the last one had no particular business, and her schedule was open. Thinking back, she spoke less and was more composed than other magical girls, and there wasn't much about her that could be annoying. It was fair to say she would be permissible to accompany him.

Ragi used a search spell to derive the contact information of the magical girl Clantail. He did sort of see this as an abuse of his position, but he shoved that thought into the corner of his brain, telling himself it was a trivial concern.

◇ Dreamy☆Chelsea

Just like many other magical girls, Chie Yumeno—Dreamy☆ Chelsea—was a fan of magical-girl anime. Chie's mother, Fuchiko, who said she'd been a magical girl before her marriage, had initially been charmed to see her daughter watching magical-girl anime. But before long, Chie's enthusiasm had exceeded what Fuchiko deemed acceptable as a parent. Chie watched magical-girl anime until her eyes became bloodshot; she refused to leave the TV, devouring VHS tapes until she wore them out, until her mother had scolded her—"Enough of this!"—and pulled her away.

That wasn't enough to stop Chie, who would get up in the middle of the night and wrap a blanket around the TV so she could watch without letting the light escape. When Fuchiko discovered her like this, she was more impressed than she was exasperated.

Such intense concentration had to be a talent. They said that those with the potential to be magical girls would occasionally manifest it in strange ways as humans, sometimes as incredible athleticism, memory, unusual appearance, or life spans so long they neared the limits of living creatures.

Fuchiko wasn't a career magical girl, but whenever she had the spare time between house chores and child-rearing—and when she didn't have the time, she would use her magical-girl abilities to make some—she would participate in magical-girl clubs and events, so she had a wide circle of friends. That was how she got a magical-girl scout she knew to check out her daughter and got the stamp of approval. "Your daughter has the aptitude to be a wonderful magical girl," she said, and Fuchiko felt quite keenly that you couldn't fight blood.

That was how Chie Yumeno became the magical girl Dreamy☆ Chelsea. Enveloped by the joy that a world of dreams and magic was actually real, she took her first step down the path of the magical girl.

And then the seasons changed, and the days flowed by…

"Look. You really need to cut this out."

"Mom…are you mad?"

"Of course I'm mad! How dare you tell me you don't want to get a job!"

"I mean…it's weird for a magical girl to get a job."

"It's not weird at all. All the characters from the anime you like have jobs. Like Cutie Healer and Star Queen. All those people are getting paid. I've even heard that Magical Daisy was going to college while also working part-time to support herself."

Chie rose up and faced her mother and puffed her cheeks out big and round. "I've told you over and over those aren't the ones I like! Those ones are all like...the kind who fight and stuff! That's no different from shounen manga or mecha anime! I like magical girls! Stories about cute girls helping people in trouble!"

Chie wouldn't say it had been better back in the day. That was because the magical girls Chie had loved since she was young were the old retro ones, the ones from the bygone days of the Showa-era '80s and earlier. However, like how the falling snow must always go away someday, that era was long gone. If not for reruns or video rentals, she never would have been able to see them at all.

But now was even worse. The magical girls Chie loved had gone even further away. No matter how much those "people who were more or less categorized as magical girls" raged about it, if you asked Chie, they weren't the real deal.

"My ambition is to be the kind of magical girl I love. Ever since I first became a magical girl, I've been helping people every day, and I'm not going to stop. If I get a job, it'll get in the way of magical-girl activities." With that impassioned speech, she clenched a fist, feeling the firm and strong will inside her that would never bend.

However, the look on her mother's face immediately struck her with the foreknowledge of her own bending. Chie shuffled back on her bottom, but the wall and windows were right behind her, and there was nowhere to run. Her mother, her face twisted in unbearable anger, stepped up to Chie and looked down on her. When she transformed, she looked like a charming little devil who delighted the eyes of those who saw her. But right now, she looked like a big devil.

Chie straightened her posture, shifting into a proper kneeling position. She placed her hands on her knees and stared straight ahead. "Um."

"How old are you this year?" her mother demanded.

"That has nothing to do with th—"

"How old are you?"

"Thirty...four."

"Would you like to know what the neighbors are saying about Chie from the Yumeno household?"

"No..."

"Get changed right now and go to the employment center."

"Yes..."

"It'll be fine. You'll manage it somehow—and enjoy yourself, too. That's how you always are."

"You're just saying that..."

"What was that?"

"Nothing..."

Chie didn't want to get a job. She thought a magical girl should only ever do magical-girl activities. If she wanted to make money, she would have to get a job, and if she got a job, that would mean responsibilities. She would start prioritizing her work responsibilities over her magical-girl activities, which didn't produce income, and her identity as a magical girl would fade.

With her desire to make being a magical girl her number one commitment, Chie had used every trick in the book to somehow get this far, but her mother's patience was reaching its limits.

She couldn't buy any more time. If she went any further, her mother would resort to force. Her mother knew a lot of people from being in the magical-girl clubs. Some kind of anachronistic route like being sent to a tuna fishery, a crab factory boat through some shady day-labor recruiter, gold panning, a labor camp, or a silk mill in the middle of nowhere might actually be real. She could even envision being introduced to some old man in his fifties with a child who was Chie's age and being told, *"Starting today, this man is your husband."*

There was no way out. Dragging her heavy legs, Chie headed for the employment center. She wanted to stop by a convenience store. Even a bookstore would do. She wanted to stand there and read. She wanted to kill some time. But there was nowhere to run. In the space between graduating from university until now, she had lost her avenues of escape.

The door of the employment center was too heavy for a thirty-year-old woman who didn't get enough exercise. While she was dragging her heels around the entrance, a middle-aged man in a suit opened the door for her. Giving him a smile like, *"Ahhh, both of us have it rough, huh?"* she went inside and followed the directions she got at the front desk to fill out some registration card. As expected, she left a lot blank. Saying, "It's so tough when there's a lot of blank spots, huh," she turned her self-deprecation to humor in a chat with the lady at the reception desk, who recommended that for people like her, there was a "support program for gaining skills useful for employment," and so she decided to participate.

In what looked like a meeting room, together with a young person of university age, a housewife-looking middle-aged woman, a homeless-looking man with a big backpack, and various others, Chie listened to a sort of lecture. The bearded man sitting next to her complimented her interesting clothes—*Miko-chan* T-shirt with a four-kanji word that was written wrong, like the kind a foreigner would wear—and she got some cookies. A bunch of the others were pulling out notebooks and writing things down, which made her panic, so she went back to the reception to borrow a notepad and ballpoint pen from the lady there. *It was something like this back in college, right?* she thought as she jotted down whatever seemed important. Apparently, it was a good idea to get your bookkeeping qualification, just in case.

Talking with the older man about how "there's actually a lot that goes into a job search, huh," figuring next they'd search on the computer, they got the lady at the reception desk to teach the two of them. The older man was struggling, but it wasn't difficult for Chie. At home, she was either on the computer, in magical-girl form and using her magic to play, watching anime, eating or sleeping, or reading manga. She was already a computer veteran with more than twenty-five years of experience—a computer guru, basically. Once she discovered how to turn on a new machine, she could do anything with it.

Salary, sponsors, conditions, people who could use key macros, people who could program, people who had driver's licenses— there was a lot of information, but nothing seemed like what she was looking for. It wasn't like she really had any qualifications or experience she could brag about, so compromise would of course be necessary. The easiest thing would be to search for the best conditions possible of those who seemed like they might hire her, but that also kind of gave her the feeling she'd get caught in something exploitative or nasty. Chie was definitively lacking in social experience, after all. Looking beside her, she saw the old man had apparently figured things out and was repeating, "I see, I see," while double-clicking. Great.

Her eyes happened to drop to her right hand, on the mouse. Her dark-pink nails reflected the fluorescent lights. She exhaled through her nose, then scrolled downward. Zoning out, staring at the screen, she thought about what she would do after this. She'd stop by the convenience store to check out the new snacks and ice cream on sale. Her mother wouldn't complain about her dillydallying around on the way home if Chie claimed she was rewarding herself. But if she was going to make that argument, she'd need to come up with some results. Had it been three days ago when her mother had mentioned that she was looking quite plump? She could make up some sloppy lie, but her mother would see through it. When her mother got serious, she was relentless in checking every detail of the story. It was probably pointless to try.

Thinking about her mother only made Chie depressed. She'd think about something else. Oh yeah, if she was going to check out the snacks, then she wanted to stand at the store and read manga magazines, too. Would that manga that was often on hiatus be in it or not? If it was, that would give her the energy to live on. While giving deep consideration to these matters, she scrolled along until, eventually, her fingers on the mouse stopped.

Chie slightly narrowed her right eye. There was some orange

text in large font that looked blatantly abnormal. Even more abnormal about it was the term "magical girl."

She scrolled down. More appeared.

Recruiting magical girls.
Only those with magical-girl abilities are able to see this text.

Oh...what's this here?

Chie touched her index finger to her right eyelid and pushed open the eye she'd narrowed. "Hey, mister."

"Hmm? What is it?" the man beside her replied.

"Can you see if there's something written here?"

"Hmm... Doesn't look like there's anything."

"Really?"

"I just got my glasses prescription renewed, so I can see even tiny print."

"Oh, okay. Thanks."

This was the real thing. They were recruiting magical girls.

Chie's mother had told her that the gate to being a career magical girl was a narrow one, opened only to a select few who were bursting with talent, and it led you down a thorny path. Chie considered her mother to be an excellent magical girl, but even she hadn't become a career magical girl and had started a family instead.

As to whether Dreamy☆Chelsea was overflowing with talent—being a magical girl for nearly thirty years would make you understand that, whether you liked it or not. Chie wasn't about to abandon her conviction that a magical girl's job was not done with strength or speed or laser weapons, but even outside of those areas, she didn't seem any better than other magical girls. The only person she had to compare herself with was her mother, who had given up on being a career magical girl, but Chelsea wasn't even as good as she was—not in experience, in her eye for people, in consideration, in strength of heart, or cooking skill.

But it wasn't like she was worse in every single way. There was her magic. It should also be fair to consider that a magical girl should just succeed using her magic.

Through her magic, Chelsea could control the stars. That sounded like she could control heavenly bodies, but of course that was impossible. When she explained that she could play by making little star-shaped objects fly around, most people would put on vague smiles, and depending on the person, they might even say something encouraging.

But it was no reason for pity. Chelsea saw it as very charming and appropriate magic for a magical girl, a gem she was quite satisfied with. She would use her stars to knock pebbles into the air, making those pebbles hit distant targets over and over, like how you'd bounce a tennis ball against the wall. The more times she did it, the higher the points. She'd been playing this "star-shoot game" since she was little, and even now she sometimes set new high-score records. If this had been a professional sport, she could have made a living on it, but unfortunately, Chelsea was the only player.

The sort of magical girl Chelsea imagined needed a magical girl–ish magic and then one more thing: luck. The luck to find magical-girl work appropriate for herself right when it counted was just what a magical girl needed. Chie lifted her finger from the scroll button on the mouse. She ran her eyes over a new line once, then did it again, then one more time.

Beginners welcome. Recruiting those who can transform into magical girls. Seeking a kind and genuine magical girl. Magical abilities or athleticism not questioned. Cleaning, cooking, and other skills are preferred. Illegal or legally evasive activity strictly forbidden. Cheerful, at-home workplace.

Chie grinned out of one side of her mouth. The world wasn't all bad.

The man beside her was startled by a strange sound coming from his computer and loudly called out to the staff.

◇ **Love Me Ren-Ren**

There's no end to the number of unfortunate people who won't realize that they are unfortunate. That was what Rei's examiner had told her. Mentally, Rei had resisted that idea, but she hadn't put it into words.

Rei Koimizu didn't consider herself unfortunate. In preschool and then school, hearing about her friends' families or even seeing her friends' mothers—they always seemed kind—when she went over to play, she never thought they were better than her mom. She only thought they were different from her mom. It wasn't even that she felt her mother was irreplaceable or more important to her than anyone else. Her mother was her mother, nothing more and nothing less. The fact of her mother being her mother was, on its own, very important to Rei.

Around the time she entered preschool—no, even before that, when Rei was just born—she must have had a father, but she remembered him only vaguely. She thought she could remember things like his back being broad or him having a loud laugh, but maybe those things might actually be an impression of him that had come later, around the time she'd learned about him.

In other words, she didn't remember her father. In Rei's memory, there was only her mother.

She would carry a stool with her to the sink and put her body weight into the knife to cut the vegetables. Busily moving her little fingers and nails, she would rinse the rice, and she also regularly cleaned out the pot of the rice cooker. She didn't think of it as a hassle or unnecessary toil. Her mother would come back late at night and then go to work when Rei was away from the house. Rei saw her mother only a few times a month, but every time she did, her mother would be drowsily looking down at the floor. Rei thought she must actually be sleepy. There was no way she wouldn't be tired.

Rei would clean the toilet and sweep the hallway, tidying things as best she could. She didn't make the sweet kind of curry—she used the medium spice that her mother preferred, although Rei herself tolerated a little bit of spice. She ran the washing machine every day so the laundry wouldn't pile up, and she always used the leftover hot water from the bath for it.

Rei found this to be a worthwhile lifestyle, but her mother didn't see it that way. She learned as such when she got a phone call from her mother, saying, "I'm not coming back anymore." The words hit her hard.

It was sad, and it was painful. For the first time, Rei was aware of how important her mother was to her. She had taken her mother's presence for granted—eating, sleeping, watching TV, occasionally telling jokes and smiling at her, but now she was gone.

She had a dim sense of why her mother wasn't coming back anymore, and that was what made her sad. Her mother was different from Rei. She wanted her own time. There were lots of things she wanted to do. There was also someone she'd fallen in love with. She must have thought that if Rei wasn't there, she might be able to get all those things she couldn't get. Rei didn't know if that was true, but ever since her mother had told her good-bye, she'd stopped coming home.

Rei was in elementary school. She'd known this sort of thing happened all over the world. She was so, so sad; the tears just kept coming, but she never considered searching for her mother or attempting to make her come back. No—maybe she had thought about it, but she bit her lip and stopped herself. She didn't want to hold her mother back. If she did something like that, people would learn that her mother had left, which would only result in problems for the woman.

But that didn't happen.

Rei was scouted by a certain examiner, and she became the magical girl Love Me Ren-Ren. She'd known you could make a living by getting someone to hire you for money, and she also managed to find someone to play the role of her guardian. Her days became even more incredibly busy than before, but Rei continued to pay rent at her apartment and go to school, and she didn't shirk in cleaning or laundry, either. She kept everything her mother had left behind untouched, but she also took care of everything so her things wouldn't get too dusty. That way her mother could come back at any time, and they could immediately go back to their old lives.

The examiner who helped Ren-Ren out with things pointed to her and said, "You're an interesting person. Look for someplace where that appeal...your character can be put to good use. I pray that will be the stage that I wish for."

Love Me Ren-Ren would summon love with her bow and arrow. With her arrow, she could firmly retie unraveling bonds.

Love Me Ren-Ren cherished the connections between people. Rei had decided she would. Rei existed, Love Me Ren-Ren existed, because her father had loved her mother, and her mother had loved her father. If something came about because of Love Me Ren-Ren, that had to be something wonderful. She made more smiles and lessened the number of crying faces. Love and bonds were the most important things to that end.

So Ren-Ren started taking jobs that involved bonds between people: She restored families that had been falling apart due to affairs, renewed relationships between siblings who had been in an inheritance squabble, and reconciled couples who wanted to make up but couldn't bring themselves to take that first step. Occasionally she would even discard her own position or benefit in the pursuit, and her reputation for earnestness spread until she was well-known. Now she was what her examiner had called a "fortunate freelancer," and work came to her even if she didn't advertise herself.

It was rare that a client brought Ren-Ren to their house. Those who hired Ren-Ren, regardless of their level of wealth or status, all wanted to keep their privacy. In that sense, this client could even be described as quite open, but Ren-Ren wasn't childish enough to be glad about that.

A mage was going somewhere to inherit wealth and required magical-girl accompaniment for it. That was all it was, but Ren-Ren was being shown into her house, and the economic situation she could infer from that dwelling was not great. Those facts put together a convincing story in her head.

The house had been built more than thirty years ago. The whole building was tilting just enough for her to barely sense as a magical girl, though she wouldn't have noticed as a human. The wallpaper was faded. It had probably been a darker yellow to begin with and was now a paler cream. Something like black soot had accumulated in the bottom of the round fluorescent light hanging from the ceiling. It resembled the apartment where Rei had lived up until it had been demolished.

But just because it resembled the familiar home she'd lived in for so many years, that didn't mean it was comfortable in the same way. The kitchen floor was slightly sticky, and the dining table legs were too high.

The magical girl sitting on the other side of the table set the tea-cup in her hands down on the table—there was no saucer—as she muttered something. Her diction was so unclear, Ren-Ren wasn't sure if it was Japanese or a spell. Either way, it was so quiet and indistinct, and Ren-Ren was completely unable to pick up what she said.

"Um…did you say something?" Ren-Ren asked.

Eyes still lowered, the magical girl muttered some more. Ren-Ren still couldn't parse what she said. Her costume was mostly black, and she had a melancholy air to her, with dull eyes and a vacant expression that seemed to reject further intrusion.

Ren-Ren had been working many years as a freelancer, but her work tended to be of a certain type. She only ever took on work related to human bonds and social relationships, and having done well at that, now she only ever got that type of work coming to her. This work was also not the sort that needed to be handled by more than one magical girl. So she'd only ever gotten more opportunities to work solo, and it had been a long time since she'd been involved with another magical girl. She wasn't sure whether she could work well with others.

Ren-Ren smiled awkwardly back at her, and the magical girl known as Nephilia went *ksh-sh-sh* through her teeth—that was probably laughter.

"L-L-Love Me...Ren-Ren...huh..." Though it came out in hesitant stutters, it wasn't like Ren-Ren couldn't barely pick it out.

"Ren-Ren is fine, Nephilia," Ren-Ren told her.

"Nephi..."

The magical girl called Nephilia looked like a *shinigami* carrying a very frightening giant scythe. Ren-Ren knew scythes were originally farmer's tools, but this big weapon with the unconcealed dull gleam of metal was still very impactful to her. But Nephilia's attitude didn't really highlight that—she actually had an air of gloom that was far from violence.

"By the way, both of you."

The two magical girls tore their gazes away from each other, Nephilia looking to the right and Ren-Ren left to look toward the voice.

"If you're gonna talk, then include me," said a woman in her mid-twenties. Her chestnut-colored hair rested at her shoulders. She didn't wear much makeup overall, with only her lipstick in dark red. Since she was slouching, Ren-Ren couldn't see below her chest, but still, you could tell she would be bending her knees quite a bit to fold her legs in her chair. The left strap of her camisole lay over her collarbone, while the right strap was coming off her shoulder, and Ren-Ren felt like this asymmetry almost symbolized her character.

Nephilia nodded silently, blank-faced, head hanging as she looked up at the woman. "B-bad...at talking..."

"Ahhh, you're bad at talking. There's no helping that," the woman replied.

"In...heritance...law...office..."

"I see. You're saying you're not good at talking because you've hardly done anything besides your specialized work."

With upturned eyes, Nephilia did that same snicker through her teeth. She seemed to be agreeing.

Ren-Ren made a particularly soft expression. "Yes, yes." She nodded. "It's the same with me. I've only ever done work relating to family issues. So I haven't worked very much with other magical girls."

Nephilia put a hand to her forehead and then gave a toothy grin. "Nervous…here…together…"

"I'm nervous, too. Since this is gonna be nasty stuff," the client said.

Nephilia raised one eyebrow. "Oh…?"

"Well, I mean. When the daughter of the mistress gets a message from a deadbeat to shamelessly barge into the event just to get an inheritance, it's gonna be nasty and a lot of trouble, am I right?" Given her appearance, at a glance it seemed like she was speaking very casually. But her fingers on the teacup handle were gripping tight, and the ends of her nails had gone white.

Emphasizing lightness in her manner, Ren-Ren put the words together. "Our business is in resolving hassles like that, Miss Agrielreymwaed Quarky."

"Agri is fine. It's way too long otherwise… Actually, I'm impressed you remembered it all." The two of them laughed together, and then Nephy followed up with that snicker of hers.

"A…Ag…," Nephilia stuttered.

"Oh, Ag is okay, too, but I'm used to be calling Agri, if you don't mind."

"Ri…"

"Ohhh, sorry. You were still in the middle of saying it, huh." Agri and Nephilia laughed, and this time, Ren-Ren was the one to follow.

Agri stood up and said she was going to the bathroom; Ren-Ren breathed a little sigh. Nephilia moved just her eyes to look at Ren-Ren, who pretended not to notice, picking up her teacup to moisten the inside of her mouth.

"So your specialty is inheritance and estates, Nephy?" Ren-Ren asked.

"H-hate…dead people…bodies…"

"I…don't really like them, either."

"Bad…at fighting…"

"I doubt there will be any fights. I would be uncomfortable with that, too." With a wry smile, Ren-Ren moved to pick up her teacup again, but it was already empty.

Nephilia lowered her voice even quieter, cupping her right hand around her mouth as she said, "Think…of…boss…?"

Ren-Ren's face tensed into a serious expression. "I…would like to help Agri as much as possible."

"If…money…work…?"

Ren-Ren folded her fingers over the table. She wondered how much she should say. She realized if she spoke honestly, she would ultimately be laughed at, but she was going to do so anyway.

"Agri feels negatively about her deceased father," she said with a knowing nod. "I don't know very much about the circumstances of mages, but it seems something like what we would call the daughter of a mistress."

"U-uh."

"I…want to help Agri come to love her father, even a little bit."

Nephilia's eyebrows knitted together, then jerked upward, then slowly returned to their original position. "Huh…"

"Isn't it sad for a daughter to hate her father?"

After about three seconds of silence, Nephilia's shoulders trembled, her voice smothered. She wasn't crying. She was holding her stomach and laughing like it was absolutely hilarious.

Ren-Ren wasn't offended. She was always laughed at when she talked about this sort of thing. Nonetheless, she didn't want to be misunderstood. "I'm not lying, Nephy."

"I—I under… Not…lie…" Nephy stopped laughing, then leaned over the table, lifting her chin to fix her gaze on Ren-Ren. Her eyes weren't vacant and half-lidded but properly open.

Ren-Ren felt overwhelmed, but she didn't let that show on her face, looking back at the other girl. "Is that…funny?"

"N-no…sorr…"

"It's not really something to apologize for… I'm used to being laughed at."

"Cool… Ego… Magical…girl…like…"

Ren-Ren wasn't sure if that was a compliment but responded with an expression that could be taken as a smile.

Nephilia slid out one hand to lay it over Ren-Ren's. Her hand was cold. "Straightforward…nasty… I like…" She smirked.

Maybe she wasn't complimenting Ren-Ren after all.

◇ 7753

When Mana told her about the invitation, even 7753, who could confidently say she wasn't good at picking up on hints, understood what she wanted. It wasn't that 7753 had gotten quicker on the uptake but that Mana was very easy to understand. Mana had no magical girls she could look to for private favors, but she was also too embarrassed to say *"I have no one else"* and directly ask 7753 to accompany her to the island. She didn't want to complain that she was lost with nowhere to turn to gain 7753's sympathy, but she wanted her to come.

7753 could understand painfully well that Mana was in trouble, and she did want to help her. There had once been a magical girl Mana could have asked for help. Whenever 7753 remembered that magical girl, Hana Gekokujou, she was assaulted by a feeling that made her want to scratch at her chest. And Hana had been like a sister to Mana, so it had to be worse for her. Thinking about this made 7753 want to help her out, if there was anything minor, even the smallest thing that was in her power.

But 7753 had work. She made an attempt nevertheless and wrote out a request for leave, and to her shock, her schedule opened up. The magical girl whom 7753 had been looking after, Princess Deluge, was transferred to "where she should be," with hardly any time to say good-bye.

And now 7753 had come to this island.

It was hot. The beach sizzled under the blazing sun, and the large rocks in the sand would make it impossible to walk barefoot in human form. 7753 was a magical girl, so she could handle that discomfort in that form, but she wouldn't have chosen to do it. The most she did was get as close as she could to the water's edge while staying out of the spray as she gazed into the horizon. She would look bad in front of Tepsekemei if she got carried away. Even if Tepsekemei wouldn't remember that she'd been brought with the promise that she couldn't be too loud, break anything, or do anything dangerous, 7753 would remember.

As for said Tepsekemei, she was high in the sky, blowing in the wind. When Mana warned her that if she went too high up, she might hit a barrier, she replied, "I already did that"—was that a good sign or not?

"Tepsekemei looks like she's having fun." 7753 turned around to see Mana gazing up at the sky with a tired expression. She held down her flapping cape with her right hand and her hat with her left, against the wind. That, with her outfit like a magical school uniform, made her look very put together but also not very cool.

"It sure is hot," 7753 commented.

"It really is," Mana agreed.

"Um…then why not at least take off the cape?"

"I'm going to dress formally when knocking at their door, at least." Letting out a heavy *phew*, Mana rested her hands on her knees to support herself. "Just so you know, I'm not being slow because I'm too hot."

"Huh? Really?"

"The gate to get here was handmade by some amateur. Of course using something like that will make me nauseous."

7753—and probably Tepsekemei, too—didn't get sick and had only thought, *Being able to teleport with just a device like this is so amazing.* It would make her feel guilty to seem unaffected, though, so 7753 pasted on a grimace.

"What about you?" Mana asked.

"I'm not so bad. I'm not the type to get carsick in the first place."

"No, I mean the heat."

"Oh, that." 7753's costume, with the motif of a boy's school *gakuran*, looked like it would be stiflingly hot. It wasn't suited to a very plainly southern island like this, but cold-weather gear and underwear were all the same for a magical girl. The air was drier than Japan, so in terms of humidity, you could even call it comfortable. "We'll have no problem. Tepsekemei spent the whole winter in that getup, after all. And that's despite originally being a creature who can't live in the cold."

"I envy that... Magical girls are so tough...," Mana muttered, maybe like a compliment or maybe an insult for their lack of sensitivity, and then tottered away from the ebbing and crashing waves.

"We're going, Tepsekemei," 7753 called out loud to the sky, and then she trotted off.

7753 tried to take Mana's arm, but Mana swept her off, saying, "Don't treat me like an invalid." Left without a choice, 7753 walked half a step behind, ready to support her at any time if she fell.

"Weddin," a voice called to her from behind.

7753 corrected her without turning back. "I'm not Weddin, but what is it?"

Tepsekemei didn't reply, and when 7753 glanced back, Tepsekemei was looking around with a somehow confused expression.

"What is it?" 7753 repeated.

"I don't know." That was vague for Tepsekemei. Floating in the air, her expression was serious.

7753 was aware she wasn't the type to think, *I've got to stay sharp*, but with the other two like this, maybe she really did have to pull herself together.

There would be a whole bunch of formidable characters like mages and magical girls on this island. More frightening for the newly arrived trio was that they had no idea what kind of people they could expect to run into. 7753 had seen a lot of magical girls and a comparatively smaller selection of mages, and she knew a lot of them were good people. However, she also knew the bad ones were nasty enough that it could lead straight to a threat to your life.

Now, when Mana lost her temper or when Tepsekemei inno-
cently did something rude, 7753 would have to be the one to cover
for them.

So for now, to avoid being rude, she removed her goggles and
let them hang from her neck.

CHAPTER 2
ON SATABORN'S ISLAND

◇ **Pastel Mary**

Pastel Mary removed the stones that dotted the path along the coast, and by the time she'd completed the first stage of work on the west side, the sun was shining high in the sky. No matter how optimistically you looked at it, she wasn't done clearing the path in time for the guests to comfortably walk to the main building. She had to finish before the guests arrived, but they would be there the next day. She'd gotten a clearly annoyed message from her boss about it. That fact put Mary in a glum mood. She had to go offer the depressing report that "I wasn't able to finish in half a day" right now, but her boss was in a bad mood before he even heard it.

This island was just too big. No matter how much she walked, she didn't reach one end of the island from the other. She figured that if she wanted to cover the main building in the middle, the annex built surrounding it, and the gates that dotted the island, she'd need more than four hours even with help from her sheep. So she'd begun the task during the dim hours of predawn, but in the end, she hadn't even finished the west side after working more than six hours, and the task was carried over into the afternoon.

Under the brilliance of the powerful dark-orange sun, she rapped twice with the knocker of the main building, and then when the large, hinged doors opened automatically, she slid on through. When she'd first started working here, the main building had overwhelmed her. It was like an old castle, with a thousand-square-foot footprint and four stories all in stone. Mary had been moved, trembling at the thought of coming to work at such an incredible place, but now that a week had passed since her hiring, she was irritated at how pointlessly large it was.

Mary went up one flight, two flights of stairs, then went down through the hall on the third floor toward the adjoining building. All the doors ahead looked similar, and she still wasn't quite sure which room was which. She stopped in front of a star-shaped nameplate with *Shepherdspie* written on it in pretentious cursive. This was the room of Mary's employer, the mage John Shepherdspie.

The estate was big, and only having just been hired, Mary simply couldn't remember the layout. After she made the same mistake over and over and failed to learn, the boss had nailed this to the door for her while grumbling, "It hurts the aesthetic." His sense of taste meant he wanted to pick a shape for it at least, and so he'd selected a star-shaped plate. This way, even Mary wouldn't make a mistake, and it was very easy to understand.

So she opened the door to report—

"Yeeeek!"

"S-sorry!" Startled by the loud shriek, Mary hurriedly closed the door. Then, after closing the door, she once again digested the scene she'd just witnessed.

…Why is there a naked woman there?

Mary checked the star-shaped nameplate again. It had *Shepherdspie* written on it. That was the name of her boss. It was an odd and also delicious-sounding name, so even Mary wouldn't get it wrong or forget it. In other words, that meant this was her boss's room. But then, for some reason, there was a strange woman in here. And she was completely naked.

Mary pondered the situation. Maybe her eyes had fooled her or something. Like it was possible there had been an obscene doll left there, or an indecent poster put up, or something like that. And then the wind had blown in when she'd opened the door, and it had sounded like the shriek of a woman. That could happen.

Had that been real, or was she mistaken? She had to make sure. Taking care not to make noise, Mary turned the knob and quietly pulled the door open a crack to peek in. There was a face right in front of her.

"Oorp!"

"Hyeeps!" With a muffled shriek, Mary landed on her bottom. On the other side of the door, she heard a sound like a frog being stepped on, and after that, all was quiet. It was completely different from the sexy shriek before, but it was basically a woman's voice.

She had not been seeing things, and it had been no mistake. Someone was there.

Desperately quelling her racing heart, Mary put her hand on the doorknob again and then remembered, *Oh yeah, I didn't knock*, and when she knocked three times on the door, a shrill voice came back at her, saying, "W-wait! Hold on!" Now she couldn't run away.

About thirty seconds after Mary had steeled herself, by her internal clock, there was a call from inside the room. "Okay, okay, okay, I'm dressed now. Come in."

"Pardon me..."

"Ahhh, yeah. Hi." The woman wasn't completely naked. She was in a bathrobe. It was too big for her, with the cuffs rolled up. It looked like she had thrown on a men's robe in a hurry. Her cheeks were flushed, steam was rising from her hair, and her skin was white, but she had no makeup on. Combined with the pale aqua bathrobe she wore, all elements were indicating that she had just come out of the bath, but her eyelashes had an impressive, natural curl.

Who is this? The one thing Mary understood was that she'd

never seen this person before. She didn't understand anything else, no matter how much she racked her brain. And on top of that, sand was scattered around the room, along with half-eaten snack wrappers, manga magazines, and handheld game consoles. None of it made sense.

Seeing Mary look around the room, the unfamiliar woman realized her blunder had been exposed. "Ahhh, was this a problem after all…?"

"Huh? A problem?" Mary echoed.

"Well, you know… I thought maybe I was a little too messy."

"Oh, no, that's not it at all. Yes, I'm sorry for being so rude and staring. I really am sorry. I just came to report that the west is done…"

"Huh? The west is done?"

"Huh? No, um."

"You mean…in a global affairs sense?"

"N-no, that's not what I mean… I'm sorry, actually the west isn't even done… It's taking more time than I expected."

"Like in a 'the Cold War isn't over yet'…kind of sense?"

"Huh?"

"Huh?"

Mary didn't get what she meant. The woman seemed just as confused as she tilted her head.

"Um…I came to notify…," Mary began again.

"Notify me? Huh? About what? About, like, your wedding?"

"No, I'm not married. But it's not that."

"Oh, I'm not married, either," the woman said, answering a question Mary hadn't asked. "Wait, hold on. Let's sort this out."

"Um, okay."

"What did you come here for?"

"I came to notify you," Mary repeated, "of the maintenance of the western side. I'm still working on it."

"Marriage has nothing to do with it."

"Nothing at all, and again, I'm not getting married."

"What about a boyfriend?"

"That…um, how should I put it, faded out."

"If you had a boyfriend, then isn't it all good? My mother's always pestering me about that, saying if I'm not going to get a job, then I should at least get married. I think that's a mean thing to say… I'm sorry, that's not what this is about."

"Yes, I thought this conversation wasn't quite right."

"Let's sort this out again. You came here just to say that the maintenance of the western side isn't done."

"Yes."

"You haven't come here to get mad about the room being a mess?"

"No."

"Phew…well, I didn't think anyone should get mad at me for making a mess in my own room, though."

"Huh?"

"Huh? What?"

"Your own room?"

"Yeah, my own room."

This was Shepherdspie's room. So then that would mean this person, who claimed this room was her own, was Shepherdspie. But she was completely different from the Shepherdspie Mary knew.

No, wait. This means that…

Mary tried thinking back on all the facts. Shepherdspie was single. From the way he looked and acted, it seemed like romance wasn't a part of his life. And he was unemployed. Mary remembered he'd said a little proudly that he didn't have to work, with his status. Having a son like that would probably make a mother worried. On top of that, this woman was saying this was her own room. Though Mary had thought she was way too different from Shepherdspie, now that Mary actually thought properly about it, the only difference was her appearance.

"Transformation…?" Mary wondered.

"Transformation?" the woman repeated. "Ahhh, transformation, huh. I always get kinda worked up when I transform, you know."

"Well…that can happen sometimes."

"Though I don't mind that. But when you want to relax, that's something else."

"Um…can you transform?"

"Of course I can."

"Yes, of course. Sorry for the strange question."

It's him! It's Mr. Shepherdspie! He's transformed with magic!

Thinking of it that way, it all made sense. Shepherdspie was a mage, so he'd be able to shape-shift. It wasn't like Mary couldn't understand the desire to transform into a young woman. Even getting around seemed tough if you were that fat, so she could get wanting to change things up.

When Mary was convinced—*I see, so that's what's going on*—there was a creak in the hallway, followed by footsteps.

She turned back, and after a short wait, Shepherdspie appeared, big belly swaying. "I heard…a shriek… *Huff, huff…* What is it…? Are you…okay?"

"Huh? Why?! There's two?!" Mary exclaimed.

"What are…you…so…surprised about?"

Mary stared at him. The thinning blond hair, the dubious mustache, the black robes, the plain wooden wand at his waist, and the way he was panting—it didn't seem to be anyone but Shepherdspie. "Which is the real one…?" she murmured.

"Seriously…what are you talking about?" After catching his breath, the male Shepherdspie wiped his forehead with the sleeve of his robe, looked at Mary and the female Shepherdspie in turn, then, with his eyebrows in an upside-down V, tilted his head. "There are a few things I'd like to ask—do you mind?"

"Huh? Uh, um."

"What is it?" The female Shepherdspie was completely calm in this abnormal situation.

The male Shepherdspie nodded with an "mm-hmm" and a deep sigh, then turned to the female Shepherdspie. "Why are you wearing my bathrobe?"

"Because someone opened the door without knocking when I was naked."

"I really do apologize for that…," said Mary.

"No, no. No need to worry," the female Shepherdspie told her.

"Don't go off on a tangent. I'm not talking about that," said the male Shepherdspie.

"And wait, isn't this bathrobe for me?" said the female one. "It was left in this room."

"This isn't your room. It's my room."

"Huh? Is it…really? Oh, um, sorry. It said Dreamy☆Chelsea on the nameplate, so I thought for sure this was my room."

"It doesn't say that. It says Shepherdspie."

"Huh? Really? But there was a star mark on the nameplate…" The woman muttered excuses under her breath. "And *che* and *she* look similar…"

"Even if you did mistake it for your own room, how could you make a mess this shamelessly?"

"It said at-home work environment… I figured it was okay to treat this like my own home."

"You shouldn't take that seriously… No, never mind. That part was my fault. More importantly, why aren't you in magical-girl form?"

"Huh? Do I have to be in magical-girl form?"

Mary inched backward in an attempt to be even slightly less stuck in between the two people talking. This made her strike the back of her head on the wall, but the other two were heedless and kept conversing.

"*Do you have to be in magical-girl form?* Listen. I hired you as a magical girl. I didn't hire you as a human."

The woman looked like she really didn't want to do it. "I always get kinda worked up when I'm a magical girl, so…," she muttered.

"What's wrong with that?"

"But it's more fun to laze around as a human…"

"Did you say something?"

"Ah, no, that's just me talking to myself. Um, well, it's just like, you know. I—I think it's weird."

"What's weird about it?"

It seemed Mary had misunderstood completely. This wasn't a conversation between two of the same person. Rubbing the back of her head, she watched, gulping.

"Um, I'm saying it's weird for a magical girl to be transformed on a regular basis," the woman replied.

The boss was visibly confused by this opinion, looking at Mary as if seeking some input, but Mary quietly looked down. The master responded with an "ahhh" or "uhhh" noise between a listening sound and a groan, then gave a little sigh at the end. "So what does that mean, in other words?"

"Look, um, you know. A magical girl ultimately lives as a normal human. She isn't going to be transformed into a magical girl on a regular basis. Being in human form while lazing around… Wait, no, I mean that's all purely about convenience, isn't it? How can you call yourself a magical girl when you're using your powers for yourself? You transform when other people are in trouble…yes, in order to handle some kind of accident. Pushed to it by misfortune, a little girl strikes back with magical powers and solves problems and brings smiles. That's the sort of underdog story that warms the viewers' hearts. It makes them think, *Wow, I admire that; I'd like to become a magical girl, too.* Am I wrong?"

Mary timidly looked up, and her eyes met with those of her boss. This time, she couldn't look away. *"Do something,"* he seemed to be telling her, but Mary shook her head.

Her boss sighed, raised his right hand, and rubbed his pinkie and ring fingers to produce a pathetic little sound. A small saucepan suddenly came flying down the hallway and smacked right into the wall, clanging loud enough to make you want to plug your ears and then roll around on the carpet. "Ah, no. Wrong item. Not this one." With great effort, the boss picked up the small pot and threw it back, and when he rubbed his middle and pinkie fingers this time, he managed a somewhat better snap than before. When a glass bottle came flying from the hall, he caught it with a little sketchy juggling. Twisting the lid off, he tossed the contents back to drink a quarter of the bottle in one go, then let out a deep sigh and threw back the bottle, making his mustache whoosh. Just this mild exertion made sweat bead on his forehead.

"Agh…maybe you do have a point," said Shepherdspie.

"Mm-hmm," said the woman.

"I agree that relying completely on magic on a daily basis isn't ideal."

"Right."

"But I don't know if I can allow that."

"Huhhh?! I think it's no big deal, though."

The boss brought his fist to his mouth and cleared his throat. "You fail to understand something."

The woman paused a moment, and then her expression slowly darkened. "Me? What? What am I not understanding?"

"We're already in an emergency situation right now. Magical girls are necessary at this juncture." The boss continued. "Soon, we'll have a bunch of mages who will require delicate treatment all gathering on this island: a mistress's daughter, a famously obstinate character, a resident of the ivory tower, a cop, and a sheltered rich girl. I will be welcoming them and satisfying them with fine cooking, but that won't be the end of it. Even after they've been fed, the upper classes will demand more, naturally. This isn't a matter I can somehow manage on my own. The cooperation of you magical girls will be vital. If this isn't an emergency, then what would you call an emergency? I won't let you say you don't need your magical-girl powers."

The woman put on another aggrieved look. She wasn't even trying to hide that she meant to arm herself with any logic to argue him down and avoid trouble.

But the boss leveled her with an unusually confident expression, and the woman clicked her tongue with an expression of resignation before nodding reluctantly. "I'm sorry... I can be in magical-girl form..."

"You seem quite unhappy about it."

"No, that's not... Well, I am, but."

"You are?"

"I am, but, well, I'll suck it up."

"Thanks. Then if you could transform right away."

"Oh, it's a major problem as a magical girl to transform in front of others, so isn't there someplace I could hide to transform?"

"Ah, yes. You can use the room next door."

The woman strode out of the room, slamming the door loudly.

The boss wiped the sweat off his forehead with his sleeve, then produced a weak snap with his index and middle fingers. A chair slid over to him, pulling wrinkles over the carpet as it came, and the boss sat down. The chair creaked but didn't break. "What a hassle... This is the problem with magical girls."

"Well, some people are like that...," Mary said.

"You're quite a lot yourself, you know."

"Huh? What? A-am I...really?"

"You're constantly falling over."

"I mean... I don't know, it's just...my frame and body ratio and everything are different compared to when I'm in human form..."

"But I can't deny that you're not as bad. Can I really leave cleaning and showing in the guests to her? I can't help but get the feeling it won't be all right."

"Oh, of course. I was thinking from how that conversation was going that maybe that was what it was. So she's a new person who's come to work for you?"

"What did you think she was?"

"Well... No, it's nothing. I think I was a little tired."

"I'm tired, too..." After a heavy sigh, the boss wiped the sweat off his forehead. "Teach her whatever she doesn't know and support her as much as possible. I don't have the time to hire a new magical girl right now. I naively thought that people would come if I just posted a recruitment ad. When I think of how I might have gotten some better personnel if I'd just made the pay a little higher..." His expression was more serious than ever before.

Mary's face grew serious, too, then stiffened, then twitched. Any new hire would naturally have more experience in the business of magical girls than her, so she'd been relieved to have a new person to rely on who could take the lead, but it turned out that was not at all the case.

"I'll have her handle serving and setting the tables," said the boss. "Best to avoid exposing her to the guests as much as possible."

He was already treating her like an object.

"Um, but…," Mary said, "I've told you this is my first time doing a job like this, haven't I?"

"Uh-huh, yes. I'm aware."

"This is a bad idea. Didn't you just bring up things about an obstinate person and a sheltered young lady? In short, all the mages coming will be fussy people, right?"

"So then, you tell me. Would you have me put *that* before fussy people like them?"

"Uh, well, that's a little— No."

"It'll be fine. They're all coming in order to inherit a fortune. They obviously won't want to start up any funny disputes. A serving magical girl tripping and falling won't be enough to get them ma…" Shepherdspie stopped halfway, closed his mouth, put a hand on his chin, then gazed at the ceiling for a while before adding, "So long as you don't trip and spill soup over their heads, they probably won't get mad."

Mary groaned and looked up at the ceiling. "When you put it like that, I get the feeling I'll actually do it…"

"No, no, no, how does that follow? Just watch out. Be careful."

"I'm always being careful. But for some reason, mysteriously—"

Mary was cut off by the sound of a door opening. She turned around to see a magical girl in a glaring color scheme posing with a stick at the ready. Her apparent age was somewhere between elementary and high school, with an appropriately small frame. Her height, body weight, the length of her limbs, and everything else was shrunk down compared to the woman from before, but she wasn't clumsy like Mary.

Her little stick had a tiny star-shaped decoration daintily stuck on the end. For some reason, it was mended with clear tape.

"So super happy to meet you!" the girl gushed. "I'm the magical girl Dreamy☆Chelsea! That's me!"

Mary backed up half a step, leaving the space between the boss and Dreamy☆Chelsea like she had before, and bowed at the waist. "Ah, hi. Thank you. For the polite introduction. My name is Pastel Mary."

A beat later, the boss also heavily bowed his head. "Hello... I'm John Shepherdspie."

"Nice to meet you, May-May!" Chelsea cried. "And Johnny Pie!"

"Ahhh, yes. I'm glad to meet you," said Mary.

"Likewise... But please don't call me Johnny Pie."

"Then Mr. Pie!"

"That's...well, it's not *un*acceptable."

Chelsea spun the stick in her right hand while doing the same with the thing she held in her left, then crossed both arms in front of her chin and stopped flat. The object she'd been spinning along with the stick was a magical phone. "Hey, my magical phone isn't connecting to the Internet."

"Keeping this place separated from the outside world was the wish of the deceased. He was an eccentric, after all. It's inconvenient in many ways for me, too."

"Awww, that's boring. But the scenery's so nice, I was thinking of posting pics on social media."

"Please don't do anything like that even if you do get Internet access."

Chelsea grumbled things like "how boring" as she tucked her magical phone away in her pocket, but once she'd lifted her chin again, her displeasure was gone, an endlessly bright smile on her face instead. "Oh yeah, that thing just now!"

"Huh? What thing?" Shepherdspie asked.

"That thing where you snapped your fingers and something came flying! Were you using magic for that?"

"No, I wasn't using magic. There's a spell cast on the main building itself. It's made so that you can do things like that by inputting special commands."

"Wow! I wonder if I can do it, too."

By the time the boss raised his right arm, Chelsea had already snap-snapped with both hands. As the master was about to call for her to stop, something was already flying toward Chelsea from behind. A magical girl moved too quickly for a mage who never got exercise to stop her.

Chelsea squatted down on the spot without looking behind her, and a red plastic gas container came flying, skimming over her head. It just about hit Mary, who avoided it in a flustered panic, then lost her balance, stumbled, and hit the boss on her way down, and the two of them wound up tangled up on the carpet.

With no one to catch it, the gas container hit the wall, contents spilling everywhere as it rolled on the floor. Clear fluid leaked out, and a sharp smell filled the room.

"Ah!" Chelsea cried, making Mary turn toward her, but the boss's belly was in her way, and she couldn't see. But she could see the lit torch flying toward them. With nobody to catch it, the torch flew along the same trajectory as the plastic container, hit the wall, bounced while scattering sparks, fell to the floor, and blazed up.

The boss screamed. Chelsea stepped on the carpet over and over in an attempt to beat out the flame, but the fire wouldn't go away, and the carpet was roaring into a blaze. Chelsea stomped on the floor harder, the room shook, the floor creaked, the furniture fell over, and she could hear the sound of something cracking—the master yelled, and before Mary could even be surprised, part of the floor had crumbled, and Chelsea, the desk, chair, video game console, and everything else fell to the floor below.

With dust, black soot, and smoke clouding the air, it was difficult to even see two feet ahead, but Mary felt the heat, and she could also hear things burning. The fire had not stopped. She pulled a piece of paper from her pocket and sketched out a sheep with her pastels. The paper swelled, and a sheep leaped out from within.

"I'm going to fill some buckets with water, so help me out," Mary told the sheep.

The sheep bleated and started running for the entrance to get outside, but when it tried to jump over the fire to get there, its fluffy sheep wool caught fire. The sheep cried out pitifully and flailed around, and doing that right near a big hole in the floor caused it to fall into the hole. The shrieks of one person and one sheep could be heard from below.

Pastel Mary hadn't considered things properly. A sheep wasn't cut out for a fire. There was nothing for it but to go alone. Making up her mind, Mary stood and raced off, but forcefully shoving aside the thing she was tangled up with meant she'd ripped a giant tear in the boss's robe, and he staggered and fell down into the hole, too.

Now two people and one sheep could be heard shrieking from the bottom of the hole. But Mary didn't have the time to save them. She had to put out the fire as soon as possible, or this little mishap could turn into the whole house ablaze. So Mary raced off but then immediately felt something slam into her forehead and staggered. Before she could understand that she'd hit the wall by the door because she'd tried to race off when she couldn't really see, she'd landed on her bottom, and when she stuck out her hands to try to catch herself, there was nothing there, and she fell straight down into the hole.

◇ 7753

After arriving through the Inspection Department's gate, they looked at the map on the invitation as they walked for fifteen minutes along an animal trail. They climbed a path up a hill that was kind of like a promenade, which curved into a downward slope with rocks all over it, and now there were trees all around that blocked the ocean from view. The ground was quite uneven, and just walking in a straight line took more time than expected. They still hadn't arrived at their destination, which was in the center of the island. They went along a deer trail surrounded by tall trees that blocked off the sunlight, making it dim even during the day. That made the temperature not as hot, which was something to be grateful for, but it was a hassle to keep an eye behind her while also brushing aside the branches that stuck out on either side.

Though 7753 did wish they would get there soon—Mana was struggling with teleportation sickness—it wasn't like thinking or wishing it would make her get there sooner. Mana would probably feel better if 7753 lent her a shoulder or carried her on her back or in her arms, but offering that would probably make Mana mad. Her pride was too great.

7753 worked for the Magical Girl Resources Department. Her job was to observe magical girls through her goggles to check their abilities, principles, opinions, family members, work history, and more. It was possible for anyone to simply equip her magic goggles and see the data it displayed, but only 7753 was capable of the swift and minute adjustment of the status to be viewed.

No one else being able to change those options satisfied 7753's ego somewhat, while also giving her more business trips. She'd gone on countless business trips to rural villages and remote locations, but she'd never been anywhere with so much nature—or such a vacation spot. Right now, they were coming from a cape over a beach into a forest, walking on and on over a deer trail. 7753 found the absolutely choking amount of green to be endlessly fascinating, thinking *wow, wow* as they walked along a path that had received only token maintenance.

For starters, things smelled different. The faint scent of the ocean lay in the air, along with the smell of young trees. The aroma of greenery was dense and thick enough to drive the aggressive salt odor into the corner. Blown in the wind, the branches swayed, and the leaves shivered. The wind pressed the short grass to the ground, while the high grass rustled and rasped against her ears. The trees and plants grew thick around the line of exposed earth. There were red and yellow flowers with a very southern feel, while beside them stood lines of trees with large hand-shaped leaves fanning out, and the trees opposite them were great coniferous trees that reminded 7753 of the pines that clustered around her neighborhood shrine. Trees that looked like sago palms rose to the heavens, while the massive ferns tall as adult men looked like those edible flowering ferns, with their heads rolled up like they were still sprouting. It wasn't simply that there were lots of plants of many different kinds. The flora ranged from tropical to cold-weather species, growing side by side despite the habitat and climate they typically needed. They must have been altered somehow to match the temperature and humidity of the island. It didn't appear as if the priority was aesthetics or the view, so they had probably been planted with the goal of being used for experiments or something. There was no such thing as natural or unnatural when it came to magic.

The cool wind stroked 7753's cheeks. Tepsekemei was high overhead, circling in the sky. It seemed she was more or less obeying her order to not go anywhere 7753 couldn't see, but the tall trees and the branches and leaves that unfurled from them did sometimes hide her from view anyway. Tepsekemei, who looked like a lamp genie, crossed over the sun, and 7753 shaded her eyes with her right hand, squinting. There was a rustling in the thicket ahead, and two brightly colored birds flew up from the direction of the sound. Spotting Tepsekemei shooting out in pursuit, 7753 called out to her, "No chasing birds!"

Tepsekemei turned back, and her form faded, then wavered. After about three seconds, when she returned to her original thickness and shape, she was tilting her head with a baffled expression. "Why not?"

"Wasn't it written in the books you read that you can't bully animals?"

"If you save the spider in the end, you're forgiven for anything."

"Making weird interpretations again… Um, listen, it doesn't have to be a spider that you save. If you save a bird, it will save you from hell and take you to heaven. That's safer than a spider's thread."

"Mei didn't know about that system…"

Learning some basic kanji had broadened the range of books Tepsekemei read, including Akutagawa, apparently, and it had influenced her in weird ways. Perhaps reading had had some educational effects, but it had mostly just created more trouble for 7753.

Tepsekemei's expression went from baffled to serious, and she slowly came down. *Oh yeah, we were stopped*, 7753 noticed, and she turned to Mana beside her to apologize and saw she wasn't looking at 7753 but staring up at Tepsekemei.

7753 followed Mana's gaze. Tepsekemei was holding a bunch of something in her right arm. They were a dull gray color, like black and white paints mixed together, shaped like ellipses four inches long. They were the fruit from some kind of plant. There were tooth marks on them—signs they'd been bitten into.

"Ahhh!" 7753 cried out. "You ate something here without asking?!"

"It was good," Tepsekemei said. "Eating gives you energy. Mei will share them with Weddin and Funny Trick."

"We don't want it. Ah, you ate so much."

Tepsekemei had bitten into two of them, and there were three with just peel left. Her cheeks were sticky with fresh juices, and chewing on the thing in her mouth made her talking a bit clumsy.

Still with her face turned up to Tepsekemei, 7753 quietly asked Mana, "Is this okay?"

"If they were important, they probably wouldn't leave them to be stolen like this," Mana said with a sigh. It seemed that rather than be exasperated at Tepsekemei's behavior, she was so tired, she didn't care about some minor crime. This was unusual for her— Mana was a rigid person who endeavored to act the inspector at all times. The saying of "the demon getting sunstroke" to describe someone who's usually strong being unwell came to mind, but 7753 kept that remark to herself.

"Do you think it's fine?" 7753 asked her. "They're not going to get mad at us? The one who owns this island does magical research, right? Wouldn't it be bad if this fruit was valuable?"

"It isn't rare…and besides, the dead can't get angry."

7753 raised an eyebrow a tick and stared at Mana. She seemed like she wasn't talking about her own business, and it wasn't simply that she was in a bad mood or tired. There was a detachment in the way she talked.

Mana coughed like something was caught in her throat, breathed a lamenting sigh, and continued. "I haven't actually met the deceased personally… It's just that my father studied under him for a very short time."

"Oh, really?" 7753 had been worried about whether she should pry about that, like maybe there was some interpersonal mage conflict going on, so she hadn't been able to ask about Mana's connection to the deceased. 7753 had been like that ever since she was a kid—waiting for the other person to say it themselves—and it had led 7753, Kotori Nanaya, to have a limited number of friends.

"Eating will give you energy," Tepsekemei said.

"Sure, maybe eating food will give me energy, but…" 7753 trailed off.

"It's the foundation of living things."

"But I thought magical girls didn't need to eat."

"You must not forget the foundation of living things." Tepsekemei's serious expression never wavered as she held out a gray fruit to 7753. The Nanaya family home used to have a tree in their garden, which had fallen due to rot when Kotori had been very small. She felt like the fruit on that tree had looked similar. She seemed to recall they had been loquats.

7753 couldn't tell Tepsekemei to put them back, but she also thought it was a bad idea to accept one. As she was waffling, an arm stretched over her shoulder, and a small hand took the gray fruit. It was Mana.

Mana pushed up her wide brim, supporting her large, pointed hat to examine the gray fruit. Then she leaned in, opened her mouth wide, and bit into it, skin and all. 7753 flapped her lips a few times, hands halfway raised. When she was finally at a total loss as to what to do, Mana nodded.

"This is a grayfruit." Mana took another bite, let out a breath, looked back at 7753, then scowled. "No, the name of the fruit is *grayfruit*. I'm not just saying that it's a fruit that's gray."

"Ohhh, that's what you mean."

"Just what do you take me for?"

Mana took several bites, dexterously making sure the dripping juices stayed inside her mouth, then sighed again. The color was returning to her pale face. Mana waved her right hand to shake off the juices stuck to it, extending her hand to Tepsekemei to accept another fruit and throw it at 7753. "Try it. This fruit absorbs magical power from the land and the earth, and each one contains a small amount… Still, it's only a minute amount. Any mage with aspirations in pharmacy…even at the student level will know a couple hundred compounds that use it. They've been planted anyway, so if you don't eat them, they'll rot. They'll go to waste."

Mana took another from Tepsekemei, while Tepsekemei, for her part, double-fisted the remaining grayfruit and chomped them in alternation. 7753 looked at the fruit in her hands—the gray loquat—rolled it around, poked it with her fingers, and brought it to her nose and sniffed it. It was sweet. She had the feeling it smelled similar to a loquat, too. Imitating Mana, she bit into it without peeling it. Her first bite was timid and hesitant, while on her second, she put more in her mouth, and she opened her mouth wide for the third. It was as sweet and juicy as she'd expected—no, even more so. The skin didn't get in the way of the fruit, with no poking hairs, but it was still soft. It was nice how it melted completely naturally in her mouth and slid to the back of her throat, and the sweet, refreshing scent that wafted from her mouth to her nose couldn't be tasted anywhere else. It even felt like heat or a kind of energy was filling her from the core of her body. Tepsekemei hadn't been lying when she'd said it would give you energy.

It made 7753 want another, but they were already gone. "This is…good."

"They're also sometimes processed and used as nutritional supplements. I've made those before, myself. It's rare for them to taste this good, though. These might be a new type," Mana said. She was no longer dragging her words when she spoke, her back was nice and straight, she looked somehow proud even though she wasn't talking about herself, and most of all, there was color in her face. She was completely back to normal.

7753 was about to say, "*So it works on teleportation sickness, too, huh,*" but held her tongue. "Huh? Then doesn't that make these valuable after all?"

"If it becomes a problem, we can just apologize. I could even have them reduce my share of the inheritance, since he's a fairly wealthy individual. There's quite the share for the unexpected daughter of a student. Supposedly."

"Now that you mention it, I was a little curious about that. It's not for his own student, but for that student's daughter? Normally wouldn't you choose someone with a closer relationship as an heir?"

"I asked my father, and he said the man was always rather odd. Though it's true enough that researchers out there are all weird in some way to a greater or lesser extent."

"Are we okay, then?"

"The man's dead. You're safe."

"Well, ah…true."

"Precisely because he was such an oddball, he might have left behind something interesting."

"Something interesting? Doesn't an estate mean money and land?"

"Art and artworks and also magical tools."

"Ahhh, so he had things like that, too, huh."

"There also may be things like unpublicized magical formulas, since he was a fairly famous researcher. I'd be glad if there were some new spells I could use for investigation. If there is, I'll ask to see if they might give me priority for it."

"Is who gets what going to be decided based on discussion?" 7753 asked.

"I figure they respect the will while also comparing with precedent, while keeping to common sense." Pulling a white envelope from her pocket, Mana took the letter from inside and tugged it open. "Identical letters have been sent to all those with the right to inherit. It will be decided at that location who will inherit the estate of the deceased. Those who fail to respond to this invitation will lose the right to inherit. Each heir should bring a maximum of two magical girls to accompany them."

"That letter makes it seem like only one person can inherit, though."

"That's the part that lacks sense. It's extremely illogical to gather multiple people and then make it so only one can inherit. If you want only one heir, you should indicate them from the start. If they're getting everyone together to decide, that will turn it into a common sort of negotiation. I highly doubt they're thinking they'll have the accompanying magical girls do ten-minute tournament matches or something."

"Well, uh…um, so the discussion will just be done among the mages?"

"I don't think we're bringing magical girls to have them participate in a discussion."

"Then what for?"

"I was wondering about that, too, and I thought about it, but…" Mana seemed thoughtful. "There might be animals kept free on this island, so I figured you're bodyguards to protect from things like that."

"Ahhh, I see."

"In the first place, if they needed magical girls for discussion or whatnot, there's a whole bunch of professionals in the Inspection Department."

"Of course. There's no need to bring your friends, huh," 7753 said, and Mana's lips stiffened slightly. 7753 wondered why and then repeated what she'd said in her head and realized, "Ah. Sorry for being rude, saying we're friends."

"No…well, yeah. It's fine. Don't worry about it. Rather, the thing you don't have to worry about is the discussion being among mages. I mean that you don't need to worry yourself over weird things… Um, I'm a sharp, experienced veteran from Inspection, too. Your worries are unnecessary; in fact, they're rude," Mana said with apparent confidence, pulling a handkerchief from her pocket to wipe her hands and mouth.

And then with an "Okay, let's go," she moved to walk in the lead, then immediately turned back. She looked angry, plus she was jabbing her finger at 7753, which made 7753 automatically take half a step back. "I want you to keep a proper eye on Tepsekemei as much as possible. Since some of them are probably going to be cranky people."

"I will. Sorry," 7753 said.

Mana pointed her index finger diagonally behind her. "And, Tepsekemei. Don't go flying off without permission. Stay close."

"If Mei isn't flying, Mei won't know if enemy magical girls are approaching," Tepsekemei replied.

"This looks like the middle of the wilderness, but it's just a quick jump here by gate. We're still a part of civilization. This is a place that's protected under the law—in other words, there are no enemy magical girls," Mana declared, then pushed aside the thicket and started lumbering along cutely.

Following after her, 7753 was relieved to see Mana recovered, but her being back to normal meant that she was as angry and bossy as usual. Praying that if she was going to cause quarrels, they wouldn't be beyond 7753's ability to patch up, 7753 followed after Mana's small back.

Glancing behind, 7753 saw Tepsekemei making herself bigger and smaller as she followed them. She more or less did as told and didn't fly up into the sky.

◇ **Love Me Ren-Ren**

Ren-Ren raised the map of the island to the sunlight. The lay of the land was just as the map said. It seemed they were going along the correct route. It had taken ten minutes to get this far, so then it should take them another ten minutes to arrive at the main building, their destination.

Nephilia's hesitant speech was easier to understand now than when they had first met. But not because she was speaking louder or enunciating things better. She hadn't become easier to hear; she had become easier to read.

Ren-Ren was good at guessing at people's intentions based on their gestures and tone of voice. It was difficult with someone she had only just met, but it became more accurate through the course of many conversations and doing things together. To give a specific example, even with something like, "Un… Ight…," which only sounded like bits of words, if you looked at her holding her palm against the sun and looking up in annoyance, you could figure out that she might be trying to say, *The sun is too bright.*

They had gone into an old, large building, using the elevator to go up and down a certain number of floors to emerge in a certain room on floor eight and a half, which shouldn't exist, then gone through some paperwork with the Magical Kingdom staff posted there so they could finally use the gate—to Ren-Ren's eyes, it had looked like a big, old wooden door—and using that, they'd come to this island.

Since it had been a long process, there had been plenty of opportunities to talk with Agri and Nephilia. They'd talked about things like how boring the movie she had seen with the free coupon she'd gotten the other day was, or how the castella from this one old Western bakery had been good, or that apparently a mascot from the Magical Kingdom had been in some local mascot contest, and other trivial matters.

Relationships were about learning what the other person wanted you to do and what they didn't want you to do. The perception and observational skills to learn these things were necessary for Ren-Ren to do her job, whether she liked it or not. Her sometime examiner had told her before that learning out of necessity means that you have a talent for it, but even now, Ren-Ren wasn't sure if that had been her honest opinion, or flattery, or perhaps an attempt to console her.

You could even come to know a person through casual chat. When you come to know a person, you will also learn what they want to talk about.

Agri had learned to pick up what Nephilia said somewhat, but she couldn't understand her as well as Ren-Ren, and she occasionally needed interpretation. Agri was curious to know if there was some kind of trick to it, but Ren-Ren knew from experience that if she honestly said it came from observing people, that would just creep Agri out, so she avoided it somehow with a smile and an evasive remark.

The wind blew along the path between the trees, and Agri held down the hood she was using to keep sun off her face. Even if she had just pulled this hooded robe from the closet and patted the dust off it—with the remark unbefitting of a young woman that it was great that it was a cream color, since the dust wouldn't stand out—wearing it made her look fairly mage-like.

There was another gust of wind, and Nephilia grimaced in the blast, pursing her lips, while Agri muttered "shit" at the blue sky, and then as if to erase those words, the wind blew through again.

When the wind blew, the trees rustled and the waves crashed in, bringing the roar of the sea to them. Even just walking, nature was filled with all sorts of sounds, more than Ren-Ren had expected: their steps on the earth, twigs snapping, leaves rustling on the branches she lifted up so they wouldn't hit the ones following her. Birds cried, then flew into the air, and when there was a wavering motion in the thicket, suddenly an all-white sheep poked its nose out and cut right across ahead before disappearing into the brush.

"Maybe it's a pet that lives free-range. That was too clean to be wild," Agri said before adding, "Well, whatever," and yawning in sincere disinterest.

Ren-Ren led the other two. Outdoor activities weren't her specialty, but she couldn't make Agri do it, and Nephilia didn't seem like she could be counted on, either. Ren-Ren moved a spider's nest to a different branch and pushed aside some tall grasses as she took the lead, making to spare the two behind her as much grief as possible. When she moved a fallen tree that was in the way off the path, she noticed a mark like an animal's bite in it. From the size and shape of the bite, it looked like it was from a carnivore the same size as a human, and Ren-Ren made sure she was focused and ready. No matter what kind of wild animal attacked, it was no match for a magical girl, but this place was a so-called magical island managed by a mage. There might be more living here besides regular flora and fauna. Bodyguarding was as out of her field as outdoor activities were, but she had to do it anyway—that was what it meant to be a magical girl.

With even greater caution than before while also never slowing, Ren-Ren pushed forward, while Nephilia and Agri started playing the word game *Shiritori* out of boredom. Around the time Nephilia's extremely persistent *ru* attack had reached its eighteenth round, the path opened up. The trees that had been shading them ran out, while instead the whole ground was covered with grass short enough to be crushed underfoot. Ren-Ren squinted in the bright light.

The smell of water tickled her nose. It didn't smell like salt. It was just water.

Some gentle, grass-covered slopes followed, and between them could be seen a beautiful circular pond that Ren-Ren eyeballed at being a hundred yards in diameter. The water's surface glared under the sunlight. Gradually, her eyes got used to the sun, and the full scene of the pond became clear. Trees grew around it, with gray things that looked like fruit hanging from the ends of their branches. Something at the water's surface made a splash. There had to be some creature beneath, as it made waves. The waves were too big to be from small fish or insects.

Any thoughts of sitting down on the grass to have lunch here was blacked out in less than a second by the sole color of caution. Ren-Ren wasn't used to being in nature, so it was best to stay away from things she didn't know anything about. Not to mention how you couldn't guarantee it was a normal creature, the island being what it was.

Right before Ren-Ren could suggest that they avoid the pond and move on, there was another splash on the water's surface. It was ten to fifteen feet closer than before.

Ren-Ren nocked an arrow on her bow, while behind her, she heard Nephilia draw her scythe.

Whatever it was, an insect, or an animal, or a fish, it was too bi—

"Heya."

The two magical girls, who had come forward to check things out, instantly turned away from the pond and leaped to positions where they could protect Agri. Ren-Ren dived low to the ground, while Nephilia drew back with her scythe held in front of her. Agri's cry of surprise came a beat later.

The magical girl who had called out from behind the group looked surprised as she waved her right hand at them. "Whoa there, weapons? That's dangerous."

Even if they had been distracted by the pond, Ren-Ren hadn't sensed her presence at all. The magical girl's costume was like a fur pelt, faint black painted over a bluish-gray with a short tail on it. Large and pointed feline ears poked out from her head, and the canines that could be seen from her grinning mouth were large and sharp, like a carnivore or a vampire. Unlike Ren-Ren or Nephilia, she didn't have a weapon. She fought with her bare hands.

The magical girl thrust her hands forward, probably showing off that she wasn't carrying anything, then hop-hopped backward to give them about ten yards. "My bad for startling you. Sorry. Still, no need for weapons, right?" She was casual in tone and attitude. She didn't seem to be hostile, but you couldn't let your guard down.

Ren-Ren slowly straightened and leaned toward Agri to whisper without moving her lips too much, "Do you know her?"

"No."

Ren-Ren's lips bent, and a sigh leaked from the corner of her mouth. She wasn't any good at conflict and hated violence. She thought that of course people should understand each other, and there was nobody she couldn't get along with. Feeling her hand on her bow tremble, she squeezed it.

Ren-Ren considered how to continue from here. This wasn't like a family quarrel. She didn't know what this person's goals were. Their goal was—to avoid a fight. Ren-Ren would let her know as peacefully as possible, but also quite firmly, that she didn't want to fight. Without causing bad feelings, and without letting their party be underestimated, she would ask who this magical girl was affiliated with. She was probably accompanying a mage who had come to this island.

Before Ren-Ren could voice this conclusion, the fur-pelt magical girl laughed. The fangs poking out of her mouth glinted in the light, and Ren-Ren narrowed her eyes slightly. "You're like, her, right? Agri-something-or-other? Am I wrong?"

Agri put her hand on Ren-Ren's shoulder. That had to mean that she would talk. "You're not wrong. But how do you know? I'm not famous or anything, am I?"

"You used the gate at the new lodging to get to this island, right? They told us about it."

"Would they normally tell you that casually? They don't have a duty to privacy or secrecy or anything?"

"I mean, it's the Osk Faction that manages that place, right? They see human rights as about as important as eye snot or dental plaque."

"Huh. So you're with the Osks? That sounds really nasty."

"But we've got some nice things to say now. My master says he wants to talk with you."

"Um…well, fine."

"Thanks."

Muttering, "What a hassle," Agri prodded Ren-Ren forward. "It's in bad taste to yell at each other from a distance. Let's get closer."

"No, but…it could be dangerous," Ren-Ren cautioned. "I wasn't able to sense her presence at all."

"Even this place is basically under the rule of law, so they're not gonna do anything weird. If you're worried, just keep your distance and get them with that arrow of yours if something happens. Nephy, you stay with me." Agri briskly started walking, and Ren-Ren was forced to cede the way to her.

Nephilia passed by Ren-Ren after, giving her a glance, then a nod. Her look said, *"We've both got it tough, huh,"* but she didn't look as anxious as Ren-Ren.

Ren-Ren walked about fifteen feet behind. She would have liked to be twice as far away, but doing that might make the other party wary. Quite unlike Ren-Ren, the fur-pelt magical girl showed no tension at all as she smiled in a relaxed manner.

Once they were about ten steps apart, the fur-pelt magical girl turned to the pond. Ren-Ren kept a cautious eye on the magical girl as she followed her gaze. The thicket rustled, making leaves fly off the trees, and something zoomed out. It was a carpet, with someone sitting on top of it. The flying carpet jetted straight toward them fast enough to make water spray up and then rain down a few seconds later, coming up behind the fur-pelt girl to spin around her like it was drifting to turn toward Agri, then stopped flat. The wind the carpet swept up flattened the grass to the ground and made Agri call out in surprise, while Nephilia snickered *ksh-shh* and the fur-pelt girl cried, "Mya!" and squatted down to avoid getting sprayed.

The man sitting atop the carpet raised up one hand with a "'Sup." His voice was thick and low. The sleeve of his robe slid down, exposing a muscular upper arm. His wrist was marked in green with a complex figure of interlocking pentagrams and hexagrams. Ren-Ren had heard before that a lot of mages had tattoos. Of course, this was for their magical meaning and not for fashion. "I'm Navi Ru. I was a student of Sataborn's, a ways back. This is Clarissa… Uh, what was your full name again?"

"Heeey, how can you forget it? It's Toothedge, Clarissa Toothedge," the magical girl—Clarissa—protested with a bow.

Hearing that, Agri nodded. "Agrielreymwaed Quarky. The daughter of Sataborn's mistress. The magical girl with the scythe is Nephilia. The one with the bow is Love Me Ren-Ren."

Nephilia stuck her jaw out, eyes fixed on the others as she bowed her head. It made her look like a mischievous child, but Navi didn't seem bothered, nodding in an easygoing manner.

While bowing her head, Ren-Ren examined Navi and gulped.

He was too rough-looking to call a mage. His receding hairline, the thin hairs that remained at the front of his head, his protruding gut, the blatant pale spot from the shave of his thick facial hair. His expression, most perfectly described as a smirk, contrasted with Clarissa's mysterious look. Before any considerations of his age, the first thing that struck Ren-Ren was how intimidating he was. Overall, he was squared, rugged, coarse, and thick.

What made Ren-Ren nervous wasn't the dramatic features that comprised Navi but something else entirely—the movements of his eyes. Before looking at Ren-Ren, Nephilia, or Agri, his eyes zipped toward the pond, then went to Ren-Ren, Nephilia, and Agri in turn, then the pond again, before immediately returning to Agri; then he snorted and folded his arms.

His attention was on the pond, and he was trying to hide it. Was there something going on with the pond? Or was there someone there? If he was trying to hide that, it surely wouldn't be anything good for Agri.

Putting on the appearance of being focused on Navi and Clarissa, Ren-Ren kept a watchful eye on the pond. Agri had a relaxed air as if talking to an uncle, while Nephilia in particular seemed beyond relaxed and even flaccid, zoning out listening to the two mages converse.

Navi remained seated on the carpet as he began. "The daughter of the mistress, huh? Nice, just the sort of thing I wanted."

"What do you look so pleased for?" Agri replied.

"Yeah, sorry. Ahhh, my bad for stopping you when you're in a rush, li'l miss."

"I'm not really rushing. We're not heading to some fun event anyway."

"Yeah, that not-fun event is what I'm talking about. Though I'm also here to get an inheritance from the old man Sataborn."

"Did you come here ahead of time and wait for me? Is this an ambush?"

"Nah, we must've come at about the same time. There's a bunch of gates on this island. Personally speaking, I'll take anyone I can cooperate with."

"…Cooperate?"

"Basically, I want to talk about you and me, both of us getting something outta this." Navi tapped on his broad forehead. "Meetings are the way of mages when deciding everything—from the Three Sages down to wood chips."

"That sounds obnoxious."

"So yeah, this part is kinda important. If we're speaking of what's gonna happen with this estate, there's one person here who really can't stand me. It's an old man named Ragi. He hates me so much, you'd think I killed his own grandkids. He'd probably even hurt himself to spite me."

The way he said it must have been funny to Agri, as her head shook with smothered laughter.

Raising one thick eyebrow, Navi looked at her, his thick lips twisting into a very fearsome smile. "It's not like I personally hate him, though. The old fart has spirit. I really love how he talks like he's a fine and important man of the upper echelons. But unfortunately, this isn't something I can just let go as a personal issue. So I'd like an ally who'll help me out. I don't care how, so long as the old man doesn't rage at me like he's ready to go down together, that's enough."

"Well, that's fine," Agri said. "But if I help you out, that only increases your share. There's no benefit to me, is there?"

"Ah, that's the thing, li'l miss."

"Could you stop calling me that?"

"How about lady?"

"Agri is fine."

"So, Agri, I think we probably want different things. We should be able to work things so that we both benefit."

"What do you want, old man?"

"Could you not call me *that*?"

"What about uncle?"

"Navi is fine." Navi rapped his forehead, Agri's shoulders shook, and Clarissa held her stomach as they all laughed together like it was so funny. But while they did, Navi's eyes flicked over to the pond. Ren-Ren sensed fear more than curiosity in his look, and she lightly bit her lip, dry from nervousness, gently moistening it with saliva. Nephilia laughed late after the other three, and she kept snickering alone for about three more seconds after the others had gone quiet.

"I don't need money, or stuff, or land." Navi smirked.

Agri gave him a questioning look in return. "Then what did you come here for?"

"I want any tech the old man left behind."

"Huh? His research wasn't anything special, though."

"Don't underestimate him. He was a pretty talented mage. Some people did laugh at him, saying the old man would never commit to anything and dabbled in everything, but there were more who would call him by his important-sounding nickname of the Almighty Mage. And going by how many techniques were named after him in a variety of fields... Well, though maybe he was dubious in his personal life," Navi added suddenly at the end, possibly in consideration for Agri, who didn't think very well of Sataborn. There was an attempt at flattery in Navi's smile, which Agri turned aside with a smile only in the corners of her lips. Probably no one else but Ren-Ren noticed that she was clenching her fist hard enough to make her thumbnail go white.

"Um, so?" Agri said. "You want those...Sataborn-brand formulas, then?"

"I'm not interested in anything he's done that's already been released to the public. What I want is new tech that he kept secretly and told no one about."

For the first time since Navi had appeared, Agri's eyebrows came together, just slightly. "Whaaat? That smells fishy. You don't even know if any exist."

"Making bets like that is what a man's life is all about."

"Well, if that's what you want to do, I won't stop you, but I don't want you telling me after, *'There was no new tech; isn't it unfair for you to be the only one going home with what you wanted?'*"

"I'm not gonna be that stingy about it."

"Mages will all become sticklers, when push comes to shove."

"All I can say is trust me. I want the old man's work, so I'll arrange it so that you can get as much money and stuff to take home with you."

"We've only just met; of course I can't trust you," Agri shot back. "If you absolutely insist, then I don't want a verbal promise. I figure we might as well make it a Nariami-style contract. Then we could both be at ease."

"Huh? Nariami-style? You want to cast a curse?"

"It's not a curse. We just offer up something of corresponding worth in case of betrayal. Nothing happens if you don't go against our deal. Or did you fully intend to go against it?"

"Of course not. But I didn't bring any of the documents for a formal contract out here."

"You have some, don't you, Nephy?"

Having the conversation turn to her made Nephilia's eyes snap open, then gradually close, and once she was back to her usual half-lidded expression, she nodded. Navi scratched his head and drew up one knee on his carpet. His robe flapped up, revealing a hairy shin. There was an old, deep scar about halfway up his shin, the one place with no hair.

Ren-Ren thought. This man's whole body had a sense of violence to it.

"I'm not really happy about the idea of leaving physical evidence of our agreement, though," Navi said.

"Ma...wor...new...template..."

"She says that she can fiddle with the template a bit to make it look at a glance like, oh, we just made some reasonable contract," Agri explained. "She'll make up the wording nicely so that if this contract gets pulled up later and people prod us and ask what it was about, there won't be a problem."

"What, you brought a specialist?" Navi was incredulous.

"I mean, this is that sort of gathering."

"True enough."

The two mages and Nephilia leaned close together, and with the contract sandwiched in a binder between them, they shot opinions back and forth, like, "Let's do this here," "No, I can't compromise on that," and "I want a little more," while Clarissa stretched like she was bored and Ren-Ren was on her own, feeling on edge. Nephilia asked the two mages' opinions while aggressively filling the contract with more words. The once-white paper now had more black than white; holding up this complete "black-looking paper" to the sun, Nephilia snickered *ksh-shh*. It looked like a small child's crayon scrawl, but however it looked, she was a specialist in the area, so that had to be how they were done.

Navi skimmed the text once more. "Can't you change this part a bit more?"

"That's an issue of nuance," Agri said.

"The nuance is what bothers me. My living depends on reputation and honor."

"So he says, Nephy. Please do the honors for this venerable gentleman. Oh, watch out to make sure I'm not losing out here by mistake. You can't let your guard down with a mage."

"'Kay…"

Navi chuckled. "Heh-heh, my bad."

"There's nothing bad about it. It's common enough to be concerned about those things. This is a Nariami-style contracting technique, after all. No matter if you try to burn it or bury it or rip it up—"

"You don't gotta threaten me. I get it…" Navi stroked a smooth line from the top of his head to the end of his chin, putting on an overly serious expression in a deliberate sort of manner, then eyeballed the contract again. "Don't forget—this goes both ways. If you break our deal, all your assets are mine."

"That's what a contract is. If you break it, then I'll be the one taking the shirt off your back."

"Well, I guess so. So then, let's call this contract complete. Let's do our best to make sure we both benefit."

Nephilia went down on her knees, then raised up the paper, binder and all. Navi and Agri laid their hands one on top of the other over the black paper and chanted a spell. Their enumeration of incomprehensible syllables repeated, accelerating as Navi's crisp chanting and Agri's resonant chanting collided like a dialogue or a shouting match, and it was so tense that Ren-Ren lost her sense of time, and then it came to a sudden end. The two mages went quiet and withdrew their hands.

They split the piece of paper in two as if peeling a layer of skin off the page, and Navi and Agri each took one half in hand. Repeating, "Countin' on you, then," Navi left, swaying on his carpet, while Clarissa walked backward while waving her arms wide.

Watching both of them go, Ren-Ren stayed hidden behind the hill, and counting five minutes after they were out of sight, she stayed low as she approached the pond to look down diagonally at the water's surface.

Little fish swam around, and a dragonfly was perched on a reed. Ren-Ren couldn't see to the bottom, and there were no shadows of large creatures moving, either. Ren-Ren breathed a sigh of relief and mental exhaustion.

"You can't be worrying so much over that old man's bluff," came a voice from behind her. Startled, Ren-Ren turned around to see Agri smiling and gesturing at the pond. "He made a show of letting you see his wrists, right? That was the mark of a mage from the Lab."

"The Lab? What's that?" Ren-Ren asked.

"A place that's ninety-nine percent full of crooks. You don't have to know any more about it, and I don't want to talk about it, either. It's nothing but rumors, and I don't actually know that much."

Ren-Ren furrowed her brow. Her concern must have registered, as Agri fluttered a hand in the air and snorted. "He was talking like us meeting was coincidence, but don't believe that. I figure he looked into me, and he thought we could work together, so he actually was waiting for me. If he's from the Lab, I'm sure he'd be able to look up pretty quick that Sataborn's mistress had a child. Of course he'd imagine said daughter was thinking it would be nice to have a more comfortable lifestyle."

Taking the hand extended to her, Ren-Ren stood up to be immediately drawn into Agri's embrace. With the soft, swelling mounds she could feel even through her robe pressed against her cheek, Ren-Ren looked up. Agri was looking down at Ren-Ren with unusual seriousness. "Do you pity me?"

"No…why?"

"You look like it."

"This…is the only expression I can make. I don't pity you." Ren-Ren knew Agri's personal fortunes were not blessed. Ren-Ren also knew that Agri hated her father. She could also tell that her mother must have suffered, and it must have been a struggle for Agri. But Ren-Ren's feelings didn't seem like pity.

"Really?" Agri asked.

"Really. I don't pity you…but I am concerned."

The two of them gazed at each other for a while. Agri was the first to look away. She quietly muttered, "Good grief," but her tone didn't sound irritated. She turned back and beckoned to Nephilia, and bringing her in as well, she took the three of them into a tight huddle. "I don't need pity or concern."

"Right." Ren-Ren nodded.

"Since this is a businesslike relationship, right? Well, just as long as you don't betray me."

"I would rather die than betray you."

Agri laughed for a while, then noticed the earnest look on Ren-Ren's face. Her expression turned serious, and she bit her lip as she averted her gaze. "Thanks," she barely managed to mutter, her voice quiet and hoarse.

Ren-Ren nodded, accidentally knocking foreheads with Nephilia when she lifted her head at the same moment. It sounded like two rocks colliding.

CHAPTER 3
GREETINGS, THEN AN INCIDENT

◇ **Touta Magaoka**

When his aunt had first told him her secret, he'd thought she was joking. Then, once she had transformed in front of him, it turned out to be no laughing matter. Magical girls were real. They were actually real.

"Whoa!" he exclaimed at the sight.

"Ha-ha-ha!" His aunt cackled. "How do you like that? You believe now?"

"Like, I thought for sure you'd be just the same, but with a magical-girl outfit on."

"If that were how it worked, I'd have quit being a magical girl in my teens..." She casually lifted the entire dresser with only her right hand, humming as she held it up to clean the tatami under where the dresser had just been. Then she turned off the vacuum cleaner, set down the dresser, went right out to the veranda, and jumped off. Before Touta could even scream in horror, she came back to knock on the front door.

And her boobs were bouncy and huge.

She was a magical girl. And she was right there in front of him. Now her evasiveness to questions about her work made sense. She was always so vague and wouldn't tell him—it was because she was a magical girl. Plus, now he understood why hard-to-reach cracks between the wall and dresser were never dusty, unlike at his friends' houses.

"Are there no male heroes?" Touta asked her. "Like riding modified motorbikes or piloting giant robots—or the type that fire beams and lasers?"

"I've never heard of anything like that. Oh, but if you mean guys who become magical girls, yeah, I've heard of some."

"So they're always magical girls… That's fine; it's a little disappointing, but I'll let that one go."

"Why're you acting like it affects you? It's just something you've gotta accept about life."

"Fine, I accept it."

"You back down surprisingly easily."

"I mean, like, you said I'm a mage, right?"

"You're the grandson of a cousin of a mage. Simply put, your, um…relative was a mage. But even if you have mage blood, if you don't learn how to use it, you still can't do anything. Oh, one more thing. I think you understand this, but if you let anyone find out or tell anyone about magic, mages, or magical girls, you'll be made to forget everything, as if they're plucked from your brain."

"Really?"

"Oh…I'm not sure. This happens a lot with magical girls, but I get the feeling like it hasn't really happened for mages."

"Huh? Then what does happen? It's kinda scary if I don't know."

"Well, you just have to remember that something scary will happen. You can't tell your friends, either."

"Okaaay."

Touta had never experienced anything supernatural. Even though a mountain of things like that appeared in books or on TV, there had been nothing mysterious in his life.

His parents had been in a traffic accident when he'd been too young to remember it, one time he'd had a fight with a kid who'd said there was no such thing as Santa Claus and Touta had cried, and he'd sneaked out one night with a friend to go to a haunted spot, but nothing had happened, and then they'd been found out after and gotten an earful for it—all those things had happened because of a lack of anything supernatural. No miracles had happened, no ghosts had been there—nothing like that. It wasn't fun. It was boring. Nothing incredible happened to Touta, and he hated that. There were strange things happening somewhere out there, and he was sure they were so magical, but they wouldn't happen to him.

But now that was over. That day, his aunt had brought him something magical. His aunt would do this for him. All he'd known about his aunt was that she was his mother's mother's little sister—she was his great-aunt, actually. He hadn't known what she did, either. From how she went to work in clothes that didn't look like what you'd wear for a normal job—a T-shirt and sandals—she'd been very puzzling to him. She was the kind of person that, when he heard she was a magical girl, he thought, *Oh, I see*, as all the puzzle pieces came together.

"Huh? You're not coming with me, Auntie?" Touta asked her. "Why not?"

"I have work I just can't get away from."

At times like these, he couldn't say, *"So work is more important than me, huh?"* even as a joke. He never wanted to see the look she got when she heard jokes like that ever, ever again.

"So I'm going alone?" he asked.

"I'll have a friend of mine go with you. No worries; she's someone you can count on. But she can be a little difficult. Well, there are a lot of magical girls like that."

"She's a magical girl?"

"Yep. She used to work harder than anyone, but she's gotten lazy lately, for a bunch of reasons. You'll wind up no good if you avoid working too much, so I come up with jobs like this sometimes to give her something to do." Then she followed with, "You should ask her for more info on magical girls, mages, and the Magical Kingdom."

Touta felt like she'd picked up that he was full of questions, and he nodded in silence. When his aunt said, "When you meet her, eat with a healthy appetite," he nodded again.

He met that magical girl another day at a sukiyaki place. Miss Marguerite was, as his aunt had said, a very fastidious person. With a hat and skirt like a noble lady and carrying a slim sword like a Western fencer, her chopsticks weren't even touching the delicious-looking sukiyaki in front of her. Despite Touta's nervousness about being around the first magical girl he'd ever met besides his aunt, he heartily ate the sukiyaki as told, and while taking care to avoid letting them notice, he also compared to see if his aunt's magical-girl form had different-size boobs than Miss Marguerite. Her boobs were normal. It seemed it was not the case that transforming into a magical girl would give anyone huge boobs.

Marguerite looked like she was in a bit of a sour mood. His aunt seemed glad about that. He figured he'd managed that conversation just as she'd told him. On the way back from the sukiyaki restaurant, his aunt praised him: "The way you glanced at our boobs to compare them was pretty good."

Though Touta was panicking about how she'd been able to tell, he pretended he'd done it deliberately and puffed out his chest proudly. But he also had the feeling that she could tell it had not been deliberate.

◇◇◇

Two days after having sukiyaki, Marguerite, who'd been told to help Touta get ready, came over to the apartment building after dark. The doorbell rang, and when Touta turned on the screen for the apartment intercom, he thought, *She's here!* Miss Marguerite, in that same aristocratic lady–looking costume, was on the screen. Could it be she had come to the apartment building in that outfit?

Touta immediately unlocked the automatic door at the entrance to let her in. His aunt hadn't come back from work, so it was just the two of them. One-on-one. Touta rubbed his sweaty palms on his pants. They faced each other with the long kitchen table between them. There was plenty of distance between them, but he felt a pressure pushing him that made him shift his chair over.

Marguerite grabbed a cup and glugged down her barley tea, then set down the cup on her saucer. Touta stood from his chair, pulled a bottle of barley tea from the fridge, and poured Marguerite another serving.

"Thanks," she said.

"You're welcome."

In science class experiments, Touta had been grouped with a kid who was bad at conversation. Whenever things felt awkward, they felt like they both needed a drink to sip to pass the time. Marguerite didn't seem like she generally loved to chat. It was probably just as Touta thought. His aunt was so nasty.

"Or maybe it's both of them…," Touta muttered.

"Is something the matter?"

"No, it's nothing."

Marguerite might also have been nervous. Thinking about it that way, his tension relieved somewhat. She talked like a teacher, and she was really pretty, but it all seemed so forced—and that was cute.

"Are you positive nothing is the matter?" Marguerite asked.

"It's really nothing."

"I see. Well then, let's get ready."

"Right."

Touta had heard that the trip would be about a week at longest. Picking up all the things he figured he'd need for about that stretch of time, he lined them up in the tatami room.

Marguerite swept her gaze over everything he'd laid out and shook her head. "It's too much."

"But I already picked out some things to leave behind," Touta protested.

"You don't need games. You don't need handheld video games or card games, either."

"Whaaat…? But…"

"You don't need them."

"So then I'll leave behind the cards for trading use. Since they're heavy and bulky. But I can just bring my deck, right? Just the deck case won't really get in the way."

"Your teacher scolds you when you bring toys to school. Am I wrong?"

"No, but…"

"You're not going to a playground. So you won't need toys for playing."

"There might be people to play against there, though."

"It will be all mages and magical girls there. There won't be any friends for you to play with."

"Are you sure…? Won't I have nothing to do in the evenings?"

"If you have nothing to do, then you should go to bed. Replenishing your strength in preparation for the next day is part of the job."

"Fiiine…"

"And then these multiple tanks… Are these…crayfish? Why something like these?"

"I have to take care of them."

"Make a friend take care of them."

"Look, I finally got these guys to molt after screwing up a bunch of times, and they're the biggest and most valuable crayfish I've ever gotten. My friends would just forget to feed them and make them eat each other and skip cleaning the tanks. They're sloppy about taking care of them."

"Then have your aunt take care of them."

"Auntie doesn't like crayfish. She says they stink like crayfish… Obviously! She never stops nagging me to put them out on the veranda."

Marguerite smiled. It was not a pleasant or gentle smile. It was 100 percent a smirk. "Insist that you can't go if she won't take care of them and just make her take them. I'm sure she'll take care of them, even if she complains."

"You think...? Then I'll do that." It looked like his aunt had shoved some work off on Marguerite, and now Marguerite was glad his aunt would be stuck with something she didn't like. Auntie had said that Marguerite was a friend, but was this how friends were? Touta's friends—now that he thought about it, all those guys would gleefully do things you hated, too. "Maybe that's just how it is..."

"What is?" Marguerite asked.

"Oh, no, nothing."

"Also, you're missing some things. A robe, cape, and hat."

"What?"

"You need appropriate attire for a mage gathering—such as a robe, cape, or hat. You should have clothing that makes you look like a mage."

"Ohhh, so you wear easy-to-understand stuff like that, huh. But I don't have any."

"I'll ask your aunt to arrange for some. And we'll also want gifts."

"You'll have Auntie get some of those, too?"

"Yes. Light snacks are fine, but the more expensive, the better."

"For how many people should we get?"

"We don't know how many people will be there. So let's get a fairly large amount. Ten should be enough."

"We can eat the leftovers, right?"

Marguerite smirked. "That's not a bad proposal."

Touta smirked back.

◇ **Miss Marguerite**

After the dinner meeting at the sukiyaki place, Marguerite asked over the phone again about what she and Touta should be doing, listening to make sure there were no implied and unspoken intentions. Once she was sure what her former associate wanted, she massaged her furrowed brow.

It wasn't as if she was being used for her combat skills to win something. This wasn't a request to educate an amateur into a warrior, either. What was being asked of Marguerite was experience. Marguerite had worked for many years for a government office, and so she knew a decent amount about the Magical Kingdom, and she also knew quite personally how to associate with mages and magical girls. She was being told to make use of those skills and also to teach Touta.

She would offer what was being demanded of her, as far as she was able. That was what Marguerite had always done. Even if she had been basically dragged into this, that was what it meant to get paid to take on a job. Fortunately, Touta was an obedient and honest boy. Marguerite had known a number of magical girls who were elementary schoolers pretransformation, and all of them had been selfish and willful. Compared to them, he was far preferable. But he might get carried away if she said she was thankful he was a good boy, and she didn't want that, so she maintained a strict attitude.

On the way to their destination, they visited the Inspection Department, saying hello to the mages and magical girls who worked there before passing through the gate installed there to arrive at the island. The whole time, Touta's curiosity was on full blast, saying, "Good morning," "Nice to meet you," "What's that?" and "I've never seen anything like that before," looking for explanations from Marguerite and using up their time, and it put off their arrival later and later.

The magical girl Death Prayer—Touta's aunt—said the reason she had Touta join this inheritance meeting was that "more than the inheritance itself, I want a record of him being officially recognized as a mage." She had saved up a decent sum of money so that things would be okay if she died at any time, but that wasn't enough to put her at ease. Touta's father, who'd had mage blood, and his wife, Touta's mother, had passed away together in an unfortunate traffic accident. But Touta's father had lived as a white-collar worker at a company. He'd ended any involvement with the Magical Kingdom and had lived without using magic. That was a fine choice, in its own way. Marguerite could understand thinking that being involved in magic and the Magical Kingdom wouldn't lead to anything good.

However, Death Prayer was in a different position. She hadn't said so much out loud, but Marguerite had been able to figure it out, and she understood what Death Prayer had wanted her to. Death Prayer was on a very dangerous job right now—one dangerous enough to make her think she might leave Touta all alone. If the death of his great-aunt left him all alone in the world, it would be best for him to have the status of a mage and also to know about the Magical Kingdom. Record of him receiving an estate would semi-formally make him a mage. And the mage who had left this inheritance was from an esteemed family, so it was safe to assume there would be people of decent status among its heirs, too. Touta could make connections with people like that, and this would make it so he could rely on Miss Marguerite in the process. That was what Death Prayer was thinking.

Marguerite wasn't enough of a recluse to refuse. Her senior had once been too ashamed to ever show weakness, and Marguerite was young enough to feel moved by her old colleague revealing the vulnerability. She also knew when to give up. Once she was dragged in, she'd say "oh well" and do it.

Marguerite would teach Touta what he didn't know. That was part of this job. At the Inspection Department, when he asked "What's this?" and "What's that?" she answered everything, and Touta nodded thoughtfully at her answers.

"You know everything, huh, Miss Marguerite?" he said.

"I don't know everything. Don't rely on me too much," she replied.

"Ohhh, so it is true."

"What is?"

"Auntie says when you get a compliment, you'll actually act cold back."

Marguerite cleared her throat while silently cursing Death Prayer, who had to be working.

That aside, one of the things Marguerite had to teach him was "how those who want to make connections should behave." Not everyone was a good person who would be sweet on him just because he was a child, and he couldn't be a child forever. Therefore, he should learn the manners and common sense that would be needed in the future while he was still a child. That was what discipline was.

Arriving at the island, what was the first thing Touta should do? Greetings. Cheerful, pleasant greetings are the cornerstone of communication. John Shepherdspie, who was managing the island, was abed because he wasn't feeling well, so they sent a message asking after his health while passing some of the gift sweets that Touta's great-aunt had gotten to the magical girl who worked for him.

Even if he was just managing the island, he was in a position where he had to entertain mages. Marguerite had thought that he might be able to help smooth things over if Touta happened to make some mistake, but it didn't seem like they could count on him if he was sick. Perhaps because their employer was ill in bed, the two magical girls Shepherdspie had hired, Dreamy☆Chelsea and Pastel Mary, seemed rattled and in a tizzy. The flock of sheep was far calmer than the two girls, making orderly lines to carry things. The way their faces pointed slightly upward, looking proud as they lifted their legs high, was just like humans.

As they left, Touta looked back to gaze up at the estate. "Wow, that mansion is like a castle... Oh, look, look! That wall over there is crumbling down." Off where Touta pointed, part of the stone wall was falling apart, damaging the majesty of the estate.

"Keep thoughts like that to yourself," Marguerite told him. "It's rude to voice such things as you point."

"Okaaay."

Chelsea and Mary told them, "We would be pleased to have you wait over there"—they actually said it with more stuttering— and pointed Marguerite and Touta to an annex that could be seen from there. Just twenty-five yards away from the main building that Touta had described as being like a castle, the annex was quite a bit newer and smaller. But it was still big enough to easily be called an impressive residence on its own. It had to have been built less than ten years ago. It inevitably looked cheap next to the moss-covered stone castle, but it was sturdily built with good materials. If Marguerite's judgment was correct, it would also be soundproofed and have reliable anti-earthquake measures as well.

"Why are you knocking on the walls?" Touta asked her.

"You don't need to worry about that," Marguerite replied.

Going through the entrance, which was equipped with sensors that would sound an alarm if a stranger was to pass through, she followed the guide map on the wall to the lobby.

Some mages were already gathered in the hall, and there were even more magical girls. The sixty-five-square-foot space was furnished as you might expect, with round tables, chairs with arm-rests, silver candelabra, a set of knight's armor holding a spear, and a soft-haired rug dyed an eye-opening shade of red. Everyone was sitting where they pleased to chat or read or whatnot, and the atmosphere wasn't bad. Touta's gifts got a decent reception, and there was the sense that they had accepted him somewhat.

"I see... Though it may be a distant relation, he does have a blood connection with Sataborn," said the old man.

"Um, yes. Though I've never met him," Touta replied.

Marguerite knew this man's name. He was famous, after all. He was the head of the Magical Girl Management Department, Ragi Zwe Nento. His job was to yell at foolish magical girls.

Ragi appeared calm—specifically, wilted. He was leaning on his twisted staff for support like he could barely sit upright. He looked so drained, you wouldn't think this was the constantly furious and stubborn old man from the rumors. Even just talking seemed laborious, and his exhaustion was apparent. Perhaps the way he sat alone and away from the others meant to convey that he didn't want to talk to anyone.

Touta wasn't really paying attention to Ragi talk, his eyes flicking in the other direction. He was curious not about the old man sitting on the sofa before him but the magical girl standing beside him. She was completely unperturbed by his rude stares, standing stiffly at attention at the old mage's side. His curiosity came as no surprise; the girl was human from the neck up, and she had the lower body of a deer.

Marguerite had known of her, even before the brief introduction from Ragi. That was because after Annamarie had lost her challenge, Marguerite had looked up every single one of Cranberry's children. But even if you didn't know her background, her strength as a magical girl was apparent at a glance. When she received a gift from Touta, she raised it above her head respectfully in thanks, and even though she was just standing there, she always kept a strict watch around her.

Marguerite had heard that Ragi was very straitlaced and hated magical girls, so why would he have brought one of Cranberry's children of all people? Being in his position as the head of the Management Department, he had to know of Clantail's background. Marguerite reminded herself not to let her guard down, no matter how weakened he looked.

The middle-aged man with thinning hair who sat in the place farthest from Ragi called himself Navi Ru. He said he worked in a department that was under the direct supervision of the highest echelons of the Magical Kingdom. If that was the truth, then he was on the elite track.

But nothing about the man himself gave a sense of his rank or career background, and he welcomed Touta with a good-humored attitude and friendly words. "So then, once this is over, wanna come to where I work? I'll put in a good word for you so you can join us."

"Um, well, uh, I'll talk about it with my aunt," Touta stammered.

"Nah, nah, nah, wait, wait," the magical girl with him cut in. "That isn't a place you'd take a kid."

"Come on, Clarissa, you're... Yeah. You've got a point. That place isn't for kids."

Even though Touta hadn't seemed that enthusiastic, learning that this place to work as a mage had apparently vanished, his shoulders slumped in visible disappointment.

Navi gave him a couple of gentle claps on the shoulders. It seemed as if Touta's reaction pleased him. "Don't be so disappointed. Look, I'll introduce you someplace else. I'm sure there's places that, like, a kid would be happier to go to, probably."

"You're just saying that," Clarissa shot back at him. "It's not like you have that kind of authority."

"Don't tell him that. Let me look a little cool, okay?"

Clarissa opened her big mouth and laughed, her shapely canines in plain view. Those fangs were sharp, which would be more appropriate for a fierce feline. And you could tell from the way she clapped her hands and bent over when she laughed that she was incredibly flexible and springy, with supple muscles that moved with ease. Though she might normally be pleasant, fun, and charming, she was the type who would become a warrior if the time came.

And then Navi. There was no way "a nice mister who looks rough but loves kids" would be able to work surrounded by the sly old foxes of the Central Authority. And the magical girl he'd brought with him wasn't just a buddy brought for chat but a fighter. Marguerite couldn't let her guard down.

The mage with the name that you'd stumble over, Agrielrey-mwaed Quarky, was a young woman. She seemed to be having a friendly conversation with Navi, but she said the two of them had only just met on this island.

Agri appeared to be more interested in Touta's background than Touta himself. In other words, what drew her interest was that he had Sataborn's blood. It was fair to say Agri was closer to the deceased than either Ragi or Navi. She was not an old academic friend or a student who hadn't visited in a long while but a direct blood relation.

"As for our relationship...are we okay calling us distant relatives?" Agri said. "I dunno if there's a more proper way to put it."

"I'm not sure," Touta replied.

"It'd be awkward if you suddenly started calling me Auntie."

"Oh, I think so, too."

Agri smiled at Touta, then flicked her eyes to Marguerite and smiled at her as well. Marguerite let her cheeks relax enough to not be considered rude, and seeing their exchange, Nephilia did an odd snicker, while Love Me Ren-Ren, who sat beside her, chided her quietly.

Agri probed Touta's situation with little bits and pokes. The pair under her hire seemed relaxed, but their eyes were sharp. They didn't look like fighters. Either they had magic or something else? Types you didn't overcome through fighting were actually more trouble in cases like these. And you could imagine what kind of mage would bring magical girls like those. Marguerite judged that the mage named Agri was a shrewd woman, but Touta was fidgety around an older lady and seemed like he'd fall for her wiles at any minute. If they had the opportunity to talk later, Marguerite would have to teach him that she was not someone to be trusted.

Marguerite snorted quietly, making sure to keep anyone from noticing. But despite her efforts, Nephilia burst out laughing, making her cup rattle on the table and black tea spill onto her saucer.

"Miss Marguerite."

Marguerite turned around upon hearing her name and saw an unfamiliar face. No—maybe it was just a face that was a little more grown than one she knew. But it still easily counted as the face of a child.

"It's been a long time, Mana," Miss Marguerite replied.

The mage girl who'd arrived even later than Touta was an acquaintance of Marguerite's. "Why are you here?" Mana asked Marguerite.

"As an escort for a mage."

"You? As escort?"

"I'm just working freelance."

"If that's how you were going to wind up, you shouldn't have quit Inspection. Your departure has weakened the whole department. One great instructor gone means basically—"

"You think too much of me."

Mana worked for Inspection. Unusually for a mage, she directly involved herself in investigations, and she had the will to polish herself as well as the desire to gain experience. Though she had a slight tendency for narrow-mindedness, by Marguerite's standards, she had the makings of an excellent inspector.

Touta was fidgety, his gaze shifting between Marguerite and Mana. Marguerite indicated Mana with her palm. "This is Mana." Mana cut off there and closed her mouth. She had introduced her by her given name. If she had been speaking as an inspector, then of course Marguerite, being in the higher position, would call her by her name, but Marguerite had quit Inspection. Despite having told her students they shouldn't neglect manners, once it was her turn, it seemed like she wouldn't necessarily conduct herself well.

Once it was clear Mana wouldn't call her to task for this, Marguerite continued. "She's an old colleague. And she is currently your aunt's colleague."

Touta nodded, looking like this basically made sense to him.

But Mana tilted her head. "Aunt?"

"Death Prayer."

"Ahhh, Prayer's."

Having to explain to both parties was a hassle, but avoiding hassles would cause even bigger hassles later. Marguerite turned her palm the other way to indicate Touta. "This is Touta Magaoka. He's a relative of Master Sataborn and my—"

He wasn't her employer. Death Prayer was the one who'd paid Marguerite. He also wasn't her ward, and it was roundabout to call him someone she was bodyguarding. He was like a companion or a friend. After a moment of hesitation, the word that came out was, "He's something like an apprentice."

"Nice to meet you, Touta. Your aunt has always…obliged me with her guidance," said Mana.

Touta must have sensed some implication in that slight hesitation, as he bowed his head apologetically. "Um, I'm sorry about my aunt… I'm Touta Magaoka."

"Oh no, ah… Well, this magical girl is 7753." Mana gestured with a palm to the magical girl sitting next to her. Being so suddenly referred to, the magical girl in a boy's school uniform bobbed her head in a hasty bow, making the goggles hanging around her neck clunk against her forehead. "She works with Magical Girl Resources."

Inspection and Magical Girl Resources didn't have a very good relationship. Marguerite hadn't heard about it improving since she'd quit, either. Unlike a freelancer, you couldn't bring 7753 over for pay. So then this had to be a personal friend of Mana's. Marguerite was privately glad that even a stubborn, short-tempered girl like Mana had someone like that, and she smiled on the inside, thinking Mana was a good girl at heart—but she didn't let that show on her actual face.

"I do have another companion here, but…" Putting a hand to the brim of her hat, Mana scanned the area and scowled. "She's not here. Hey, where did Tepsekemei go?"

"Um…she took that tin of cookies she just got and wandered outside," 7753 told her.

"I told you to keep a proper watch on her," Mana scolded her.

"I-I'm sorry. I tried to stop her, but she slipped out."

"Good grief… Um, it sounds like she's gone out to play. I'm sure there will be opportunities to introduce her later. 7753, this is Miss Marguerite… Hana's master."

When Marguerite had heard that Hana Gekokujou had died on the job, she'd thought it had to have been some mistake, but she had to accept it upon hearing Archfiend Pam had died in the same incident. Hana had been one of the most outstanding of Marguerite's students and an excellent magical girl, but even she could never have survived a battlefield where Archfiend Pam had fallen. In fact, Mana was far more the unusual case for having survived a situation like that, but Hana had surely been the one to accomplish that. Mana's expression when she said "Hana's master" and 7753's expression when she heard those words were telling.

Mana exchanged a few words with Touta, bringing Marguerite into it as well, occasionally making 7753 panic when the discussion was turned to her, and they finished a decently peaceful chat. Marguerite felt like Mana had become gentler and kinder than before. Maybe that was thanks to 7753, or maybe it was the influence of the other magical girl who wasn't with them.

After leaving Mana, Touta said to Marguerite quietly, "Hey."

"What?"

"Am I your apprentice, Miss Marguerite?"

"You don't like it?"

"Oh, no…actually, it's exciting."

She didn't get what he meant or what he intended there, but if he wasn't unhappy with it, then that should be fine.

The mage they met after Mana was a unique-looking girl with strong visual impact. Though she couldn't be much different in age from Touta, she spoke like an adult.

"It's very good to meet you, Touta. My name is Yol," she said.

"Yeah. Nice to meet you," Touta replied.

Her hair was voluminous, made poofy with large spiraling rolls. Just doing her hair probably took forever. She wasn't a magical girl, so it wasn't a part of a transformation. It was possible to do intricate hairstyling through magic; the higher you went up in class with mages, the more they tended to see time-consuming grooming as a virtue. Unlike the other mages, her pointed hat and robes were elaborate, with her family crest patterned in gold thread, the sort of attire chosen only by those both wealthy and pedigreed enough to brag about it. And the wearer came off as luxurious in the way of some Western dolls but put into human form, and adding to that a haute couture robe that would be recognized by those in the know was a powerful enough sight to make a timid mage automatically prostrate themselves before her.

But Touta spoke to her without any shyness at all. It seemed like he wasn't nervous around girls his own age. And the girl, Yol, didn't criticize Touta for it, gladly accepting the gift he'd brought. The charming joy of a girl of that age saying, "Oh my, I'm so glad" and "Thank you," would bring anyone joy. There was a human goodness different from a magical girl's coquettishness. Touta tried to act mature, saying, "Oh, it's nothing much," as he scratched his head, but there was a smirk on his face. Still, it was different from the nasty self-satisfaction of an adult. It was childlike and pleasant, too.

But the servant who stood beside Yol didn't seem to think that way; she was practically glaring at Touta. When Touta happened to look up, he noticed that glare and lowered his eyes like a child being scolded over something done wrong. He hadn't done anything bad enough to deserve that, though.

Marguerite glanced at Yol's servant—the one who stood on Yol's right side and had been glaring at Touta. Noticing that, said servant glared at Marguerite next. Though her robes might have seemed confusing, since they featured a family crest about a rank down from Yol, she and the other servant were both magical girls.

The other of Yol's two servants was letting her eyes wander all over uncomfortably, but nobody was going to save her. Her black hair, straight bangs, and round glasses were very plain for a magical girl, but her facial features were beautiful.

Noticing that Touta was acting strangely, Yol turned to look back and finally realized that one of her servants was glaring at him. "Whatever are you doing?" she asked her servant.

"I am merely looking straight ahead, as usual, miss. Just…"

"Just?"

"I would say that those who have something to hide will often avert their eyes thoughtlessly."

"You're always saying things like that, Maiya."

Marguerite furrowed her brow. Now that the name had been said out loud, she couldn't pretend not to have noticed.

Maiya didn't miss that, either, the corners of her mouth twisting.

Marguerite mentally clicked her tongue, to which Maiya replied, "It seemed you meant to pretend you wouldn't notice, Miss Marguerite."

Marguerite knew that if she noticed Maiya, it would mean trouble. But if she admitted she'd meant to pretend she never noticed her, it would plainly mean even more trouble. "...Not at all. I only just noticed you. Your attire was different than the Maiya I know."

"Hmph, you came prepared with that excuse..."

The Maiya whom Marguerite had met before had carried a staff that was exceedingly humorous in appearance and color—it looked like a candy cane—and matched its bearer's clown-like costume.

But the murderous aura that welled up from Maiya's whole body, as well as her expression of smothering those feelings, made everything about her that should have been humorous instead eerie, fathomless, and frightening. Not a single person who had faced Maiya had thought of her staff as silly.

At a glance, Maiya appeared empty-handed. But upon closer inspection, there was a little lump under her right arm. She was hiding the staff under her robe. She would draw it immediately if her mistress was in danger. And then she would wield it without mercy, brutally enough that you wouldn't be able to tell who was the victim anymore.

It wasn't clear whether Yol had noticed the mood between Marguerite and Maiya; she clapped her hands to get their attention. "So you're acquaintances."

"I wouldn't go quite that far," said Maiya. "We unfortunately keep bumping into each other."

"Don't say that. Aren't you the one who told me you have to value your friends, Maiya?"

"If they are friends, they should be valued, but that's not the case for those who are not friends."

"You have this nice opportunity to see each other again, so you should rekindle your friendship. We'll go have a chat in my room." Yol stood and took Touta's hand, dragging him to his feet. Maiya's eyes widened in shock, but Yol ignored that, leading Touta toward the door at the back. Maiya started reaching out one hand but stopped halfway and retracted it, then called out "Rareko" to the magical girl next to her, who hurriedly followed after her master and Touta.

At the hall exit, Navi called, "Ohhh, a couple of young people are stepping out of the party together? Getting frisky!"

Yol laughed. "Oh, Uncle, you always say such funny things."

Navi tried to add something else, but noticing Maiya's murderous look, he shrugged and chuckled. "Heh-heh."

The two children and one magical girl left the hall. Marguerite and Maiya remained standing there, staring at each other. Maiya was really closer to glaring. Her face contorted even more as she bitterly spat, "Eugh. I never expected to see your face in a place like this."

"I could say the same thing," Marguerite replied.

Marguerite had run into Maiya many times during the Archfiend Cram School's events. Since they had both been outside participants and not members of the school, Marguerite would hear things about her whether she liked it or not. She'd heard Maiya had a position like a nurse and home tutor in the house of a mage, and that the reason she gave for participating in events was "I can't have my skills become rusty if the time comes when I must protect my master." Most people participated in those events for letting off steam or for simple pleasure, like a hobby. Marguerite had thought making your job your excuse really made you such an extreme workaholic, but now that she reconsidered it, she had actually done the very same. She sighed at herself.

Tracing back through her memories of Maiya rekindled indescribable bitterness, anger, and vexation in her heart. She knew it wasn't any fault of Maiya's, but looking at Maiya made Marguerite remember and brought a frown to her face.

Around when had that been? There had been no established rules back then, and they hadn't had the media exposure, either. Which meant it had to have been quite a long time ago.

Marguerite had been participating in an Archfiend Cram

School event. The school was a gathering of battle-mad magical girls who flocked to the strongest of them all, Archfiend Pam. Calling it a part of diligent training and to make them stronger, they had periodically held large-scale combat tournaments.

The rules had been primitive and violent. The participants would wander around a plain and clash with each other, and the last one standing was the victor. Since the participants were all hooligans with primitive and violent ends, nobody would ever complain indignantly about how awful it was and storm off. They gleefully threw themselves into a banquet of barbarism, enjoying hitting and getting hit.

Marguerite had reasons she couldn't enjoy herself there. She hadn't joined in for personal pleasure—she was participating as an instructor of the Inspection Department.

Sometimes she had trainees whom she wanted to gain combat experience, but they weren't ready to risk their lives in actual fights, so she would take them to Archfiend Cram School events to give them a sense of what real combat was like.

Archfiend Pam herself declared it safe, and Marguerite supervised, too. Compared to real fights against criminals, it wasn't like this couldn't be called safe-ish. If everyone they were up against would be great fighters, that was decent enough.

Marguerite had brought only one magical girl that time. Most years, there would be three or five, but there was only one pre-newbie apprentice that year. Year after year, the Inspection Department was becoming less and less popular. The pay was too low for how much of your time it demanded, and more than that, it was too dangerous. Of course there wouldn't be more willing candidates.

But even if she didn't have a great quantity of candidates, she wasn't exactly lacking in quality. The apprentice inspector Annamarie was good enough that she could even pass as a new student at the Archfiend Cram School. With her bullfighter-style costume, carrying a muleta made of a stick and cloth, two banderillas at her waist, a saber, and a brilliant capote, all crossed with a flamenco dress, she was flamboyant enough to hurt the eye.

In contrast with her fantastical appearance, the way she fought was grounded and solid. She was a defensive fighter, focusing on blocking and evasion to find a weakness in her enemies and finish them off. She was resilient mentally and physically, and she'd never once given up, not even in the Inspection Department's infamous hell training.

In hindsight, that had to mean she'd been training to defeat a particular enemy, but at the time, Marguerite hadn't thought to pry into her personal situation. Annamarie had just been an apprentice worth training. Her style had a lot in common with Marguerite's own, being a fencer using a rapier, so there were many techniques she could teach her.

But the problem wasn't techniques or physicality. It was something mental.

As was not uncommon with strong magical girls like her, Annamarie could be vain about her strength. Marguerite had taught her with pain that there was a stronger than strong, but that just ended with Annamarie acknowledging that Marguerite was stronger than her, and her faith in her own strength never wavered.

It's important to believe in your own strength. If a magical girl loses that and her spirit breaks, she'll meet her end before long. But it was still a problem for her to believe that she was stronger than everyone else, and Marguerite was an exception. That would kill her quickly, too.

Having her apprentice join in this event was supposed to have corrected that tendency at least a bit, but contrary to Marguerite's expectations, Annamarie chalked up nothing but victories.

Handling her magic muleta like a part of her body, she blocked attacks and trapped weapons or tied up enemies directly. Her magic muleta that could change its hardness at will was a powerful weapon as well as armor.

Marguerite knew that some of those magical girls were actually very strong, but the stronger they were, the more wary they were of Marguerite, who stood behind Annamarie, and their distraction led to their defeat. Or more like Annamarie tended to actively use Marguerite's presence as bait. She really fought like a bullfighter, creating openings in her opponent.

She was confident in her own strength and yet would also use some sneaky moves that would make some scowl and accuse her of unfair tricks. The more Marguerite tried to hide herself, the more those who were skilled in combat would turn their attention to Marguerite, and they would be defeated without having the chance to fight with all their strength.

Annamarie would be overjoyed with each victory, and then her instructor escort would admonish her, but Annamarie would be glad anyway. Plus, when Annamarie smiled at her, Marguerite smiled back instinctively. Then Marguerite would make a face and say, "You'll get a lecture once we get back."

That was when Maiya showed up.

She appeared in a completely natural manner, practically gliding toward them from the shadow of the trees. Her core was firm, steady. She wasn't just strong—she moved like a magical girl with mastery in martial arts.

Marguerite recognized her. Her face and name were already well-known. She was a master of staff techniques, and she was as good as the top members of the Archfiend Cram School graduates. Even for Annamarie, who could pass for a new student at the cram school, this was the wrong fight to pick.

Maiya swiped from right to left, and Annamarie blocked with her muleta and riposted with her saber—Maiya pushed back, right leg stepping forward to catch Annamarie's foot, and next Annamarie threw a banderilla, making Maiya jump back as she swiped it aside with her staff as Annamarie immediately went for a follow-up strike.

There was a triple stab from Annamarie's saber, but Maiya turned each thrust aside with butter-smooth blocks as she slid in range. Annamarie responded by coming forward as well. There was almost zero distance between them.

The triple stab was the bait. By deliberately making a wide move to offer an opening, she drew Maiya in.

Annamarie made her real attack with the muleta. Once she was close to her opponent, she hardened the cloth part of the muleta and swung it as a single board perpendicular to the ground, aiming to crush the top of Maiya's foot. With a cry of, "Olé!" she struck sharply. But Maiya had already moved. She'd shifted her leg back by one foot's length as she simultaneously grabbed the edge of the muleta with her right hand to push it downward, along with the force of Annamarie's swing.

Two people's worth of force made the muleta stab deep in the ground, leaving Annamarie's face defenseless. Her mouth opened in shock, but it was already too late. Before she could soften the muleta and pull it out of the ground, Maiya's stick hit her. She fell in a single attack. The muleta was still thrust in the ground beside her like a grave marker, but she wasn't dead—merely unconscious.

Maiya had read her utterly. Marguerite didn't think Annamarie had used her magic in front of Maiya before, but Maiya had used her movement, flow, rhythm, eye movement, everything as material to carefully read her aim and lay her trap. Annamarie, who had been enjoying the strike and riposte with her opponents in the rhythm of a flamenco, must not have understood she was going down until that very moment.

Maiya withdrew her staff in a flowing motion and turned to Marguerite. She'd had an eye on Marguerite all through the fight, ready to be attacked at any time. *It's quite something that she beat Annamarie so thoroughly anyway*, Marguerite thought, privately impressed as she spread her palms toward her opponent, raising them on either side of her head. A revenge match for her student would be counter to her goal. Annamarie had lost, so Marguerite's job as her chaperone was to carry her to the medical tent.

Maiya gave Marguerite a murderous look. That look said, *"If you're not going to fight, then don't come to a place like this."* Scowling and with her staff pointed toward Marguerite the whole time, she left.

When Annamarie woke up in bed, she pressed a hand to her forehead and said, "Aw, I lost." She didn't look as defeated as her words said.

Marguerite also had lots of things she wanted to say, but for now, she figured, *Oh well*, and nodded generously.

"I won't lose when it's for real," Annamarie said.

Her saying "for real," that had to refer to, in other words, the incident she would later cause. If Marguerite had been considering things more seriously, she might have been able to figure that out. But she hadn't thought about it deeply at the time, her only insignificant impression being, *She's tough, after being beaten that badly.*

It was a strength for a magical girl to be resilient and never get discouraged—especially for investigators working for the Inspection Department. At the time, Marguerite had thought that if Annamarie grew in the areas where she should and work on her weaknesses, she wouldn't only become strong but would become a first-class investigator.

Now, she could understand. She had made her own assumptions about what sort of magical girl Annamarie was. That had been hopeless arrogance on her part.

Marguerite had run into Maiya at many events after that. Annamarie had been with her at some of them, but there had also been times without her. But now only the times with Annamarie kept coming back to her. Every single one of those memories tortured her. Looking at Maiya made her remember how she'd been then, made her think of Annamarie with pointless thoughts of, *If I'd only done this, if I'd only done that,* racing through her head. She almost sighed, but she swallowed it.

Marguerite was too polite to say honestly, *"Seeing your face makes me remember things I don't want to,"* and she maintained a vague expression as she was forced to converse with Maiya. "It seems you're still in good form…"

"That goes for both of us," Maiya replied. "Though I heard you quit Inspection."

"I did."

"You're freelance?"

"I am."

"Is that your current employer?"

"It's mean to call him 'that.'"

"'That' is enough for insects who approach the miss—well..." Maiya casually grabbed the tip of her pointed hat and gripped it. It formed wrinkles in the brand-new hat, and looking at the brow underneath it, you could see bitter lines there, too. "There's actually a worse insect."

"What kind?"

"Filth that deserves to be addressed as the kind of massive, toxic vermin that writhes around at the bottom of a night soil jar. That *thing* keeps approaching in an attempt to butter up the miss. Never mind contact, it's noxious to have that thing anywhere close. Agh, absolutely vile."

"...Is that person here?"

Maiya spoke quieter. "Listen, Marguerite. Work with me. Don't let Navi Ru approach the miss. If you cooperate with me, it may be possible for me to establish your client's position."

In events, Maiya was like a wild animal that knew only the hunt. Now, she looked like a working adult dealing with lots of problems. Had time changed her, or did she put on a different face depending on when she was off or not?

Marguerite nodded, prompting her to continue.

◇ **Touta Magaoka**

"Weren't those two glaring at each other? Are they okay?" Touta asked.

"It's fine, it's fine; we should let those old friends chat together." Yol walked briskly on ahead—still holding Touta's hand.

Her fingers were soft, smooth, cold, and chilly, but they were gradually warming up. When Touta realized that was because he was warming them up, he yanked his hand away. Yol turned back to him with an expression like, *"My,"* and smiled right back at him. Ahead of where she indicated with a "Go ahead" was an open door, and Touta realized they'd come to her room.

It was way bigger on the inside than he'd expected. There was a sofa smaller than the one they'd been sitting on before, a long table, some kind of cabinet with alcohol and wineglasses in it, and two more doors on the other side of the room. Maybe that was where she got changed and slept and stuff. The words that he imagined of his own accord—"getting changed" and "sleeping"—made Touta blush, and he hurried on into the room.

Yol moved her cape to the side to sit, while Touta sat on the seat opposite her, and the magical girl in glasses who had been called Rareko went to stand behind Yol.

"So then, let us begin," Yol said.

"Begin...what?" Touta asked.

"Tee-hee, why don't we stop pretending we don't know?" She was acting rather strange—somehow different from before. She seemed bolder or something, like a rival character from anime or manga. "I've been researching how magic is treated in worlds other than the Magical Kingdom—how the existence of the technology we call magic, which shouldn't even be known about, has been received and grown culturally."

"Ah, yeah."

Yol suddenly leaped to her feet, cape fluttering. On the inside of her cape shone countless somethings... Touta narrowed his eyes and examined whatever they were. Looking closely, he recognized them. "The Hellfire-Burnt Queen," "Dream of the Extreme," "The Lady Knight's Anguish," "Devilish Twin Angels," "Robot's Treasure," "Anonymous Seraph"—attached to her cape were cards from the wildly popular trading card game Magical Battlers. It was packed with rows of difficult-to-acquire promotional cards or rare cards that were too expensive for him to get his hands on.

"Touta Magaoka," Yol said. "I immediately recognized that name. You're a duelist as well, aren't you? You won third place in the fifth annual national Battlers elementary school tournament."

"Huh? How do you know...?" Touta wondered. "Oh, is it 'cause my name came up in a magazine?"

"It's an unusual name. In my pursuit of other cultures, I fell to the temptation of dueling..."

"Oh, I see."

"Now come, Touta! Choose the regulations you're most skilled at! Now, let the curtains rise on the game of darkness!"

"Sorry, I didn't bring my deck."

"Huh?" Yol's eyes widened. She stared back at Touta with her mouth half open. "Why not?"

"Miss Marguerite told me not to pack anything that would get in the way..."

"My goodness... But the deck might be called the soul of a duelist...!" Yol cried out, throwing her hat to the floor. Rareko dithered, unable to do a thing, but it wasn't like Touta could do anything, either, as Yol stomped on her hat over and over. "But I planned to show off my Satacon!"

"Huh? Satacon? You mean General Satan Control?"

"That's right. Of course you must know about it. Using the Control Deck typical in Battlers, you hold out however you can using counters and bounces until you can play the high-cost demon General Satan—"

"No, I know that... But you can't play Satacon now, right?"

"Why not? My darling Satan can sally forth anytime—"

"General Satan's a banned card now, though."

"No way?!"

"Last week, there were some special revisions aside from the regular revisions, a bunch of errata came up, and they announced like an afterthought that General Satan's been made a banned card... I heard that all cards related to General Satan have gone down in price across the board, and card shops aren't doing buybacks."

"This can't be... How absurd!" Yol fell to her knees. The set of cards attached to the inside of her cape hit the floor with a thump, and her hair, in an incredible state, wafted down together with it. "I can only acquire information from *Monthly TCG*... So if it happened last week... No... Could it be...there is an upheaval in the scene...?"

"Yeah."

"Dreadful… This is simply too dreadful… But my Satacon… It was so finely tuned! I read every single dribble of meta, and the meta on the meta…" Yol was on her hands and knees on the floor, shoulders trembling. She was in shock.

Touta looked over at Rareko and saw she was still completely flustered. It didn't seem like she'd be useful. In other words, he had to be the one to do something. "U-um…isn't this an opportunity, though?"

Yol looked up. It revealed her face, which had been hidden under her hair. There were tears in her eyes. "Opportunity…for what? My darling Satan is gone now…"

"That was gonna happen anyway. They've been saying that ninety percent of the top-of-the-world tournament was face-offs between similar Satacons… But you know, now that it's been banned, new decks can come into play…right? I've heard that, now, famous deck builders are coming up with the decks that will dominate the new scene."

Yol straightened up into a formal kneel on the floor. At some point, she'd stopped crying and sucked it up. "In other words, you mean…this is an opportunity to come up with the new strongest deck and carve my name into Battlers history…?"

"Huh? Yeah. Well, maybe."

Yol stood with her hat in hand, swept the dust off it, straightened it up, and put it on her head. She clenched her right hand in front of her chest. With her eyes focused on the ceiling, she cried, "True opportunity lies in times of crisis!"

"Ah, that's the catchphrase God-Emperor Iizuka used a lot in the second season of the anime."

"Now that it's decided, it's time to build a deck. You help, too."

"Oh, sure. Are the cards that aren't in your deck pinned to your cape, too? Isn't that hard to use?"

"But it's cool."

"True, it is cool."

"I had it specially made."

"Awww, nice." She wiped the sweat off her forehead in relief and glanced at Rareko.

◇ **Dreamy☆Chelsea**

Poor Mr. Shepherdspie was stuck in bed. He said unlike magical girls like Mary and Chelsea, mages weren't any tougher than humans. The double-punch of falling down a floor and inhaling smoke, plus the little fire and damage to the building, had weakened him both physically and mentally. Saying that he didn't want to do anything anymore, he had crawled into bed and stopped moving.

Chelsea felt kind of bad, too. She'd gotten a little overexcited about her first job. So after reflecting on her actions and with her boss self-confined to bed, she decided to do her best to improve his view of her as much as she could by giving him the energy to get up, at least. So for starters, she took Pastel Mary out to fix the place that had been damaged.

"No, no way, no way," Mary rambled in a panic. "There's no way we can fix this. We need to get a carpenter."

"Yeahhh, huh. An amateur couldn't do this, huh."

Failure already.

After discussing with Mary, they decided they would try to clean things up, at least. Mary drew some sheep and used them to cart away rubble, while Chelsea strung a yellow rope around the trees of the area and hung up signs saying No ENTRY. While they worked on it, mages who said they'd come to visit the island showed up now and again, and each time, the two magical girls told them, "Shepherdspie is in bed right now, since he doesn't feel well," and had to guide the guests to a different building.

I see, so this is work, Chelsea thought. This work thing was more of a monotonous drag than she'd expected. But when she saw Mary looking like she might drop dead at any moment, Chelsea really couldn't leave it all to her while she took a break.

But maybe a short break would be fine while she went off to the kitchen to leave a gift from a guest there. So with that thought, she left their work site. The gift was a paper bag from a well-known department store. Inside, wrapped in the paper of an equally well-known bakery, was a box. Chelsea's instincts were telling her this was an assorted cookie set. If she was at home, she would just open it and have some, and if her mother complained about it after, Chelsea could apologize then, but even she didn't have the guts to do that at work.

She seemed to recall that the white chocolate cookies from this shop were really good. If she could get online, she could have checked the reviews or the product description, but now, she could only gaze at the box. *What a shame, what a shame*, she thought as she stared at it. *I suppose there's no harm in just cutting the seal.* If she did that, though, she knew she'd take one automatically, and so she stared helplessly at the box until she figured she should get back. She left the temptation alone on the table and turned away to find Mary, peering out from behind a pillar and staring at her.

"...I'm not going to eat them, okay?" Chelsea said.

"Really...?" Mary was leery.

"Of course I'm not going to eat them, geez. More importantly, why are you here?"

"You took so long coming back, so I thought maybe you were stealing a bite..."

"I'm not gonna, I swear! It's all good, okay?"

Maybe Pastel Mary was sharper than Chelsea had thought. Mentally revising her evaluation of her, Chelsea returned to her work. But once they were done removing the debris and cleaning up where the fire had been, there was hardly any work left.

Once she was done stringing the ropes and looked up, thinking she was done with the job, she saw the hole on the wall of the estate. It was the spot where she had stepped through the floor and had fallen along with it. "Ahhh, I forgot about that."

"Wouldn't it be best to cover it with a plastic sheet or something?" Mary pointed out.

"Oh? You think?" Chelsea was doubtful.

"It would be bad if rain or something blew in through there, right?"

"It's so sunny, though. I doubt it'll rain anytime soon."

"But the wind will blow in."

"I think that'll be nice and refreshing."

"It doesn't look very nice seen from the outside, though."

"You don't think it's cool in a sort of avant-garde way?"

"Chelsea…are you trying to reduce your workload?"

"No, no, not at all! I'm totally raring to go… Huh?" Something crossed a corner of her eye. A translucent human figure resembling a lamp genie was carrying a tin of cookies, picking out one of them to crunch—

"Hey! You! You magical girl or whatever person over there!" Chelsea cried.

The translucent girl in lamp genie–themed attire looked right, left, down, and then pointed to herself. "You mean Mei?"

"You can't just eat those cookies! And how did you get them?"

"This is Mei's now, so Mei will eat them."

"Those aren't yours! They're Mr. Pie's!"

"I don't know any pies. Funny Trick gave them to Mei. This is Mei's." She sharply turned away from Chelsea like she was ready to fly off. At this rate, the cookie thief was going to slip through Chelsea's fingers. Even Chelsea had resisted the urge, but a magical girl whose name she didn't know was going to run away with those delicious brand-name cookies.

Chelsea looked down at a rock at her feet. Should she kick it? But if that girl was to dodge it the wrong way, the rock could hit the cookie tin by mistake. If the cookies inside were broken, it would all be for nothing. The girl's semitransparent coloring was also curious. When that type of enemy appeared in video games, physical attacks wouldn't work on it.

Chelsea switched gears, going after the cookie tin. No way in hell that could resist physical attacks. And she wouldn't use her magic. Basically, the best idea was to steal the tin from the girl. She would get close and snatch it away.

"Wh-what do we do, Chelsea?" Mary asked.

"No worries! You just leave this to Dreamy☆Chelsea!"

Chelsea confirmed the enemy position. She was getting away— already twenty-five feet up, thirty-five feet away from the building.

Using the wall, that was close enough to make it. With her first step, Chelsea leaped off the ground, then she set one foot against the wall of the estate to run up the side of it. Hop, hop, hop—snagging uneven spots in the wall with her toes to race up, she ascended until she'd reached the same height as the lamp genie. Bending her legs all the way to ready for one final horizontal spring, there was a nasty creak, and her footing crumbled away. The wall came tumbling down, throwing Chelsea to the ground, where she managed to catch herself in a roll.

Mary, however, was making her escape into the forest astride a sheep. She was twisting her head to look back with an expression of desperation as she yelled, "Up! Up!"

Looking up as instructed, Chelsea saw the collapsing stone wall of the estate slowly falling toward her. Chelsea ran after Mary, then overtook her, and the wall came down—rather, part of the building came down, spilling into the trees in the area with a loud crash, sending a cloud of dust billowing up as fruit and nuts rolled, as well as crushing the rope she'd worked so hard to put up, too.

Mary, Chelsea, and the sheep all managed to escape to safety. They weren't hurt. But Chelsea didn't feel like she'd been saved—because the scale of destruction was just so big. Mary's lamenting "Ahhh…" like she was digesting the event shoved the seriousness of the situation in Chelsea's face.

Chelsea considered how she could talk her way out of this and decided to foist it off on the cookie thief. That would work best.

◇ **Love Me Ren-Ren**

Mages were all important people. Without them, magical girls would never have been created.

Having a lot of people around was very nerve-racking. None of the magical girls were standing. The half-beast Clantail; the pair wearing mages' robes, Maiya and Rareko; and Miss Marguerite—who was in the style of an aristocratic lady—all stood beside their employers.

Thinking she should do so as well, Ren-Ren made to stand, but Agri grabbed her hand and stopped her. "Where are you rushing off to?"

"No, um," Ren-Ren began.

"Right now is a time for talking, so you should talk. Okay, talk."

Taking Ren-Ren and Nephilia with her, Agri shifted to a new seat. Mana and Yol were very charming, while Ragi seemed rather worn out, perhaps because of his age, and Touta seemed unused to things, like some random elementary schooler brought in and forced into mage clothes. Common to all of them was the sense that they were not bad people.

After a brief chat, Agri returned to her spot across from Navi. "He's a little different from what I heard," she said.

"Ahhh, the old man." Navi nodded.

The two of them were whispering together. Their conversation was protected by magic so the other mages and magical girls wouldn't overhear.

"I heard he was a fiery old grump, though," Agri said.

"Who knows…? Maybe it's age." Navi shrugged. "Rumors say he has plenty of rage left to spare, though."

"If he's going to be like that, then we don't have to bother going to talk to him, right?"

"Yeah, I'm good as long as he stays quiet."

The others didn't seem like bad people, but it was a bit hard to tell. At least, Ren-Ren had trouble saying for sure either way.

"What about the others?" Agri asked Navi.

"I know Yol. We're on good terms. But that magical girl she's got really has it out for me. The best thing would be to avoid letting that one offer any opinions."

"Why does she hate you?"

"I dunno. She's viscerally repulsed by me or something. Women are irrational."

"Don't just lump women all together."

"I don't hate women in general. I'm actually thankful for them."

"Hold on." Clarissa cut in on their conversation, rising from her seat. "Didn't you hear something?"

"No, did you?" said Navi.

"I didn't really hear anything," Agri added.

Ren-Ren and Nephilia said they hadn't heard anything, and Clarissa closed her eyes, her big ears trembling minutely. Navi grabbed her arm and muttered, like he was talking to himself, "There are things only Clarissa can hear." She probably had excellent hearing, just like she appeared.

"I'm not sure…," Clarissa said. "It sounded like something collapsing."

"From where?" Navi asked.

"From the estate."

"Hey, hey, that can't be good."

"There was a spot that had come down, right? That's got to be it," said Agri.

"Nobody better have been caught in it. We might as well go take a look." Navi smacked his knee with a large palm and stood up. In a voice far louder than the whisper he'd been using to discuss, he called out, "Hey, everybody," and gathered all attention on himself. "It sounds like the main building—"

There was a clatter from the corner, and a cup and its contents spilled out. It was diagonally across the room, some ways away, but Ren-Ren judged what had happened in a single glance.

A table had flipped over. Ren-Ren and Nephilia stepped in front of Agri, and Clarissa spread her arms out to cover Navi. Marguerite, near the exit, put a hand on her rapier, while Maiya pulled out a colorful staff. 7753, who'd been sitting comparatively closer, staggered to her feet. And then Clantail scooped up Ragi in her arms. Ragi had fallen, knocking over the table.

"Hey, old man, you oka—?" Right as Navi tried to approach him, he pitched forward and crumpled. Clarissa immediately caught him. Agri slumped against Ren-Ren, who hastily caught her in her arms.

Ren-Ren scanned the room. 7753's arms were around Mana's shoulders. Maiya and Marguerite had raced out the back door.

"What...?" Agri moaned. Ren-Ren stayed alert as she held Agri close. "I...feel so weak... Getting weaker..."

"Please don't force yourself to talk," Ren-Ren said.

Something felt off. *Whose voice was that?* she wondered, but it was just her own voice. Agri's body, limply slumped against her, felt heavy—even though there was no way a magical girl would find the weight of a single adult woman as heavy.

Holding Agri, Ren-Ren checked her right arm. It was not a transparent clear white with long, graceful fingers. It was a human arm, with fine hairs on it.

She looked over at Nephilia. A girl in a blazer-style school uniform of about high school age was looking at her in surprise. Her eyebrows were well maintained and on the defined side, with dyed soft brown hair in a straight cut that went down to her back and glossy lips. There wasn't much about her that was the same as Nephilia, but Ren-Ren could tell. She was Nephilia. She was the only one who would look amused in a situation like this.

A petite girl in braided pigtails, glasses, and a sailor uniform fell into the sofa along with Ragi, and the one lending her shoulder to Mana—a woman in pajamas in her midtwenties—lost her balance, too, diving into the sofa. A girl in a skirt with suspenders was almost crushed under Navi. Once she somehow managed to crawl out, it was clear she was about elementary or middle school age, maybe younger.

"What is the meaning of this?! What is going on?!" That one had to be in her forties. A woman fashionably attired in a fine gray business suit was yelling. She held a limp Yol in her arms. So that was Maiya. The young woman in black-rimmed glasses and a maid outfit following her appeared to be trembling and nervous, suspiciously looking all around the room. That would be Rareko. Her attitude was the same as when she was transformed, and her appearance was plain. Touta, who appeared next, was looking at Yol with concern, but he was able to walk on his own. The woman in her late twenties behind him who was glancing around the room— that had to be Marguerite. Her casual attire of a long T-shirt and skinny jeans was completely different from her magical-girl form, but her utterly alert stance and calm gaze was the same.

"I'm asking what's going on!" Maiya repeated furiously.

The magical girls—now no longer magical girls—looked at one another, saw that nobody was going to answer, and grew visibly confused. They had no idea what had just happened. The one thing they did understand was that they were in big trouble.

CHAPTER 4
MAGICAL GIRLS IN REGULAR CLOTHING

◇ **John Shepherdspie**

In any era, mages tended to look down on food and beverages, and some even thought enjoyment of such was a sin. Many would disparage such things: "There's no need to fixate on the mere intake of nutrients!" "It's a waste to spend time on cooking and eating!" "One should put that time to use in study and research!" "That's just lazy pigs touting 'culture' as a plausible excuse!" among other complaints. Shockingly few would endorse gourmet cuisine. Whenever a mage showed an interest, it ended up being something like, "Let's create food with magic, and if we're going to do it anyway, it might as well be good." But the creation of food and drink with magic is equivalent to the process of automation, and a personal touch is necessary for achieving fine balance and revolutionary innovation.

Shepherdspie's opinion on the matter was simple and straightforward: "Nothing beats delicious food."

*　　*　　*

Those words echoed in Shepherdspie's mind. No sooner had his eyes flared open than they squinted in the light of the sun seeping in through the gaps of the curtains.

Yes. Nothing at all beat delicious food. In order to obtain it, he had to work, though. He couldn't stay in bed forever. Shepherdspie stirred and propped himself on his elbows in bed. He felt too weary to be simply fatigued. He'd sustained nothing worse than bruises when falling from the floor above, and he hadn't broken any bones. Perhaps this wasn't harm to his body but to his inner self.

It was true that he'd experienced an emotional shock, but he couldn't be lying around in bed forever. He had an obligation. He swept off the blanket.

Shepherdspie had been preparing for this day, and that preparation wasn't a hardship. He had never put full effort into exercise, study, magic, arts, or anything else like that, but the one thing he could passionately devote his energy to was food and cooking. He heaved himself up.

He'd researched all the most excellent ingredients with the utmost thoroughness. In addition to the local products such as the vegetables, pork and pork bones, green pheasant, and fish, he had also made orders for beef shank, beef bones, celery, green onion, bouquet garni, and various other ingredients. It all looked delicious. And it *was* delicious. True gourmet was already beautiful in the ingredient stage.

Ahhh, what beauty!

Slicing and shaving off the meat. Breaking and crunching the bones. Delicately and sometimes boldly. Such craftsmanship—no, this was art—could not be accomplished by using magic with an eye only to convenience. He focused his eyes to skim the broth with as much precision as was humanly possible. The bouillon was brimming with gold, the clear amber essentially a masterpiece. The broth and the sauce—the essence of a dish, some might say—would cause problems for cooks because of the subtleties that wouldn't last in the fridge, but putting them in the storage here could keep them in a freshly made state forever. Shepherdspie made precise use of magic in such specific areas in pursuit of the pinnacle of cuisine, something beyond a mere advancement to amateur craft. He would not only entertain as the host; he would bring the guests joy as a chef.

I'll channel all the techniques I've learned...!

His excitement grew. He raised himself up on the bed.

He had covered every contingency when deciding the menu as well.

He'd avoided anything too oily, which would be hard on older people, while also including food that children would favor, such as pudding and ice cream as petit fours. Additionally, some of the guests were commoners. Rather than course cuisine that demanded formal manners, they would probably prefer to eat casually in a buffet style while mingling with the others. He made the drinks with lower alcohol content, selecting a popular apple brandy over some pretentious antique wine. For the children, there was freshly squeezed juice of various fruits. Without trying to show off or be officious, he nevertheless enlivened the eating. The individuality and taste of the chef was expressed in the aperitif selections, too.

That's right... There are people waiting for me...for my cooking!

Gritting his teeth, putting his hands on his knees, Shepherdspie forced himself to rise.

Not making it a standard multicourse dinner would offer more freedom in the menu, too. The dish Shepherdspie loved the most, the one he'd made his own name, shepherd's pie, was too much a home cooking item to serve to mages, but it was actually perfect for a buffet. Plenty of mashed potatoes. And then ground beef—Shepherdspie's own preference was lamb, but he would nix that this time out of consideration for Mary—Époisses de Bourgogne, fermented butter, bacon smoked with sakura wood chips, a little olive oil, and cream as the secret ingredient.

Heh-heh, fwa-ha-ha-ha-ha!

Just imagining it, he couldn't stop drooling. Absolutely delicious. He was willing to bet his whole fortune on this. Shepherdspie had just that much confidence in it. Anyone who ate it would sing its praises. It wasn't as if Shepherdspie really loved or respected his guests. He wasn't particularly fond of the men and women he was working himself to the bone to please. But he wanted their compliments. He wanted them to acknowledge that Shepherdspie was exceptionally talented in the field of cuisine. He wanted applause, cheers, praise, cries of shock and awe, that sort of thing.

Tossing off his nightcap, he slung his robe over his pajamas and forced his dragging legs, lifting them up and down to get to the door. When he undid the knob lock and opened the door, light poured in. It was blinding. Shepherdspie squinted, holding his right hand up to the light. The beautiful light of the sun, as if indicating his exultant future—

"...Huh?" he blurted out.

No wonder the light was blinding. There was no wall. Or rather, it wasn't that there was no wall at all. It was still there. But it wasn't doing its job. Not only was the light coming in from the outside, exposing the miserable aftermath of destruction, but wind was blowing in, too. Looking up, it wasn't just the first floor—the second and third beyond were all gone, too. Blown in the wind, Shepherdspie staggered and reached out to put his hand to the wall, but before he could, he stopped. The wreckage looked like it would crumble if he leaned on it.

Shepherdspie gently closed the door behind him. His heart was at the opposite pole of gentle, but if he let himself close the door like he felt, the rubble was bound to collapse. His eyes swept right to left, but there was less that was still standing at this point. Rubble that looked like it had originally come from the wall had been piled into a number of large mounds, so there had been some cleanup done. Shepherdspie put a hand to his head. How long had he been asleep? What had to have happened while he was asleep for things to have wound up like this?

Shepherdspie headed to the kitchen, scolding his body and heart that seemed about to falter. He would have liked to lean on the wall for support if he could, but he couldn't do that, either. It was too dangerous.

The surrounding trees had all been flattened. The basement entrance was a ruined mess. The ceiling of the hallway to the courtyard had come down. Had there been a duel between two mages who hated each other or something? Or had something exploded on accident? Had a herd of wild bulls charged through?

Oh, the guests.

Were the guests who had been invited to the island safe? As the host, Shepherdspie was obligated to protect them. Then he thought of the two magical girls. Were Chelsea and Mary safe? He trembled, and the flesh of his belly hit his thighs. The suspicion crossed his mind that maybe Chelsea's and Mary's safety was the wrong thing to worry about. Instead of concerning himself with that, it seemed not at all unlikely that those two had been the cause of this destruction—Shepherdspie shook his head. Smoothing his mussed hair with his right hand, he started walking ahead once more. True, Chelsea had made the floor cave in and Mary had pushed Shepherdspie down a floor, but they hadn't done anything this terrible. Or rather, this kind of destruction could only be done deliberately.

Despite his denial, the doubt wouldn't disappear from his mind. Just like the stubborn burn mark at the bottom of a poorly maintained cocotte, it wouldn't go away, no matter what.

"Ohhh! Mr. Shepherdspie! You're awake!" she said, roughly throwing down the wooden box she'd been holding. Looking surprised, she sprang over in his direction. It was a human woman. What was the name of that undergarment that was the length of about 85 percent of the body and showed the ankles, again? He thought it had been used in the name of a movie, but he couldn't remember it. Her white dress shirt not only had dirt on it, but the cuffs were torn, too. Her wavy brown hair was tied up in the back, but he figured it was normally a semi-long cut that curled inward. She was about twenty years old. Her fingers were long, and her nails were cut evenly. There was a protrusion like a callus on her index finger.

Shepherdspie narrowed his eyes. He was ashamed to admit if

there was a woman, he would find himself observing her, even at a time like this. But the lines of any women, magical girls included, were without exception artistic, which was also reflected in the cuisine Shepherdspie preferred.

While he was pondering on and on, the woman ran up to him, then stopped. It looked like she tried to say something, but she was panting and couldn't quite talk. She had her hands on her knees, shoulders heaving.

Shepherdspie breathed a short sigh, then took ten times that to inhale again. "Mary?"

"Huh? H-how—how could you tell?!" Surprised, the woman staggered and wound up on her bottom. Shepherdspie thought about offering her a hand, but he didn't feel well enough to do so. The woman stood up, then tapped twice with the toe of her pumps to remove the mud that was stuck on her shoes. The mud was already dry; she must not have noticed the mud until she'd fallen over and her shoes were in her field of view.

"You're...Pastel Mary, yes?" said Shepherdspie.

"Yes, I am...but I'm not transformed right now, right? How can you tell?"

"Well, um." First of all, she had the same energy. And he also figured from the callus on her index finger and her art-student attire that she was an artist either by trade or as a hobby. Furthermore, when she'd called him Mr. Shepherdspie, he'd been just about certain of her identity.

But now was not the time to be babbling on about that, and since he'd had experiences before where he had talked smugly about things like this and received an unfavorable reaction, he was appropriately evasive and didn't say how. "I made a good guess."

"Ohhh."

"First impression is the most reliable for things like this."

"Oh, really?"

"Basically. You need an eye for people when hiring, after all."

"I see."

"And when you fell over, I knew it was you."

"That's my most distinguishing feature? Don't tell me that!"

"You have no one but yourself to blame, considering how you said you carry yourself differently as a magical girl…" Shepherdspie looked down at her. "You're not much different at all."

"I *am* a bit different."

"Other magical girls who are more different go without falling over."

"It's a really subtle difference. One you can't tell from appearances alone."

People who make excuses must look like this to others. That had to be the same for himself as well, he thought with a nod, and he would look quite the disgrace. You always need a reverse teacher, no matter how old you get.

Shepherdspie sighed deeply. He was surprised he had enough energy to talk. Or rather, he didn't have the time for suffering, since it was too much effort—wasted effort. "That really doesn't matter right now."

"Ah! Right! This is a disaster!" the woman cried.

"It's quite obvious at a glance there's been a disaster."

"Not that; there's an even bigger disaster!"

Shepherdspie just about passed out. There had been a disaster big enough to destroy half the main building of the estate and then an even bigger disaster on top of that? He didn't want to think about it. But he had to ask. "What happened…?"

"Last night, all the mages collapsed, and all the magical girls were detransformed."

Now that she mentioned it, the sunlight was shining in from the east. This was the morning sun. This was too long for him to have slept, even if the injury had knocked him out. Did it have something to do with how the mages had collapsed? Was it illness, or gas, or something else? Shepherdspie had learned a fair amount about the systems in the main building, but he couldn't really say he knew everything about the whole island.

"That really is a disaster," Shepherdspie said.

"That's why I told you it's a disaster."

"Just what on earth is going on?"

"Mr. Shepherdspie, you don't have…any ideas about the cause?"

"No. I have no idea."

"There's some weird magic cast over the estate, though. It's not that going out of control?"

"When magical power goes out of control, it's more obvious to see… Oh, like an explosion or a fire."

"What about something he was researching leaking out?"

"I don't think so…" Since it would be distributed as the inheritance, Shepherdspie had gathered all magic items into the storehouse of the main building. He had also assessed the catalog of them, but not being the specialist, he didn't understand all the effects each item might have. The more specialized the item, the more things about it he wasn't sure of.

"Is this the only area that's collapsed?" Shepherdspie asked.

"Yes, it's just what you can see around here," the woman replied.

In other words, the storehouse was safe. It didn't seem like it had to do with the magic items—but magic was magic, so he couldn't say that for sure.

"I'd like to ask a specialist's opinion, if possible," said Shepherdspie.

"Like I said, everyone is down."

"How bad is it?"

"Aside from one boy, the rest of the mages are all moaning and groaning. And then there's the magical girls who went to the gate to get help… Actually, I'm impressed you can walk, Mr. Shepherdspie, even though you're a mage."

He did feel sluggish, but it wasn't so bad that he couldn't move. Was it thanks to his fat, or was it his obsession with cooking?

The word "cooking" rose in his mind, and he looked up. "Cooking…yes, cooking."

"None of the mages are in the state to eat," the woman explained, "but when magical girls can't transform, they get hungry, right? So we decided to have a meal to start before investigating the island, so we had the food that was in the kitchen, but… That was okay, right?"

Shepherdspie staggered. He almost collapsed, but he pulled himself up with the utmost effort. He felt dizzy. This woman was saying that they had eaten the food that had been in the kitchen. And that meant, in other words— Shepherdspie raced off. Or more precisely, his emotions were racing. His body and heart couldn't keep up, so functionally, he was just walking quickly, but anyway, he was hurrying.

The voice of the woman came after him from behind. "And everyone was wondering! If maybe you don't know something! And they want you to tell them what you know! Can you hear me? Mr. Shepherdsp—aaaaah!" The woman, who'd been chasing after him, cried out, followed by the sound of hitting the ground. She must have tripped over something and fallen.

Shepherdspie didn't turn back, and of course he didn't extend a hand to try to save her, either. He gritted his teeth. The ingredients were ultimately nothing more than ingredients—they were not cuisine. The fond and the bouillon had taken time, but they hadn't been made to be eaten just like that. It was the efforts following that which would make them true cuisine to serve the guests. And that plan was falling apart because of magical girls.

Shepherdspie loved cuisine, and he respected the people who created it, but that didn't mean he respected all non-mage humans. He was neither a philanthropist nor a humanitarian, and he despised foolish and worthless people—the types of people who would treat food crudely and who would make a mockery of eating. In that sense, he wasn't fond of magical girls, as they didn't need food, either. But it wasn't as if they chose to not require food and drink. Those who had designed them like that were the ones to be despised, and it was barking up the wrong tree to be complaining to magical girls. But forgiving them for blasphemy against food was a completely different issue.

He heard footsteps coming from behind. Occasionally, they stumbled. Shepherdspie kept moving forward, not turning back. He opened the door to the kitchen, looked at the pot on the stove, moaned "Ahhh," and fell to his knees. The whole pot of bouillon was completely gone. There was a bag packed with vegetable scraps, too. So they had used those as well? The plates piled on the table were marked with sauce. He leaned in to sniff them. It was canned tomato sauce. They had used it on his carefully selected ingredients without even checking for taste, without any adjustment or addition to the store-bought sauce, just *because it was there*. Another cry of "Ahhh!" spilled from him.

"Ahhh! I can't believe you're still here!"

When the footsteps that had been following him reached the kitchen, an accusatory voice immediately rained down. There was no reason Shepherdspie should be criticized. When he raised his chin in indignation, the woman who'd called herself Mary was glaring down somewhere else, looking upset or angry. With the mountain of plates in the way, Shepherdspie couldn't see anything. He leaned one hand against the table and slowly stood. Beyond the plates was a woman in a bathrobe hunched all the way over, cradling a soup bowl. He knew that woman. That was Dreamy☆Chelsea pretransformation.

The woman in the bathrobe held a spoon in her right hand and a soup bowl in her left and was scowling. "You've got the wrong idea. Look. This isn't my fault."

"This isn't about fault," Mary replied. "We can't be the only ones slacking off when everyone else is busy doing all sorts of things. But the moment you got the chance, you came back to the kitchen to have soup. Even though we just finished breakfast time."

"I needed nutritional supplementation."

"Everyone else was satisfied from dinner and breakfast."

"I have poor fuel efficiency."

"That's just nonsense... Ah! The soup is completely gone! You ate it all!"

"That was unavoidable; I mean, this soup is really good... Ah, Mr. Pie!" Looking up from the soup bowl that appeared to have been licked clean, the face of the woman in the bathrobe sparkled. It was a joyful expression, like someone lost in a desert who'd found an oasis. "This soup is great! The best! I've never had anything so insanely delicious before! Amazing! Hey, tell me your recipe! I'll have my mom make it when I get home."

"At least say you're going to make it yourself…," Mary grumbled.

"My mom's a better cook than I am."

"Well, um, even if that is true…"

The woman in the bathrobe went on—talking about how delicious the soup had been. How there was no point in living if she couldn't have any more of this. How if she just had this, more energy would always well up inside her. "If you have welling energy, then do some work," Mary muttered.

Each time the woman in the bathrobe praised his soup, Shepherdspie's plump cheeks relaxed, and before he knew it, there was a faint smile on his face. An invigorating sense of satisfaction filled his heart. He pulled out a chair, sat down, and hung his head, completely out of energy. The expression on his own face, reflected in the glass door of the dish cabinet, looked more peaceful than anything he'd seen on himself before. He could just about be satisfied enough to die right that moment, but then he thought, *I can't die now*, and shook his head.

◇ **Kotori Nanaya**

She had made a big mistake. Lately, staying in magical-girl form had generally brought woes to both her work and private life. If she never detransformed, her dress pretransformation would naturally get sloppier, and she would stop using makeup and stop doing her hair, and she wouldn't even put on shoes, and with the excuse that she didn't need it if she was a magical girl, Kotori had gotten sloppier and sloppier. And all of that had led her to now. She hadn't planned to detransform, so she hadn't brought clothes. She'd brought a swimsuit because she'd heard they were going to an island, but how could she wear that now? And that was in 7753's size anyway, so it would be too small.

Everyone else was in school uniforms and formal wear. They were so put together. Some were in casual wear, but it was still clothing they could go outside in. The one in the maid outfit couldn't be wearing it for fun; that had to be her work uniform. In other words, it had a dignified air.

The only one in her pajamas with no makeup was 7753— Kotori Nanaya. Everyone else surely had registered her as being "the hilarious pajama woman" or "pajamagical girl." But this situation was dire enough to have made Kotori's disgrace trivial in comparison.

Something unclear had happened that had caused the mages to collapse and the magical girls' transformations to come undone. This unclear event could only be expressed as *something*, and despite having a lineup of veteran magical girls who seemed like they would be far more reliable than Kotori, they all had no idea. Even if they wanted to try asking the mages, Ragi, who seemed like he would be the most knowledgeable, followed by Navi, were both completely unconscious. Yol was struggling to keep her eyes open at all, while Agri and Mana could somehow wring out words. But despite the differences in their symptoms, they were all incapacitated. Only Touta was walking around without any particular difficulty, but he was basically just a normal little kid, and it wasn't like he had any help or knowledge to offer.

All the mages—even if this didn't seem like an immediate threat to their lives—were in a fairly serious state. And though the magical girls were mobile, they were in a serious situation of their own. They'd taken their physical abilities and magic for granted, but now they couldn't use them. They were a few defenseless women stuck on an isolated island in the middle of the ocean where there were wild animals running loose, too.

Though they'd met up with the two magical girls who worked at the estate, they were basically just as clueless. They didn't know anything about the island, either. They said their employer should know, but he was still asleep and wouldn't wake up. So they decided to eat to get their strength up first, but Kotori couldn't even process the taste as good or bad and just forced it down.

Time passed uselessly as they wandered around in confusion

until nightfall, and since they couldn't be walking around in the dark, they decided to take a break for now. But the coming of dawn didn't resolve anything, and the mages were still fast asleep. Tepsekemei hadn't come back, either.

Kotori was worried about Mana, but she was also worried about Tepsekemei. All the other magical girls had been human to begin with, so they'd been able to gather together—Tepsekemei was originally a turtle and would have a hard time coming to them. But then this island was so big, it would be difficult to search for a single turtle. If her transformation had come undone while she was flying through the air, then worst case—considering this far, Kotori shook her head.

It'll be okay, it'll be okay, it'll be okay; Mei is strong. And she's lucky, too. She's not going to…

Nephilia, Love Me Ren-Ren, Rareko, and Maiya armed themselves with a poker, hatchet, shovel, and crowbar and headed out for the gate first thing that morning. They would use it to return to the outside world and seek help. Dreamy☆Chelsea and Pastel Mary would investigate the estate, while Kotori kept an eye on the mages in the annex and stood guard there. Though Clantail and Clarissa Toothedge stayed behind, too, they were both too small to defend anything. The only ones she could rely on were Miss Marguerite and herself.

Kotori's gaze dropped to the object in her hands. The hammer shone dully under the light of the sun coming in from the window, and it felt heavier than it actually weighed. Her left hand held a pot lid. She held both objects by their wooden handles but felt no warmth from either. She'd been handed these in order to protect herself from beasts, but just how useful would they be? Even in magical-girl form, she wasn't any good at rough stuff. Could she use these for anything other than carpentry or cooking? Just thinking about it made her heart and stomach feel heavier. She would have at least felt better if she could have transformed, but she couldn't even do that.

Ever since the incident in B City, she'd been spending more

time as a magical girl, even outside of work hours. She'd lost her old habits of detransforming to go shopping or to get her hair done at a popular salon. Every time she remembered the faces of the magical girls she'd met during that incident, it hurt like being cut open. As long as she was in magical-girl form, it would ease the pain.

Maybe that was just running away. Kotori couldn't deny that. Living with Tepsekemei, a magical girl from B City, forced her to remember all the time. No—she was sure that was an excuse, too. The incident would have lingered in her mind whether Tepsekemei was there or not.

There was no escape on this island. Kotori remained frightened and human, worried about the missing Tepsekemei and Mana, who couldn't get up, and all she could do was stand there patiently at the annex entrance.

"Um."

Kotori turned around to see the girl in glasses and braided pigtails standing there. She couldn't really tell if the girl had an expression or not. She had the stature of a middle schooler or younger, and her face read as middle school or first year of high school at most, but she seemed superficially far calmer than Kotori.

"Um...you're Clantail, right?" Kotori felt like it was weird to call a human by a magical-girl name, but she didn't know her name as a human, and it would be weird to ask now, so there was nothing for it but to call her this. "Did something happen?"

"A call."

"Huh...? Ahhh."

This wasn't just a girl of few words—these weren't enough words here. There was no subject and no verb. But Kotori figured it out. There weren't many people here who would call for Kotori specifically.

"I'm sorry—can I ask you to handle things here for a while?" Kotori bowed to Clantail, who nodded. Then Kotori strode down the corridor to open the door to the large hall. There were a bunch of sofas there where the mages lay limply. Maybe it would have been better if they rested in the beds in their separate rooms, but since they didn't have enough people to watch four mages separately, they were forced to lay them on the sofas in the hall and put blankets on top of them.

The girl in a skirt with suspenders looked over at her and stuck up her right thumb to indicate behind her. It was a totally incongruent gesture for an elementary schooler, but when you imagined her original form, it actually felt right. The woman in the long T-shirt with plain English letters printed on it glanced over at her, then immediately returned to her task of fanning the old man. Though she couldn't have been much older than Kotori, she seemed far more dignified.

Kotori passed by Touta, who was wiping the sweat that was gushing down Navi's forehead (though it was hard to tell how much of that was forehead), and went to the girl who lay on the sofa at the very back. "Mana?"

"Have a request...," Mana said, like it was a struggle. It was painful just to look at her, and Kotori wanted to tell her, *"Please take it easy and rest now,"* but the firm light of will shone in Mana's eyes. She hadn't called for Kotori because she was in pain or because she was suffering. That was the look of someone with a goal.

"Take me...my room," Mana wheezed. Even just getting out a few hoarse, broken words was absolutely the most she could manage. Kotori brought her ear to Mana's lips.

"Take me...to my room," Mana repeated.

"Will you be all right?" Kotori asked her.

"Pharmacy is...my...specialty. In my bags..."

"Oh, so then I could bring your bags here—"

"No." A clear rejection. She said that a bit louder, too.

Kotori brought her ear away from Mana's lips and looked at her. Mana's expression was firm, saying that she wouldn't change her decision.

Kotori cleared her throat, took Mana's arm, and brought it behind her own head. Putting an arm around Mana's shoulders, Kotori somehow got her to stand, but Mana was hardly holding herself up at all. Circling her other arm behind her thigh, Kotori lifted her with a heave. Kotori wasn't all that strong, but Mana was as light as she looked, and it seemed like she could barely carry her to her room.

"Hold on there; where are you going?" a voice called out from behind.

Without turning back, Kotori replied, "Mana says she wants to check if there is anything useful in her bags."

She sensed movement from Marguerite's direction. "Wouldn't it be better to just bring her bags, rather than forcing her to move?"

"She said she didn't want others moving her things… I'm sure there are drugs that would be dangerous if mixed and things like that."

She sensed a presence standing where she'd seen Touta before. "Um, I'll help…if you don't mind."

And now Touta. Kotori was grateful for his kindness, but she didn't want him following right now. "It's okay, it's okay. I'm stronger than I look." Kotori lumbered heavily to emphasize her strength even more.

But a presence behind her rose to her feet and approached. Kotori heard a child's carpeted footsteps and trembled. "Oh, and besides, Mana doesn't like to be touched by other people," she said. Then she followed that with, "It took a long time before she'd let me touch her."

The presence behind her stopped, then returned to its original position and sat down. Kotori silently apologized to the vaguely dejected presence. She'd become a better liar than she used to be. When Tepsekemei asked questions that were difficult to answer, she would avoid them with sloppy answers, and despite knowing Mana was looking into the B City incident, Kotori kept her mouth shut about having been in contact with Pythie Frederica for a mission for Magical Girl Resources. It was all miserable and shady.

Kotori had made it look like she was calm while in the big hall, but once she came out of the courtyard, she was panting as she carried Mana. Even if she wasn't heavy, Kotori hardly ever got exercise while human, so she was quite literally an unbearable burden. Panting hard, she opened the door to Mana's room, but she still didn't toss her down, laying Mana gingerly on the bed. Mana's luggage wasn't girlish at all, a black Boston bag and a milk-white suitcase, but you couldn't deny they were very Mana.

"Is this it? This one?" Pointing to the bag, Kotori followed Mana's direction—her nod—and opened it up. Kotori checked over the items within one by one until she pulled out a dark-brown plastic case from the Boston bag. She dug her nails into the case clasp to pry it open. She wasn't used to handling tools like this, so she was weirdly nervous, wiping off the sweat dripping down her cheeks with her thumb. The tiny case was just four by six inches, with a row of slim ampules inside. Mana still had more instructions. Aside from the ampules, she'd also brought needles and thin black rubber tubing. Mana tried to prop herself up on her arms, and Kotori hurriedly went to help her.

Kotori raised up the bespectacled Mana and followed her instructions—her voice was as quiet as a mosquito's buzz—rolling the sleeve of Mana's robe up to the shoulder and then tightly wrapping her left biceps with rubber tubing. Kotori couldn't do the rest, even with instructions. Breathing heavily, Mana broke an ampule, inserted the needle, and drew up the contents. She brought the needle to her arm with trembling hands, and though she hesitated a few times, she stuck it right into a vein that had risen from the rubber tubing's restriction. The plunger pushed in the translucent fluid, decreasing in volume until it was depleted. Kotori watched, unable to stop her. She didn't even know if this was a good thing or a bad thing. Once before, Mana had strengthened herself with drugs to fight an insanely powerful magical girl. Then she'd passed out afterward and gone straight to the hospital. Of course, she wouldn't be using the same stuff as that time. At least, Kotori didn't think so, but she couldn't say for sure.

Mana slowly lifted her chin and looked up at the ceiling. She pursed her lips and blew out a breath that eventually became a long sigh as Kotori watched, sweating buckets. Mana exhaled especially deeply, and then when she turned to Kotori, she looked a little refreshed and invigorated, and there was pink in her cheeks.

Kotori let out a long sigh as well, grabbing Mana by the shoulders. "Are you all right? There's nothing funny going on, right? You're not using any weird drugs?"

Mana's bright-eyed expression immediately turned to a scowl as she brushed away Kotori's hands. "Stop worrying about nonsense!"

"I mean, of course I'm going to worry. You wound up in the hospital from doing that before, didn't you?"

"This is a different type of drug. The one I used this time is just a nutritional supplement."

"Just a nutritional supplement… Isn't that what everyone who uses dangerous drugs says?"

"What would be the point of lying about something like this? It really is just a nutritional supplement. But not for the body. It's replenished my magical power."

"Your magical power?"

"This must mean that the reason the mages all collapsed and the magical girls' transformations were undone was their bodies' magical power drying up. I'm going to try testing a little more." Mana pulled out a second needle. Withdrawing the liquid drug from an ampule, she tried to take Kotori's arm, but Kotori panicked and waved off her hand.

"What are you doing? Don't!"

"It's not poison! Relax. If this makes you go back to being a magical girl, then we know the cause." Mana took her wrist hard enough that it hurt and drew her close.

Never once as long as Kotori could remember had she ever liked needles, but she couldn't possibly refuse this. She looked back fondly on when she'd been a child and could say straight out that she hated needles.

"Um, what about disinfectant?" Kotori asked.

"It's not necessary with these syringes."

"What about using a rubber tube, like you did before?"

"You have thick veins, and they're easy to see."

Kotori gave up, scrunching her face and closing her eyes. She felt a literal stabbing pain and the feeling of a foreign object going into her arm, cold, disgust, unease, and various other negative feelings, and when she felt the needle come out, she finally opened her eyes. Though her left arm still hurt a bit, that was all. When she looked down at her arm, there was a little red dot. Maybe Mana was better at giving injections than the doctor Kotori usually went to.

Kotori waved her arm around. She didn't feel any worse, but she didn't feel better, either. If it was as Mana said, then she should have recovered a little magical power, but it wasn't like she'd felt a sense of loss or fatigue when she'd become unable to transform in the first place—the transformation had just come undone spontaneously, and then she'd been unable to turn back again. Kotori tried transforming so she could say, *"It doesn't look like you can resolve this with just one needle,"* but it worked. Like when her transformation had come undone, Kotori was completely naturally able to transform into the magical girl 7753.

She was dumbfounded for a few seconds. Then, seeing her arms and legs, her costume, her voluminous hair, and her goggles, which you might call her lifeline, she cried out, and Mana leaped on her and covered her mouth.

"Don't yell. Quiet."

"No, but, I mean—"

"You're allowed to be wowed or surprised, but keep your voice down. You got that?" After that warning, Mana removed her hand. 7753 turned around, but when she reached out to the doorknob, this time, Mana captured her wrist. "Listen to me. Don't make a fuss. Stay here."

"But we have to tell everyone."

"Only when we figure out who it's okay to tell."

7753 started to protest, *"Is this the time to be doing something like that?"* but then closed her mouth. Mana looked extremely serious, and she wasn't going to hear any arguments. Mana, who you'd think would be the far weaker one, pulled her close, and 7753 sat down beside her on the sheets.

Mana leaned close and lowered her voice. "I'm going to have you check them."

"Check them?" 7753 didn't get what she was trying to say. The mages were out on the sofas groaning, and they had to save them as soon as possible. And the magical girls had left the mansion and could be in danger out there, so of course it would be good for them to be able to transform. It would be safest for 7753 to go out and help. And to save Tepsekemei, too—

Mana smacked her own thigh, interrupting 7753's train of thought. "Don't rush. Prioritize checking with your goggles over everything else."

"Like I said, check what?"

"Check if someone caused this mess. We can tell people about the cause and how to fix it after we know for sure they didn't do it. We should pretend to be helpless, too, until then."

7753 chewed on the meaning of Mana's words, and it took her a few seconds until she had digested them. Her eyes widened. "Wait, you mean someone caused this?!"

"Don't yell."

"Oh, sorry."

"Maybe someone did this, and maybe not. That's why we're going to check. If someone did cause this, I'm not gonna let them get away with it."

The mage girl who'd been laid flat and groaning was gone. Now, there was an investigator who, as a member of the Inspection Department, wasn't going to let a villain do as they pleased. 7753 bit her lip with a little nod. There were creases in the white sheets.

7753 was also supposed to be one of the magical girls who had fought in B City. Even if it had been for only a brief time, she had abandoned considerations of her personal safety to stand against fearsome enemies in order to protect the city, in order to support the girls who had protected the city. She'd been running from those memories because they were painful and difficult, and this time she'd gotten herself all worked up thinking of this like a vacation or a fun trip, and as one of Mana's companions, she was all in a confusion.

Mana was different. She didn't run away, and she didn't try to forget. She was trying to be a stronger investigator—surely, one great enough that Hana Gekokujou would not have been ashamed of her.

"Understood. I'll do it. I'll go." 7753 was about to get up, and this time, Mana grabbed the hem of her costume.

"How are you going to explain it if you go as a magical girl?"

"Oh, of course... But what should I do?"

"Take off your goggles and undo your transformation. You leave the goggles separate, as an item."

"I see... Um...so in other words...I adjust the goggles' settings beforehand, then check people through the goggles when they're not looking?"

"Now you get the idea."

"What parameters should I set the goggles to look for?"

"Can you make it so they check the level of understanding about this incident?"

"I think that could be checked through the number of hearts displayed."

"Then make it that. If they're the culprit, then of course their level of understanding will be high. And even if they're not the culprit...if this situation was caused by some kind of coincidence and they know and aren't saying anything, you can call that close, half-guilty."

First, 7753 would look at the people still at the annex. If they were all clear, then Mana would share as much of her drug as she could. Next, 7753 would head out and go after the group that had headed to the gates and check if they were clear or not.

"But regardless, be quick," said Mana. "It's not good to leave things like this."

"Yes, of course."

"The others aside, the old man will die."

"But..." 7753 couldn't say that she'd heard that he was way more vivacious in his old age than a mage who never exercised and only had youth on their side. After some hesitation, she decided to put it slightly differently. "...I've heard that he's a spry old man in good health, though."

"Apparently, there are some concerns about his health."

"Oh, really?"

"We all got a health check a few years ago, and when he got his results, he was ranting on about how 'this must be some kind of mistake; don't give me this nonsense...' So I heard from my father."

You'd think he wouldn't be like that about his own health, but he was being outrageous there, too.

"So then I'll act fast," said 7753. "Um, how long will this drug last?"

"I don't know. I wasn't expecting something like this. I don't even understand what's going on in the first place. It would be best not to waste it, if possible... But we should tell those on our side that we're on their side. I wouldn't call sharing it for that purpose a waste."

7753 changed the settings on her goggles, took them off, and placed them on the bed, then undid her transformation. All that was left then was the goggles.

Goggles in hand, Kotori stood, and Mana grabbed the sleeve of her pajamas. "You won't have anywhere to hide the goggles with an outfit like that."

Kotori wound up borrowing Mana's robe. It wasn't her size, but being a loose-fitting design, it wasn't like she was going to burst through it.

Kotori put on the robe and left the room. When she told the story Mana had suggested—"Mana lent this to me when I complained about not wanting to wear embarrassing clothing this whole time"—Clantail and Clarissa were completely convinced, and Touta nodded a bunch of times.

Though she had been aware of it herself, everyone else acknowledging that her attire had been embarrassing was humiliating. But she didn't let that discourage her and did her job. Ragi, Navi, Agri, Yol, Touta. And then Clarissa, Clantail, and Miss Marguerite. None of them knew what had caused the situation, and Kotori was relieved.

◇ **Rei Koimizu**

Rei went back the way she had come as a magical girl, now in human form. Though it had to be the same path and sights, everything looked different. The wind was blowing dirt and dust up, and the sun was gradually beating down hotter. The large leaves splaying from tree branches looked sharp, like they would cut if touched. The way was unpaved, and she felt like she would stumble on rocks and uneven spots on the ground. And then there were wild animals. She'd seen birds flying in the air and fish swimming in the pond, but the only large animals she saw were sheep. Though it was just that she hadn't seen any large animals, and it didn't mean there weren't any. The guests had been explicitly told to bring magical girls, so you would naturally assume there was something. Everyone else thought so, too.

A walk down this path was a casual stroll for a magical girl, but not for a human. The group's progress was slow. Maiya, carrying a crowbar, walked in the lead, while Nephilia, with a shovel, guarded the rear. Rei was second to last, while Rareko walked ahead of Rei. She was constantly hearing complaints from ahead, like, "Is this really all right?" and "Agh, why is this happening?" There were sighs. About one in every five times, a scolding flew back from the lead of "Be quiet, Rareko."

Just doing it in human form was more stressful. The wind and sun were kind to magical girls but harsh on humans. How many of the people here had anything to prevent sunburn? Most of them were wearing minimal makeup or none at all. But there was a pressing enough threat to their lives that such things didn't even matter. They didn't know what was going on, but they had to go out to head for the gate anyway. This was kind of like a suicide squad, in a way.

Rei continued to observe how everyone talked and acted. They were different from when they were magical girls. If she got them mixed up, she might get hurt.

Get hurt?

What sort of hurt would that be? How did she reach that assumption? She already had her answer, but she could pretend she hadn't noticed. What would Agri want in this situation? Was it all right for her to do as Agri wanted?

There was a poke at her back. Still walking, Rei turned to see the brown-haired girl—Nephilia—looking at her curiously. Wondering what this was about, Rei faced forward again, and then there was a stroke along her spine. Now she was sure this wasn't her imagination. Rei turned back to look Nephilia in the eye. She didn't look guilty about it at all, tilting her head.

"What?" Rei asked her.

"What do you mean, what?" She spoke more clearly than when she was a magical girl. But Rei didn't understand what she was after.

"You just touched my back, didn't you?"

"No."

Rei faced forward again. Before she had the time to wonder what that was about, fingertips rapped her back in succession, and Rei turned around. "What is it?"

Expression not changing at all, Nephilia muttered, "Anyway," basically declaring that she was going to change the subject, and Rei scowled. "That's a cute uniform. You in middle school?"

"No, I'm in high school," Rei replied.

"Huhhh. Your skin is so pretty, I thought maybe you were in middle school."

"Well...thanks."

"First year?"

"I'm in second year."

"So we're the same age. Surprising. You have such a cute baby face."

This wasn't necessarily entirely a compliment. Rei offered a vague smile in return. She hesitated, wondering if she should face forward again or not, and looked back at the other girl. Though it looked as if Nephilia was speaking to her in a pretty friendly way, she was completely expressionless. Her appearance was neat and trim, with sharp pleats in her skirt. Her hair was dyed from the roots, with no black inching in. Her eyebrows were thick—normally that would give the impression of sloppy grooming or a hot-blooded and emotional disposition, but with her, it gave her an air of elegance like Heian-period court nobility. Looking at the whole picture, she was even more inscrutable than the magical girl Nephilia.

"Hey, tell me your LINE," said Nephilia.

"Huh?"

"Or are you using magical-girl social media? Magitter? MINE? Or Lightningram? That works, too."

"I really don't…"

"You don't have them?"

"No, now just isn't the time."

"But it seems like things'll get busier later."

Their whispered chat must have been noticed, as a call of "You, stop fooling around" flew at them from the lead, and Rei faced front again. Hearing the muffled snicker of *ksh-sh* from behind, she thought, *Ah, that is Nephilia.* It actually put her at ease.

Keeping alert to their surroundings, the group made their way along, pausing over slight noises only to be relieved that it was the babbling of a river or the rustling of leaves, looking up at the beating sun with irritation as they headed for the gates. It took them triple the time it had taken to get there. Passing through the wet lowlands, they ascended a gentle hill, and when they looked down from its crest, a brown, square object was visible beyond the trees. Someone let out a weak *phew.* That object was the gate. Everyone else besides the one who'd made that sound upon finally reaching it sighed, too.

Restraining their feet's urge to hurry and scolding their hearts' tendency to race, they resumed their slow and gradual march. They did relax their attention a bit, just from their goal being right ahead. Ten minutes after that.

When they finally got to the gate, it wasn't working.

"Just what is the meaning of this?!" Maiya was enraged,

swiping her crowbar this way and that, but it wouldn't resolve the situation.

Rareko said she knew "more than totally nothing" about these things, and she tried touching the panel and knocking on the parts of the device, then lay on the ground faceup with a toolbox beside her, clacking and rattling around as she fiddled with things like a car mechanic, but when she got up, her expression was still grim, and she shook her head without a word. According to her explanation, none of the parts looked broken, and she thought it was just that there was no energy supply. She also said she couldn't repair it. Maiya got mad again, but regardless, it wasn't something that could be fixed.

There were two gates on this island: the one Ren-Ren's group had come through and the gate on the other side—on the south side. The group decided that if this one was no good, they'd try going to the other side and so headed in the opposite direction. Their steps were heavier than before. Though Rei figured this wasn't going to work anyway, she followed along without opposing it. It wasn't like she had any alternative plan.

Looking at the situation, it made sense that there was no energy being supplied to the gate. The magical girls couldn't transform, and the mages were groaning and unable to get up. It seemed unlikely that the south gate alone would be intact given the situation, but they still had to check anyway.

Nephilia caused mischief like an elementary school boy— touching Rei's hair, flipping up her skirt, always picking some new target or trying some new thing, but Rei ignored her. It was partially because she had other things to think about right now, but also because she didn't want to get yelled at by Maiya any more than she already had.

Normally, you would be able to see the connection between someone's human form and magical-girl form. They were the same person, so there wouldn't be a dramatic personality change. Things might be different if it was the rare case of an animal or a guy becoming a magical girl, but Ren-Ren had never met a magical girl like that. Rare cases should fundamentally not be taken into consideration for anything.

Maiya was strict with herself and others. Her muscle, incredibly thick and lithe for a woman of her age, was visible even through her suit. Her legs were also thick and muscular. In other words, she trained as a human, too, not only as a magical girl. The way she swung a crowbar wasn't amateur, either. She may have been emotional, but her body had been trained. And even that emotionality, Rei could imagine came from Yol's dire situation—in other words, it was professionalism.

As for Rareko—surprisingly enough, she could use a weapon. Unlike Nephilia and Rei, she handled it like she knew how to defeat an enemy with it. Properly speaking, they would have liked to leave her with Yol, but if she was able to handle the gate system, there was no reason not to bring her. Put it the other way, then that would also mean trusting Marguerite, who seemed to be an old acquaintance of Maiya's. When she had talked to Marguerite right before leaving, it had to be to tell her to protect Yol—or something to that effect. Rei thought back on how sharp and vigilant Marguerite had looked and breathed a little sigh.

The party went back the way they had come, and then once they had reached the hill where the annexes and main building would be in view if they ascended, the two in the lead stopped. Rei looked up front, wondering what had happened, but it was just the path ahead, and there wasn't anything in particular. Looking at Maiya, her head was tilted upward. Since Ren-Ren was behind her and couldn't see her face, all she could tell was that "it seemed she was looking up." Rei followed Maiya's gaze. There was a figure. She knew that figure. She seemed to recall it had been in the main building. But it had disappeared before being introduced. It was the magical girl dressed in a dancing-girl costume.

"What are you doing?" the girl asked.

"That's my line," Maiya shot back, almost cutting her off, weapon at the ready.

But even if she did raise her weapon, it wasn't like she could do anything to a magical girl. It looked silly, but Rei felt like she had to do something, too. All of them raised their weapons and pointed them at the magical girl—Rei thought she'd been called Mei. It was strange that she was able to stay in magical-girl form in the first place in this situation. Rei also thought it was very natural to assume that she would know something about the situation, when she was the only one transformed when nobody else could do it.

Mei calmly approached the ground, and the group backed up, surrounding her in a circle. Rei observed. Mei didn't show diffidence or smile sadistically—she remained cool as a cucumber, chewing on something. Her mouth munched along, then swallowed. "Mei just had a close one."

"Why are you transformed?!" Maiya demanded.

"This is a valuable food."

"What are you talking about? I'm asking why you're transformed!"

"Mei is kind. That's what Weddin said. So Mei saved ants, too. And spiders. This time, Mei decided to save birds, too. If Mei sees the Toshishun, he'll get saved, too."

Maiya stopped trying to talk to her. All that she was getting was nonsense and something from Akutagawa stories. It was clear to see that Maiya suspected this person was funny in the head. It was hopelessly hopeless for someone who could casually kill all of them if she wanted to be crazy. Nephilia covered her mouth, shoulders shaking. This was frightening enough that even she would try to restrain her laughter.

Mei's face was extremely difficult to read. She didn't try to communicate nonverbally what she was thinking. She was different from any humans Rei knew. She was also different from any magical girls Rei knew. Never mind classifying her, Rei couldn't even search for anyone similar.

"In other words." That wasn't Maiya. Nephilia, shoulders shaking, opened her mouth. The tone and inflection of her voice was quiet and calm. "You're kind, so you'll help us out?"

Mei nodded. Having managed to communicate with her even

slightly was like a miracle. She floated toward them. This time, none of them tried to back away. They timidly came closer instead and looked at the metal box Mei thrust out like she was trying to show them—it was a cookie tin—which was crammed with gray fruit—

"Mei!"

On top of the hill. Rei thought it was a mage, but it turned out it wasn't. It was 7753, who had stayed behind at the main building. She'd been wearing pajamas before, but she was wearing mage robes and a cape now. She must have borrowed them because she didn't want to be in that embarrassing attire forever. Probably from Mana.

"You're all right! What a relief!" she practically shouted. Nigh tumbling down the hill, she raced down the slope, spreading her arms wide to embrace Mei, but then passed through her. 7753's shout turned into a yelp, and since Maiya and Rareko stepped smoothly aside, there was nobody there to catch her, and she fell and went rolling farther down the hill, tossing up dust as she went.

This time, Nephilia didn't cover her mouth as she snickered *ksh-shh*.

◇ **Miss Marguerite**

The problem was on the way to being solved. There were enough of the "gray fruit" that could be picked from the "gray trees" that grew wild on the island, even with a large number of people eating them. The mages were all revitalized, and the magical girls were able to transform again. Even if they didn't know what had caused things, even just knowing a method to handle it made a big difference.

"Hey, Miss Marguerite?" Touta said.

"What is it?"

"Why was I the only one who could walk around and talk normally?"

"I figured you're not being treated as a mage."

"Aw, seriously...?"

Though this had produced one disappointed person, rather than getting down about it, said disappointed person was glad of the other mages' recovery and looked to be enjoying a chat with Yol that was rather sprinkled with specialized terminology. They were apparently talking about a card game. Marguerite felt mildly guilty about having ordered him to leave the cards behind because games were unnecessary, but from another angle, you could also say that made it so they would play another day. It would be perfect to help Touta make connections.

Though it remained an issue that they couldn't use the gate, John Shepherdspie, who managed the island, told them: "There's an external battery. If you put that in, you might be able to make it work." So Maiya and Rareko pulled out the six-inch black cube as well as some cables and such from the storehouse and headed for the gate.

Agri, Nephilia, and Love Me Ren-Ren stayed inside to discuss something. This inheritance meeting couldn't be said to be proceeding according to plan at this point, and it would probably be canceled. They would have to try again at a later date, and Marguerite assumed there would be a wait until then. Was the trio discussing a new contract for that time, or were they talking about something else? In Marguerite's opinion, the mage named Agri was clearly fishy. Even if they hadn't only just met, Marguerite wouldn't trust her. Marguerite had asked Mana and 7753 to station themselves in the large hall of the annex. The only way out of the annex was to exit through the large hall, so there was good reason to put them there.

When Navi saw the destruction of the main building, he was in shock and groaning. *Why is he so depressed when it isn't his...?* Marguerite wondered, but she remembered that this place could become Navi's. Maybe he'd been gunning for it. He ordered Clarissa to investigate the scene, but it seemed things did not turn out how he'd hoped, and his shoulders slumped.

Ragi, on the other hand, had become more energetic. Or rather, it was less energetic and more enraged. He yelled at Shepherdspie for failing to manage the island properly, while the portly man shrank away in shame. They still hadn't even figured out the cause of this, after all. While in contrast with her apologetic boss, one of the magical girls who Shepherdspie had hired, Dreamy☆Chelsea, argued back fiercely. She doggedly opposed Ragi with rather incomprehensible counterarguments—like would you blame the landlord if a satellite fell and hit your head?—and with the dispute rapidly heating up, Pastel Mary attempted to stop it by creating sheep, but she must have made too many, as the master couldn't keep them all under control, and some went wild, and though everyone else managed to dodge or avoid them, Navi was the one person left squatting there, swallowed by the herd of sheep.

Clantail transformed her lower body into a goat to herd the sheep together, and though Ragi was still angry, he was shown to the "management room" to investigate the cause of the incident. Shepherdspie apologized to him as he led the way, while Navi—who was getting hit over and over again—had Clarissa looking after him. When Tepsekemei came flying down, Chelsea pointed at her and yelled about it, and Mary tried to stop her and fell, going headfirst into the mud. Touta and Yol laughed as they went to go save Mary.

Marguerite was the one person apart from the others, watching. There was a lot of commotion, but it was the commotion of peace. Things were heading to resolution, and everyone was sighing in relief. They were at ease that they weren't headed to disaster. It should be fine. There were no problems.

Marguerite put a hand to her hat and pulled down the brim. She was always the one person worrying even when things were going well—it was necessary for her to worry. There was more sense in this than everyone smiling optimistically. But she couldn't deny that this disposition caused her suffering.

Marguerite averted her gaze from the scene before her and looked back. It was the forest. The layers of trees kept her from seeing through it. Marguerite focused her hearing on the forest. Something was coming this way. It was fast. Too fast for an ordinary creature to move. She put a hand on her sword. Even if it was sheathed, she could draw it out without a moment's delay.

She could clearly hear footsteps. They were panting hard. She could see them. Those mage-style robes—it was Rareko. Her expression was twisted up as she ran. Her eyes met with Marguerite's, and she gave her an imploring look. Avoiding trees and roots, Marguerite trotted into the forest to face Rareko.

"It's bad... It's bad...real bad," said Rareko. "The gate...the gate is broken."

Marguerite scowled in spite of herself, increasing her bitter feelings. "The battery didn't work?"

"No, that's not what I mean."

"There was an accident? Or was it too old and worn out?"

"It's really not anything like that. It was like the door was totally cut in two."

She was saying it had been broken in a way that could only possibly be from deliberate destruction. Marguerite consciously brought her eyebrows together. She made her expression blank, settled her tone of voice low, and asked, "Where is Maiya?"

"She's run off to the north gate to secure it. She told me to come back here and only tell you..."

Not a bad decision. Or so it seemed to Marguerite. So then what should she do? She hadn't been granted enough time to fully consider this matter at length. "Don't tell anyone that the gate has been broken."

"Huh? Oh, right."

"And keep watch to see if anyone is doing anything strange."

"Yes, right. Underst—"

Marguerite ran off without listening to the end.

Mana had whispered into her ear, "I had 7753 investigate to see if anyone knew about what caused this situation." Marguerite had been impressed, thinking Mana had managed some good work despite her incapacitation—but then Mana said she'd just been overthinking it. In other words, the result of her investigation was *none of them*. None of them had deliberately caused this. So then was someone trying to take advantage of this situation to pull something? Agri's trio was in her rooms. Mana and 7753 were in the big hall, Shepherdspie and Ragi were at the management room, and Maiya and Rareko had headed for the gate. All the other mages and magical girls had been under Marguerite's eye.

Mages would sometimes have demons serving them. They would be capable of destroying a gate without leaving the main building. And magical girls had magic. They could use it to destroy something far away. All of them were equally without alibi.

These gates couldn't be destroyed so freely. They were magic gates, made to endure despite continual exposure to wind and rain. If what Rareko said was correct, then someone had destroyed it deliberately. Marguerite bounded off the earth and leaped between the trees. How possible was it that Rareko's report was incorrect in the first place—no, that was unlikely. Marguerite did ultimately trust Maiya, and upon realizing that she also trusted Rareko, since Maiya had faith in her, Marguerite snorted. Rareko had chosen a poker as her weapon, and she knew how to use it. The way she wielded it, her footwork and stance were all the same as Maiya. It was fair to assume Maiya had been the one to teach her how to use a staff. Maiya teaching her own skills meant she recognized Rareko as one of her own, a subordinate. You wouldn't teach someone you can't trust how to fight. That was basically telling them your weak points.

Marguerite leaped over a thick root and jumped diagonally off a bare stone face.

She didn't properly understand what was going on in the first place. She was standing atop something terribly vague—without knowing if this was earth, concrete, asphalt, or if perhaps she was over thin ice, she was standing here because it would support her weight for the moment. Being in a situation where she had to trust someone "because someone worthy of trust believes in them" was making that even worse.

Ocean salt tickled her nose and quickly became a strong, unconcealable smell. The woods came to an end, and Marguerite emerged in a rocky area. She saw the gate immediately—and bit her lip hard. Violence and brutality were apparent in its twisted, destroyed remains, as if it had been ripped open aggressively. The touch panel had been crushed, and the top and bottom of the door were in separate pieces. Marguerite was alert as she drew her sword. She sensed no one.

Sliding her feet along the ground, she approached the door and noticed that behind it was a pool of red liquid. It was dark. She knew what that liquid was. The question was whose blood it was— but she discovered that quickly as well. There was a woman in a suit lying facedown. A stick lay in an indentation just a few feet away, and it was wet with seawater.

Its passion-pink and white-striped pattern was vivid to the eye, like some kind of candy. It was unmistakable. That was the magical steel staff Maiya used.

Marguerite touched the body and turned it over. Its expression was horribly contorted in agony. It was Maiya.

If her steel staff was lying there, then she must have been transformed. She had died while transformed and dropped the stick, and it had tumbled away.

The waves rolled in, crashed against the rocks, and scattered in spray. The seawater mingled with the large pool of blood.

Maiya had been a true master of the staff. They said that facing off against her, she would bewitch you with the movements of her body, her footwork, and the way she handled her staff. She had fought on par with the most active of the Archfiend Cram School graduates who were at the top of the school, and her name had always been ranked near the top in their events.

Who was capable of killing Maiya? This wasn't a feat a demon or homunculus could manage.

And what's more...

If you were to take this wound at face value, that meant she'd been killed by a slice to the front. Killing Maiya with a direct frontal attack would be fairly difficult, even for Marguerite.

Marguerite apologized to Maiya in her heart, picked up the staff, and ran for the main building. You could say she apologized for abandoning the body, and you could also say she apologized for taking away her staff, but ultimately, it was most accurate to say she apologized because she wanted to.

CHAPTER 5
TROUBLE TO TROUBLE

◇ **Ragi Zwe Nento**

There was a folding chair, a plain metal table, and a diamond-shaped information terminal with a few cables extending along the ground. Ragi reexamined the stone-walled room once more: It was extremely barren, with nothing else, not even a window.

The magic cast on this building and the annexes, the island environment, and various other things could be comprehensively controlled and operated from this management room on the fourth floor of the main building. The environmental controls regulated sun, rainfall, and such for the healthy growth of the island flora, so such changes in the environment would also affect mages and magical girls. In other words, this was the most suspicious spot as to these incidents.

The string of incidents that had occurred the previous afternoon—the magical girls' transformations coming undone and the mages passing out—had been resolved by consuming the grayfruit that grew on the island, and they judged that passing out a few to each person had more or less fixed that for the moment. But the fundamental cause hadn't necessarily been elucidated or amended.

Before going to work, Ragi pulled one dull-colored fruit from his sleeve. He would feel better when he ate a fruit, but then his health would gradually go downhill—in other words, this indicated the issue wouldn't be resolved through a single intake. Eating fruit as needed to manage his physical condition was a hassle, but he didn't want to wind up in that state again.

Ragi leaned his staff against the desk and sat down on the chair with a heave. Opening his mouth wide, he bit heartily into a fruit like a much younger man. His teeth cut through the fruit, the juices running down his throat. Its invigorating sweetness and scent moistened his dry mouth, and it was as if its vibrancy filled every corner of his body. The weariness he'd felt only moments ago evaporated entirely.

Once he was done eating his second grayfruit that day, skin and all, he wiped his mouth with a handkerchief and checked in his hand mirror to see if there was juice in his beard. Sataborn had developed and improved a wide range of products, from masterpieces to junk, but Ragi thought this qualified as one of the former.

Once he'd made sure there wasn't even a spot of stickiness in his beard, that worry gone, Ragi began his task.

He started with chanting the password and tapping the terminal touch panel to boot up the device, then typed in the second password. The room went dark, and the edges of the cramped little space disappeared. The old mage was the one thing sitting alone in a vast, all-black space—even if he reached out a hand and turned around, there was nothing to touch, and even if he walked around or ran around, he wouldn't get anywhere, either.

Ragi selected a simple magical formula for extracting information to get a grasp on the systems, and one after another, magical figures of every color rose into three dimensions. From here, he should have been able to get inside, but things didn't go that easily.

It was made in an unusually complex way for a mere environmental management system. The creator—Sataborn—had not even considered that someone else would be using it after his death. Despite having written up a will in preparation for his passing, the man had left this part out entirely.

Sataborn had made use of new technology in every aspect of the island, and this was also a custom installation, with more and more things being added after the fact turning it into one big black box. He must have gotten really into it as he was making it. It's fun to incorporate new elements when you're making something—that much Ragi could sympathize with. At some point, Ragi had also started to enjoy reinforcing his own office security, poring over the latest thesis papers as well as literature on traditional defensive techniques in order to create an absolutely impregnable magical fortress. Ragi hadn't made any considerations for his own successor for when he left his position, either.

But there was one key difference between Ragi and Sataborn.

Ragi was alive. When he let someone use that office, he could explain things to them.

Sataborn was dead. He couldn't explain this system.

The mages had passed out, and the magical girls' transformations had come undone. They didn't know the cause. Though Ragi wanted to investigate this, he wasn't even sure he could get the information to display in the first place. Magic he didn't think he'd ever seen or heard of was running continually, while the information in the magical figures was being refreshed in units of milliseconds.

There was no point in continuing this. Ragi undid the simple magical formula. The magical figures disappeared one by one, and the whole enclosed space flickered, the darkness leaving to become just a small room again. Operating the terminal atop the metal table, Ragi closed the windows that had popped up, and in the end, the terminal went back to only having the standby light on, and Ragi sighed and stood from the chair.

Contact with the systems was difficult, and he didn't know the cause of the incident. It wasn't like there were no methods to brute-force analyze it, but he didn't have the manpower, the tools, the materials, the magic power, the time, anything. That didn't seem like something he should be doing right now. If he was going to investigate the cause in earnest, they should send everyone straight off the island, then bring in specialists once they were ready. *Aren't you a specialist?* a voice inside him said irritatingly, but he restrained his anger by laying out a clear plan: He would lead the experts who came back to this island once they had the preparation and support, and he would work on uncovering the cause.

Ragi nodded. That was best.

When he emerged from the room, Shepherdspie and Mana were standing in the hallway and talking for some reason. The two of them stopped their conversation and looked at Ragi.

Ragi didn't try to hide his bitter expression, shaking his head. "Forget resolving the malfunction. I can't even guess as to the cause." Seeing them both disappointed made him all the more privately irritated, but that wouldn't change the facts. "That blasted Sataborn has been shoving in all his own new techniques, one after another. Studying it will require preparations and more. Can you arrange for about ten dozen magic gems, right now?" He glared at Mana and Shepherdspie in turn.

Though Mana seemed overwhelmed, she didn't avert her gaze, while Shepherdspie got flustered and looked down. Mana was young, but being an investigator in the Inspection Department, she had spunk. Shepherdspie wasn't even worth consideration. Sataborn should have used one-tenth of his passion toward research to educate his nephew.

"If we're not going to dispose of this island by sealing it away, then the cause must be investigated and removed. I will offer my help at that time." Ragi started to say, *"For what that may be worth,"* but became irritated with himself for being too self-effacing and said no more.

Pressing his lips shut, he made to pass by the pair, but one of them circled ahead of him. Mana was standing in Ragi's way. "So then…," she said like she was carefully choosing each word. "Then what sort of underlying cause…or reason could there be…behind all the mages collapsing and the magical girls' transformations being undone?"

Ragi's brow relaxed slightly. His wrinkles became shallower and fewer. "The most natural assumption is that the magical power in our bodies was lost."

There had been differences in symptoms among the mages, too. Ragi had been feeling poorly before his collapse, and he'd remained unconscious from then until recovery. He'd also heard that Navi Ru had been fine right up until he had passed out but had remained out following that. Yol had maintained semiconsciousness but had been unable to talk, while Mana and Agri had been able to squeeze out some words. Shepherdspie had felt unwell but had been able to walk around, while Touta had been talking and moving around completely normally.

It was fair to say that the condition of each of these individuals, and its severity, was proportional to their magical power. You could tell at a glance that Touta had no magical ability, and you'd understand Shepherdspie was an incompetent from his clumsy use of magic. Agri and Mana were decently average, while Yol would be a little above that. As for Navi Ru, Ragi had known him since he was a newbie. His decency as a person aside, he had talent as a mage. You couldn't get into the heart of the Osk Faction just through flattery and sucking up.

In contrast, the magical girls' symptoms were all about the same. Magical ability between mages and magical girls may have seemed similar, but they weren't. Magical girls didn't need magic to live, and its disappearance wouldn't affect their well-being. Having magic enabled them to transform into magical girls. If that magical power was gone, they wouldn't be able to transform anymore, that's all.

Listening to Ragi, Mana nodded deeply. She wasn't reacting like she was surprised over a new revelation but like this confirmed what she already thought. Basically, she decided she was right based on comparing her own guess to what Ragi had said. Ragi started to get angry, but seeing Mana's serious expression, he couldn't bring himself to express that anger, and he left the two behind and walked off. Mana didn't block his way or call him to a stop again. When Shepherdspie called after him, "Thank you very much," Ragi didn't reply and kept walking.

Was Mana's seriousness out of professionalism? It didn't seem like that was the whole story—Ragi shook his head. This wasn't the time to be thinking about that. There was surely something Mana wanted to do. He should just let her do it.

Ragi had his own unresolved thought—one that was so trivial, he couldn't even call it a real concern. Now that he was done with the immediate task in front of him—though issues of the inheritance were still left undone—he was free for the moment, bringing that trivial thought to his mind once more. And now it wouldn't go away.

Ragi had been feeling poorly ever since he had arrived at the island, and he'd had his hands full. So he'd been unable to consider the others around him, but thinking back now, Clantail hadn't spoken with anyone but Ragi.

This hadn't been the case with everyone else. Maiya and Marguerite had conversed like they knew each other, and Mana had introduced 7753 and Tepsekemei to the others. Navi Ru had smiled and clapped Agri's back, and Yol had taken Touta off to her rooms. As for Shepherdspie... Ragi really couldn't help but get the feeling he was unnecessarily intimate with the magical girls in his employ. Dreamy☆Chelsea, who had lashed out so sharply at Ragi, had been a woman of marriageable age in a bathrobe pretransformation, with sexual appeal and a rather alluring air—so Ragi had overheard Agri and Navi Ru discussing when they'd been relaxing in the great hall of the annex. Ragi had been privately irritated, thinking, *Can't you pipe down a little while you gossip?* As he lay on the sofa of the same annex, Ragi had figured that Chelsea was probably Shepherdspie's mistress. What indecent nonsense.

Shepherdspie's disgraceful behavior aside, those girls had had some interactions. They had seemed to enjoy chatting among magical girls, between mages, or between magical girls and mages. Clantail hadn't had that. As Ragi walked, his brow furrowed. The light of the sun slanted in the windows, lighting the dust that danced in the corridor.

Pulling his hat low over his eyes, Ragi held his breath and swept into that dust.

Clantail was a taciturn girl. She wouldn't initiate conversation. *But...*

If they went straight home after this, then only Clantail would have not gained any new acquaintances, and it would have ended as a job for her, while the others were all making friends.

Then *"so what,"* was the question, and it wasn't like it mattered— but it bothered him. It was difficult to verbalize why, which made his irritation even worse. He shouldn't be having any sort of concerns over Clantail—they didn't have that sort of relationship. Just because someone he'd hired to come with him had nobody to have friendly chats with, how was that a problem?

After a lot of thinking and getting nowhere, Ragi was struck by a flash of insight. He reeled in the rope of his thoughts. It wasn't that he was worried about Clantail. The problem was that "only the magical girl Ragi had brought was leaving without talking to anyone." Nodding to himself like, *"Yes, that's it,"* Ragi picked up the pace. Though he had been shuffled there against his will, he was still the head of the Magical Girl Management Department. He continued to fight off challengers to his authority on a daily basis. If those sorts of petty thugs knew that "only the magical girl Ragi had brought left without talking to anyone," wouldn't it call into question his suitability as the head of the Management Department?

Yes, that's what it is, when you get down to it.

He would be mocked for being that Management Department chief who could bring only a magical girl with zero communication skills. That was bound to create even more challengers.

It was fair to say he had a general understanding of the issues that would come about from Clantail being left out of the circle of association. So then what would be the procedure to resolve it?

Should Ragi put in a good word about her with someone else? Should he introduce her, at least? But an introduction from the head of the Management Department would surely make anyone feel wary. And even assuming he would introduce her to someone, was there anyone he could introduce to her in the first place? The only mage here Ragi knew was Navi Ru. And he was a reprobate. Ragi didn't know anyone else. There was just one magical girl he did know. That was 7753, the one accompanying Mana. There weren't many magical girls with numbers at the beginning of their names and even fewer whose names were just numbers. It stuck out to Ragi every time he worked on the register. *That's an unusual name. It's nice and easy to sort*, he thought. Afterward, he discovered that she was a highly capable individual who worked for Magical Girl Resources.

Ragi took a firm step forward and smacked his foot down in the hall. So then what? She wasn't even an acquaintance. He knew of her, but he was no one to her. It wasn't the sort of relationship where he could introduce someone to her.

Despite knowing from experience that this kind of worrying never produced answers, Ragi couldn't help ruminating on it. Pulling his robe up slightly so the hem wouldn't drag on the floor, he walked down the hallway and down the stairs, where he happened to look out the window on the landing. Clantail was there. She was not alone.

Nephilia was standing at her side, petting her back. Clantail was staring straight ahead, letting her do as she pleased. She wasn't reacting. Nephilia was letting out an eerie, muffled snicker. She seemed to be enjoying herself.

Ragi wondered if that meant the two were friends.

Coming to no conclusions after some consideration, he decided to call it better than nothing.

◇ **Clantail**

Clantail was in the courtyard. She'd decided that if anyone asked, she'd tell them she was enjoying the sun. But that wasn't actually the case.

From this position in the courtyard, she could watch to see if anyone tried to go into the management room on the fourth floor, where Ragi was. She could also go straight to him in a single bound if anything happened there. In other words, she was basically standing guard.

If she was going to guard Ragi in earnest, it would be best to follow him into the room or stand in front of it. But considering the old man's personality, following him around constantly would make him explode in a fit of temper. There was already a lot going on, and he had to be mentally and physically tired, but there was still work only he could do, and they had to have him keep at it.

This island was not kind to the elderly, so as long as they remained here, she would avoid causing him unnecessary anger when guarding him. There were some perplexing things going on, and there was no guarantee that they had come to a rest. At times like these, muscle was ultimately the most useful.

Anyone who saw Clantail would surely assume she was zoning out—good, because she was deliberately trying to appear that way. Her mouth was open slightly, her eyes aimlessly pointed upward toward the fourth floor.

A breeze happened to stroke her neck. She turned to the wind, and the sound of footsteps came shortly after. The person didn't seem to be trying to hide their presence. They were being open about it.

"Ksh-shh..." The magical girl covered her mouth as a low snicker slipped out. It was the girl with a reaper motif and a large scythe over her shoulder—Nephilia.

Lowering her head, Clantail didn't smile back. She didn't have a specific reason for feeling the way she did, but she didn't think she'd get along with Nephilia. Then again, it was rare Clantail felt she would get along with someone. Fighting was something else, but this was about socializing.

"He...o...," Nephilia murmured.

"Hello."

"Mind...if I...?"

"...Go ahead." Clantail was standing guard under the pretense of sunbathing, so there was no reason to refuse. Maybe she could have made up some reason to refuse on the spot, but she wasn't any good at things like that.

"Want...to talk..."

"Yes." Right after saying that, Clantail thought that "yes" was a weird thing to say, but once the word was out of her mouth, she couldn't take it back. She smacked her own bottom with her tail.

"Work...magic... Hear voices of the dead..."

Nephilia was saying she could hear the voices of the dead with her magic. Clantail's tail swung wider. Her heart stirred. Hearing voices of the dead—what did that mean, exactly? Did she make contact with what they called "the other side"? Would Clantail be able to speak again with her old friends who had lost their lives?

There were so many things she wanted to ask, but she couldn't get them out. No matter how she thought and thought, she couldn't sort out what she wanted to ask or how.

Nephilia looked up at Clantail's face and smiled. "Could I... pet...?"

"Yes." This wasn't the time for petting, but if Clantail said no, that would make it more difficult for her to ask any questions. Nephilia placed her right hand on Clantail's back and slowly stroked it.

"So...," Clantail started to ask, then closed her mouth. She cleared her throat quietly. "So, um, this magic to hear the voices of the dead..."

"Playing back...their voices from life...that's all..."

Ahhh, Clantail thought. So it wasn't like you could talk with the departed on the other side. Clantail kept her mouth shut to keep from blatantly showing her disappointment and nodded. Nephilia didn't look at her face at all but her bottom. Her eyes were on Clantail's drooping tail.

Expression serious, Nephilia gave her a tiny nod. "Often...get hopes up...and disappoint..."

"Oh, no."

"Sorry..."

"No, I'm sorry."

After a beat, Nephilia opened her mouth slowly, as if she was going to say something of grave importance. "Was called…clean up…Keek incident…work."

Clantail felt even more sharply distressed than before. Now she knew why Nephilia had come to talk to her. But she didn't know what Nephilia was after. She figured she had to say something, but the more she thought about it, the more her head was thrown into disarray.

"That…," Clantail began, then shut her mouth. Footsteps. Coming down the stairs toward them. After a little while, she saw a figure in the window. It was Ragi. He was watching them with an unusually kind expression.

"Let's talk…later…," Nephilia whispered. Her breath was slightly moist.

◇ John Shepherdspie

Ragi went off in a huff. He said he didn't know what was behind this in the end, but Shepherdspie was relieved, regardless. Being around the old man made him nervous. For a high-class idler like Shepherdspie in particular, a sharp-tempered old man was basically his natural enemy.

The old man's back went out of view down the corridor, and when Shepherdspie's eyes shifted to look down, next his eyes met with those of a girl. She had the gaze of a passionate professional. Despite her youth, being the species that worked on the front lines, you might also call her a natural enemy to a high-class idler. A high-class idler had lots of enemies.

"Just to confirm this once more," Mana began, "you have no guesses as to the cause?"

"Not at all, to be perfectly honest."

"And nothing like this has ever happened on this island before."

"I haven't been living here that long, you know. This is the first I've experienced such a thing."

"I see…" After asking this much, Mana's expression suddenly relaxed. "Well…we're past the time for inheritance and wills now, huh."

Oh, Shepherdspie thought. He'd been tense, thinking this was an interrogation, but apparently he'd gotten the wrong idea. Shepherdspie wasn't so bad at chatting. "I really don't know what to do. And we have no idea what's caused this mess, either."

"Master Ragi seems to be struggling a lot, too."

"Well, this is my uncle's mess, after all."

"Even Inspection had been considering formally adopting Sataborn's barrier formulas."

"Talent was the one thing he had in spades, unfortunately."

"Was he an odd person?"

"He was an absolute eccentric."

There was a moment of silence. When Shepherdspie looked back at Mana, she seemed more serious. "No matter what an eccentric he was, don't you think the demand that we bring one or two magical girls was suspicious?" She had a different air to her now. Even Shepherdspie, who was slow in all areas, felt it. Turns out it was an interrogation after all. Going back and forth between acting casual and aggressive was bad for his heart, but this conversation wasn't going in a direction for him to coldly push back by saying she was being rude.

"Huh? Suspicious? What is?" His voice cracked.

"I can't see what conferring the estate would have to do with magical girls."

"Well…true," Shepherdspie acknowledged. "I suppose I'm forced to admit it's suspicious. But you know—perhaps you're not aware of this—my uncle Sataborn was such an oddball. He could have put in an article demanding that everyone come to the island walking on their hands, and I might just have thought, *Well, this is him*. He really was that sort of character."

"But still…"

"Look—if there's anything dubious, you should just do a thorough investigation after leaving. I would be quite grateful myself if you would handle it, as a professional. We have no idea what's behind all these strange events, so we can't leave things like this, after all."

"Indeed."

"And it's quite awful to be stuck on an island with bizarre things happening for unknown reasons." Swallowing the remark, *"I wish I could have left with Maiya and Rareko,"* Shepherdspie nodded.

Mana still looked unsatisfied, tilting her head, but Shepherdspie figured overthinking things was the nature of people of her profession. Her job required her to face down those who would do harm, so it was quite appropriate for her to regard others with suspicion.

"Are we done?" Shepherdspie asked.

"Yes. Thank you very much."

"Due to the accident, we won't have much more time left here, but if you could use that time in a way that suits you, um, I'd be happy—as the host."

"Of course."

"I doubt you'll want to take a dip in the ocean, but you can at least enjoy yourself in the garden. There are quite a lot of plants on this island with beautiful blossoms."

"Yes, I'm sure."

Feeling fairly satisfied that he'd spoken appropriately for the elder in this exchange, Shepherdspie nodded. He did not add, *"I still have work left, so this isn't the time for me to slack off."* Talking with a younger person actually required more consideration than talking with your elders.

"Well then, pardon me," Shepherdspie said as he passed by Mana, but after going five steps, she called him to a stop from behind. He was very careful when he turned back to her to keep a *"What else do you want from me?"* expression from showing on his face. "Is there something?"

"Thank you very much for the meal. I've never had such delicious soup before."

This time, he took care not to let his joy show blatantly, nodding generously at her with the self-important attitude an elder should have. Shepherdspie turned away from her, and once he was heading off again, his cheeks relaxed. Despite telling himself off—*someone might think of you as a soft uncle who gets all pleased just from compliments about his food*—he still couldn't help but smile.

◇ **Mana**

Once she tried talking to him, Ragi didn't seem like a bad person—and neither did Shepherdspie. They were peculiar mages, but Mana couldn't be criticizing others about peculiarity.

Being the host and a blood relative of the deceased, Shepherdspie was in the greatest position of control over the island, but he didn't have the air of someone who would do such a thing. He didn't come off like a conniving person who was pulling the wool over her eyes with incredible acting, either.

But still, the situation was suspicious, and it bothered Mana.

After watching Shepherdspie disappear around a corner, she opened the door of the management room that Ragi was investigating. The hinges weren't oiled properly, and they creaked unpleasantly. Peeking in, the tiny room of about ten square feet contained only a chair, desk, and terminal with cables coming off it. There were no windows, and it was dusty. When she reached out to the terminal, pins and needles momentarily ran through her fingers. Mana drew back her hand and rubbed her fingers. This was a common type of "warning." If she was to ignore the password and the set procedure and try to reach out again, she wouldn't get off with just a warning that time.

She let out a quiet huff. This wasn't the sort of thing an amateur could meddle with.

Closing the door behind her, she let out another huff through her nose. She didn't like any of this.

She started to walk, wrapped up in her thoughts. She had a mountain of things to consider.

The letter's demand to bring a magical girl bothered her like a little fish bone stuck in her throat. Though she'd basically written that off to herself before, figuring it had to be for protecting the heirs from wild animals, things were different now. They'd basically never encountered any wild animals since coming to this island, and she had nothing but doubts as to whether magical girls were really necessary. And then her thoughts flew to how each of the heirs treated magical girls. All of them were nothing but oddballs.

Navi and Agri had been talking about how Shepherdspie had a magical girl for a mistress. And now that they'd pointed that out, Chelsea had indeed been very like a mistress, being shamelessly in a bathrobe in that situation. There was also something dubious about her calling her employer Mr. Pie—and from how she'd flared up at Ragi, telling him not to speak badly of Shepherdspie, it seemed like there was a little more feeling there than a relationship connected purely by cash and contract. And as their host, Shepherdspie had recognized the personhood of the magical girls, doing his best to make them welcome. And his cooking was good.

Yol had spread out some sort of cards from a game and was in enthusiastic conversation with Touta. She'd clearly fallen for the charms of foreign culture. Mana had gone through a phase like that, too. At that age, everything was so brand-new and hopelessly fun. Yol didn't act particularly arrogant even with Touta, who couldn't use magic, and Maiya, the magical girl attached to her household, also seemed to be serving her with absolute sincerity. Her family had to recognize and value magical girls.

Agri seemed to have friendly relationships with magical girls, too. She said she'd paid them to come with her, but their relationship didn't seem as calculated as that. She was easygoing and generous with them. The child of a mistress would generally have a hard time, so perhaps that was why she was generous with the people below her.

Ragi initially came off as a disagreeable mage, but it seemed like his anger came from a position of regarding magical girls as equals. In the first place, when magical girls dared attempt information theft, he should have dealt with them the proper way—getting their records and reporting them to the authorities. His decision to take them on personally was so childish, but at the same time sportsmanlike, in recognizing those magical girls as challengers. Had he always been like that, or had he become that way through working as the chief of the Management Department?

As for Navi—in terms of his résumé, he was a real-deal elite who someone like Mana could never hope to reach, but he wasn't at all arrogant. Even when his subordinate Clarissa made fun of him, he just laughed. He didn't take her to task for it. And with the other magical girls, as well—though he could be a bit crude—he talked, smiled, and clapped their shoulders like a neighborhood uncle. Mana had heard that the Osk Faction was harsh on magical girls—were not all of them like that, or was he just the type to draw a clear line between business and his personal life?

Touta wasn't even a mage in the first place. But still, seeing how a magical girl of Marguerite's caliber was earnestly guarding him, Mana thought he had to be of rather good character, even if he was a child. Marguerite wouldn't get so serious just because he was related to Death Prayer.

She did wonder if she was overthinking this. Shepherdspie had said they'd be able to go home soon. That was correct. He was right. But Mana still couldn't help but think about it. A normal person would see this as needless. But even if it was, thinking about it made a chill run up her spine. Not knowing the cause made her even more uneasy.

She'd been this way ever since that time. After that incident, Mana always felt anxious about things happening for reasons unknown to her.

She knew why she was like this—it was that incident in B City.

Something had happened. But she still hadn't managed to get a grasp on it. Back when they'd been trapped inside that barrier, if she had been able to get even half a step closer to something like the truth, wouldn't things have turned out differently? Mana had tossed and turned in bed many nights with thoughts like this before going to sleep. She'd solved the B City incident in her dreams more than just a few times, with Hana at her side saying, "That was tough, huh"—and then she woke up.

Just thinking about things like this made her jaw clench in an attempt to digest her regret and frustration. But Mana was still alive, and the regrets and frustration of the dead had to have been even worse. Their deaths weighed down on her one after another, and in order to withstand their weight, she had to clench her teeth and move on.

Voices coming from outside drew Mana back to reality. They were cries and yells.

Looking down and out the hallway window, she saw people crowding. It looked like they were surrounding someone. It wasn't just one person being angry. She could also hear crying.

She ran. Racing along the stone corridor, she jumped eight steps, but she failed to take the impact of landing and staggered. She somehow caught her weight on the railing but then fell on her knees. She couldn't be giving in to pain now. Scolding her legs, Mana got up and ran again.

The voices were getting closer and closer. Making sure not to touch the crumbling wall, she made it outside. Ragi and Shepherdspie were already up ahead. Ragi looked like he'd swallowed something sour as he clenched his staff. Shepherdspie was in such a dither that Mana felt bad for him.

Shepherdspie must have heard her coming, as he turned back. As soon as he saw Mana's face, he moaned, "Ahhh. It's terrible. A terrible thing has happened." His voice cracked.

Mana lowered her voice, meaning to calm him as well as herself. "What happened?"

Shepherdspie's gaze wouldn't settle, restlessly moving right, left, then back. Mana looked beyond his obese figure to where his attention lay—on a clump of people. Agri, Nephilia, Navi, Clarissa, Clantail, and 7753 were all turned away from them. Ren-Ren was standing idly by the open hole in the wall of the main building. The one slumped in the center—was that Rareko? Marguerite stood to the side with a stricken expression. Yol was clinging to Rareko and sobbing, while Touta was rubbing Yol's back.

"That's…," Mana began.

"Maiya is, um, how do I put it—she's passed," said Shepherdspie, making Mana's face stiffen, and she looked back at Shepherdspie. He staggered as he flinched back, his gaze darting around restlessly before he eventually looked down at the ground. "Um, according to Rareko and Miss Marguerite, the gates have been destroyed, too… Ahhh, oh dear, why—how has something like this happened?"

"The gates? Both of them?"

"No, um…yes. The south and the north, both have been destroyed."

Dreamy☆Chelsea poked her head out from the main building to see what was going on. She tried talking to the group, but nobody would explain. Ren-Ren was closest, so she pressed her for information; then she heard the news.

Mana drew in a deep breath. She tugged the brim of her hat down to hide her face, letting out an exhale that was longer than her inhale. Once she was sure her heartbeat had slowed a little, she lifted the brim of her hat and showed her face. "You're saying that Maiya has passed away?"

It took Shepherdspie a few seconds to realize she was speaking to him. His eyes flicked all around again, and then with a surprised look like he just remembered that he'd been the one talking with Mana, he nodded. Mana bit her lower lip as she waited patiently.

A few seconds before Mana reached the limits of her patience, Shepherdspie started talking. "Ah, yes. They said Maiya, um…was killed."

"Was it murder?"

It took Shepherdspie a further few seconds to reply. It probably wasn't that he didn't want to reply or that he was being careful with his wording but that he was just confused. "Ahhh, yes. Since I'm told she'd been slashed open and was bleeding…"

"She wasn't caught by a security installation on the island or something like that?"

"Ah, yes...I mean, no. There isn't anything that would stab a person. Or rather, never mind killing someone, there just isn't anything that would harm a person."

The one who managed the island was saying it wasn't some security system. The only other option Mana could think of would be the wild animals that were apparently on the island, but no wild animal could kill a magical girl. In other words, she'd died in a manner that could be nothing but murder.

But despite her ominous feeling being proven correct, Mana couldn't at all bring herself to think, *Look, I told you so.* All she thought was, *Why did this have to happen?* Things you didn't want to happen would generally happen. That was what the Inspection Department existed for.

Mana gazed upon the magical girls and mages of the group in turn. 7753 was just as upset as Shepherdspie, eyes wandering in every direction. Navi Ru's right hand was over the upper half of his face with his chin turned up at the sky, while Clarissa was looking at him with an expression like she had swallowed lead. Agri had gone pale and was cross-examining Rareko about something, while Ren-Ren, now done explaining to Chelsea, was trying to comfort her. Yol did nothing but cry, and Touta also looked like he was on the verge of tears as he stroked Yol's back. Ragi was tired to the bone, sitting down heavily on the stone steps, while Clantail stood at his side. The only one who was the same as always was Tepsekemei, who was drifting in the sky as Dreamy☆Chelsea yelled at her, "Stop floating around!"

Mana touched her own face. She probably had a miserable expression, too.

Nephilia was talking to Marguerite, who looked sour as she responded. Marguerite seemed to have a hard time hearing what Nephilia was saying. She leaned an ear close, and they exchanged a few words, and when she looked up again, her eyes met with Mana's. The two of them gazed at each other for a few seconds at most. Mana was the one to avert her eyes and turn to look behind her, leaving the group and walking a few steps before turning back again to face everyone.

Nephilia was speaking to Agri. Marguerite, who had been at her side, was gone.

Mana put her hand in her pocket to take the tiny stone there in her palm. The crowd was still caught up in the confusion and turmoil, with nobody able to give any decent instructions. But it was always good to make doubly sure. You couldn't be sure none of them had a listening ear perked up.

Mana rapped her middle finger three times on the center of the stone, the part that was slightly indented. The commotion of the group over there suddenly became muffled. It was as if she was hearing their voices from a distance. Now she wouldn't be heard, either.

They said these rocks had originally been used among aristocrats. They'd been convenient for private conversations at balls or parties. They were in general circulation these days, and the Inspection Department made regular use of them as a magic item. They would change the flow of the air and make it so voices wouldn't slip out.

"Maiya was killed from the front." From behind Mana and to the side came Marguerite's voice. Times like these, both of them having come from Inspection would make this process more efficient. She knew what Mana wanted to ask.

"Was Maiya strong?" Mana asked.

"I don't know if I could have beaten her in a fight," Marguerite replied.

"That's significant. Could anyone here have beaten Maiya in a fair fight?"

"You never know which way a fight between magical girls will go."

"Is it possible that Rareko could have killed her?"

"Maiya was probably Rareko's combat teacher. It looks to me like she still hasn't surpassed her teacher, but…"

"You never know which way a fight between magical girls will go."

"Exactly."

Mana sighed. That a fight could have gone either way was a useless piece of information. So she started over and asked about the gate. "Can't we repair the gate? How was it broken?"

"It was physically destroyed. Apparently, some parts were taken away."

"Parts? What do you mean?"

"Someone actually tried to repair the gate once. Rareko. Her magic to fix broken things would be perfect for this situation, but she says she can't repair the gate because the whole part that connects to the power is gone. Her magic can't create a device from nothing."

"What if the culprit wanted the parts…? No, there's no way. No robber would cut off their own escape. Does that mean someone who knew about Rareko's magic broke it so that it couldn't be fixed?"

"Or Rareko herself did it."

"Was it an outsider who did this? Or one of us? What do you think, Marguerite?"

"If it was one of us, they must have done something fairly strange. Everyone was here when Maiya was killed. Rareko was the only one who went to the gate with Maiya."

"So then someone we don't know?"

"We can't be certain of that, either. It's called magic because it does the impossible."

Mana cracked open the corners of her mouth, letting out a breath slowly, so that nobody would notice her sigh. Marguerite stopped talking then, so maybe she did notice after all.

A question slipped from Mana's lips with the tail end of a sigh. "So we can't prove anything?"

"When it comes to either magical girls or mages, you can only ever acquiesce and say, '*That's just how it is.*' You should know that, too."

"Yeah, yeah, I know. I know." After a pause, Mana continued. "Let's have 7753 investigate."

"With her goggles? You planning to do the same thing as before?"

"We change the settings, of course. To Maiya's murder and the destruction of the gate. And…" Mana's lips snapped shut. She locked eyes with the old mage looking at them. Mana quickly moved her fingers in her pocket, returning the airflow to normal. Ragi's voice became audible. The old man was talking fairly loudly.

"...is. Then we should have 7753 use her magic. If we're going to investigate these matters, we must first make sure none among us is scheming something."

Mana remembered that the old man was the head of the Management Department. It wasn't surprising for him to know what 7753's magic was. Mana's eyes shifted from him to the others. Everyone was looking at them. 7753 was giving her an imploring look, too. Mana wanted to sigh, but with all these eyes on her, she couldn't do something so unseemly.

◇ 7753

Whenever 7753's goggles were needed, it was always for checking something bad. It was fair to say there were basically no occasions when she used them in a decent and amicable way, and everyone walked away happy. It was being aware of this that made 7753 so miserable about this situation, but it wasn't like she was okay with the fact that someone had been killed, either. It was just that it would always feel nasty.

7753 had sneaked looks at subjects with her goggles before, but this time, everyone was looking at her. She couldn't be taking sneak peeks now. And not only that...

"Oh no, no, no," insisted Navi. "That's not happening. It's an invasion of privacy."

No matter what sort of emergency or bloodbath was going on, someone would always bring up the most convenient line: *invasion of privacy*. Even if they made it through this safely and went back home, he could be socially assassinated if his bad deeds were exposed through 7753's magic, after all.

Navi kept repeating, "Can't have that. Nope, not happening."

Ragi snorted, making his full white beard jump as he thrust the end of his staff at Navi. "Because you're up to no good, no doubt. Just accept that there's nothing to be done about your bad deeds being exposed over this. There will be mercy if you resign yourself and let yourself be arrested."

"Hold on there, old man," Navi shot back. "I wish it were just about me. But you can't say it won't stir up trouble for the whole faction. I could say, '*I was just following orders. Master Osk told me to do it*'—I don't know whether that will pass with the other factions until I try, but I don't even want to make an attempt."

Ragi's face turned red startlingly quickly, and he began swinging his outstretched staff but then staggered, and Clantail caught him. Leaning on Clantail, Ragi swung his staff around. "Talking as if Master Osk is the don of a gang of criminals! You garbage! You don't have a smidgeon of respect! That's right—you're dag-nabbing trash! How dare bottom-dwelling filth take Master Osk's name in vain!"

"That's going a bit far. I am more or less a member of the faction, you know. I'm gonna say the boss's name."

"Then leave the faction! It's because of you miserable lot that the honor of Master Osk has been besmirched!!"

Mana stepped forward. It seemed 7753 wasn't the only one worried that if they let those two continue, it would never come to an end—Shepherdspie looked a little relieved, and Agri's fed-up expression faded a bit, too.

"You can change the settings to make the goggles display different items, right, 7753?" Mana asked.

7753 seemed flustered about having the discussion turned to her, but she nodded. "Yes, yeah, yes, that's right. I can't see absolutely everything all at once."

"So she says. So then could you make it show only about Maiya's murder and the destruction of the gate?"

Navi groaned something under his breath, looking distressed. Agri raised her hand and followed with, "If that's how it works, I'll let her see," and Shepherdspie nodded again.

Finding out that he was the only one against it, Navi nodded as well, reluctantly. "If that's all it is, then fine. It'd be a hassle to have everyone suspect me," he added, like an excuse.

7753 set the goggles and let everyone see what she'd done. She lent the goggles to Navi to show him that she couldn't see anything aside from those settings and had him look at Mana and 7753 through them.

"Well, this should be fine," Navi said.

Investigating whether anyone had destroyed the gate or whether there was anyone who had killed Maiya, each time she changed the settings, she would get everyone to check again in detail, and the result was: nobody. 7753 breathed a deep, heavy sigh. Though the mood among the group had eased a bit, and they'd started to talk, it was just slightly better than before. They weren't exactly relaxed or calm. There was still someone lurking on the island who had killed Maiya and destroyed the gate.

"No, hold on." Dreamy☆Chelsea raised a hand. "You haven't checked everyone yet, have you?"

"Huh? Haven't I?" 7753 counted down on her fingers. Navi and Clarissa. Ragi and Clantail. Touta and Marguerite. Yol and Rareko. Agri, Ren-Ren, and Nephilia. Shepherdspie and Chelsea.

"The sheep girl isn't here," Mana commented from beside her.

"Oh, now that you mention it." 7753 recalled the incident where Navi had been swallowed up by sheep. She'd been so overcome by the sight of the charging sheep that she had forgotten that situation was due to a magical girl.

Chelsea said, "Huff, huff!" out loud, pointing to her own heart. "Chelsea'll be mad if you forget May-May."

"Ohhh, no, sorry," 7753 apologized. "I didn't mean to forget... Is she in the main building?"

"Yep. Mr. Pie told her to clean up the kitchen."

Shepherdspie nodded and added, "I thought I asked you, too," but Dreamy☆Chelsea interrupted her boss before he could finish.

"May-May isn't a bad girl, so she wouldn't kill anyone or break anything, though!" she declared with full confidence, putting her hands on her hips. She followed that with, "Because no magical girl is a bad girl."

"Do you think the sheep person is the culprit?" 7753 whispered to Mana, beside her. "She really doesn't seem like she'd be the one."

"Not on the surface, at least… Marguerite, do you think Pastel Mary could have killed Maiya?"

Marguerite tilted her head right, then left, then put it in its original position. The blank look on her face gave the gesture a sort of surreal humor. "That girl would lose her balance just from running normally. She couldn't possibly defeat Maiya with martial arts."

"And with magic?"

"If she ordered her sheep, she could kill someone far away… perhaps. But Maiya would never be killed by a sheep."

"She didn't look as if she was handling the sheep very well, either," said 7753.

"What about if all that was acting, and she's been hiding her true nature…?" Mana said.

Marguerite lowered her chin at a vague angle that might have been a nod and might not. "Though it seems unlikely, it's not impossible."

Mana and Marguerite both looked at 7753 at the same time. Overwhelmed by their two hard expressions, she felt ruffled but nodded. "Then I'll investigate the sheep person…Mary as well."

Mana told that to Shepherdspie, and he ordered Chelsea to go call for her. Chelsea continued to complain, "May-May would never do something like that," but she went back to the main building.

Learning the culprit behind the destruction of the gate as well as Maiya's murder was not among them finally eliminated the obstruction to the group's cooperation—and source of suspicion.

Mana touched her right index finger and thumb to her chin. She looked thoughtful. "If we can work together, then we have to be completely thorough…"

"Yes, of course," 7753 agreed.

"We must be united against external threat, or even more could die."

"No way do we want more of that."

Mana looked up. 7753 was drawn to look up, too. The sky was red. The sun was starting to set. Magical girls could see in the dark, but most likely, whatever they were dealing with was a magical girl or something like it. They should assume things would get more dangerous. Mana was about to say as much when Agri raised her hand.

"Hey?" Seeing nobody was stopping her, Agri continued. "My Nephy says she can hear dead people's voices. If we could hear Maiya's voice, maybe we could learn something."

It looked like Nephilia said something after that, but 7753 couldn't hear it. Nephilia tugged Agri's sleeve, with her lips pulled down in reluctance as she shook her head. Clarissa pointed to that, saying, "But, like, it looks like she doesn't want to do it, though?"

"Nephy hates using her magic," Agri explained. "She doesn't like touching dead bodies. But this isn't the time to be saying stuff like that. I think we should have her do it, even if she doesn't like it."

Nephilia nodded a few times and said something, but it was so soft, 7753 couldn't hear it.

As if prompted by that, Mana lowered her voice, too. "The voices of the dead? What do you mean by that?"

"Like I said," Agri began, "that's what Nephy's magic is. She can hear the voices of dead people."

7753's heart leaped out of her throat—or it felt like it did. The words "voices of the dead" sank into her ears. Before her head could even absorb the words, she hugged her arms around her body. If the dead could speak, what would they say to her? What would they want to say? This wasn't fear. It wasn't exactly remorse, either. Indescribable feelings coiled within her and wouldn't go away.

Looking angry and upset, Mana pressed her lips shut. Marguerite stepped forward from the side to stand by Mana and lean toward Agri. "You mean like a séance?"

"No, she said she doesn't ask ghosts questions or anything like that," Agri told her.

"Sounds fishy," Ragi spat quietly, but Agri just flicked a glance over to him, ignoring that to turn back to Marguerite. "Um, so. By…touching the bodies of dead people? She apparently hears the words the dead person said. Basically, it's like, she just plays out a record of the sound, as is."

7753 heaved out a breath. She hadn't even realized she was holding it. Wondering about Mana, she looked over at her to see she was biting her lower lip, looking even more serious than before as she listened.

Scratching his head, Navi cut in. "So she can't ask the dead questions, and the dead can't start talking as they please. It's just repeating exactly what they actually said?"

"Yeah, that's it," answered Agri.

"Maybe this'll sound rude, but that ain't gonna work, is it? She's probably said something like *gwaagh* or *augh*, and not words that mean anything."

With her head hanging, Nephilia mumbled something, and Agri, whose ear was close, nodded *"mm-hmm"* and then looked up. "She says that by touching a person longer, she can go back to hear what they said earlier."

Navi groaned, expression grim—7753 felt like she'd seen him like this multiple times that day—and seeing that, Agri closed one eye. "What will we do? In order to use Nephy's magic, she needs, um, Maiya's body." That slight hesitation may have been out of concern for Yol. She was a slight distance away in Rareko's arms, shoulders trembling.

Marguerite reacted instantly. "It's too dangerous."

"Of course it'll be dangerous. I know that. I can't let Nephy go alone," said Agri.

Mana tilted her head. "So do we all go together? To the place where Maiya was lying."

Ragi poked the ground with his staff. "It would be a bad idea to leave this place unattended. Let the management terminal get broken by some rapscallion and just you see, it would be a disaster."

"So we send a few people over?" Mana suggested.

"B-but—but listen," spluttered Shepherdspie. "Wouldn't splitting up here be t-too dangerous?"

"If we can get it done quickly... How long does Nephilia's magic take?" Mana asked Agri.

"She says it doesn't take long."

"Now hold on there. Is it even worth doing all that to hear Maiya's voice?" Navi griped.

"We won't know that unless we hear it. Stop opposing us over every little thing, mister," Agri shot back.

"I'm just talking about what's reasonable."

Though the exchange went on, in the end, they decided that Nephilia and a few magical girls would go to the place where Maiya had been lying. Agreeing that they would hurry back if anything happened, Nephilia, Marguerite, Tepsekemei, and Clarissa would head to the scene, while 7753 stayed behind with the rest, praying in her heart that things would look up even slightly.

◇ **Touta Magaoka**

Somehow, it didn't feel real at all. Maiya had been totally fine just a while ago, and now they were saying she'd been killed. They said the gates had been destroyed, and they couldn't go back. Touta was scared, of course, but it was like none of it was real. Comforting someone else had provided a bit of a distraction, but now his mind was spinning in circles. Things like a murder and the gates being broken to keep them from getting out were happening in real life— even though this was a bright, sunny, and warm southern island where it seemed things like that would never happen.

His head and his heart were spinning around, but his feeling of wonderment was enough to blow all that away. He'd heard that magical girls' magic was amazing, but seeing them actually do it surprised him and made him think, *I saw something like this in anime!* The magical girl called 7753 pulled out a pair of magic goggles and claimed that you couldn't hide anything from her when she looked through them.

Some of the adults looked like they really didn't want to do it, while others were more vocal with their anger. 7753 seemed uncomfortable and flustered—and just having a bad time.

Seeing 7753, who he'd been so amazed by, pitiably bowing around to everyone made him remember. This wasn't a situation to be feeling amazed about. Yol was still crying. She said that Maiya had always been with her and that she always nagged her—but if they'd always been together, that was just like family. For Touta, that would be like his great-aunt. If he heard she was dead, of course he would cry. He hadn't known Maiya very well, since they'd only just met, but seeing Yol sad made Touta sad, too. Though she'd only been standing tall and talking about how "meet meta is part of strategy," now her back was hunched.

That was why Touta stayed by her side. Marguerite had told him to cheer her up, but he understood that without being told.

When he looked at Yol, he thought, *I want to comfort her, but I don't know what to say* or *I want to protect her, but I don't know what I can do*, and he just didn't know, but he rubbed her back for her anyway. But he figured it would be better if he could manage something else.

7753 apologized, and other people got mad, but in the end, things wound up with everyone deciding to work together in lieu of there being someone frightening. If this were a detective manga, it would have gone more like, *"There's a culprit among us!"* but 7753's goggles kept that from happening. They could unify as a group to struggle through. *Magical girls are amazing*, Touta thought.

The adults were discussing, saying, "Let's do this" or "Let's do that." They'd decided that first, they would have Nephilia use her magic to hear the voice of the deceased. Marguerite looked serious as she told him, "If anything happens, depend on an adult. But if it's hopeless, then take Yol's hand and run," and Touta nodded back with an equally serious look. She told him one more thing that sounded very difficult: "Be brazen like Death Prayer...like your aunt. You're a blood relative, so it shouldn't be impossible for you." But Touta nodded anyway. Marguerite remained stone-faced as Touta looked back just once, and when he looked up front again, she was already gone along with the other magical girls.

Touta paused, letting those words sink in. Then he said, "I'm going over there for a sec," and left Yol and Rareko. He approached 7753, who was behind Mana. "Um, can I talk to you a minute?"

"Pardon?" 7753 lifted her goggles up over her school hat. She wasn't *constantly* looking at everything through her goggles.

"Would you mind...checking me?"

"I already did. It's okay. You don't need to worry."

"No, I mean if I have a potential for magic."

7753's eyebrows went into an upside-down V, pulling firmly downward. She was clearly feeling awkward. She flicked a gaze at Mana, who was talking with the other adults. Mana's appearance resembled a child's, but when she talked, she had the air of an adult. Maybe that was because she was a mage.

"Well then, let's take a look." 7753 brought the goggles down to look at Touta.

Touta stood at attention and looked back at her, fingers straight as boards at his sides.

"Um...not yet, it looks like," 7753 told him.

He was disappointed to hear that. He was so downtrodden that he couldn't consider that "not yet" meant it might grow in the future.

"What about a potential to become a magical girl?" he asked.

"Pardon?"

"I heard that the potential to become a mage and the potential to become a magical girl are a little different, and, um, I was told that even guys could occasionally become magical girls."

7753 lowered her goggles, then raised them again faster than before. "It seems like basically no."

"...Did you look carefully?"

"I did... Oh, are you unsure because I was so fast? It's just that whether someone has the potential to be a magical girl is something I check a lot, so I can set it really fast."

Touta was disappointed. Bowing with a "Thank you," by the time he trudged back to Yol and Rareko, Yol had stopped crying. But when he saw her sad, sad face and their eyes met, he thought, *Ahhh, maybe I've gone and messed up things.* She had that sort of look. Touta regretted leaving her behind. "Sorry."

"It's all right," Yol said. "What did you ask?"

"Um…" It was difficult to admit that it was whether he had the potential to be a mage. Yol and the others all took for granted that they were mages, but Touta had his hopes dashed—at the very least, he couldn't mention it without shame.

"I was asking if maybe I have the potential to be a magical girl," he told her finally.

"A magical girl? Why?"

"If I could become a magical girl…" It was too embarrassing to say something so arrogant like, *"Then I could protect you."* He could never say that. He couldn't offer other reasons like how then he'd be able to console her or that he'd be able to encourage her. He couldn't say anything like that. Marguerite had told him to be brazen like his aunt, but this probably wasn't what she meant by that.

"…I thought maybe it'd be safe and convenient," Touta said.

"It's difficult to become a magical girl, you know. Especially for boys."

"Yeah. But I heard it happens sometimes."

"I couldn't become a magical girl, either."

"You too?"

"If you ask, you can get them to test you. There are a lot of people who will administer a test whether you're an adult or a child. I got some medicine and took it, but nothing happened…"

When she talked about the past, Yol looked a little cheerier than when she had been crying on and on. When Touta flicked his gaze up, he saw Rareko was now the one with tears welling up in her eyes.

◇ **Rareko**

Maiya was dead. That meant radical change for Rareko's life. Not in a good direction, of course. That would never happen. Her life was going to change in an overwhelmingly bad direction. If she stood around crying like Yol, nobody was going to comfort her, and even if there had been someone, tears wouldn't fix anything. Right now, she had to act, with her sights fixed on after Maiya's death.

But what made it hard was that it would be a bad idea to do anything too blatant. If she wasn't standing by Yol's side sadly looking down or something, people would think she was an ingrate who didn't even mourn her master's death. Maybe Rareko really was an ingrate, but that was Maiya's fault. The way she'd done things, Rareko would never consider her debt a true one. But even if Rareko insisted that, nobody was going to listen.

It was best to just pretend to mourn the death of her benefactor. There was nothing to gain from being thought an ingrate. The appearance of mourning Maiya's death wouldn't harm her.

Rareko kept thinking to herself. What she had to do right now was think. Letting Yol and Touta's stupid, boring chatter go in one ear and out the other, she immersed herself in careful deliberation.

Maiya had been Rareko's teacher and her sponsor. Despite being a magical girl, Maiya had behaved like a mage, and she hadn't been criticized for it, either. She'd been the most senior in service of Yol's household, and she'd been treated about as close to a member of the family as you can get.

It was Maiya's high position in the family that had permitted her selfishness. If a regular servant was to bring in some dirty brat from who-knows-where and say, *"Starting today, I will make her my apprentice,"* she would be fired on the spot.

Rareko had been allowed to live in that house because she was Maiya's apprentice. With Maiya gone, she could no longer live there like before. She would probably be tossed out. She'd been taken in by Maiya so young that she could hardly even remember anything before then, living only for training, house chores, and errands. Even if she went somewhere else now, she didn't know what she could do.

Rareko was an orphan without a single person to rely on—not parents, children, brothers, sisters, relatives, or a lover. There was no home for her to go back to. She knew better than anyone that she wasn't strong enough to be able to make a living as a magical girl. She would never be as good as Maiya in staff combat. Her magic had decent utility, but she'd been forbidden to use it freely, and she hadn't had the opportunities to consider how to make it useful, either. Even if she was to try making a living on her magic now, she had no idea how feasible that was.

Maiya had been strict. She'd worn a severe expression ever since they'd first met. Rareko could easily have died on any occasion back then—she'd be tossed this way and treated cruelly, tossed there and worked to the bone—so you'd think Rareko would have clearly seen Maiya as a savior, but Rareko didn't feel at all like she'd been saved.

Maiya had controlled Rareko with yelling, hitting, and kicking. Her educational practices were more than just a generation too old—they were two or three generations out-of-date, and Maiya never even doubted those methods. She believed that was the best way because she'd been raised like that herself. Not that she ever said that out loud, but Rareko had to assume that was what it was.

Since Maiya would resort to the rod when it came to matters of cleaning or kitchen work, it went without saying that was also the case for martial arts. Maiya had always had a staff, while Rareko had been given a staff after the fact, so they were at two completely different starting lines—but Maiya didn't care, adopting the Spartan approach of, "Of course you can do it. You're just lazy."

If you train, you'll get stronger. But it's not like it works like that for everyone. Rareko would never surpass Maiya through training methods that were harsh all of the time—not in a hundred years could Rareko win. Everyone understood that, even Rareko herself, but Maiya was the one person who still didn't get it, and so Rareko had spent every day in endless training.

She recognized she was still alive, but it wouldn't have been surprising for her to die at any point. Rareko knew about an organization of crazy magical girls who would train until they almost died, but they did it because they liked it. They weren't being forced into it.

Rareko was not someone from three generations ago; she was living in the here and now. Getting hit and kicked wasn't okay anymore, and each strike built up her resentment and anger further. It was because of Maiya that she had come to worry about what other people think. It was Maiya's fault that she'd become a two-faced person. It was fair to say that she had managed to survive somehow by making everything Maiya's fault.

This quiet anger that didn't show on the outside—that she didn't dare express—had only ever caused her stress, but it was good that her anger kept her from being sad about Maiya's death. Thanks to that, she could think clearly.

She mentally ranked her priorities. First was her own life. She had to be alive, or everything else was meaningless. Second was to get off the island alive. That was important. Maiya hadn't been a good master or someone who should be commended as a person, but she had unmistakably been strong. And not just compared to Rareko—she had rarely ever lost to any magical girl. If Maiya had lost, that meant her opponent was exceptional. Rareko should avoid fighting them at all costs.

It wasn't like none of the magical girls here seemed strong. Miss Marguerite in particular was an old acquaintance of Maiya's, and Rareko had heard they'd run into each other a number of times at Archfiend Cram School events. A magical girl who would go to an Archfiend Cram School event couldn't be weak—in other words, Marguerite was strong. Maiya wouldn't even acknowledge the human rights of weak magical girls, but she'd spoken to Marguerite with decent respect. So even if she wasn't as strong as Maiya, she had to be at a similar level.

Even if it was impossible for Marguerite on her own, maybe she could defeat the enemy if she had some backup. Of course, Rareko didn't plan to be that backup. She would play the poor magical girl who had been crushed by Maiya's death and pray that with luck, Marguerite would finish off the enemy. If someone as capable as her couldn't win, then Rareko just had to buy some time until help came.

Those who died were weak, and those who survived were strong. This was the one thing Maiya had taught her that she liked.

Rareko's eyes flicked down at the two children. Touta must

have said something, as Yol's lips were quirked up a bit. With the basic assumption that she would leave the island alive, next, she had to think about her future course after escape. If she could curry favor with Yol, she might somehow be able to ask about continuing her employment. So then what should she do to get into Yol's good graces? She was unused to flattery and adulation, so should she forget that and search for another way to live?

Rareko once again threw herself into the ocean of thought.

◇ Miss Marguerite

Fortunately, no problems cropped up.

With Marguerite leading the way, they soon reached the place where Maiya had lost her life. Her body was still there, untouched.

It was just as miserable on the second look as the first. Marguerite wanted to tear her eyes away, but she couldn't let herself do that. On the way, she watched out of the corner of her eyes how the other magical girls moved. Tepsekemei flew in the sky, so it went without saying that Marguerite needed to keep a watch on her, but Clarissa was also fast, with a mastery in the movements of her body. Marguerite could assume she had far more experience than you'd expect from her human age. Nephilia, on the other hand, was a little slow, but that was just compared to the others here; she was about average for a magical girl.

Before their group came here, Mana had seemed to be worrying about various things. Marguerite couldn't say for sure that her worries were baseless. That was precisely why they would be relying on Nephilia's magic, on the hope that it would be some kind of clue. Marguerite knelt down and prayed awhile, then beckoned for Nephilia. Nephilia retreated a half step and drew her chin back. She didn't seem very happy about this—in fact, she looked reluctant. She was muttering to herself.

Marguerite leaned her ear close to pick up what she was saying. "What? ...It's too...gruesome...so you don't want to touch it...?"

Clarissa booed. Marguerite put her right hand on her hip and looked down at Nephilia. They were clearly not going to let her return without doing anything.

Nephilia still wanted out of it, but she must have sensed that she wasn't going to be allowed to back out, as she dragged her chin up, and though she was as slow as possible about it, she got moving.

She slowly descended into a formal kneel beside the dead body and timidly reached out to Maiya's head—she drew back once, then extended her arm again, taking plenty of time until she touched her and finally began to stroke her. Once Nephilia had begun stroking her, the negative emotions disappeared from Nephilia's expression, and she picked up speed, stroking the body's head. It had stopped bleeding by now, but the ground was still dirty. Nephilia's knees were wet with blood. She paid them no mind.

Marguerite watched Nephilia but kept her attention fixed on the other magical girls as well. Tepsekemei remained continually blank-faced before the gruesome body as well as the change in Nephilia. Since this one was Mana's companion, she probably wasn't a bad person, but she was unquestionably an oddball. Clarissa was what you'd call "creeped out," her catlike ears slightly lowered as she watched in disgust. Whether that was a good reaction or not, she was easier to understand.

Then Nephilia cried out. It was the shriek of someone dying. Marguerite automatically put her hand on her sword hilt. But it wasn't Nephilia's shriek. It was Maiya's voice. Tepsekemei spun once in midair, and Clarissa cried out in astonishment. Nephilia ignored the others' reactions and continued to stroke. She looked kind of abnormal. What with the sound of Maiya's voice, it looked as if she were summoning a spirit. Even though Marguerite knew she wasn't, that was what it looked like.

"All right, then. If you'll resist, I'll show no mercy." That was Maiya's voice. It had come clearly out of her mouth. It was not Nephilia's hard-to-hear muttering.

"What are you talking about? Figure that out yourself."

It was going back in time.

"Who are you? What are you doing on this island?"

It kept going back.

"You…"

Nephilia stopped moving. Her eyes focused again, and Marguerite got the feeling their color darkened somewhat, as well. "After this…talk…Rareko…"

"You mean after this is a conversation with Rareko?"

Nephilia nodded. She looked like herself, the Nephilia Marguerite knew—sleepy-looking, no longer seeming possessed.

Marguerite played the "words from Maiya" that Nephilia had emitted backward in her mind.

Maiya had said, "You…" when she'd encountered someone. It was fair to assume, "What are you talking about? Figure that out yourself," was in reply to something the other person had said. And then before that, she'd said, "Who are you?" In other words, it was someone unknown to Maiya and also just one person. And from how she'd asked the question, it was something or someone that was humanoid, or at the very least it had to be someone who looked like you could talk to them. And…Marguerite was about to think further, but before she could, a voice came from behind her. It was Clarissa.

"I get that you wanna think about it, but like…" Marguerite turned back to see Clarissa with a crooked smile, jabbing behind her with a thumb. "Wanna go back? Standing around here is risky and scary, and I did basically leave my boss back there."

Marguerite didn't even have to consider it. Clarissa was quite right.

Regretting that she'd gotten lost in her thoughts, Marguerite nodded, then lent a hand to Nephilia to help her to her feet. The four magical girls headed back the way they'd come, while Marguerite mentally apologized to Maiya for having used her body.

◇ **Love Me Ren-Ren**

The explosive air had dissipated. It really was a relief. Ren-Ren was the worst at handling that kind of tension, the sort that would pop if you pricked it. She wanted everyone to get along, even if it took a few lies. She knew some people would disagree with her, but that didn't change her mind. That was ultimately just her opinion, and it wasn't like she would force it on anyone else.

It was a huge boon to learn that the culprit wasn't among them, and she could really understand just how strong and incredible 7753's magic was.

Agri started to talk a little more cheerily, too. She was the one Ren-Ren was the most concerned about right now. Ren-Ren receiving money, her being hired was nothing more than the impetus. Agri said that she hadn't been blessed with regards to family, and Ren-Ren wanted to put that in the past. Ever since coming here, Agri's eyes had been trailing the other mages' backs. They moved in flickering glances to examine hems and sleeves. *She's looking at their robes*, Ren-Ren thought. Everyone else's robes were beautiful and well tailored, while Agri's were old and frayed. She put on an act like she wasn't bothered by such things, but it was getting under her skin.

Ren-Ren thought that unhappiness was the accumulation of little things like that. She wanted Agri to be happy from now on and forever. That was Ren-Ren's wish.

Agri occasionally looked at Navi. He was tilting his head and cracking his neck as he looked off in the direction Clarissa and the others had gone. Ren-Ren thought he had to be worried. Ren-Ren was worried about Nephilia, too. They knew someone scary was out there, but they wouldn't get anywhere unless Nephilia went— even though she wasn't a fighter.

Yol was able to talk now. Someone dear to her had just been killed, so of course her heart was reeling. But still, what mattered was that she'd stopped crying and that she was talking. The most important thing was that she was well, and the second most important thing was how others felt. Ren-Ren hadn't spoken much with Yol, but it only took a glance to see how cute she was. Smiling always suited a cute girl better than crying. Seeing such a cute smile would make others happy, too.

With 7753's magic, they'd learned that at least there was no culprit among them. That had enabled them to bring the whole group together to cooperate against an outside enemy. This was quite important. Agri was firing off propositions, too: "Let's make the main building our base… How about we try making some kind of alarm clappers?" Everyone was brainstorming together.

But there was still one magical girl they hadn't checked.

Ren-Ren glanced at Shepherdspie. He was the one person looking glum and digging his toes into the ground. It seemed even he thought Chelsea was taking too long.

Only Pastel Mary, who materialized pictures of sheep she drew with her pastels and controlled them, still hadn't shown up. Dreamy☆Chelsea, who'd gone to get her, also hadn't come back.

The mages discussed a magical defense, while the magical girls were talking about a rotating watch and doing rounds. In order to get off the island, first they had to protect themselves. They decided that repairing the gates and contacting the outside could come after they'd largely perfected their defenses.

As they were discussing, they heard a nasty cough that kept going without a break. Clantail rushed to her employer at a trot, lending him a hand to make him sit on the steps. Ragi seemed to be quite unwell.

Ragi was basically the specialist when it came to magical defenses, and he couldn't keep going if they left him like this until he passed out—and that would also be a problem, ethically speaking. And Ren-Ren thought everyone should be well.

Shepherdspie went back to the estate in order to fetch the grayfruit they'd stockpiled, and when he came back, Chelsea was with him. He was dumbfounded, and Chelsea was disconcerted.

Chelsea muttered, "Mary isn't there. She isn't anywhere."

Shepherdspie groaned. "They're gone. The grayfruit we picked are gone."

Ren-Ren put on an expression of surprise, opening her mouth wide to look back at them.

CHAPTER 6
ALL SPLIT UP EVERYWHERE

◇ **Dreamy☆Chelsea**

All the vegetation around the main building and annexes had been removed, making a sort of yard. And now, all the guests who'd been invited to the island had congregated there. Even the visibly weakened old man wouldn't submit to their urging to go rest inside—partly because they were still waiting for the magical girls who had gone to hear Maiya's voice, and also because it seemed like he would be helpless on his own. What seemed more likely was that they wanted to ensure he could safely escape if something attacked. Chelsea did think he was being pretty stubborn, though. There were plenty of other reasons, too, and so Chelsea had to make an announcement in front of everyone.

It was starting to get dark, and the light of the main building at their backs cast all the faces in front of her in shadow. She already didn't want to tell them what she was about to say, but the backlighting gave everything even more of a grim vibe.

Pastel Mary was gone.

Chelsea had checked all the empty rooms, opened up all the wooden boxes stacked in the closet, and checked the contents, even opening up the lid of the toilet in the lavatory to look inside. She'd looked in the bathroom, too, checking behind the shower curtains, to no avail. Chelsea had even pulled books from the shelf, but no hidden rooms had appeared. And on top of that, the grayfruit the two of them had picked together and packed into a box had vanished. When they'd learned of the effects of the fruit, they'd immediately been ordered to gather the ones that grew around the main building—that had been the first job since coming to this island that Chelsea hadn't dragged her heels on. Without grayfruit, they'd be in all sorts of trouble, after all.

Everyone looked quite unhappy to hear Chelsea's announcement. She never wanted to trouble them with it, either, but the facts were the facts. Not telling them wouldn't change things.

Chelsea felt as if she were standing on top of clouds. Though she was clearly present, she felt far away. It was as if she were looking in through a TV monitor from somewhere else. Not being able to find Mary, the box of the grayfruit they'd gathered being missing—it felt like none of it was happening in real life. Maybe that was why she didn't feel angry or sad. She was weirdly calm, but her mind was full of doubt.

However, not everyone there was a flighty character like Chelsea. Agri erupted in rage at the news. She yelled and screamed, shaking Shepherdspie by the collar. "Look, you!" she spat. "What's the meaning of this?!" She threw in a, "Seriously! Bullshit! Damn it!" Spittle flew out of her mouth, her face contorting terribly as the vibrant beauty of a young woman became something dreadful directed at Shepherdspie. Her expressions of rage felt like they had *"Take that! And that!"* packed into them as mental punches.

Shepherdspie was wavering about. Chelsea felt sorry for him. He had no clue what was going on, unable to even make a decent excuse for his behavior. *That* made Chelsea angry—but not with him. She felt indignant toward the mages who were yelling at him and shoving responsibility for every single thing on him.

Before she could even think about it, she lost her cool. "Hey, how are you making everything Mr. Pie's fault?!" Chelsea leaped out in front of Shepherdspie and spread her arms wide.

Agri flinched, then immediately glared at Chelsea. "Listen, I don't know if you're his housekeeper or his mistress or what, but right now isn't the time for that. Drop the show of loyalty to your man and butt out."

Chelsea really didn't get what that first part was about, but she did get what "butt out" meant, and it sent her rage skyrocketing.

Chelsea was quite furious.

"Chelsea isn't gonna butt out of it! 'Cause Dreamy☆Chelsea is a friend to all people in trouble!"

She would never say something like that as Chie Yumeno. Chie clammed up when someone was angry with her. She thought it was rude to cut in and that you should wait for the fires to cool. She would vent her feelings or wait for time to pass, and all these little things would lessen the tone of her anger bit by bit, until finally by dinnertime, she'd had conversations like, "Oh well, watch out next time." "I will, I'm sorry."

But Dreamy☆Chelsea was different. When a friend was being unfairly accused, she had to protect them, or how could she be a magical girl?

Agri spat with irritation, "Oh, I see! If you're a friend to all people in trouble, then why don't you fix the gates or defeat the killer?! We're really in trouble here, right this very moment!"

"Not all of that is Mr. Pie's fault! Chelsea's trying to say there's no reason for anyone to be yelling at him!"

"Don't change the subject!"

"You're the one who changed the subject!"

Navi stood up and laid a hand on Agri's shoulder. "Hey, leave it at that. More importantly—"

"You're so obnoxious. Shut up, old man," Agri cut him off with just one remark, and he dejectedly went back to where he'd come from and sat down.

Instead, the horse—Clantail—approached, hooves clopping. "Pardon," she said as calmly as if she hadn't at all been listening to the yelling match just now.

Agri tilted her head all the way over and glared at her, not in the least trying to hide her irritation—like Clantail was being an absolutely provoking, massive hassle. "What?"

"I'm going to go gather fruit."

"Wait, hold on." Mana reached out and waved her hands side to side. "It's too dangerous. You should wait for Marguerite and the others, at least."

"But—"

Someone coughed. The coughing went on for a long time before coming to a hoarse stop. Chelsea's maternal grandfather had coughed like this. He'd made his visitors smile by saying, "I'd like to have a big steak once I get out of the hospital," but he'd never left the hospital in the end.

Clantail rushed to the source of the coughing and stroked his back. The old mage still had his handkerchief pressed against his mouth in distress, and when he removed it, the white handkerchief was stained red. Clantail stood, bowed, and then ran to the annex without another word.

The annex? Why?

When Clantail returned, she was carrying a large tube of rolled-up cloth. "I'm borrowing this," she said to Shepherdspie, and before he could say if that was all right or not, she strode out. Her equine lower body was enveloped in light, and a moment later, it had become that of a leopard. Her hooves became sharp claws, and her tail bounced with supple grace. Her overall frame was shorter, and her stance was even lower.

Her unexpected transformation surprised Chelsea, and there were cries of surprise from the others, too. Mana took a step forward, surely to stop her, but she moved too slowly. She seemed like she was hesitating. Maybe she wasn't sure if she should stop Clantail from trying to go into the forest to save the ailing Ragi. Chelsea could understand that feeling. As Mana was hesitating, Clantail sped up, and then even the end of her tail was out of sight.

"Should I bring her back?" 7753 timidly asked, and Mana flatly shook her head. "But does she even know where the grayfruit grow?"

"That...should be all right." Everyone there but Ragi, who seemed on the verge of collapse, looked at Shepherdspie. His shoulders trembled, and he looked around, then cleared his throat. "It's not a rare fruit on this island. They can be found surprisingly easily if you look by rivers and forests or by the paths. But still, a single tree doesn't bear much fruit. Gathering a decent amount should take some time... Oh yes, having a map of the island should help."

"Wait, so then was what Clantail just took..." 7753 trailed off.

"That would be the tapestry...I think."

I see, Chelsea thought. Now that they pointed it out, there had been a tapestry with an aerial view of the island on the wall in one room. Using that to search would be far better than looking haphazardly.

"Can you tell that from just that, though?" 7753 asked.

"More precisely, I think that's what is drawn on the tapestry, so it's probably better than nothing... And as I said before, they grow all over the island, so they shouldn't be that difficult to find. It's just that we already gathered most of the fruit around the main building, so she'd have to travel a bit..."

She's actually smart, for someone who's half-animal, Chelsea thought, impressed. But Mana was angry, saying it was selfish of her to run off at a time like this, and Agri was angry, saying it was because there'd been a thief, and Mana said angrily yeah but still, while Agri angrily said that prioritizing securing fruit was pragmatic as they butted heads. None of the other mages and magical girls attempted to interrupt or intervene in their dispute. With the ire no longer directed at him, Shepherdspie breathed a sigh of relief. *Isn't that nice, Mr. Pie?* Chelsea thought.

After yelling at Shepherdspie and Chelsea, next, Agri was going at it with Mana. It was like she didn't even see Chelsea anymore. Maybe she was fine with anyone, as long as she got to yell.

Chelsea had heard from her mother that mages were smart. Now that she was actually associating with them, it made her tilt her head dubiously. None of them seemed very smart.

A situation where one person has killed another was too far

from reality; it was like a TV drama, manga, movie, anime, or light novel—it was some kind of fiction. It didn't feel at all like it was happening to her. And Ragi being on the verge of collapse made her think, *Aw, that sucks.*

If anything, her attention was on the direction Clantail had run. That had been very courageous and cool. Ragi was the type of man Chelsea wouldn't want living in her neighborhood—he was basically a nasty, stubborn old man, the kind of person Chelsea would find obnoxious. But Clantail had risked her life for him anyway by going into the forest to search for the grayfruit.

She was doing everything she could for the sake of her friends and allies. That was very like a magical girl.

Clantail was a magical girl, but her aesthetic wasn't to Chelsea's preference. If a magical girl like Clantail appeared in anime, Chelsea might post a comment on social media like, *I don't think that kind of weird attempt at a new design is great for a magical girl. With the times we're in, what people want out of magical girls is the classic look, not reinventing the wheel.* But still, despite that, Chelsea's preferences aside, she was a magical girl. When her employer was in trouble, she leaped into the forest to look for the grayfruit, heedless of danger to her own life.

Yes, that was obviously how a magical girl should be.

One gust of wind, then a second stroked the ground. Chelsea reflexively hugged herself. Realizing that wasn't a very magical-girl-like gesture, she immediately unfolded her arms again. When she happened to bring her palm up to look at it, it was trembling slightly.

She stared at the sky. The sun was about to set beyond the forest.

Chelsea looked at Agri and Mana. She could hear what they were talking about more clearly than before. They weren't just "yelling at each other." Agri was yelling angrily that Mary had stolen the fruit and disappeared, wailing that this was a question of Shepherdspie's responsibility, and she was even saying the string of incidents might have been caused by Mary.

Chelsea slowly closed her trembling hands and squeezed them.

Her long magical-girl nails, neatly groomed and painted in vivid red, bit into her palms, and it hurt. It hurt, but that pain brought Chelsea clearly back to the real world.

Chelsea wasn't the kind of person who would stay silent when nasty things were said about her friends. And Chelsea also wouldn't let Clantail get the juiciest moments.

"You're wrong." She said it out loud. Mana, Agri, and all the other mages looked toward Chelsea all at once.

Chelsea puffed out her chest and looked them all right back in the eyes. "You're wrong! May-May doesn't steal!"

Her mother had said, "You dream too much when it comes to magical girls." She said that magical girls live in reality, too, so they're tainted by reality. But if Chelsea was to agree, then Dreamy☆Chelsea wouldn't be Dreamy☆Chelsea. Even if her dinner was taken away, even if her monthly allowance was decreased, this was the one thing she would never back down on.

"Don't talk about May-May like she's a thief!"

Putting it into words made her mind clear, and she knew what she had to do. Since coming to the island, Mary had been more friendly to her than anyone. She was a friend. She wasn't a thief at all. There was absolutely no way she could be the one behind everything. Chelsea was a magical girl, and magical girls believed in their friends. She would always believe in them, no matter what. In other words, Mary hadn't betrayed her, and she hadn't stolen anything. She hadn't disappeared to escape the consequences of her actions. That meant that Mary had been taken away by someone or that she'd been forced to flee, and she was in a very dangerous situation.

Chelsea stuck a thumb up and jabbed it at herself. This was an expression of her determination and a display of her will. This was saying that she was a magical girl.

"I'm going to go save May-May."

There were a lot of people here. They were all together. It wasn't that dangerous here. It was different with Mary. She could be captured by someone. She might be hiding and crying. She might be about to be killed. Chelsea was a magical girl and her friend, so that meant she was going to save Mary.

Turning her attention back to each one of the faces that watched her with surprise, Chelsea felt magical-girl power swelling up inside her. She'd been snacking on the grayfruit a lot when Shepherdspie hadn't been watching—they were good—so she would probably last longer than the other magical girls.

Shepherdspie flapped around, waving both arms wide side to side. "S-stop this!"

"I don't wanna!"

Mana stepped forward, extending a hand to Chelsea. "I'm telling you, it's too dangerous!"

"I know that!" Nimbly avoiding Mana's hand, Chelsea kicked off the trunk of a tree, then landed on her toes on one of the countless tree roots that creeped along the ground. "Leave it to Dreamy☆Chelsea!"

She posed, and then with the dumbfounded expressions of every face present seeing her off, she raced away.

Chelsea was absolutely going to save Pastel Mary. She'd made up her mind.

◇ **Miss Marguerite**

Marguerite looked up at the main building. The lights were on in the upper floors. Was that an attempt to make things just slightly brighter? But the atmosphere here was dark.

The information Maiya's body had brought them had been a little positive, that "the culprit was not someone Maiya knew," but it was fair to point out that was just reinforcing the information gained from 7753's goggles. It didn't feel like it had any effects such as improving the atmosphere or morale or getting them all to work together. When the magical girls got back, they all ran to their own patrons, abandoning the others to make whispered reports.

Touta had done well. And Yol, who had been constantly crying before, had now cheered up enough to bite into the grayfruit that was offered to her. Her eyes were red and her cheeks were white, and it was difficult to say she was in good health, but still, she was managing to eat what she had to in order to live.

Marguerite was about to pet Touta's head but stopped her hand right before she could. Treating him like a child wasn't a good way to express her respect.

"...What's wrong?" Touta asked.

"Oh, just that you've done well." Marguerite patted his shoulder twice. Touta was looking up at her curiously—he seemed to be doing better than she'd thought. Marguerite massaged his shoulder with that hand, and Touta scowled like it hurt, so she withdrew her hand.

"Everyone just does whatever they want! Seriously! Agh!" Mana was in a huff.

Agri had her arms around Ren-Ren and Nephilia, and the three of them were talking about something in a huddle. Clarissa and Navi were the same. It was clear something had happened. And that something was nothing good.

Marguerite offered one of the grayfruit she carried in her right arm to Mana. "On the way back—"

Mana snatched the grayfruit away. She turned away from Marguerite and handed the fruit to 7753, then turned back to Marguerite with a slightly gentler expression than before.

Marguerite watched 7753 over Mana's shoulder. She walked over to the old man, whose face was pale as a corpse, and said to him, "They picked up some grayfruit on the way back."

Marguerite handed another to Mana, who gazed at it for a while before sweeping her eyes around the area. She was probably making sure there was enough to go around. She exhaled, then bit into it with a grimace. "Oh...thanks... In all seriousness, I really am grateful."

"We just happened to find some," Marguerite said. "We couldn't take too much time, so we don't have many."

"Even if it's not many, they're in high demand right now."

"What happened? There are fewer people here."

"The fruit we picked is gone."

"...How did something like that happen?"

"Pastel Mary disappeared."

"She took them?"

"That was what we were discussing, but..." Mana's expression soured further. It must have been a yelling match they were calling a discussion. "And then Dreamy☆Chelsea ran off."

"Why?"

"She said Pastel Mary isn't a thief, and someone must have kidnapped her, so she left to go save her."

Marguerite put a hand to her temple. The headache was not her imagination. Who was it who had said that you had to be a little bit crazy in the head or you wouldn't be able to do the job of a magical girl? "Nobody stopped her?"

"Nobody could."

After all, it wouldn't be fair to tell mages to stop a magical girl.

"...Where's Clantail?" Marguerite asked.

Mana glanced behind her. 7753 was squatting by the old mage, helping him eat the fruit. The fruit did seem to be more or less going into Ragi's mouth, but who knew if he was actually chewing it? When his hat started sliding down from his head, 7753's arm snapped out to hold it down.

"The old man was coughing up blood," Mana said. "I haven't given him a proper examination, but I think he was close to his limits. He wasn't going to last any longer without grayfruit, so Clantail went into the forest with the tapestry."

That was a reckless thing to do, but it was at least more rational than Chelsea's wild behavior.

Marguerite took a bite of a grayfruit. The flesh and juices mingled with her saliva to slide down her throat. It eased the hunger that she shouldn't have been feeling, so long as she was in magical-girl form.

She couldn't say it to Ragi, but the old man's condition was now kind of like an indicator. When the mages had fallen unconscious and the magical girls' transformations had come undone, Ragi had been the first to go. In other words, their transformations wouldn't come undone until Ragi was down. That was the literal deadline. If the "enemy" attacked when they were human, they wouldn't be able to fight back. They'd die, no doubt. They all understood that. That was why Agri, Navi, and all the magical girls were eating the grayfruit.

But...this is...

Marguerite hadn't been precisely measuring the time, but hadn't the interval gotten shorter, compared to the last time Ragi's health had gotten worse and he'd had a grayfruit to recover? Had the grayfruit become less effective, or was the situation getting worse?

7753 stood up and headed to Rareko and Yol. Ragi must have gotten comfortable despite things as he was sitting up on his own, though he was leaning on his staff. Exhaustion was apparent on his face, and he also seemed mentally befuddled.

Marguerite tossed the last of the fruit on her palm into her mouth and swallowed it without hardly chewing it. She was disgusted about making a weakened old man their canary in the coal mine and irritated at having been forced to do that. Clantail was impulsive for being unable to stand by and dashing off into the forest, but she wasn't wrong, as a magical girl.

Although Marguerite might silently condemn herself, she couldn't abandon her post. Everyone was all off on their own groups around their mage clients, discussing. Even though they had to all come together, they weren't coming together.

"Leaving aside the theory that Pastel Mary is the culprit, we should get more organized as a group," said Marguerite.

"About that." Mana sounded even more bitter. "I think we should find out what all the magical girls' magics are, as well as the mages' areas of specialization."

They knew that nobody with them now had killed Maiya or destroyed the gate. In that case, it would be best to get a grasp on what the others could do in order to work together more effectively. This really should have been proposed earlier, when they'd had 7753 use her magic, but Mana hadn't spoken up about it then.

Marguerite didn't need to ask to figure out the reason why. Mana had kept 7753's abilities a secret to investigate the others' abilities privately. However, that scheme had fallen apart when Ragi had made 7753's magic known to all of them, and now everybody knew that Mana had been able to order 7753 to do just that. It wouldn't be strange for some to wonder, *Did she actually try doing—? No, wait, she definitely did.* Anyone with a bit of smarts would arrive at that thought.

Coming from a position where she had wronged them in a way made it unsurprisingly difficult for Mana to make this proposal. And on top of that, it seemed like she'd been arguing with someone while Marguerite had been gone. That would make it even more difficult for her to suggest learning more about one another's abilities.

Marguerite withdrew her finger from her temple and touched it to the end of her chin.

She hadn't come as a guest but as an accompanying magical girl, so it would be a bit presumptuous for her to make such a proposal. Depending on how it was taken, it could cause offense. In the Inspection Department, nobody would hold back over the difference between magical girl and mage, but this wasn't the Inspection Department. There was Touta, but even if he was more or less an invited guest, the others would have realized by now that he couldn't use magic. It would be odd if he had been pushing for this.

Perhaps a good compromise would be to go through Touta to ask Yol. Though she was young, she had a good character and family background. Even if she was immature, she had a strong presence. But Marguerite couldn't impose further on a young girl who'd just been stricken with such a major emotional shock from Maiya's—

"Ummm."

Marguerite withdrew her finger from her chin and turned around. John Shepherdspie, his large frame scrunched up as much as possible, was standing there. Then she remembered: *Oh, right, he's here.* He was far more suitable for the role than the very young Yol.

"What's happened to Pastel Mary?" Shepherdspie asked. "Have you seen any trace of her in the forest, or..."

"Unfortunately..." Marguerite trailed off.

"I see..." He sighed deeply, not even trying to hide it, and bit into a grayfruit. He seemed highly anxious. Maybe he was suitable for the role, but Marguerite also wondered if she should be forcing him to shoulder any further burdens. Still, he was better than Yol, who'd been crying her eyes out over Maiya's death.

Shepherdspie took his time swallowing. "Mm...right, and also about Maiya..."

"Yes?"

"Where did you bury her?"

Marguerite stared back at him. Shepherdspie flinched and thrust his hands in front of him. "Oh, I do believe that it's most reasonable to return her to Miss Yol in the end, but if we're going to do that, then we should know where the body is... I don't mean anything badly at all by it."

"Not at all... We've left the body as is."

"A-ahhh, I see...is that the situation?" Shepherdspie backed down apologetically.

Marguerite stroked her face from top to bottom, returning it to what she figured was her original expression.

Burying the body. Ordinarily, of course that was what you would do. But none of the magical girls there had proposed burial. Marguerite hadn't even thought about it. She did feel no small amount of grief for Maiya, but it still hadn't even come to her mind. She wouldn't consider digging a hole to bury a body when they might be attacked by an enemy at any moment. The most she'd been able to manage was picking up some supply resources as an afterthought, since they'd been growing on trees on the way back.

If you judged Shepherdspie to be maintaining a decent level of humanity, then Marguerite was on the abnormal side. She silently apologized for putting him lower on the priority ranking than Yol—not just that, she'd forgotten he even existed—and then looked at Mana beside her.

Mana must have picked up on what she was thinking, as she gave Marguerite a little nod, then bowed her head to Shepherdspie. "I'd like to make a request of you. May I?"

"What is it?" he replied, looking more confused than annoyed. But if they were going to ask someone, Shepherdspie was it.

Marguerite was about to explain her request when there was a sudden call of, "So hey," making her turn around.

It was Agri. She held a half-eaten grayfruit in her right hand. Her left was free, index finger pointing at the grayfruit in Marguerite's hands. After distributing one each to everyone, there were three left over—but put another way, there were *only* three left over. "Like, wouldn't it be good to gather more? There's totally not enough."

"You got that right," Navi replied with a nod, which Clarissa mimicked, albeit more rapidly. "I think it'd be a good idea to put together a team like before to go gather some."

"Yeah, I agree. So…" Agri passed the grayfruit from her right hand to her left, then tossed it backward to Love Me Ren-Ren, who caught it in both hands. "I think the people gathering them should be the ones holding on to the inventory. How about that?"

Sweeping her gaze around to meet the eyes of each person there, she stood up straight and touched her right hand to her chest. "For instance, if we get attacked, us mages aren't gonna be useful in a fight, whether we're awake or not. But we'll be in trouble if the magical girls can't transform. So then we should prioritize the magical girls over the mages when distributing the fruit. Am I wrong?"

"Nah, nah." Navi shook his head, and Clarissa shook hers, too. Her big catlike ears swayed side to side. "If a mage knows they're gonna be useless, that's fine. But listen, I'll be useful. I think it'll be bad for everyone if I can't do my job when the time comes."

"Huh? What?" Agri put a hand to her hip, bending at the waist to lean her face close to Navi. Navi didn't back off, puffing out his chest, and the two of them glared at each other in those weird poses. "You're telling us to treat you special 'cause you're gonna be useful?"

"C'mon, lady. You're the one planning to get a bigger share for yourself because you're employing two magical girls."

"What? That's completely unjustified speculation. Just because you have nasty ideas like that, don't assume others are the same."

"But well, you know..." Navi's gaze flicked elsewhere. He was looking at Ragi, sitting slumped. "If it were just about changing the distribution, that wouldn't be a bad idea. But I think differentiating based on whether you're a magical girl or a mage is unfair discrimination. If the standard is whether you're useful or not, then, well. That's not discrimination; that's differentiation."

Yol and Touta seemed confused. Rareko seemed entirely at a loss, looking alternately between the two mages. Shepherdspie was in a dither, Ren-Ren looked apologetic, and for some reason, Nephilia was the one person smirking in amusement. 7753 gave Mana a sidelong glance, cringing away like she was frightened. And then Mana—you didn't even have to ask what sort of mood she was in. Deep lines furrowed between her eyes, and her teeth could be seen from the corners of her lips. She was mad about these two squabbling over trivialities in an attempt to gain even the slightest advantage. She was going to explode in under five seconds.

Marguerite was mysteriously coolheaded. She asked herself why but didn't come up with an answer. Unable to work together in a situation that necessitated it, they were trying to cast off the weak and scrabbling for even the slightest personal benefit. This was just about as bad as you could get, in terms of true character being revealed in a crisis situation. Normally, Marguerite would become angry like Mana. But for some reason, she was coolheaded. There was something difficult to verbalize, something strange—

A voice came from above. "It's here."

She followed Mana's gaze up to see a magical girl floating in the air—Tepsekemei, the one Marguerite didn't really understand. That had clearly been her voice. But her face wasn't pointed toward the two nastily bickering mages but the other way—toward the main building. She wasn't actually looking at the main building; her face was just pointed in that direction. Her eyes appeared as if they were looking somewhere else beyond that.

"What's wrong, Mei?" Mana asked.

Still with her face pointed to the main building, Tepsekemei muttered, "Pukin."

Various emotions crossed Mana's face. Confusion, loathing, surprise—what came out strongest was fear.

Marguerite narrowed her eyes. She knew the name Pukin. The name had come up a number of times in the documentation of the incident that had happened in B City. That was the magical girl who had caused Hana Gekokujou's death. She'd been an incredibly powerful fighter, and even if you used all your fingers and toes, you wouldn't have enough to count Pukin's victims in just B City alone.

But Pukin was gone. It wasn't even that she'd gone back to prison. She was dead.

Mana let out a shallow breath and inhaled again. She was nervous. "What…about Pukin?"

"It's like her," Tepsekemei said.

"Like her?"

"It's like her. That's what's here."

Marguerite opened her mouth to ask what Tepsekemei meant, but she didn't say anything. She felt it.

It was there. Something was there.

Her heart was pounding hard. Marguerite drew her sword. She figured it was past the main building, between fifty and a hundred yards away. Even from that distance, it penetrated her with enough lethal intent to make her feel like she'd been attacked, and her body moved. A beat later, the ground rumbled. A piercing sound made everything tremble, and then trees flew up high in the air, along with massive clods of earth. Some hit the spire of the main building, crashing through the wall to destroy the tower. There were sparks and steam gushing up from behind the main building as hard as a geyser.

"The power generator is back there!" Shepherdspie called, and not even a split second later, the main building's lights went out all at once.

Marguerite tried to go to Touta, but he wasn't where he had just been a moment ago. Rareko was running into the forest. Yol was in her arms, and since Touta was firmly holding her hand, he was swept into the forest as well.

From the corner of her eyes, Marguerite saw Clarissa running off carrying something large. That was probably Navi. Shepherdspie was flopped on the ground behind her. Agri's group was already gone.

The air felt tense now. It had become oppressive in a flash. It had sent people fleeing, but she couldn't be sure that was true of everyone. In fact, some probably saw this as a good excuse to move onward independently. It was clear to anyone that there wasn't enough grayfruit. They needed more of it faster and faster. Plus, the main building, which had been their base, was destroyed— and with it, their reason for staying in one place. On top of that, this had come right after that dispute that had clearly announced "we're a disorderly rabble." Anyone with common sense would be losing the will to cooperate.

And everyone had to have their own reasons, too. For Rareko, that would be cowardice or a sense of her duty to keep her master safe no matter what, now that Maiya was dead. Agri and Navi both wanted to be in charge. It was common for mages to want to stand above their peers, no matter what the occasion. Their motive would be the desire to keep others from controlling the situation and restricting their own behavior or because of something like, *I don't want any more to get seen through those goggles*—Marguerite huffed to herself. This wasn't what she should be thinking about in a dire situation like this.

With the rubble of the main building, clods of earth, and even trees dug up by the roots and man-size rocks raining down, Tepsekemei didn't try to avoid any of it and took it all in the face, but everything passed through her body without causing a single wound. Marguerite didn't use her sword, using only minimal movements of her body to evade the shrapnel-like flying objects. Though 7753 cried out *ow, ow,* she stood in front of Mana and Shepherdspie, hunched over with both arms as a shield, firmly guarding her upper body as she held her ground.

"Marguerite," said a voice from behind the cloud of dust. "You're not going to run?"

"What about you?" Marguerite asked. "You're not going to run...Tepsekemei?"

"Mei is good at running, so Mei will stay till the end."

"I see."

"Mei got away from Archfiend Pam, too."

"Oh my... That's incredible."

"I get lots of compliments."

"You should write that on your résumé. A history of having been able to escape from the Archfiend alone would have you instantly welcomed into any department as an asset. Inspection in particular never has enough people..." Marguerite closed her mouth. The presence that she'd felt all this time beyond the main building, in the forest, wavered slightly. It didn't seem like it was going to attack a couple of magical girls who were chatting and making themselves open for it in a deliberate sort of way. It wavered, and eventually faded, and disappeared. Marguerite remained on guard, counting until it felt like it had been a full five minutes, then finally sheathed her sword. She made the noise deliberately loud to show off that she had sheathed her weapon, but the presence still didn't return.

She took her hat in hand. The inside edge was damp. When she touched her hand to her forehead, her bangs were stuck to her skin with sweat. Thick sweat also flowed down her back, toward her butt. 7753 let out an anxious, rattling breath and just about collapsed when Mana caught her.

Tepsekemei took a bite of the grayfruit in her right hand and stared at the fruit. "Is this congee with sweet potato?"

"Congee?" Marguerite repeated.

"Or a cucumber sandwich?"

Marguerite couldn't understand what she was trying to say. She looked at 7753, but she was swaying and seemed on the verge of tears. She didn't seem calm enough to translate. Marguerite closed one eye. She knew a lot of magical girls would repeat things or do things often that seemed very meaningful but were actually meaningless.

Marguerite didn't respond to Tepsekemei's question, asking back instead, "You said Pukin."

"It was like Pukin," Tepsekemei said.

"What do you mean?"

"Different from us."

"...Do you mean not a magical girl?"

"Different from us."

This made more sense than whatever she'd been saying about congee—since Marguerite had experienced the same thing. Marguerite had seen a variety of magical girls who were *superior beings*. They weren't simply strong—there was something fundamentally different about them. Maybe the fitting description for them was "terrific." She hadn't actually seen this. She had just sensed its presence, but it had sent a shiver down her spine anyway. Maybe it was less that her body had moved before she could think and more that *it* had moved her.

Had that not been a magical girl? But it was difficult to imagine that it wasn't. There were rocks, rubble, fallen trees, and clods of earth scattered all around, and the main building was half-destroyed. It was probably no exaggeration to say the other side of the building was a disaster. It had accomplished this much destruction and emitted that sinister aura to keep Marguerite frozen on the spot. *Could anything but a magical girl do this...?*

"Was Pukin...not a magical girl?" Marguerite asked.

"She was a magical girl. But she was different."

Marguerite had heard that the old magical girls were made differently. Was that the difference between Neanderthals and Cro-Magnon, or was it as different as birds and reptiles?

"What do we do?" Mana asked as she lent a shoulder to 7753, who was staggering from having been struck by the things flying through the air—she seemed heavy, but it felt like it would be tactless to help.

"Go find those who have fled...," Marguerite answered. "But first..."

"But first?"

"We need grayfruit."

"Ahhh, yeah."

Marguerite put her hat back on. The sweaty parts were cold in a moist way and felt gross. It would get colder at night, even on a southern isle. She looked up to see pale clouds above and a hazy moon behind them.

Though the bad situation could excuse them, these were not the most reliable allies, to scatter and run rather than stand and fight. Still, they had to have numbers, or things would get even worse. The enemy that had come to them was no ordinary opponent. It was a magical girl—no, a *something*—so strong that Marguerite understood how Maiya had been killed. Even knowing it was there, Marguerite's legs hadn't moved, and she'd just watched it go. She had no clue if they had any chance of winning.

She was worried about Touta, but on that front, she had no choice but to pin her hopes on Rareko. If there was one point where Rareko was superior to Maiya, it was that she could flee faster than anyone without a moment's hesitation—in other words, she had no unnecessary pride. Marguerite prayed that even if she ran into the enemy somewhere, she would manage to get away.

Marguerite looked around the area, but Ragi was gone. Had a kind someone pulled him by the arm, or had he somehow managed to escape the scene of disaster? Marguerite scooped up the fallen Shepherdspie in her arms and slung him over her shoulder.

Seeing that, 7753 timidly asked, "Is he...okay?"

"...He doesn't look injured," Mana answered. According to her brief diagnosis, he had no injuries, so he must have passed out from the shock. However, Marguerite couldn't determine yet whether that was fortunate.

Their plan was to search for grayfruit first, and so they decided to go to the place Marguerite's party had found on their way back, where there had been some growing. There hadn't been enough time before to harvest all of them. There should still have been a few left. With Tepsekemei in the lead, the party started walking.

Coming up behind Tepsekemei, Marguerite said, "Wait. Wait, Tepsekemei."

"What is it, Marguerite?"

"It would help if you could choose a route I can actually follow."

"Over the pond?"

"I can't exactly walk on water."

"Understood."

Marguerite followed after Tepsekemei.

◇ **Love Me Ren-Ren**

Trickling between the trees was a creek narrow enough that even a five-year-old could step over it. Ren-Ren flew upstream. She followed the flow of the meandering creek, going up a cliff and through a culvert to its source. Eventually, she reached a large rock, and confirming that water oozing out at its foot was what made the creek, she breathed a deep sigh.

She'd come from the center of the island and was now pretty close to the eastern edge. The night had grown darker, too. She could hear insects buzzing in the thicket. That cry from the tree-tops had to be an owl.

Ren-Ren had a cabinet in her heart. She divided up all the humans, mages, and magical girls she'd ever met by type and tucked them into the drawers of her cabinet to pull out when necessary. No two magical girls were completely identical, but they would be similar in some way. Even with a magical girl she had never met before, she would respond to them based on the information in her drawers.

But some she couldn't classify, like Tepsekemei, who lacked the intent to communicate her thoughts and feelings to others. And the *thing* they had just encountered—yes, though Ren-Ren hadn't seen it directly, it felt as if they'd had some kind of encounter. Just remembering it started her trembling from the inside out, and she felt sick enough to bring her food up. She would have preferred not to remember. There had never been anyone else before who could make her feel that way, when she hadn't even seen them.

Ren-Ren had met violent people. She'd met self-serving people.

She'd met people who loved nothing more than disparaging others, and she'd met those who would feel pleasure to see someone else moaning in pain.

But she'd never met anyone like *that*.

"Ren-Ren. Hey, Ren-Ren." Agri's voice interrupted her thoughts.

"Ah, yes. What is it?"

"You're squeezing too hard. If you squeeze me with your strength, you're gonna break my little arms."

"Sorry."

"Uh-huh. Or, like, you can let me down already. Thanks."

"Ahhh, right." Ren-Ren gently let Agri down from her grasp. The sensation and warmth of the thighs she'd been supporting in her arms went away. Agri laid her back against a tree and inched her way upward, and once she was fully on her feet, she swung her arms around and stretched her back like she was doing morning calisthenics.

Ren-Ren let out a deep breath and looked at Nephilia. Nephilia was looking back at her, too.

"That...that thing just now—" Nephilia interrupted herself with a shake of her head, the gesture and her unusually serious expression showing a refusal to speak.

Ren-Ren gave a little nod and turned to Agri. "Um, about that thing just now."

"Yeah?"

"That was, um, what Maiya..."

"I think that's what attacked her."

"Of course..."

"Can you beat it, Ren-Ren?"

Ren-Ren hadn't exactly been able to measure it. And even if she could ascertain its strength, she doubted she could win against it. Even if she said she was giving up because it was so much stronger, she didn't know *how* much stronger it was. Perhaps it was ten times stronger or a hundred times. Ren-Ren saw the regular students of the Archfiend Cram School, as well as the graduates and their leader, all as one category of "incredibly strong people." The only ones able to differentiate the stronger and weaker of them were those in that group.

"Not possible?" Agri asked.

"Well, um, ah…I'll do my best," Ren-Ren replied.

"Yeah, that's a good answer. And, Nephy? Can you do it?"

"…No way."

"Yeah, that's a good answer, too." Agri smiled unsuitably brightly for the situation. The hysterical woman who had been snapping at people over every little thing in front of the main building was gone.

"Um," Ren-Ren began.

"What?"

"We left all our things behind, though…"

"It's fine; it wasn't anything much anyway. And actually, I wouldn't have wanted you to go get my stuff then."

"Right."

"This is all we need at the moment." Agri took a grayfruit in hand and opened her mouth wide. When she was about to bite into it, she stopped, moving just her eyes to look at Ren-Ren, then Nephilia in turn. She closed her mouth without taking a bite, wiped the fruit on her sleeve, and gave it to Ren-Ren, then pulled out another to toss to Nephilia. "You guys should have them instead."

"I couldn't," said Ren-Ren.

"Didn't I say before? I was being somewhat sincere about all that. If something happens and I collapse, it'd be a big mistake for you guys not to be able to transform."

Ren-Ren looked at Nephilia to see her gladly chomping into hers. Ren-Ren hesitantly brought the fruit to her mouth and bit in. No matter how many times she ate them, she never got tired of them. They were sweet. And tasty.

"So here's the place, right?" Agri confirmed.

"Yes. I think so," Ren-Ren replied.

"It doesn't seem like she's coming, though."

"Well…" Once Ren-Ren was done eating her grayfruit, Nephilia, who'd been gazing up at the sky with a peaceful look on her face, suddenly turned sharply and placed her index finger to her lips. Obeying that finger, Ren-Ren put the conversation on pause and perked up her ears. She could hear the sound of leaves against leaves. Then footsteps. It was coming closer. It wasn't just one person—no, it *was* one person, but the other sounds had to be from a number of four-legged animals. The insects stopped buzzing.

"She's here," Ren-Ren announced, and then without even enough time to blink, the person of the hour had arrived.

"I apologize for taking sooo long! I'm sooorryyy!" Pastel Mary leaped toward her almost like she was sliding to a base, and Ren-Ren caught her in a stance like a martial artist receiving a tackle. Mary buried her face in Ren-Ren's chest. Feeling the heat of her breath, Ren-Ren automatically tried to peel off Mary, who squirmed, firmly attached to her with unexpected strength.

"Mary. Mary. Listen," Ren-Ren said. "Let go for a moment."

Mary muttered something incomprehensible and shoved her face into Ren-Ren's chest. Ren-Ren turned to Nephilia for help. Though Nephilia was smirking the whole time, she did help, and with the strength of both magical girls, they somehow pulled the two girls apart.

"Mary, listen," Ren-Ren began. "Will you hear what I have to say?"

"Ohhh, Ren-Ren. I'm sorry. It's just that we were apart for so long. I was lonely. So I just..." Mary was embarrassed. She still wanted to squeeze her, but she took a step back anyway. But then she stumbled over a rock and started falling, only to be caught by the body of a sheep, sinking into its wool.

The love created by Ren-Ren's magic was infinite in variety, depending on the person. Pastel Mary's version was comparatively restrained. Ren-Ren decided that had to be because of her reserved and cautious personality.

"Mary," Ren-Ren said. "Why did you take the grayfruit everyone picked?"

"You told me to go pick some grayfruit...," Mary replied. "Was that bad?"

"No..."

Mary's head was bowed apologetically as she examined Ren-Ren with upturned eyes. Ren-Ren had asked her to "pick the nearby grayfruit and come." She'd only wanted Mary to gather grayfruit from the nearby forest, but Mary had misunderstood and taken it further, going so far as theft.

"You should've been more specific about your request," Agri said with a sigh.

That had been Ren-Ren's mistake. Agri didn't know everything about Ren-Ren's magic. Ren-Ren was the only one on this island who knew how people would wind up when they were pierced by her arrow and fell in love with her.

So Ren-Ren should have chosen her words more carefully.

Agri had thought they should gather grayfruit; Ren-Ren had also agreed that was the right idea. Agri had said they had to keep it a secret from the others, though. "Shouldn't we work together with the others now and avoid conflict?" Ren-Ren had asked. "Just Ren-Ren and Nephilia might not be enough against this killer, and we don't know where they are." But her attempts to convince Agri had only made her even more heated, and Agri had argued her down.

The grayfruit they all shared were worthless. The grayfruit Agri monopolized would become more valuable down the line. Time would continue to pass, and once they exhausted their supply—if they only had the grayfruit that Agri had kept hidden—they would be able to profit off those. Agri would be able to get everything she'd yearned for but had never been able to acquire.

The look in Agri's eyes seemed swept away in enthusiasm, but the words coming out of her mouth projected a strange chill. Even when Ren-Ren had tried to convince Agri that her own life could be in danger, she'd replied, "I don't think there'll be any more deaths." Her statement was baseless but seemed convincing for some reason, and the words seeped into Ren-Ren's heart. When Agri clasped both of her hands and said please, Ren-Ren couldn't do anything but agree.

They'd had to go secretly gather grayfruit. And to that end,

Pastel Mary, who could control lots of sheep, was suitable. What Agri had proposed was against law and ethics. But Ren-Ren wound up agreeing anyway. Knowing that Pastel Mary would be forced to go alone into the dangerous forest, Ren-Ren had agreed. She had circled around behind where Pastel Mary had been working in the main building, sneakily nocked an arrow, aimed, and loosed it. Ren-Ren's arrows wouldn't hurt her targets physically; it would just make them fall uncontrollably in love. Ren-Ren had made her request of Pastel Mary and then had surreptitiously kept watch on the entrance so that Pastel Mary could get out of the back gate. That was all Ren-Ren had done.

But even that small action had caused a serious incident. Ren-Ren failed to do her due diligence. She hadn't considered adding detailed conditions to her request to Pastel Mary. So when Pastel Mary had secretly tried to gather lots of grayfruit, she'd started by carting away the grayfruit stored in the main building—because that was just what she had been ordered.

Agri had panicked. Ren-Ren had panicked, too. She didn't know how Nephilia had felt about it, though.

Agri had played the emotional mage blowing her top, wailing and causing conflict, telling them about Nephilia's magic and making them go to Maiya, just doing whatever she could to put off things, until when the deed had finally been exposed, the "enemy" had appeared. It seemed less like the timing had been good and more that it had been *too* good, but Agri had said, "Well, I guess that's how it goes," just nodding like it made sense to her somehow.

Though things hadn't gone perfectly as planned, in the end, they'd gathered some fruit. Sheep with bags and boxes on their backs came following after Mary. It was quite a number.

"It was pretty valuable that they didn't know your magic, huh, Ren-Ren," Agri said. "Then it was worth creating a mood that would keep people from bringing up the idea to share our abilities."

"That's true," Ren-Ren agreed.

"But it's still not enough." Agri made a little smile with the corners of her lips.

Ren-Ren swallowed. "Not enough…? You're going to pick more?"

"Uh-huh. More is better. But maybe we should avoid using the sheep openly. Since everyone's scattered all over the island, and they might get seen. It would be an issue if someone followed the sheep."

"That's too dangerous. Any more than this would be…"

"It'll be fine. It's not too dangerous…probably. I don't expect our killer will want to cause any more problems—at least I didn't get that impression after I saw that expression." Agri cocked her head.

She was talking like she knew something. *Could she be…the one who killed Maiya…?* Ren-Ren thought, but then she remembered 7753's goggles. Agri couldn't be the culprit.

"Um, do you…know what's happening?" Ren-Ren asked her.

"Oh, I've just been thinking about it looong and hard. Like, maybe *this* is what happened."

Just what do you mean? Ren-Ren was about to ask when there was a poke from behind, making her reflexively arch backward. It was Nephilia. *Is this the time to be doing something like that?* Ren-Ren thought and turned back to see Nephilia looking up at the sky. Ren-Ren followed Nephilia's gaze up. She wasn't looking at the sky. It was atop a rock. With the hazy light of the moon behind it, something person-shaped was standing atop the rock.

"Chelsea! Has! Arrived! …Hey, can you hear me?!"

Ren-Ren knew that voice. And she also knew what she was after.

Ren-Ren ran her finger over a box and tapped on it twice. The finger that had poked her in the back tapped twice in response. Ren-Ren nodded, and she sensed Nephilia nodding back.

With a leap and a beat of her wings, Ren-Ren shot into the air, crossing over the rock and the person standing atop it to look down on her from above. Nephilia stood in front of Agri with her scythe at the ready, both of them backing slowly into the thicket. Mary seemed frightened, clumped up with her sheep like she was ready to run.

Ren-Ren said clearly in her mind that she would manage somehow. To Ren-Ren, that meant, in other words, to charm them by shooting them with her arrow. Dreamy☆Chelsea posed just like she had right before running into the forest and fixed her gaze on Ren-Ren.

The sheep Chelsea held by the base of its neck in her left hand was flailing. Her hand popped open to release it, and the sheep practically tumbled its way down the rock to flee.

So she followed the sheep here...

"Chelsea's found you, villain! Give back May-May!"

Chelsea spoke and posed in a theatrical manner. It was like she was performing in a magical-girl show.

"We can't return anything to you..." Ren-Ren flapped her wings a second time and used that movement to cover how she was nocking arrows behind her back. She nocked one, two, three arrows. "We just found Mary, too."

Chelsea crouched down and slammed her right fist into the rock at her feet, sending cracks running along its surface as she buried her fist in the rock. The cracks spread. Once her hand was buried to the wrist, Chelsea pulled it out and stood straight with her fist still clenched, squeezing it in front of her face. It was trembling with the tension.

"Dreamy☆Chelsea..." She opened her right hand. In it lay brown rocks with twisted points. Right as Ren-Ren realized that Chelsea had grabbed some rock to crush it into star shapes, she somersaulted in midair, drew an arrow, and fired it in the same motion. The three arrows were aimed straight for Chelsea's face, heart, and stomach, but none of them made it. Ren-Ren saw a flash, and then Chelsea was posing with all the arrows in her left hand, each arrow sandwiched individually between her fingers. "...has it handled!"

With a flap of her wings, Ren-Ren ascended while firing off more arrows. Her first went straight, the second was concealed in the shadow of the first, and the third she shot to be faster than the first two so that it would collide with the other arrows on its way and change their trajectory—but that third arrow never connected. Chelsea's right toe sprang up to strike it aside, sending it spinning in the air to vanish behind her.

Chelsea lowered her raised leg, then cutely bent it backward. Bringing both hands to her mouth, she posed. "Chelsea won't forgive you!"

Star-shaped stones flew from Chelsea's right hand. Ren-Ren prepared to dodge, but the stars didn't come toward her, instead drawing a strange zigzag path as they went around Chelsea.

Chelsea leaped into the air. Even then, she was posing dramatically. With a cute gesture, she used a star as a stepping-stone and bounded off it, ascending unimaginably fast for the way she was moving, making another star circle ahead of her to bounce off that next, and with a speed that belied her cuteness, she was right up in Ren-Ren's face.

When Ren-Ren fired arrows in retaliation, a star repelled the first as Chelsea flashed yet another cute pose with the stick in her hand, which knocked away Ren-Ren's curved shot. Then Chelsea theatrically raised her leg and brought it down.

Ah!

Ren-Ren made it by a hairbreadth. She lifted her right leg to block Chelsea's incoming shin and was flung back in the opposite direction she'd flown in from. Ren-Ren slammed toward the ground.

That couldn't be called a kick. Chelsea's leg had just touched her in the course of moving her leg into that unnatural pose, but its strength and speed were incredible. Ren-Ren's shin was screaming in pain. It felt like muscle had torn.

Ren-Ren put on the brakes. Even a magical girl would die if she hit the ground at this speed. Rolling the other way in midair, she was flapping her wings hard to slow herself down when something struck her in the back, and now she was definitely being slammed down to the ground. Chelsea was stomping on her from above. Even if Ren-Ren knew it was coming, she couldn't evade it. That big flap before hitting the ground slowed her down a bit but didn't stop her, and she rolled along the ground.

She took the fall properly, slowing the speed of her landing. Rolling along, even though she barely avoided the foot stomp that came while she was down, Chelsea's next kick sent her flying upward, then another strike slammed her into a rock.

Ren-Ren coughed and clutched her chest, racked with pain as she fell to her knees. With a glance, she grasped the situation. Chelsea was facing her from a little over ten feet away, while Mary and her sheep looked on from farther away, frozen and trembling. She couldn't see Agri and Nephilia. Ren-Ren was in some serious trouble, but considering how strong Chelsea was, she considered herself lucky she wasn't dead.

Chelsea was still posing. She completely ignored efficiency in a fight, committing her effort entirely to cuteness and magical-girl-like movements. But despite not trying to fight properly, she was still too much for Ren-Ren. Even when prancing around ridiculously and prioritizing aesthetic, Chelsea was simply so much stronger.

Ren-Ren noticed the rocks circling around Chelsea were moving in the shape of a star. There probably wasn't any purpose to that, either. It had to be because it looked nice.

This was crazy—Ren-Ren was crazy for fighting when there was no reason to, and Chelsea was crazy for striking her opponent like this was an extension of play. It was all crazy. Ren-Ren swallowed the blood pooling in her mouth.

Ren-Ren expected Chelsea to keep going, but she turned to Mary instead. "May-May! Don't worry!"

Mary seemed confused for a moment, but her expression immediately turned to relief as she spread her arms to Chelsea, and then, pulling an arrow of Ren-Ren's from her sleeve, she stabbed—or almost did, but Chelsea's right fist moved through a pose to strike her hard in the side, and Mary passed out from the pain. She crumpled in the middle of her herd of sheep and could no longer be seen.

"Agh, geez!" Chelsea huffed. "Even making May-May do something like this! This is just—I'm really not gonna forgive you now!"

Chelsea had read every move of theirs thus far. Sneak attacks and trick attacks wouldn't work. No matter how absurdly her dancing around was, if she won, that made it the right approach. That held true for more than just magical girls.

Holding her stomach and dragging her feet, Ren-Ren tried to circle around to the right side, but Chelsea jumped ahead of her, scattering the frozen herd of sheep with a kick—one that was elegant like a ballet dancer.

"Chelsea thought you were trying to take a weirdly long time. Heh-heh, Chelsea's got it all figured out."

The box that had been hidden by the herd of sheep was revealed. It was packed full of the grayfruit—spilling out over the sides from how many were inside—which were basically a lifeline for the magical girls right now. Ren-Ren watched in despair. Those supplies were their only advantage. With that exposed, the one way they had the upper hand over Chelsea was gone—or at least that was what Chelsea thought as she reached out to a fruit in the box. The fruit suddenly flew upward.

Nephilia, who had been hiding inside the box, sprang out and jumped on her. It was a pincer attack. Chelsea spread both arms wide, lifted one leg, raised herself up on her tiptoes, and spun as if she was dancing. The way the dreamy girl saw it, maybe she actually was dancing.

Chelsea blocked Nephilia's scythe with her knee and knocked it aside with her hand. Nephilia lost her balance, Chelsea hooked her fingers into her opponent's collar to fling her at Ren-Ren, who crouched down and bounced Nephilia up with her back as she went for Chelsea. Chelsea grabbed the arrow in Ren-Ren's right hand to stop it and slapped the arrow in her left hand out of her grasp. Behind her, Ren-Ren heard the sound of a blade ripping through the air. That was Nephilia's scythe—Nephilia had flung it while flying backward, and it skimmed over Ren-Ren's wings only for Chelsea to casually lift one leg to kick it away. That same moment, Ren-Ren attacked with her final arrow, an arrowhead grasped in her tail, and swiped up from below Chelsea's thighs—Chelsea did a backward somersault in the air to get away.

After three spins in the air, Chelsea landed on the edge of the box, then looked down at her feet. It was just a bit, but there was blood oozing from her toe. The arrowhead that had been fixed to the side of the box had left a wound you couldn't even call a scrape. Nephilia had been the one to set the trap. She must have thought that Chelsea might carelessly touch the box and cut her hand. She couldn't have expected Chelsea to have hopped onto it in such a pointlessly dramatic gesture, but even if it was unexpected, now they had won.

The look on Chelsea's face gradually turned vacant and dazed. Though Mary was still groaning among her herd of sheep, she stood up and called out, "Stop this already, Chelsea."

"Yeah, I'll stop," Chelsea answered instantly. She ran to Mary and helped her up. "Sorry for everything!"

Mary told her it was okay as her eyes shifted over to Ren-Ren, who nodded back and moved away from the two of them. Chelsea fidgeted as she continued to apologize to Mary. Her expressions of love seemed somewhat docile and not too bad.

That had been a close one. Chelsea was stronger than Ren-Ren had thought. She shouldn't have assumed that Chelsea wouldn't be anything much because she normally seemed so airheaded. After all, she'd been hired for the job, so they shouldn't have underestimated her. Not only was it simplistic to assume she was just her employer's mistress, but it was dangerous.

"Are you all right?" Agri asked Ren-Ren.

"Yes...somehow." She tried to smile at Agri, who had popped her face out from the thicket, and Nephilia, who had gotten up, but pain ran through her side, making her right cheek twist up.

"Are you really okay?"

"I can still move."

"Okay, then... But wow, your magic, Ren-Ren. It sure is amazing."

"Thank you very much."

"It's amazing...but maybe a little inconvenient."

"Well...yes."

Mary reluctantly embraced Chelsea, who paid no mind to Mary's discomfort over Chelsea gleefully rubbing her cheek against her.

Ren-Ren's magic would make anyone pierced with her arrow fall in love. But only the first person would fall in love with Ren-Ren. The second person would fall in love with the first, and the third would fall in love with the second. And that would lead to an ongoing chain until eventually, it would get completely out of Ren-Ren's control and run wild...which was something that had happened twice before.

"But if it's just two people, it'll be all right," Ren-Ren said. "It can work."

"Uh-huh. And the third?" Agri asked.

"That...well, we'll manage somehow."

"Good, good."

Nephilia snickered. Agri nodded with satisfaction and waved her right hand to indicate ahead. "All right, let's get out of here. We made a lot of noise, so we might get some uninvited guests."

"You mean...the enemy," Ren-Ren said.

"No, not the enemy. I don't even know in the first place if there is an... Well, whatever. Anyway, let's move. C'mon."

Nephilia followed Agri, and Ren-Ren sent Mary a signal with her eyes. Mary's sheep gathered around Chelsea, who wouldn't leave Mary, and practically carried her away as they all walked off.

The insects must have decided the commotion was over for the moment, as a second later, they began hesitantly buzzing.

CHAPTER 7
NUTRIENTS, NUTRIENTS, NUTRIENTS, NUTRIENTS, NUTRIENTS INSUFFICIENT

◇ Clantail

Though the map drawn on the tapestry was quite simplified compared to reality, Clantail was able to get a rough grasp of the island overall. Checking the branches above one by one, she passed between trees, and after a minute of running, she came out to a little path along a hill. From here, she would head for the forested area.

She didn't hesitate. She didn't have the time for that. Following the tapestry, she chose to run through the places with the thickest greenery, looking for grayfruit on the way, but she didn't find any. Figuring they might be growing someplace that couldn't be seen from below, she raced into the trees but didn't find any there, either. Shepherdspie had said they were dotted all over the island and that they weren't rare.

Was she looking for them the wrong way? The clock wouldn't stop for her. It ignored Clantail's impatience, slowly and steadily edging along. No matter how far she kept going and going through the forest, she didn't find the fruit she was looking for. She came to a stop. If she was going to change her methods, she needed to do so sooner rather than later. She also expanded her search to include Pastel Mary.

Clantail checked the tapestry again and raced into the forest. After coming out to a rocky area covered in dark-orange stones, she looked at the tapestry once more to make sure she hadn't gone in the wrong direction.

Arriving at the base of a large and particularly tall rock that towered in the center of the rocky area, Clantail canceled the leopard and transformed her lower body into a different creature.

The coloring of its wings was terribly plain, just a pale and spotted brown—Clantail's main body actually had far more decoration. At a glance, the slim, fragile legs and the large wings that scattered dust looked like those of a butterfly, but the width of its torso and thickness of its fur proved it was not that. She was not the beautiful butterfly beloved by many but an insect some would scowl to see—a moth. Since the insect was scaled up to match Clantail's size, her torso was as thick as a small oil drum and her wingspan greater than ten feet. The sight alone might make someone who hated moths faint.

Clantail fluttered her wings and came up to land on the tip of the pointed rock to rest her legs there. She hadn't transformed to leap into the air and observe from above. Flying creatures all maintain a fine balance to stay airborne. Changing the head to Clantail's torso in flight hampered speed, strength, and stability, and it would distract her focus, too.

Her goal was not flight. Clantail perked up her ears. She could hear. The mages and magical girls were all clustered together at the main building. There was a splash in the pond. Those things on four legs chewing grass had to be sheep. There were other things moving, too. Clantail leaped up and flapped her wings. She was not fast or strong; it was absolutely the most she could do to just keep her balance.

There was a type of moth with an extremely wide range of hearing. It could hear at least as well as a bat or a dolphin, and it would pick up sound waves that humans couldn't perceive. Conveniently for Clantail, unlike bats and dolphins, moths sensed sound through an organ on their torso, not their head—a feature that Clantail, who could transform the lower half of her body into different animals, found the hardest to come by.

Once, Clantail had been unable to find "someone who hid herself." All the animals with the best senses, across the board, had those organs on their head—eyes, nose, ears, tongue, etc.—making Clantail unable to copy their sharp senses. And so what Clantail had wanted to protect, what had been dear to her, had slipped from her grasp—because she'd been unable to find that someone who hid herself.

Thinking about what had happened that day made her feel like her whole body was burning, going up in flame. Despite all her struggle, she'd failed to keep hold. No matter how awful it was or how much it hurt, she could never allow herself to forget that.

Clantail—Nene Ono—had researched animals because it was fun and because she enjoyed it, and she had learned all sorts of things about them. But after that incident, she'd changed the way she thought about it and how she did it. She wasn't really interested in insects; she would research them as well in order to gain what she needed.

Knowledge alone wasn't enough for her to transform. So that winter, she'd gone to an insectarium that was three prefectures over. There had been a nasty disease or something going around, so a lot of the insects had died and about half of the facilities had been closed, but she'd still been able to see a number of types of insects in person.

Clantail never wanted to let someone she should protect slip from her grasp again. The warmth of her body cooling in the water, her breathing and the bubbles getting smaller, and eventually disappearing—never again. No way.

With the "ears" at the bases of her wings, she focused on the sounds around her.

She was capable of emitting sound and using its echoes to detect the shape and location of objects. But there was a lot of cover in the forest to begin with, and it seemed as difficult as she'd imagined to try to search for the grayfruit, since they would be hidden by branches and leaves.

Clantail scowled. There was too much auditory information. The rustling of the leaves, the buzzing of insects, the cries of an owl, the wind and water—listening like this, it was surprisingly loud. Even eliminating all that background noise, she could hear animal sounds in more than just a few places. When she'd heard there were supposed to be wild animals on this island, she'd been looking forward to maybe being able to observe some rare creatures, but no animals had shown themselves since she'd come. But even if she'd never seen them, they apparently were there on the island. Footsteps that were not sheep's hooves, the crunch of biting into a tree, lapping at water—there were quite a few animal sounds like these.

They said that Cranberry, Musician of the Forest, had heard sounds with greater precision than the eye could see. Clantail didn't have magic specialized to sound like Cranberry, so she wasn't very skilled at listening. But she had to try.

Leaping from rock to rock, she went back into the forest, flying at low altitude. The densely growing foliage in the forest made it more difficult to pick up sounds there than the rocky area, requiring more delicate attention and analysis of the information.

She flew extremely slowly with her eyes locked on the scenery, attentive to all the incoming information. She must not forget about the killer who was supposed to be on this island. There were things she would have to do if she discovered something that looked like them, but right now, the grayfruit was more important—of course for Ragi, but for Clantail as well, and all the other mages and magical girls would absolutely need the grayfruit in order to face the unknown enemy. Weaving between trees, Clantail flew over a thicket and passed along an animal trail to come to the crest of a hill. This reconfirmed that the tapestry wasn't useless as a map, but she still couldn't find any grayfruit or Pastel Mary.

She flapped her wings a bit to slow down at the border between the forest and the wetland. She was changing direction to aim for a different green area when, suddenly, her field of view was covered in darkness. The smell of the trees, the earth, the leaves, and the nighttime dew, plus every single sound instantly became distant. Her moth half disappeared, and of course her wings went along with it. Clantail plunged to the ground headfirst, covering her upper body with both arms as she rolled along until she hit a tree back first, bending it and coming to a stop. She gasped in pain and rolled over to lie faceup. Her arms felt completely weak. When she tried to move them, a piercing pain ran through them. Maybe they were broken.

It took her a few seconds to realize her transformation had been undone.

Even just trying to get up hurt. Resisting the pain, she sat up, got onto her knees, and tried to stand, but her arms hurt, and a moan slipped out. She couldn't see anything. It was pitch-black. The taste of blood was spreading inside her mouth, and it hurt when she ran her tongue along her cheek. It must have gotten cut.

Her right arm hurt even more. Her left one was a little numb, but she could move it now. She ran her left hand over her face and head. It wasn't wet, and there were no lumps or swelling, and it didn't hurt where she touched. And her glasses were gone.

Though it was hidden behind the leaves and branches of the tall trees, the light of the moon and stars did reach her. Her eyes gradually adjusted, but that couldn't miraculously help her see without her glasses.

Nene looked around. She'd been fully occupied only a moment ago just managing all the information, but now she was standing in a world where she could hardly see or hear. She wasn't even sure where she was. She didn't know what lay beyond the darkness. She squeezed her scarf and clenched her teeth to keep from screaming.

If her transformation had come undone because the effects of the grayfruit had worn off, that meant disaster at the main building, too. She had to get back somehow and meet up with the others.

A tree branch shook, and a bird flapped its wings to vanish into the sky. Nene clenched her scarf even harder and let out a ragged breath with her shoulders heaving. She couldn't properly gather her thoughts. The only thought spreading in her mind was that she had to get back.

Cautious and wary, she slowly crouched down and placed her left hand on the ground. She needed her glasses. She had to find them. The tapestry was also gone. It would be best to look for that, too.

Dropping to her knees and slowly groping with her hands, she searched the area. Every time her fingers touched something, she jerked her hand away, then slowly reached out to touch it again, and then once she realized it was a rock, tree branch, or something else that wasn't her glasses, she resumed her task.

She couldn't find them. It never ended. Her throat produced a low groan. She smacked her hand over her mouth, and this time she moaned from the pain in her right arm. She had to find her glasses, and she needed the tapestry, too. Slowly running her hands over the ground, she searched. She heard the *drip, drip* of droplets falling onto the earth. She didn't even know anymore whether it was her tears, sweat, or snot—rather than wiping and wiping at it, searching came first.

A sound came from the thicket behind her. Nene shuddered and rose up to one knee, then rotated around 180 degrees. The sound of swallowing spit came from herself. The buzzing of insects stopped. The sound of rustling leaves came three times, with pauses between, telling Nene that it wasn't her imagination.

Sliding her fingers along the ground, Nene gradually backed up. From kneeling, she went into a crouch, then readied to run.

She heard a loud noise—like something exploding in the distance. Startled, she turned toward it, then immediately retreated again into the underbrush.

She couldn't hear the sounds of the thicket anymore; her thunderous heartbeat drowned out everything else. She'd stopped breathing a long time ago. Sweat dripped through her eyebrows and caught in her eyelashes, but she didn't even try to wipe it away. She avoided making any noise as best as she could as she backed away from that place. All thoughts of her glasses or the tapestry were gone.

One step, another, then one more—she heard rustling leaves and a snapping twig, and then something leaped out from the thicket. Nene swallowed her spit again. Its cries, smell, and silhouette were like those of a dog, but it was far bigger than what she'd imagined. It was as big as a calf, though her vision was blurry, so that was all she could determine. Nene tried to slowly back away, then stopped when something hard hit her heel. There was a tree behind her. She couldn't back up any farther.

Even without her glasses, she could smell the animal and hear its growl. Her shriek and its howl sounded at the same time.

The beast jumped; Nene instantly crouched and leaped straight to the side. The beast slammed into the tree she'd been right in front of, crying out in a way that didn't sound like a normal animal at all. Already exhausted beyond her limit, Nene was chilled to the very depths of her heart by that sound.

She was going to die. It was going to devour her.

She didn't have the time to think about what you're supposed to do when you're attacked by a dog, or where a dog's weak point is, or anything like that. It was the most she could do to just move her body. She snapped dried branches underfoot as she pulled herself up through a gap between two trees, and then the beast was thrusting its face between the trees to try to leap on her, showering her with its drool. Her hands reflexively reached out to the ground. Running a palm along it, she grabbed a full fist of earth and flung it against the snout that was trying to snap its fangs together.

Its next cry was very understandable. They flailed around, breaking branches and scattering leaves of the underbrush, and Nene was practically flung away to roll over the weeds.

She came to a stop when she hit something hard on her left shoulder. With a moan, she reached up with her right arm, which made her moan again. Despite her groans, she propped herself against a tree to get to her feet.

The odor of the beast rose in the air, cutting through the smell of the earth she'd flung at it. It was angry that it had been obstructed, angry that it had been hit with something nasty, and maybe it was even hungry. All of that was about to hit Nene. She could hear it sliding over the weeds. Though she couldn't see it readying to leap, she could sense it coming.

Nene stood up, turned away from the beast, and grabbed a tree with both hands. The tree bark was rough, and it felt like the sharp bits would pierce her skin. But since it wasn't slippery and smooth, maybe she could climb it.

She was good at tree climbing. Her small frame actually made climbing easier. She'd scaled trees that stretched high above, which surprised even her. Whenever she'd thought, *I want to see a cicada buzzing up close*, or, *There's a big cavity there—I wonder if there's a bird's nest inside*, or, *Maybe a squirrel or wild mouse lives there*, she'd grabbed its branches and set her feet on its protrusions to satisfy her curiosity.

The beast howled behind her. Nene tensed her core muscles.

The last time she'd climbed a tree had been in elementary school. She hadn't grown much since then, but it had still been a while since she'd last done it. And her vision was terrifyingly bad, too. Would she be able to grab the branches? Her whole body hurt from hitting things and falling. Her right arm in particular hurt just from moving it.

She yelled out loud from the pit of her stomach. The beast's howling faded, and Nene set one foot on the tree and leaped up. She reached out an arm to grope for something sticking out and grabbed a branch.

Her foot slipped, but she somehow maintained hold, pitching forward, since the footing she'd thought was there was gone, got control again, and kept going. Getting a grip with her fingers, she pulled her body up with both arms. She felt the sound and vibration of an impact, and her fingers started to slip, but she fought it and held tight. Her right leg wouldn't move. The beast was biting her shoe. Nene kicked it away and slid out of her sneaker, and the beast fell backward, tossing up dirt. Her arms hurt, but she ignored it. Bringing up both legs along with her arms, Nene put her socked toe against the tree to raise her whole body.

Her hand touched a branch. It was a thick one—even thicker than Nene's arm. Her arms and legs and head were all screaming that they were at their limit. This was the end of it. Bracing all her limbs, she pushed her body up over the branch. Then she sat on the branch and hugged the tree trunk with both arms. Her chest hurt. Even panting this hard, her heart continued to leap wildly and wouldn't settle down.

An even louder howl and the grating sound of claws scraping resonated terrifically through the tree. Nene clenched her teeth. Repeating three times in her head that no way was she going to die here, she clamped down on the fear that was trying to force its way out.

◇ Touta Magaoka

Touta hadn't wanted to get separated from Marguerite, but Rareko had pulled Yol, who'd been holding Touta's hand, so they'd all wound up running away together. Rareko ran around all over the forest, finding one grayfruit on the way, while Touta clung to Yol, frantically trying not to get dropped. In the end, they came to the coast, and Rareko searched for someplace inconspicuous. She punched and kicked at the cliff to dig out a cave, and the three of them went inside and huddled together.

Touta didn't really get what was going on, but he was terrified. He couldn't even complain to Rareko, *"How could you run and leave everyone else behind?"* He'd wanted to run, too. He just didn't want to be separated from Marguerite—staying behind with her back there would have been far more reassuring than getting separated from her.

But then that would mean getting separated from Yol. She seemed like she would feel more hopeless than Touta, so he didn't want to leave her for other reasons. He hadn't had the time to say anything as they'd been fleeing, but after ten or twenty minutes of being still in a fifteen-foot-wide cave, he calmed a little. He regained enough presence of mind to talk.

Touta said, let's go back. He said it would be better to be with everyone else.

Rareko said it was too dangerous. She said they had no idea what that scary thing would do, and it would be best to stay here to protect the miss…to protect the both of them.

Before Yol could say anything, a man appeared. It was sudden. When he popped his head in to peek at the entrance, Touta heard Rareko gulp.

But it wasn't like Touta could get himself to say anything. He would have liked to hug Yol close protectively, but more accurately, he was startled—he freaked, rather, and clung to her automatically.

Well, of course he would be surprised. Both he and Rareko were. They were surprised enough that until Yol cried, "Uncle!" they didn't even realize that it was Navi.

The smiling face that raised a hand with a "Yo" looked not only quite tired but also dirty—but it was indeed Navi. His clothes were Navi and his physique was also Navi, so you'd think they'd know at a glance it was Navi, but right that moment, he was soaked with bright red blood from the top of his head down to his neck. His collar was a mess, surely because it had absorbed the blood. Of course that would freak out Rareko, and it would freak out Touta, too.

"What happened?!" Yol cried.

"Ah, getting away was a bit of a struggle," Navi replied.

"Your head!"

"Come on, I was balding to begin with."

"I don't mean that!"

Following Yol's gaze, Navi smacked a hand against his forehead and looked at his palm. He scowled at his red palm, then wiped his face with his sleeve. "Stuff was flying around and hitting me all over the place. I figure some chunks hit me. Well, I got this far fine, so I'm sure it's no big deal."

"No, it is a big deal," Yol shot back, and Touta and Rareko both nodded.

They sat Navi down in the middle of the cave, and Rareko wiped him with a towel as she looked at his wounds. Navi snorted and said, "Nothing but hassle." Maybe he was talking about his own situation, or maybe he was talking about people worrying about him when he was okay. When Touta thought about the time he'd been told to stay at home when there was an important Battlers tournament, just because of a little fever, he could understand that "nothing but hassle" feeling. But what Navi had been suffering was more than a little fever.

"D'you know where the others went?" Navi asked them.

"No…we all became separated…," Yol answered. "And we haven't seen them since."

"'Bout the same on my end. I'm having Clarissa look, though."

"Isn't that dangerous?"

"If what's out there is something her fast legs can't outrun, then all of us are really outta luck. Well, I'll just do what I can for now." He smacked a bulge in his sleeve, then when he tilted it toward the ground, something rolled out. It was grayfruit. There were one, two, three, four of them.

"So many!" Yol cried. "We could only find one, and that took so much effort." The one grayfruit they had found had already been split by Yol and Rareko and eaten.

"No need to hold back, kids. I already secured some for me and Clarissa before sharing." Navi held up the sleeve on the other side and showed them. That one was also bulging. It had to have grayfruit tucked in it.

Touta let out a breath of relief. He didn't need them, but he knew they'd really be in trouble if Yol collapsed or if Rareko couldn't transform. Touta would have liked to find some himself, if he could, but getting them from someone else still helped, and he was grateful. He stood up and bowed his head at an angle that would look sharp. "Thank you very much." It was simply proper manners to thank someone with a bow when they helped you out.

Yol and Rareko bowed after him, and Navi scratched his head shyly. "Hey now, like I just said, I'm only sharing a bit." Navi smiled, then happened to look down and catch that Yol and Touta were holding hands. He narrowed his eyes, then smirked and smacked Touta on the shoulder, making Touta cough.

"What is it, Uncle?" Yol asked.

"Naw, nothing. We've all got to work together to tackle this."

Touta thought there was a teasing twinkle in his eye. Times like these, Touta normally might have let go of her hand automatically. But this time, he squeezed harder instead, making Yol yelp, and he apologized, relaxing his grip.

Navi's smiling grew even more clearly gleeful than before, and his eyeballs rolled into his head as he looked up. "Aren't you done yet, Rareko?"

"It seems the bleeding has stopped."

"Despite how my blood's always rushing to my head, eh? Well, get it done."

"Yes, as quickly as possible."

Of course there was no doctor's bag and no first aid kit, either. They didn't even have a toy first aid set. Still, Rareko wiped off the blood with a towel and such, making Navi's head even more sparkling than when Touta had first met him. Reflecting the light of the moon and stars, it sparkled like a second moon.

"Well then, guess I'll get going." Navi slapped a thigh and stood up with a *hup*.

"Going…? Wherever to?" Yol asked.

"C'mon, we won't get anywhere if we don't meet up with the others. I'll hide if things get dangerous, so no worries there. Well, since I got polished this shiny, maybe I'll give up on hiding, though." He laughed like he was amused. He looked much more at ease compared to when he'd first come. Maybe talking had relaxed him a bit. If that was the case, maybe Touta had been a bit useful, too.

"Listen, don't leave this spot. Just settle down right here. It looks like there's someone up to nasty stuff." Then with a flutter of one hand, Navi disappeared into the darkness.

Looking at him go, Touta thought, *Adults really are reliable.* Touta had considered him as like the misters who sold chicks, goldfish, or slider turtles at street stalls at night, but maybe people like that who seemed bad would be reliable when things got tough.

In the books you could borrow from the library, there were lots of stories featuring the exploits of children who could put adults to shame, but right now, it didn't seem like Touta could accomplish anything that would put the adults to shame. It was frustrating, but the reason Touta couldn't accomplish great feats was because he was Touta.

If Marguerite was there, would she say something thoughtful to console him? Touta figured she wouldn't be able to say anything thoughtful and would just put a hand on his head or something, then kind of regretted that thought. It was rude for him to imagine such a thing.

"Will he be all right...?" Yol wondered. "No, I do think he will be all right...but Uncle doesn't value his own safety or things of that nature very much."

"Really?" Touta asked.

"He'll write it off saying it will all be an amusing story afterward, so it's fine."

"Do you know him well? Is he your actual uncle?"

"No, my family will occasionally make requests of him. They say what those requests are is grown-up talk, so they won't tell me what it is, though."

"Hmm..." He didn't really understand why he'd gone and asked that. But now that he had, he agonized over it. *Agh, why'd I have to open my mouth?* Now he had to smooth things over. Nervously licking his lips, Touta said, "People like that...um, who don't consider their own safety much, you know..."

"Yes?"

"My aunt says that just means they'll only be exuberant and generous so long as they're successful."

Touta remembered about himself. When Navi had pulled out a bunch of fruit, Touta hadn't been happy about it. He'd felt more frustrated at first, like he could shout out, *"Damn it!"* He thought it was probably like that. Touta had felt that way even though it was obviously best for there to be lots of fruit for Yol and Rareko. He'd found himself thinking, *I wish I'd been the one to bring in lots of grayfruit to make Yol happy.* He'd felt frustrated that Yol had been cheered by that chat with Navi, too—even though it should have made him happy that Yol was feeling better.

He was sure that wasn't good. That was exactly why Touta had blabbered on with a bunch of irrelevant stuff in an attempt to cover himself and to keep it from being noticed that he was trying to cover himself. He was so scared, his whole body was shuddering, and he knew there was no helping that he was scared, but that still didn't stop it from being frustrating. He wanted to look good in front of Yol, and he wanted Marguerite to praise him—even though crazy things were happening, and he was scared. Touta even thought himself—he was hopeless.

"Your aunt talks about difficult things," Yol said.

"She said unfortunately, some people will keep on succeeding their whole lives, right until the end."

Yol sighed. "I'll pray that's what happens."

Beside them, Rareko kept nodding.

◇ **Ragi Zwe Nento**

It was as if a haze lay over everything. But it wasn't painful. His loose grasp on his senses brought him peace rather than suffering. Rather than living life clearly conscious and tortured by pain, it was better to be in a cottony peace and slide into an easy death. The reason and knowledge he'd relied on his whole life put up the white flag against violent pain.

Suddenly, Ragi realized. He was not at peace right now. His

mind wouldn't stop coming up with distractions one after another. How was Clantail doing? What were the other mages and magical girls doing? Had they found a way to get out?

The pain that had kept racking his body, making him collapse, was gone now. When he opened his eyes a crack, his whole field of vision twisted and wavered, gradually forming a clear image, and the outline of his thoughts sharpened with it. He coughed a few times, and it stung the back of his throat, but it improved the airflow somewhat. There was a sweet taste in his mouth. A fruity sweetness filled it from his nostrils to his throat. It tasted and smelled like grayfruit. It really was too sweet for Ragi's taste.

He drew in a whole lungful of the sickly sweet air and sent oxygen to his brain.

Ragi sat up. His back hurt. His rear, too. The cloth laid over his body was probably his own cloak. Underneath him was rock. It was hard. Being laid down in a place like this, no wonder his back and bottom hurt.

He focused his eyes and looked around, but all he could tell was he seemed to be in a small space that was all stone—something like a cave. He couldn't see in the dark, after all. Wind blew in from one side, while air on the other side was still, which had to mean there was one entrance. He carefully felt around, but his right hand immediately reached a wall. It was rough and angular. Rock. The back of his left hand knocked into something, and he yanked it back. Timidly reaching out again to touch the object there, he felt wood that was far smoother than the rock and grabbed it. It was his usual staff.

Ragi heaved a great sigh.

He ran a hand where his head must have been lying when he was asleep and touched a lump of cloth smooshed into a ball. He picked it up and pulled it open and found it was his hat. *This isn't to be used as a pillow,* he thought as he patted off the dirt and put it on his head. It felt like it was certainly crushed and a disgrace, but as a rare fortune in this situation, it was too dark to see it. But before any of that, anyone who saw Ragi now would notice—

"Oh! You're up!" He heard a voice from the windy side. That high-pitched voice particular to magical girls reverberated within the cave, irritating Ragi more than necessary. Her brazen stride with absolutely no care at all for others doubled his irritation. "That's great, Grampy."

That nickname irritated Ragi beyond the point of no return. But still, he didn't complain out loud. Currently, Ragi was not unconscious or close to it. He wouldn't even consider choosing an easy death over a life full of pain. In fact, he was irritated at himself for having thought that a moment ago. He was fully conscious, and from the lingering taste and smell in his mouth, it was clear that he'd been intaking grayfruit. Since Ragi had been unconscious and there was no way he would have found any himself, someone must have saved him. The odds were that savior was the girl before him now.

He should thank her, but he was too irritated to do it. Times like these, Ragi's mouth, his tongue, his throat would not move to say thank you. Against his own desire to offer thanks first, but in a sense following it, he did not bow his head in thanks but rather demanded imperiously, "...Where am I?"

"Hmm?"

"Where is everyone else? Why am I in a place like this?"

"Oh, I see. You don't know what happened, huh." The magical girl Clarissa Toothedge, who had ears that were pointed like a wildcat, clapped her hands. Ragi narrowed his eyes and looked at her. They weren't completely in the dark. There was light coming in from the moon and the stars outside. Clarissa was hunched over, but the tips of her ears were still touching the ceiling of the cave. If Ragi had thoughtlessly tried to stand up, he might have hit his head.

"Someone scary came to attack, and everyone ran off on their own," Clarissa explained.

"Someone scary?"

"I think it's the same as what got Maiya."

Ragi's head hurt. He didn't remember exactly when he'd fallen unconscious, either. Riding the hazy waves of his thoughts, he saw something. When he'd heard someone scream, had that been a dream, or had that been reality?

"What's going on…? What's going on?" Ragi muttered.

"Like I said, we just got all split up."

"Any dead?"

"Maybe. I don't really know."

"Atrocious…" He was even feeling like he was the one person thrown in from a different timeline. "What about Clantail?"

"Was she the girl who is a horse or a leopard or whatever on the bottom?"

"That's her. Where is she?"

"She left everyone before we were attacked."

"She did? Clantail went off on her own?"

"She couldn't stand waiting while you were in such bad shape, so she went off to go pick some grayfruit. That was a little before we got attacked by the scary person."

"Why would she have to do that? We had a store of the grayfruit."

"Pastel Mary took 'em and ran."

It was all a miserable mess. There wasn't a shred of discipline. Magical girls were chaos. They couldn't be bound by rules or laws.

Ragi clenched his right hand, which was placed down on the bare rock. The sand on the stone gathered from his fingertips to his palm and made an annoying scraping noise. Every single little thing was so irritating.

His bad mood must have showed. "You don't have to get so mad," Clarissa said lightly, and that made Ragi even angrier.

"How could I not be angry?!"

"Well, true. That's fair enough. But it's times like these when you've really gotta be positive."

"Positive? Ridiculous, telling me to be positive in this situation."

"Instead of getting mad and complaining, it's better to get done the things you can do, one by one, right?"

Sometimes, even if you were saying something reasonable, the tone would hurt the message. And more than that, most of all, the sole fact that she was a magical girl who had been brought here by Navi Ru hurt it enough that you could basically call it ruined. Ragi's mouth twisted inside his beard. Yes, Clarissa was employed by Navi Ru.

"Hey," Ragi barked.

"What is it?"

"Where is your employer? Aren't you saving the wrong person?"

"It was the bald mister's orders that I save you, you know."

"What do you mean?"

"It doesn't mean anything. You were in bad shape. He told me, 'I can manage myself somehow, so if anything happens, you can leave me and save that old fart.' Whoops, sorry, the venerable Master Ragi."

Ragi's lips twisted even further. Being indebted to Navi was a regretful disgrace—a humiliation.

As Ragi was wordlessly making his stick rattle, Clarissa nimbly circled around behind him, put her hands on his shoulders, and gently massaged them. "I heard that you guys don't get along, but like. There's no point in getting into a spat now. Both you and he are in the Osk Faction, after all. So I think that's all the more reason you need to get along."

It didn't matter how much time had passed; Ragi would never be able to forget what Navi Ru had done. When the faction had split into two camps, he had infiltrated one camp to leak information to the enemy side. He had learned their dirt and, through threats and bribery, broken the opposition. Ragi knew himself that Navi Ru hadn't done that of his own accord. Someone else had given the order, and Navi Ru was merely the one to execute that order. But someone who is beaten down without hardly being able to resist is never going to see it coldly and rationally, like, *"He was just following orders."* Mages who were ignorant of the ways of the world and only knew life in the ivory tower couldn't put up a fight against Navi Ru's wiles, and after fully capitalizing on his aptitude, he'd seemed satisfied with the results he'd won. He had gained a suitable position from it—which brought them to right now.

Ragi somehow relaxed his clenching jaw and managed to ask, "…What is he after?"

"Pardon?"

"I know full well he's not the type to help anyone out of the goodness of his heart."

After a moment's pause, Clarissa clapped her hands and laughed. She had been like this before, too—her laugh was breezy and cheery, not at all what you'd expect from someone who was stuck in a place she could die, cut off from the outside world. Magical girls' personalities were all detached from the real world like this to a greater or lesser extent, which was just one more thing that irritated Ragi.

"Come on, now, don't be so mad." Clarissa laughed for a while, then waved one hand at the sullenly silent Ragi. "You're not wrong. Yeah, he's after something."

"…You're honest."

"Ah, you're still suspicious. But it's nothing that complicated. That mister has a high opinion of you, Grampy. Your skill as a mage."

"…Oh?" Ragi had the sense that Clarissa smiled.

"He's thinking he'll make use of you sometime, once he's become important. He's putting you in his debt now for when that happens. Even if it puts his own life in danger."

Ragi was about to yell back, *"Like hell I'm going to let that bastard use me for anything!"* but Clarissa raised a palm in front of him. Ragi held his tongue.

"I think that sort of relationship is fine." She was still in a good mood.

Ragi did not share her sentiments at all. "What relationship?"

"You guys wouldn't even be able to get along if you wanted to, so you should just think about it like using each other. It's way healthier than being at each other's throats, and it'd be useful to the Osk Faction, too."

Ragi could tell she was puffing up her chest. She seemed proud.

She had to be thinking she was brandishing the correct argument. She didn't even realize how irritating that was to Ragi—or she was doing that on purpose. Her attitude and casual manner of speaking didn't seem to come from a genuinely shallow character, but rather that she was deliberately trying to make herself seem so.

"'Kay then. Stay put. You were real sick to begin with, so if you move, you'll run out of energy right away. I'll leave some fruit here, though." Clarissa rolled something over. Bending his back, Ragi turned it over with the end of his staff, and when he picked it up, a sweet smell wavered at the end of his nose.

Clarissa's footsteps moved one step away, two, and then Ragi struck the wall with his staff. "Wait. Where are you going?"

"We've gotta find the others. I'm gonna go look and see if that dangerous person is there or not, too."

"We're not done talking yet."

"And I'll look for Clantail, too, as much as I can."

"Hey!" Ragi yelled, his words reverberating against the stone walls to bounce back to him. There was nobody to hear them.

He smacked words of anger along with his staff at the wall, and the impact made his hand go numb, and he dropped his staff, and then he clenched a fist and was about to strike the stone wall but stopped right before he could. Thankful that he still had enough good sense to stop, Ragi inhaled a large breath and scooped up his staff, and then when he heard the skitter of something moving behind him, he turned his whole body around.

Seeing a centipede about as long as his biceps move from under one rock to another, he let out a really large sigh this time. Absolutely everything about this was miserable.

◇ **John Shepherdspie**

Upon regaining consciousness, the first thing Shepherdspie saw was the starry sky through the canopy of trees. The sight of the surrounding scenery and the wavering light just about drew a sigh from him. This had to be the kind of beauty that would inspire poetic sentiments. If he'd had a pen and paper at hand, maybe he would have wrung out a line. Shepherdspie let out an *ohhh* and heard murmuring around him.

He was gently lowered down. Someone had been carrying him on their back.

Some girls were looking down on him. Their beautiful faces formed a circle around his field of view with the moonlight filtering through the branches in the background forming an evocative scene—if you just cut out that part, you might think you were in heaven or something despite their similarly grim expressions.

The back of Shepherdspie's head hurt, his stomach rumbled, and his back felt cold and gross. "Where am I...?" he moaned.

"There was an emergency, and we left the main building," Marguerite said simply.

"Do you think you can move?" Mana asked with concern.

7753 spoke next. "Um...are you okay?"

"Mei wants fruit," Tepsekemei said.

Just from asking one thing, he got answers back from four different people. Not only had Shepherdspie just awoken, one incident happening after another had exhausted him mentally, and he no longer had enough mental space to carefully consider and digest the answers from four different people. The one he should address was probably Mana. He had a bit of a cold impression from Marguerite—rather, that she was a bit scary and hard to approach. Tepsekemei was kind of incomprehensible to him, and 7753 didn't quite seem like someone you could count on.

Shepherdspie pushed himself up and wiped his forehead with a handkerchief. "Why did you leave the main building?"

"It was attacked," Mana answered.

"Huh? What? Huh? It was attacked? By who?"

"The one who killed Maiya and destroyed the gates, most likely."

"Hold on; hold on just one moment... Huh...? I can't believe it. Give me a moment." Shepherdspie looked from one girl to the next, but they were all equally serious. It seemed this was no lie or joke. Then he realized something was amiss. There were not enough people here by far. Ragi, Navi, Agri, Yol, and Touta were missing, and aside from Marguerite, not a single one of the magical girls those people had brought were there, either. "Huh…? No way. It can't be… The others…"

"No, they ran away." Mana corrected his assumption. "They're scattered all over the island, but we don't know where they are."

"Oh, I see. That's good… Well, it's not good that we don't know where they are, but it is good that they're safe… *Is* it good?"

"…Well, better than getting injured or being dead."

"Ohhh, yeah. Of course."

Through asking for additional information and explanation, gradually, Shepherdspie got a grasp on the situation. They had been attacked by the bad guy who had gotten Maiya, and Shepherdspie had passed out. Those who weren't with them had all run off in different directions, and those who remained had carried the unconscious Shepherdspie while searching for grayfruit. Shepherdspie was initially thankful for his fortune, thinking it was a good thing he hadn't died, but his feelings turned somber when he remembered this wasn't really good fortune but more of a silver lining. But whatever they were going to do, first, they had to find some grayfruit.

Shepherdspie stared at the sky. It wasn't a good spot to look from, with tree branches and clouds hiding the starry sky from him. Were Pastel Mary and Dreamy☆Chelsea safe?

Had Mary been taken away by someone, or had she run away with the grayfruit? With things like this, the latter would be better. If she had run off with the fruit, then this was Mary, so she would surely have done it out of feeling helpless and scared, getting into a panic that had led her to the deed. She'd probably fallen a few times while carrying the fruit, too. Shepherdspie would have wanted her to say something to him before running away if possible, but he really couldn't be confident that Mary saw him as an employer she could count on. All Shepherdspie could do was pray that Chelsea had found her, at least.

◇◇◇

Now that Shepherdspie was awake, he immediately came to share their problems.

Miss Marguerite had thought that it would be better to get some grayfruit first, instead of staying any longer in the half-destroyed main building, and Mana had agreed. Some fruit had been discovered on the way back from hearing the voice of Maiya's corpse, so they'd headed to gather that handful of grayfruit that still remained unharvested. They'd been hesitating about moving the unconscious Shepherdspie too thoughtlessly, but they had figured leaving him there would be even more dangerous. Unfortunately, their search had been fruitless. The grayfruit that should have still been on the tree had all been plucked away by someone else.

Now Mana and the others were in trouble. They didn't know anywhere else to find it. Nearly all of it around the main building had already been harvested. Shepherdspie had come to right when they were really stuck as to what to do, which brought them to the present.

"Um…do you know someplace where there might be a lot of grayfruit growing?" 7753 asked timidly.

"Well…if I knew that, I would have said so when we were at the main building," Shepherdspie replied.

"Of course…sorry."

Even if he did know some things about the island, it was just slightly more than the other heirs. His knowledge couldn't be compared with that of the original owner of the island, his uncle Sataborn. Ragi had to know more about the island's systems, while Rareko would know more about the gates. The one thing Shepherdspie had confidence about was the kitchen, and that kind of knowledge wasn't going to be useful right now.

"But…" Shepherdspie trailed off.

"But?" 7753 echoed.

"I did take a casual look around the island, more or less. I think I did see some grayfruit then."

"Oh?"

"I don't remember it very well at all."

"Ahhh, yes. Sorry," 7753 said.

"But," Mana followed up, "even a vague memory is still a memory."

"Well, I suppose," Shepherdspie said.

"That's got to be more reliable than what we have, which is nothing."

There is the saying that a drowning person will even cling at straws. That felt apt to this situation, but Shepherdspie wouldn't say so out loud. He folded his arms, drew back his jaw, and groaned, making his mustache swish. "Hmm… My memories are extremely vague, you know. Well, um, we can go and give it a shot, but wouldn't it be bad if it winds up being a waste of time?"

"Let's just give it a shot, even if we think it's unlikely," Mana said. "We have no other options."

Shepherdspie nodded and got to his feet. They had to get some grayfruit, or they really would be out of options. As Mana said, even if they thought it was unlikely, going was better than not trying at all.

"Then let's go." Shepherdspie chanted and waved his hands but then whacked his fingers on a tree in the process and groaned, interrupting his chant. Clearing his throat quietly, this time he checked there was nothing around before chanting and tracing a magic square and ancient language with his fingers. After storing up the power, he touched his right index finger between his eyes. It wasn't like he was doing much. It was a spell to energize the mind. It would help him remember a little.

His mind cleared. Or it felt like it did.

"This way…probably," Shepherdspie said.

Originally, the memory had been dim and vague, as if he was being pulled hesitantly in multiple directions, but that was still better than nothing.

For the first time in a long while, Shepherdspie was putting his full effort into something other than cooking. He summoned up memories he normally wouldn't even recall, like the time he'd rented some guard demons to look around the island, twitching in anxiety all the while, or when he'd tried to read his uncle's old records, only to give up after a few pages on island flora.

"Oh, I'm glad you were with us, Mr. Shepherdspie," 7753 said. Her words added even greater pressure. He felt his stomach lurch.

Following his dim memory of *I think it was this way; this should be it*, he moved his feet forward. The magical girls' expressions were tense and alert.

Then Tepsekemei spun in the air, stuck her nose to the sky, and sniffed. "This smell." She came out in front of Shepherdspie, taking the lead instead of him.

Any mage would know that magical girls had sharp senses. He'd also heard that the first one to have gathered grayfruit and eaten one had been Tepsekemei. Shepherdspie mentally clenched a fist, thinking, *This sounds pretty hopeful.*

But Shepherdspie's hopes were quickly dashed.

"You're sure this is it?" he asked.

"Yes," Tepsekemei replied.

"Ah...it looks like these were just picked. You can see the signs," Mana said.

"There's a shred of fruit left over here," Marguerite added.

"They took everything," Shepherdspie groaned.

They had to go through the absolute disgrace of gathering the scraps and licking the remaining juices off the places where the fruit had been plucked, but they did replenish themselves minimally, and Shepherdspie set off in the lead again.

After going awhile, Tepsekemei spun in the air, stuck her nose to the sky, and sniffed. "This smell."

Privately, Shepherdspie was thankful for this rare fortune. It was already fairly lucky to have found something once based off his vague memories, and now they'd discovered grayfruit twice in a short span that night. This had to be partly because Tepsekemei had a good nose, but it was still lucky.

When they rushed into the spot in high spirits, they found— yet again, everything had been thoroughly plucked from the tree and taken away.

"Again…?" Mana groaned.

"The manner of harvesting seems rougher than the last time," Marguerite commented.

"Oh, one dropped here…," 7753 said. "Hey, Mei! We're sharing those! Don't just eat without asking!"

Why was something like this happening? How had it come to this? Shepherdspie didn't know. He looked up at the sky and hoped the buzzing of insects hid the sound of his sigh.

◇ 7753

Upon striking out a third time, the group of five had a discussion.

"Just what is going on here?" Shepherdspie wondered.

"The cut on this fruit is exactly the same as the one before," Mana pointed out.

"Someone is gathering grayfruit?"

"Um…," 7753 cut in. "Maybe the enemy who attacked us before is doing it."

"Well, whatever they are, if they're a magical being, they'll need it, yes," Shepherdspie agreed.

"Mei is tired."

"It's also plausible that someone aside from the enemy is doing this," Marguerite pointed out.

"Everyone does need grayfruit, after all," Mana agreed.

"So then isn't that another reason we should find the others?" Shepherdspie suggested.

"If it's someone we can meet up with, then indeed."

"Stop constantly making implicative statements, Marguerite," Mana shot at her.

"The odds are not so low that they will reject joining us."

"I know that."

"Oh yes, that's right, you know, um, the cuts are fresher than the last time. So then doesn't that mean we're getting closer? If we hurry a little, we might be able to catch up. Mr. Shepherdspie, do you know if any places near here have grayfruit?" 7753 asked.

"I told you, I don't remember that well."

"Yes, well, but... I'm sorry, please lead the way."

With Shepherdspie in the lead, the group set out. After a while, Mei spun in the air, sniffed, and muttered, "There are lots of smells," this time like she was pleased, but without any expression on her face.

"Ohhh, lots of smells might mean a lot growing," Shepherdspie said.

"It looks like we can be hopeful," 7753 said.

Tepsekemei went ahead again, and the group moved along. When Shepherdspie smacked a mosquito that chased him through the underbrush to squish it, Mana scolded him for making unnecessary noise, while Tepsekemei continued swiftly onward as if she didn't even hear the quarrel behind her, then came to a sharp stop.

The sudden stop made 7753 boot Mana in the bottom, and she wound up having to apologize again.

Marguerite slipped smoothly in front of Tepsekemei. "So it was you."

The glaring colors of her costume were highly visible, even in the dim forest. The magical girl who Miss Marguerite had called out to was dropping grayfruit into the plastic bag in her right hand. She sluggishly turned around to look at Marguerite. Her eyes were unfocused, as if she was gazing somewhere else.

Something was strange. 7753 was about to bring her hand to her goggles when Dreamy☆Chelsea gave her a sharp glare, and 7753 jerked her hand away again.

Shepherdspie tried stepping forward. Marguerite blocked him, but he just called out anyway, "Chelsea! So this was where you were!"

"Chelsea is...," Chelsea began.

"Hmm?"

"Chelsea is a wonderful magical girl. That's what Chelsea thought."

"Uh, what are you talking about?"

Marguerite held Shepherdspie back with her left hand as she

placed her right hand on the hilt of her rapier, and 7753 swallowed her spit.

Chelsea continued in a faltering manner, as if she wasn't even looking at what Marguerite was doing. "But that was wrong... Chelsea had to learn about real magical girls... Chelsea didn't know love."

"Chelsea, what's wrong?" Shepherdspie pressed. "Did something happen?"

"Chelsea is a different person from yesterday. Now Chelsea knows love."

"I'm not going to understand unless you talk to me properly."

"Chelsea actually never wanted to be alone. Chelsea wanted to be together forever. But there's no helping it. None of the others can keep up with Chelsea, so it'd be faster for her to go out on her own."

"The others?" Shepherdspie continued, probing for what had happened.

"You can do it, Chelsea. Don't give in, Chelsea. Even if you're alone, our hearts will always be together."

"What happened to Mary? You don't know?"

Chelsea's big eyes opened even wider, and her expression contorted. 7753 took one step back, covering Mana behind her.

"Hey, don't you dare! You people have to call May-May 'Pastel Mary'!"

Shepherdspie staggered at Chelsea's sharp rebuke—Mana tried to catch him but couldn't take his weight, and 7753 circled behind her to support the both of them. Caught between the two of them, Mana groaned painfully.

"Tepsekemei, keep an eye around us." Marguerite took another step forward. She had drawn her rapier, the blade reflecting the moonlight.

Dreamy☆Chelsea lifted her heels and floated up into the air just like that. She stopped a foot above the ground, ignoring gravity to hover there.

It was magic. 7753 wouldn't know what kind just from that.

Chelsea had reacted to Pastel Mary's name—was Pastel Mary controlling Chelsea? What was she after? Were the "others" who Chelsea talked about backing her up?

7753 quietly reached out to her goggles. There was a lot of information she had to know. As she brought them from her hat to her eyes, they were violently flicked away.

The goggles rolled away from her, and then something shining zipped out to knock them farther.

7753 followed the goggles with her eyes, then immediately returned her attention to Chelsea, eyes locking on her. Chelsea was making a little heart shape with her hands. The way she had moved looked like nothing other than using her magic—Marguerite tossed up fallen leaves as she lowered her stance, muttering to 7753, "Don't move."

7753 looked into the thicket, where her goggles had been flung, and back to Chelsea again. At this point, there was nothing for it but to leave things to Marguerite.

What...is this...?

Chelsea actually moved with sharp agility. But there was pointless stuff mixed into it, too. It didn't make sense. Figuring she had to have activated her magic, 7753 stayed on guard, but nothing happened.

The two magical girls faced off wordlessly.

Chelsea let her heart shape come apart and slowly spread her opened palms. Sticking up her index and middle fingers, she balled the rest of her fingers. With a full-faced smile on, she made peace signs on both hands.

A gust of wind blew through, toying with the two magical girls. But both remained in the same stance, not even twitching. Chelsea kept her double peace thrust out at Marguerite, while Marguerite stared back at her. 7753 was having a hard time keeping up with the action.

The first one to move next was Chelsea, again. From the double peace, she opened her right hand, her left flowing over her face to pose in a sideways peace sign. Marguerite shifted her center of gravity slightly to the left.

The wind blew harder, stirring the blades of grass. The peacock feather that decorated Marguerite's hat swayed over and over, like a toy on a spring. Chelsea was smiling beatifically like a magical girl in an anime. It was as if that same face had never been twisted in anger.

7753 couldn't interfere. Shepherdspie twitched, and 7753 felt his motion through Mana.

7753 had seen countless magical girls, including tons of them who were good at fighting.

But she had never seen a stance like this.

A span of time as slow and unclear as mud went by. 7753 didn't dare breathe. Chelsea was frozen in the sideways-peace pose. Marguerite was still not moving, either. Both of them still, never relaxing their tension, while all that time passed. 7753 realized. The plastic bag Chelsea carried was stuffed full. It had to be full of gray-fruit. On the other hand, Marguerite had only licked some juices and sucked on some skins. If time kept passing like this, Marguerite's transformation was bound to be undone first.

It was a bad idea to just wait. And if 7753 realized that, then Marguerite also had to have realized—but she didn't initiate, staying patiently at the ready. Despite thinking, *I have to do something*, 7753 couldn't move. Her impatience gradually spread until it even became difficult for her to stay still; her throat felt choked, and her chest ached—when suddenly, an electronic sound rang out. 7753's heart jumped, and she just about fell, but she somehow caught herself.

She didn't realize it was an alarm on a magical phone until she heard Chelsea say, "Oh! That's my date!"

Still with her sideways peace up, Chelsea slid backward in the air until she disappeared into the trees. When Tepsekemei started flying after her, Marguerite called out, "It's fine! Don't follow her," then blew out a breath and put a hand on the brim of her hat. Her sword was back in her sheath without 7753 even noticing her put it back.

"...She's strong," Marguerite seemed to mutter in spite of herself.

Mana scowled. "You couldn't beat her?"

"If she were someone I could beat easily, I would have cleaned things up quickly on the spot. That's probably..." Marguerite's eyes looked to where Chelsea had disappeared. "That's not any fighting style I know of. She's also replenished plenty of nutrients from grayfruit, too. She's probably been a magical girl longer than me, and her physical abilities are superior. Even with Tepsekemei's support, I might have wound up guarding two mages and a magical girl in the battle. I'm repeating myself here, but if she were someone I could beat easily, I wouldn't have let her get away. We should be satisfied that we even secured a few grayfruit."

"Could you beat her *not* easily, though?"

"If I were allowed to kill her, at least." Marguerite glanced at Shepherdspie, who shook his head in a fluster.

"No, I can't have you killing her. Actually, you know, she seemed odd. What was that?"

"It seems she's being controlled."

"Controlled...by who?"

"The way she became worked up when she heard Pastel Mary's name would make Pastel Mary the most suspicious...but right now, I can't say for sure." Marguerite narrowed her eyes, her eyelashes falling slightly.

7753 heaved out a big breath before something suddenly occurred to her. She turned to the thicket. Not having her goggles was practically like she was missing half her body, and she felt anxious like she'd lost even more than that. 7753 crouched down and shoved her upper body into the thicket, spreading the foliage with both hands. She couldn't quite find them. While getting caught on branches, she moved through the underbrush until she found the band part caught on a root and pulled it up.

The torn band was all that remained. The actual goggles were gone.

CHAPTER 8
GODDESS

◇ **Dreamy☆Chelsea**

Dreamy☆Chelsea stood on tiptoe atop her stars as they flew at high speed. Since she'd been playing on the stars every day since she was little, she would never lose her balance, not only when shifting her body weight or changing her stance but even when doing the kind of trick riding that would put an acrobat to shame. She bent her knees and leaned forward like she was doing a ski jump as she kicked up the stars' speed a notch. Mowing down grasses and breaking branches, she sped through the forest, not even glancing at the scenery blurring past her. The only thing Chelsea was looking at was Pastel Mary's smiling face in her heart.

When she thought about Pastel Mary, she felt exhilarated. No matter how much stress weighed on her, as long as Pastel Mary was there, she would blow it all away. Someone who would comfort her just by thinking of her existed in real life. Chelsea had been blessed by the song of praise made up of the wonders of love—how

264 MAGICAL GIRL RAISING PROJECT, Vol. 14

precious it was to fall for another. She was experiencing it for real. This had never happened before in her thirty-four years of life.

Through elementary school, middle school, high school, and university, Chelsea had never once lost her heart to an infatuation. When Chie was in preschool, her childhood friend had spoken enthusiastically about how he would absolutely marry her. He'd apparently forgotten all that big talk by middle school and had shamelessly dated another girl. Romantic feelings were ultimately quick to change, and compared to Chelsea's passion for magical girls, it was fragile and fleeting. That incident had deepened Chelsea's convictions, making her believe she should prioritize being a magical girl over anything else.

Sleeping or waking, she thought about magical girls, simulating her own grand activities in her mind as she aimed to be her ideal magical girl. Romance was superfluous to that end. All through her days as a student, Chie had remained determined that even if someone confessed to her *I like you* or *I love you* or whatever, she would refuse no matter what. She'd gotten no confessions in the end but had put her wholehearted efforts into magical-girl activities, and Chelsea herself had never imagined she would fall in love at this point in life.

There was the second half of season two of *Rikkabell*, the Kotarou episode of *Hiyoko-chan*, and then *Miko-chan*, which had the will-they-or-won't-they between her and her childhood friend as the main theme; *Mysterious Ran-Ran* had made the pretty-boy transfer student a regular character to prop up the show, and there were various other magical-girl anime with romance plots, but Chelsea had never enjoyed them. They had only ever made her say to herself, "You girls are far more attractive than a boring childhood friend or a pretty boy." But in meeting Pastel Mary, she finally understood how they felt. She was just as good as any of the magical girls of anime Chelsea had always known and admired, even the heroines she loved most—in fact, in some ways, Pastel Mary was superior. She was just that attractive. Language couldn't convey *how* attractive she was. There was no point in trying. Pastel

Mary couldn't be compared to anything else, and she couldn't be expressed in words in any other way but "Pastel Mary." Pastel Mary was very herself, and that was precisely what made her so attractive.

Soon, she would be able to see Pastel Mary. Even if she had been the one to ask it of her, it was so painful to work while apart from her. The magical girl with the rapier, Miss Marguerite, had made Chelsea anxious with her intense pressure and stressed her out. That was not a good magical girl. She was of the same type as Chelsea's mother—she would use violence to shut you up in the end or imply decreasing your allowance to silence your opinion— basically she was the type who was good at resolving things with methods other than discussion. For a magical girl, that would make her the "nasty rival" character at most. It wouldn't be fair to Pastel Mary to compare that girl to her. Yes, Pastel Mary was the one proper magical girl on this whole island. That was why Chelsea was helping her with her goal. She was originally supposed to have been taking orders from Shepherdspie, her employer, but he'd probably forgive her if she apologized after the fact. He was kind of soft that way.

Chelsea tensed her right hand, squeezed it tightly, then looked down at it. Unfortunately, the band part of the goggles with the cute heart-shaped meters must have torn off, but it was still a totally unique treasure, even with that flaw. Mana, Marguerite, and 7753 had centered their activity on these goggles. Ren-Ren, Agri, and Nephilia had been talking about them, too. It had seemed like they'd been wary of them. Everyone either valued the goggles or were afraid of them.

Chelsea had heard about what kind of magic power these goggles had. You could see various things by looking through them. In other words, she could find out how Pastel Mary felt about her.

Pastel Mary had to like her back. Since coming to the island, their relationship had been the longest and deepest. The time the floor had caved in and the time the wall had come down and the sheep had gone out of control, the two of them had worked together to overcome the crisis. It wouldn't be surprising to get the so-called suspension bridge effect from such dangerous things happening. Plus, Pastel Mary had seen her naked. That was a vital event if you were the heroine of a rom-com. In other words, to Mary, Chelsea was the heroine, and there was no doubting her affection.

Yes, there was no doubting it, but her anxiety continued. Pastel Mary would sometimes talk with other people. Even if Chelsea knew they were only talking about work and it meant nothing, she couldn't stop worrying. She knew she was thinking too hard, but Pastel Mary was just too attractive. There was no way other people wouldn't fall for her, too, and if they did, since Pastel Mary was easily pressured, if by some mistake, she was to be moved by their affections... Chelsea didn't want a love triangle like that. As long as Pastel Mary was Pastel Mary, the deep suspicion that lurked in Chelsea's heart would surely never disappear. But—but!—if she had these goggles, then Chelsea could make objectively sure if the feelings were mutual and find any nasty rivals for Pastel Mary's affections. She could be completely and entirely at ease.

"Ah..." A moan slipped out of her. She couldn't take it. She wanted to see Pastel Mary's face. Whenever she thought about Pastel Mary, everything was dyed in Pastel Mary colors. Chelsea had shot the goggles from 7753's hands to keep her from using them back there. She hadn't been thinking about stealing them for herself. But when she'd had her peace sign up, she'd caught the goggles lying in the bushes out the corner of her eye, and she'd realized, *If I use these...* And so she'd immediately shot off a star to catch them for herself.

Stars sparkled around Chelsea. They whizzed lightly through the sky as if reflecting her excitement, sparkling under the reflected light of the moon as she flew around.

"Ahhh..." Imagining Pastel Mary being happy, another moan leaked out.

Opening her mouth wide while in motion made some drops of night dew catch in her mouth, and she choked on it, but she didn't let that get to her, and she just swallowed. The lukewarm air, the moisture like she was swimming around in mist, the smell of the earth and the strong grassy scent—it was all blessing Chelsea and Pastel Mary's future. This was the vibe you got when a magical-girl anime was going straight for a happy ending. Once the mood got worked up like this, then a magical girl would always be victorious, no matter what trials were in store.

Pastel Mary was all that occupied her heart. The frightening magical girl, the grayfruit, everything, the past and present and future, all of it just became Pastel Mary, and Chelsea was so happy about it, she did three somersaults atop her flying stars.

◇ **Ragi Zwe Nento**

The further Ragi fell deeper into thought, the more worked up he couldn't help becoming. It wasn't uncommon for him to get angry while racking his brain. The reasons for it had changed since he'd been assigned to the Magical Girl Management Department, but the more he got lost in his thoughts, the angrier he became. But even if this wasn't unusual for him, he couldn't easily ignore it.

Things he had to think about and things he had to get angry about rose in his mind one after another, despite how unbearably cold his bottom felt in the cave and how awful the stuffy air was.

It was irritating that the other mages and the magical girls had all run off in different directions. What point was there in running off on a small island like this? Ragi wasn't about to tell them to face the enemy and die. It was better to live for tomorrow than die a pointless death. Nonetheless, everyone running off on their own was keeping them from working together, and just staying alive wasn't going to point them to seeing another day. He recalled Clarissa had mentioned that she was searching for the others, but if she was capable of that much, then she could also conceal herself from the eyes of any ruffians as she went to handle matters. What Clarissa and Navi were doing was entirely inconsistent and haphazard. It didn't seem like they were aiming to resolve the fundamental concern.

Ragi was thinking. Yes, he was managing to think. Since

coming to this island, he'd been feeling about as terrible as a sick, bedridden patient. It had reduced his cognition and had often made him feel unsteady. But the grayfruit Navi had shoved at him had gained him the mental bandwidth for thought for the first time in a long while.

Why had the gates been destroyed? If it was to lock them in, then why was it necessary to lock them in? To kill all of them? Ragi could think of no reason to kill all the relatives of Sataborn. Additionally, this was too thorough to be the whims of a madman.

There was no need to go along with what that person wanted. They had destroyed the gates, so that meant they didn't want the heirs leaving. That was all Ragi had to understand.

He stood up. He took a bite of a grayfruit and stuck the rest in his sleeve. The grayfruit were more useful than he'd imagined. Sataborn had made a rather fine item. It really was a shame he'd lost his life before he could announce his results. Ragi would escape this island with the grayfruit, and showing off this new type that Sataborn had made would ease the regrets of the dead a little.

No, wait. This wasn't a new type.

Ragi's lips twisted inside his long white beard. Pulling a grayfruit out from his sleeve, he dropped it into his palm and gazed at it. The fruit rolled over like it was turning its back on him, and he stopped it with the wrinkly pads of his fingers. This was no new type. It had just been bred from an existing one. Ragi stared down at it. The grayfruit, of course, lay there with no reaction. It wasn't going to change from him squinting at it.

Ragi knew about the original grayfruit—the type Sataborn had bred this from. It was a common fruit that was used as a nutritional tonic. It was so ubiquitous, he hadn't even considered it.

When the grayfruit this was based on happened to cross a corner of his mind, Ragi tried to push the thought aside—this wasn't what he should be thinking about right now—but something bothered him, and his mind paused there. Back when he'd been a researcher, he'd called these mental moments a flash of insight, and no few theories or formulas had come out of them.

Despite his ongoing irritation, Ragi thought back on each and every thing he could come up with regarding the fruit these were based on.

The original grayfruit hadn't had such dramatic effects. It would extract a very minute amount of magical power from the earth and air over a long time and accumulate it. And they didn't grow en masse like the grayfruit of this island, either. Cultivating multiple trees on a small plot of land would cause them to rob magical power from each other, and they would stop bearing fruit. It was fair to say the fruit cultivated on this island were revolutionary in every way.

No...I see, so this is...

His sudden flash of insight was taking form. The grayfruit wobbled in Ragi's hand. All the listed facts were pointing to one answer. Should this fruit be called a panacea? No, he couldn't praise it without reserve at all.

I see... I see, I see, I see... I've got it...!

Ragi glared sharply at the fruit, but it was silent and would not speak. No matter how irritating it was, he had to rely on it right now, and that fact just made him all the more irritated.

Ragi dropped the grayfruit back into his sleeve. Putting his hat firmly on his head, he thrust the end of his staff in the earth and slowly headed toward the light. Before leaving the cave, he used a few drops of blood from his fingertip and a condensed chant to cast spells for seeing in the dark and invisibility, making sure to blend in with his surroundings. With a spell for brushing aside branches, he lopped off the vines that had been strung up over the entrance— that had to be Clarissa's camouflage. As he waved aside the sliced vines hanging from above, he scowled a little at the animal bite marks on the bark as he finally emerged from the cave.

Though it was called an invisibility spell, it was a simplistic version that was abbreviated from the original formula. So naturally, it didn't hide him completely. He would have to move slowly and quietly, from shadow to shadow. It wasn't like he didn't have any aces up his sleeve if it became necessary, but he didn't want to use them actively.

First, to rally forces. They'd all run off in different directions because they'd been too panicked to consider the safety of others. In other words, they were even divided mentally. That had been unavoidable, with Ragi unconscious and no other mage to act as their leader. *It's an old man's job to guide the young,* Ragi encouraged himself as he slowly stepped out. Going over a root that rose from the earth and avoiding slippery-looking wet leaves, Ragi was calming his heart while walking along when he felt a clap on his shoulder.

"That's no good, Grampy. I told you it's dangerous to go outside."

He turned around to find Clarissa right there. She was smiling, but it really looked more troubled than pleased. Suddenly, Ragi's arms felt odd. Without even realizing it, his wrists had been tied with rope. He lost his balance and just about fell but then realized his legs wouldn't move. His legs were also tightly bound.

"What in the blazes are you doing?!" Ragi bellowed.

"It's a bad idea to yell."

"What in the—? You devil, how dare—"

"But like, I mean, if you're gonna try to leave like this, then tying you up is my only option. It seems you're going to wander about even if you say you won't, so you leave me no choice. It's too dangerous." Not listening to Ragi in the slightest, Clarissa went back to the cave he'd gone through all that trouble to leave, and now he'd even lost his freedom to move. She tossed him back in, and he voiced loud protests, rebukes, and curses, but the single remark, "If you're too loud, bad guys'll find you," kept him from any more of that, and he was left unable to do anything but be indignant.

Clarissa left with entirely soundless footsteps. Ragi didn't try to force his way out of the ropes. This material wasn't going to tear from an old mage's struggles. There was no need to move around right now. Ragi's role was not moving his body. And honestly, raging in vain wasn't his part, either. Ragi's job was intellectual labor.

Ragi considered. Clarissa, as well as her employer, Navi, didn't think of Ragi as an asset. Did they just see him as an object for protection? But if that was the case, they were going too far. He knew Navi had no love or respect for the old. If he was planning to use Ragi down the line, like Clarissa said, there had to be a somewhat better way to do that. Navi Ru was a villain who only cared about utility, but that was just what made this feel off.

Ragi didn't bother trying to tell Clarissa his conjectures about the grayfruit. He couldn't say that none of his distrust for Navi Ru came from personal grudge, but that wasn't all of it. Even if 7753's goggles had told them Navi was not the culprit behind the destruction of the gates or Maiya's murder, you couldn't be sure he wasn't involved with the grayfruit, and besides, at this point, Ragi didn't know how much he should trust 7753 or the goggles themselves. And when it came to Navi Ru, it was right to suspect everything about him. Clarissa, too, of course.

It would be easy to destroy the gates from the inside, but whoever did so would also be trapped on the island. The magical girls on the island had had their transformations undone, and the mages were weakened. If the culprit was neither a mage nor a magical girl, that was something else, but then there would be no way for someone to sneak onto this island—Ragi muttered a curse and cut off that thought. He doubted he was going to come to any conclusions from thinking on and on now. Making efforts to leave the island came first.

I could make a new gate.

If the properties of the grayfruit were as Ragi surmised, then making a disposable gate wouldn't be entirely impossible. But he wouldn't be able to do it alone. He would need cooperation from another mage. And if the one who had killed Maiya, the one who had destroyed the gates, tried to get in the way, then he would also need magical girls to guard them.

Ironic.

There was nobody he could trust, but he needed people to work with.

That reminded him that in Sataborn's will, there had been the strange condition that they needed to be accompanied by magical girls. At this point, it really did seem like they would need magical girls, but it couldn't be that such a situation had been foreseen, could it? Ragi wanted to reject that idea, to say that could never be so, but he had no logical reasoning for such an argument.

If it were Sataborn...

Ragi knitted his brow. He didn't have enough memories of Sataborn to be able to imagine anything about him. Ragi had heard many rumors about his behavior and character. He'd been famous. And he hadn't been famous only for being an excellent researcher but also for being an eccentric.

But those were ultimately just rumors. Ragi couldn't unquestioningly accept stories he'd just heard about the man through the grapevine. But still, if even one-tenth of the stories about him were true, he had been quite the eccentric.

The wrinkles in his brow deepened. He had no proper memories of the man. It was like having seen Sataborn standing there, or sitting on the corner at a public hearing, or seeing the man apparently forced to come to a buffet party and in quite the sour mood— Ragi only remembered having seen him.

When Ragi had been younger, the two of them had exchanged some words at academic gatherings, but Sataborn had never talked much in such situations and had left right away. Once, Sataborn had come to ask the opinion of a mage who Ragi had studied under, but that had basically just been Sataborn passing him by. It was nothing you could call a memory.

The one thing Ragi could barely remember had been another buffet party. It was supposed to have been a get-together for the announcement of a new barrier formula, but it had been nothing but mages working themselves up through whispered political machinations, and Ragi had been quite furious. Angry, he'd drunk wine, and angry, he'd reached out to some boiled lobster, when another hand had grabbed the same lobster at the same time.

He'd looked at the other person automatically. It was the deeply wrinkled face of an old man. Sataborn. He was also looking at the lobster with irritation. The two old men at the party venue who weren't trying to hide their foul moods looked at each other and then, for some reason, smiled wryly at about the same moment, and Ragi drew his hand away from the lobster and indicated it with his palm, saying, "Go ahead." Sataborn said, "Thanks," and took the lobster.

The wrinkles in Ragi's brow became deeper than ever before. It couldn't be that Sataborn had invited him to this inheritance meeting in order to repay the debt of having ceded the boiled lobster to him? Impossible. But if he was as eccentric as they said, Ragi felt like anything was possible.

Wondering about an eccentric would get you caught in circles. All you had to know was that he was an eccentric. Ragi smacked himself in the forehead.

Regardless: First, he had to get out of this cave.

His current problem was that Clarissa was ready to use force on him to suddenly tie him up. That was beyond unacceptable. And then when Ragi had slipped out of the cave, she'd immediately approached him to capture him.

It was difficult to imagine that she was keeping watch nearby. Clarissa and Navi didn't have that much time on their hands. Had she caught Ragi leaving via magic? That seemed plausible.

Ragi had basically come to a conclusion. He could see what had to be done, too. He felt reluctant, but there was nothing for it but to do it. With his legs still tied, he stood and raised his wrists up to the ceiling. He rubbed the back of a hand against the rock to make it bleed, then used that as a catalyst to chant a rope escape. The rope came off his wrists and fell to the ground. He rubbed his ankles together, and that rope slid down, too, and he hooked his toes on the rope to kick it aside. He stretched his neck to the right, then to the left, and circled his shoulders.

"Now, then." He pulled out a grayfruit and swallowed it, hardly chewing it at all. Chanting a magic-detection spell, he confirmed there was magic on the vines hanging over the entrance. This had to be how Clarissa had sensed him leaving before. Ragi recast the invisibility spell, then crawled on the ground to get outside without touching the vines. Looking all around, he made sure Clarissa wasn't there and then slowly, but faster than before, walked off.

◇ Pastel Mary

Ren-Ren was close enough that Pastel Mary could just about touch her, if she reached out a hand. Her serious expression as she discussed something with Agri and Nephilia was so dignified and beautiful, it was enough to draw a sigh just from watching her. But more than the physical distance, Pastel Mary felt the distance of their hearts. Though it was only one tall boulder between them, plus some of the shards of the rock Chelsea had broken when she'd been going wild, it felt like she was so far away.

There is the saying, a sort of romantic theory, that the more barriers there are to love, the brighter it will burn. Pastel Mary thought surely only someone watching in amusement from a third-party perspective could say that. Whether it be *Romeo and Juliet* or Ozaki's *The Golden Demon*, you could enjoy it as entertainment because you were an onlooker with no stake in the situation. Someone right in the middle of a romantic disaster would never think, *More obstacles really do make a romance more fun.*

Pastel Mary was dealing with a number of obstacles right now, and they were not in the least enjoyable. And Dreamy☆Chelsea, who kept coming up with any excuse to glue herself to her, was at the top of the list.

She wasn't a bad person. She had no ill will, either. She would just, without malice, cause problems. That sort of thing had happened many times since she'd come to this island.

Ren-Ren had told Pastel Mary that the time might come when they could use Dreamy☆Chelsea's combat abilities. Now was the "time to hold firm," and even if they would never need Dreamy☆Chelsea's abilities, it would be good to have them. Most of all, if Ren-Ren undid her magic now, Chelsea was sure to become hostile toward them, and they wanted to avoid that. Ren-Ren, along with Agri and Nephilia, was trying to solve the problems on this island. When Ren-Ren had told her what she planned to do, Pastel Mary had decided to cooperate, and she had done a bunch of things on Ren-Ren's request. She had created sheep and had carried grayfruit. If they turned Chelsea against them, that would all be in vain. Ren-Ren's request would come to nothing. If they failed here, then they wouldn't resolve what had to be resolved.

There had been that much of a kerfuffle just to capture Chelsea. Trying the same thing again might not work. Chelsea would learn and be warier, too. So then it would be best to have her as an ally so that she wouldn't do the same thing again. And Pastel Mary's efforts were important for keeping Chelsea.

Ren-Ren had gently put her hand over Mary's clenched fist and said, "I understand that you love me. I love you, too... You understand, don't you? Chelsea is crazy about you. She'll do anything you say. If you can do a good job controlling her, then she will be very useful."

The cold of Ren-Ren's hand seemed to seep into Pastel Mary's flushed skin. Feeling like she was rising to heaven as she listened to Ren-Ren speak, Mary figured out what her job was. She would act like she was interested in Chelsea and give her orders. That was the role Mary had to fulfill. She couldn't let it be found out that she and Ren-Ren were in love. In other words, while Chelsea was looking, Mary had to keep her contact with Ren-Ren to a minimum.

Even though Ren-Ren was right there, Mary couldn't approach her. It was painful. But that was the more bearable pain, compared to betraying the expectations of her beloved Ren-Ren. Mary kept her head from turning to look at Ren-Ren, kept her legs from trying to walk to Ren-Ren, at least sending her sheep to Ren-Ren, sidling up to Ren-Ren when Chelsea wasn't around, drawing close to whisper of love. Was this what you called a love triangle? It was completely different from what she'd seen in TV dramas and movies.

It wasn't just the love triangle stuff that was different.

It didn't matter that Nephilia snickered crudely or that Agri would look at her like she felt sorry for her. To Mary right now, even the tall, rugged boulders of their provisional base that lacked any romance was like a romantic getaway where lovers could enjoy a fleeting tryst.

Love Me Ren-Ren had the motif of an angel and a devil. She was enchanting like a devil and also pure like an angel. The sheep Pastel Mary created were often given as offerings to the gods that devils and angels served. Pastel Mary was the sacrificial lamb to be offered to Ren-Ren.

Ah, so many feelings...

All the times she'd fallen in love before now seemed less vivid. A lover whose passions would burn out was no lover at all. A child might call anything love or romance, but that was a misunderstanding or in their heads. True love was colored by choking passion. Once before, when Mary had heard the heroine of a TV drama make an exaggerated speech about her love, she'd thought, "Oh, that sounds kind of silly." But that had been no exaggeration. True love was so big, no matter how much you said, it wasn't enough. Mary had finally learned that.

She wanted to touch Ren-Ren's horns, stroke her wings, touch the hexagram on her forehead, to grab hold of her and enjoy a stroll in the sky together, and as thanks, Mary would arrange a bed of sheep for her, and enveloped by the fluffy bed, the two of them would entangle their fingers as they—

Right as the wings of Pastel Mary's imagination were about to fly off into eternity, Chelsea came back and pulled her thoughts to reality.

Reluctantly, Mary was forced to accompany Chelsea.

Mary restrained her heart from its desire to run to Ren-Ren right this minute, suppressing her affections with the thought that doing such a thing would make Ren-Ren hate her. That would hurt as bitterly as being unable to breathe right. She wouldn't be able to take it. She had to meet Ren-Ren's expectations.

Mary faced Chelsea with great care, but Chelsea looked down, fidgeting as she dug at the ground with her toes, then turned away.

"I'm gonna go look around over there." Then, without saying what she was going to do, she briskly left.

What luck! Mary cried with joy in her heart. She was about to immediately go to Ren-Ren, then stopped.

A sheep held her sleeve in its mouth and was tugging her.

"Huh? What? I want to go to Ren-Ren now, though," Mary told it.

The sheep shook its head and pointed its snout in the direction Chelsea had gone.

"You're telling me that Chelsea is acting strange?"

The sheep nodded.

"Hmm…I wonder."

Pastel Mary was a carefree magical girl with her head in the clouds. Her sheep were cowardly and cautious creatures by comparison. They were far more sensitive to changes in the situation than the easily distracted Mary. She took a moment to reflect on what Chelsea had acted like before. Now that she thought of it, she really had been acting strangely.

Chelsea would find every excuse to chase after Mary and follow her around. She wouldn't have let an opportunity for that go so she could voluntarily do rounds. Ever since she and Mary had been hired by Shepherdspie, she'd been slacking off or snacking all the time, constantly giving in to her urges. Had she ever once acted like the kind of hard worker who would volunteer to go patrol?

If she had some other goal…what would it be? Hmm…like playing games, romantically speaking?

It was just a random idea, but that might actually be what it was.

Temporarily hiding herself to get Mary's attention, to make her realize how valuable Chelsea was as a magical girl. It was a concerningly shallow ploy, but thinking about it now, Chelsea had never once *not* been thoughtless since they'd first met.

And whenever Chelsea did something thoughtless, it always caused disaster. You wound up with a fire, or a cave-in, or a wall coming down—Mary scrabbled at her upper arms. Mary was also guilty of causing trouble for their employer, Shepherdspie, but she was doing better than Chelsea. Mary's blunders were mild enough that she'd be forgiven if she apologized. That was why she'd decided she would apologize after. What she was doing now would help Shepherdspie, too, in the end. Chelsea's deeds were beyond reproach.

If Chelsea caused some outrageous situation here, it would cause trouble for Ren-Ren, too.

With a look at Ren-Ren talking with Agri and Nephilia, Pastel Mary smothered her reluctance to part and peeled her gaze away again to turn to the forest, where Chelsea had gone out of sight. The thick, waist-deep underbrush at the edge of the forest was rustling, even though there was no wind.

Mary ordered her sheep to stay on the spot as she took cautious step after cautious step on tiptoe to keep from making any noise as she approached. She could hear a sound like fiddling with a mechanical object. She looked down at the underbrush. Chelsea was lying on her stomach there, fiddling with something.

"...Chelsea?"

Chelsea made a sound like she'd gotten a mochi stuck in the back of her throat and just about dropped the thing in her hands, juggling it a few times. That object was something Mary had seen before, too.

"Chelsea, those goggles," Mary said.

Chelsea pushed herself up and gave Mary a smile that seemed pasted-on. The goggles in her right hand were those that magical girl named something like 5 or 7 or 8 or something had been wearing.

"Why do you have those?" Mary asked.

"Oh, it's not, um...," Chelsea stammered. "Oh yeah, these are, you know. They're a present. I stole them from the enemy for you."

"Um...I don't really get it, but thanks." Pastel Mary offered the bare minimum of gratitude as she accepted the goggles.

Seeing Chelsea look so happy was irritating for some reason. She wanted Chelsea to put herself in her shoes, having to pretend she was glad even though she wasn't.

Pastel Mary's heart was already far away from Chelsea and headed toward Ren-Ren. As for the magic goggles—she didn't know how she would use them, but maybe a mage like Agri could look into them. And if they would be useful, that was sure to please Ren-Ren, and she would acknowledge Mary's efforts.

She feigned surprise. "Huh? Did something move on the other side of that rock?"

"Huh? Really? I'll go look." Chelsea flew off.

Mary took that opportunity to beckon a sheep to her, and still facing Chelsea, she reached behind her back to hand the goggles to the sheep. There was no need to tell them who to hand the goggles to. Every single one of Mary's sheep adored Ren-Ren. They would understand, even if she didn't tell them who to give the goggles to.

In the moment Chelsea was away, Mary pretended to stretch as she watched Ren-Ren, who was on the other side of the rocks. Ren-Ren picked up the goggles, looking serious as she discussed with Nephilia and Agri. She didn't have only an adorable smile. Her serious expressions were dignified and cool, too. Pastel Mary fell in love with Ren-Ren all over again as she filled up her Ren-Ren meter to satisfy herself.

"Looks like there was nothing there."

Suddenly being spoken to, Mary jerked around to see Chelsea staring at her. It was close enough that she could practically feel her breath. Too close. And she'd come back too fast. Mary had planned for Chelsea to take a bit more time coming back, while Mary would move away from Ren-Ren, but that was already off track.

"Ah, I think it might have moved behind that rock this time!" Pastel Mary exclaimed.

"I'll go look!" Chelsea chirped back.

Pastel Mary let out a sigh of relief, and when she looked over at Ren-Ren again, she was holding the goggles as she discussed something. She'd managed to get them over to Ren-Ren for the moment. Now, to just—

"There was nothing there after all," Chelsea told her.

"So fast!" Pastel Mary cried.

"Fast? What is?"

"Oh, sorry, it's nothing."

Dreamy☆Chelsea's intuition was so sharp, she could avoid attacks while hardly looking. Even if Chelsea wasn't fully conscious of it, Mary couldn't let her guard down. Mary broke her attention away from Ren-Ren and pretended like she couldn't hear bits of her attractive voice to face Chelsea again.

But Chelsea's gaze was over Mary's shoulder—at Ren-Ren. Mary leaned against Chelsea, trying to block her from doing that, but Chelsea ignored that, pushing her aside as she cried out, "Ahhh! It's those! Why do you have them?! I gave that as a present to May-May!"

Mary got up and clung to Chelsea's arm.

Chelsea made a frightening cry like a moan or a howl as she swung her arms and Mary clinging to her along with them, stomping on the ground over and over, too, and kicking away rocks, which shattered and rained down like shrapnel that destroyed other rocks around or snapped off trees. Some of the rock bullets went far over the tops of the tallest trees, flying away into the distant sky and out of sight before they even began descending from their arc.

"No! You have the wrong idea!" Ren-Ren cried as she thrust both hands in front of her. The goggles were dangling from the pinkie of her right hand. "I was just holding on to these for a bit!"

Chelsea paused in her destruction, panting hard as she stared at Ren-Ren. Still hanging off Chelsea's arm, Mary looked back and forth between the two magical girls. If Chelsea was going to commit further violence, then it would be Mary's job to stop her.

Ren-Ren glanced over, and seeing Agri down on the ground watching how things would go, and then Nephilia, standing in front of Agri with her scythe at the ready, she let out a relieved-sounding sigh and continued. "Since...I am a magical girl who uses magic tools...I'm just a little more informed about them than others. Pastel Mary asked me to look into these goggles, so she let me have them for a moment just to check them...that's all."

Using the full name of "Pastel Mary" made them come off

more distant. Mary understood that Ren-Ren was doing that deliberately, but it still prickled her heart painfully.

Chelsea snorted scornfully. "Then you should've said so to
begin with."

"I'm sorry," Ren-Ren apologized. "That was misleading, wasn't
it? I will take care in the future."

"So is it done? Um, your check or whatever."

"Yes, I'm basically done. It seems that it will be difficult for
anyone aside from their owner, 7753, to use them properly. Unfortunately..." Ren-Ren held the goggles up over her head politely and
then bowed her head to approach Pastel Mary like a servant as she
handed them over. Being close for the moment she handed them
over made Pastel Mary's heart flutter for a second, but Ren-Ren
immediately backed away, leaving her disappointed.

Splinters of wood and dust still hung around them as Chelsea
smiled. She sat Pastel Mary down on the destroyed rocks, then she
sat down beside her as she began babbling on about magical girls
and about herself.

Pastel Mary looked toward Ren-Ren. She wished she could join
Agri and Nephilia's whispered conversation, but she couldn't leave
Chelsea, and so despite feeling dejected, she listened to her talk.

◇ **Touta Magaoka**

There was the crack of trees and branches breaking, the slam of
something being blasted away, and then a sharp whoosh of air and
a shuddering that made him wonder if there had been an explosion. Maybe there really had been an explosion. It was dim in the
cave with just the glow of the moon, but Touta could tell Rareko
was growing even paler.

"These are...rocks! Rocks are being fired like bullets!" Rareko
cried.

It didn't end with the first. They were hit with two, three shots
of the "rocks." The whole cave rocked unsteadily, then creaked, and
little stones pattered down.

Rareko rose to a crouch and looked outside. Outside was dangerous for other reasons. But it would also be dangerous to stay here. Touta understood that. The third strike of pelted rocks was the last, but there was a big crack in the wall of the cave. And it was still creaking.

Touta held Yol's hand tight, and she squeezed it back.

Rareko was on her feet, hunched over, while Yol and Touta remained sitting, quieting their breathing as they waited patiently. Nothing happened. There wasn't another attack, and nobody came. Five or ten minutes or even longer passed like that as they waited, but still, nothing happened. On no particular signal, they all sighed in succession.

"Is it over...?" Touta wondered.

"I wonder if Uncle and everyone else is all right," Yol said.

"What was that to begin with...?" Rareko muttered.

There was a nasty sound. Rocks were pattering down. There was a large crack running along the ceiling, too. The crack made noise as it spread, making Touta gulp.

"Quiet...," Yol whispered. Her face was pale, and her voice was trembling. "It seems like one wrong move will bring it down... Can you repair it, Rareko?"

"I'll try." With trepidation, Rareko stood and reached up to the ceiling, and when her hand was two inches away, a rock the size of an adult's head clonked down. Rareko smacked it aside, but more kept rattling down one after another as the ceiling began caving in, and Rareko covered Touta and Yol with her body.

Touta smothered a shriek, and with Rareko covering him, he covered Yol in turn. Lying there, Yol fluttered her cape to unerringly pull out three cards from the deck equipped in it. The cards were all black with dense patterns over them, and not the Battlers cards Touta knew. Yol *smack, smack, smacked* the three cards down in an evenly spaced line on the ground, followed by a *tunk, tunk, tunk* as she suddenly produced four-inch metal pegs to pin the cards. Despite being thrown by the hands of a child, the pegs drove about halfway into the ground to nail down the cards as if she'd driven them in with a hammer. Hearing the sound of crumbling, Yol choked on rock dust and bent her fingers over and over in signs with her hands. Her movements gradually slowed, and her expression seemed pained, her breathing ragged and shoulders heaving.

Rareko was on all fours over the top of Yol and Touta to cover them. She patiently took the shower of rocks falling from above on her shoulders and the back of her head, looking like she was in pain as she rocked her body back and forth. A grayfruit fell with a plunk from her chest. "Give it…to the miss…!"

Touta's hand immediately shot out to grab the fruit and gingerly bring it to Yol's mouth.

Yol's eyes widened, and she moved just her head to chomp into the fruit, finishing it in three bites. The gesture was so bold and aggressively unlike her very much refined rich-girl appearance, it seemed exaggerated. The life returned to her eyes, and she resumed her hand signs. At the end of a flowing sequence of gestures, she put her hands together and pointed them toward the cards and pegs, and the cards burst into flame like a magic trick, burning up instantly.

Touta had thought it was "like a magic trick," but if he really thought about it, it was actual magic.

Touta realized. The sounds had stopped. Rareko pushed herself up, and the rocks that had rained down on top of her body rolled off onto the ground.

Bit by bit, the rock dust cleared. Touta's eyes widened in shock. Lines of light were packed into the cracks and missing spots of the ceiling and walls, supporting it like spreading roots. It was like the nets they put up in areas with the risk of falling rocks or something.

"M-miss, this is reckless…," Rareko stuttered. "It's truly not a good idea to be so impulsive."

"I should ask if you're all right, Rareko," Yol said.

"Magical girls are resilient." Rareko gently patted off Yol's hat and cape, then patted off her own head and shoulders, taking off her glasses to examine them from many angles. It seemed she was more worried about her glasses than herself. Seeing her do that, Touta remembered he was dirty as well, so he dusted himself off.

"That grayfruit you had me eat was the one I gave to you, wasn't it?" Yol asked. "Wasn't that the last one? We'll be in trouble if you can't transform anymore."

"I should have a bit more time left until my transformation is undone. It will be dawn soon. Once it's light out, let's hurry to gather fruit before that happens. Um, ah, though I do feel it's, um, deeply inexcusable for me to rely on your magic when I'm supposed to protect you, miss."

"Your protecting me or not isn't what matters." Yol placed her right hand over Touta's hand on her shoulder, then stuck out her left thumb and held it up as she turned her head to look back. She was smiling boldly just like the duelists in anime. "I can't sit around being protected, can I? I have to show my best, too."

Her eyes were red. There were tear tracks still on her cheeks. Touta clenched his teeth. Even though there was no way she could feel cheerful, she was doing her best to act that way for Touta's and Rareko's sakes.

All he could do right now was to lighten the mood by acting happy and bright. Even if that was all he could do, it was better to do it than not. Touta took Yol's hand, circled in front of her, and knelt down. "Oh yeah, you were a mage, too, huh."

"*Oh yeah?* Did you forget?" Yol pouted.

"Well, I'd never seen you use magic before."

"What a mean thing to say. It was the right idea to show my best, after all."

"Yeah, it was great. The way you pulled out those cards was cool."

"Heh-heh," Yol chuckled smugly. "I tucked some magic talismans in there thinking something like this might happen. It took me even longer to practice drawing them out stylishly than it took me to learn the spell."

Touta smiled, and Yol smiled back. They were speaking as quietly as possible to keep from being heard outside, but still, they were able to laugh out of enjoyment for the first time in a long while.

"Miss," the voice of an unfamiliar woman interrupted them. Yol and Touta both turned to the back of the cave. Where Rareko had been was a human woman in a maid outfit. She was not a magical girl but an adult woman. She was looking even worse than Rareko had been a moment ago. She was pale and sallow. The woman patted at her face, making sounds like "Ah, ah!" as if checking.

Yol pointed at her with a trembling hand. "Rareko, you…" Her voice was trembling far more than her hand. And the woman—Rareko—was trembling even more than Yol. If Yol was trembling, then Rareko was shuddering violently.

"Why…? It's happening faster, compared to before," Rareko said.

"What about your spare fruit, Rareko?" Yol asked.

"The one I gave to you was my last, miss…"

Yol looked toward the entrance. Picking up her staff, she made to stand up, and Touta grabbed her upper arm from behind, while Rareko grabbed her wrist from the front to stop her.

"It's my fault that we don't have any more," Yol declared. "I will go find some fruit."

"No, don't act like that!" Touta cried. "If you hadn't used your magic, we would have been buried alive!"

"Then what should I do…? Bring it up?"

"Bring it up?"

"From my stomach."

"Miss!" Rareko wailed.

"Don't—don't do that, Yol. There's probably no point." Touta desperately tried to convince her, still keeping a firm grip on her arm.

Yol's arm stopped pulling and relaxed, and Touta hesitantly released her. Yol slumped over, hands on the ground. Rareko looked somehow relieved, wiping sweat off her forehead.

Still looking at the ground, so quiet she could barely be heard, Yol muttered, "What do we do…?"

Touta waffled, looked down, then raised his chin again to put on as bright an expression as he could. "Once it's light outside, let's go search for fruit. Mr. Navi might come, too."

Rareko nodded weakly, and Yol muttered, "All right."

◇ John Shepherdspie

Mana was constantly in a bad mood. She was on edge just walking. Furthermore, she didn't bother trying to hide her irritation, making even Shepherdspie, who had nothing to do with the cause of her bad mood, uncomfortable.

7753's shoulders were slumped like she'd lost her energy. She was blaming herself, making it her fault for being completely useless because she'd lost her goggles.

But so far as Shepherdspie could see, 7753 was not the primary cause of Mana's mood going downhill. 7753 was probably about a third of it, but Mana was angrier about Marguerite. Mana kept bringing up how she'd let Chelsea get away, assuming that Marguerite would have been able to win if they'd had a real fight. And when Marguerite took it gently, Mana got mad at her and said, "Enough excuses." Marguerite had said, "I can fight her if I'm allowed to kill her," but if that was the case, then they couldn't let her fight.

Tepsekemei was busy sniffing at the head of the group, with no attention to spare to their conversation. Though it seemed like she was a magical girl of few words to begin with, so she probably wouldn't have tried to join in even if she'd been able to.

7753 was just slumping wholeheartedly, so she wasn't about to say anything.

This forced Shepherdspie to be the one to patch things up. When Mana tried to bring it up again, he changed the subject, making an effort to redirect her anger as much as he could. Despite being hungry to begin with—and hunger is the greatest evil of all—he was forced to make the effort. When Mana started to say, "Back there—" he cut her off by saying, "Oh yes, so…"

A quiet voice from behind prompted him, "Go ahead." Mentally sighing in relief, with a "Pardon me," Shepherdspie continued, "it's been quite some time since the sun has set."

"True," Mana replied grumpily.

Hearing that, Marguerite followed up with, "It shouldn't be too long before sunrise."

Shepherdspie nodded. "Unlike magical girls, I can't see in the dark, you see. So I'll be very grateful for morning to come. And I'll be able to help to search for fruit, too... For whatever my efforts are worth."

Following right behind Marguerite and walking in her footsteps kept Shepherdspie from stumbling. But there was no way he could keep an eye out in every direction to search for grayfruit while walking.

"Thank you very much," Marguerite replied.

Her thanks made him feel awkward, since he hadn't been speaking all that sincerely to begin with. He had plenty of things on his mind. *I'm hungry. Give us a break already. I want to go home. I want to have a good sleep. I wish it was all just a dream. I just want to die. Get me to safety.* It was all fundamentally worrying about himself and nothing that he could say out loud and have heard.

"Well, hmm, it really, really, really won't count for much, though...," Shepherdspie said.

"So then as I was going to say," Mana cut in, and while Shepherdspie was privately exasperated, thinking, *So you're going to say it...*, he obviously wouldn't cut her off a second time.

"First of all," Mana continued, "assuming that we're going to gather grayfruit, what will we do after that? I don't think everyone will come together."

"Hmm?"

"Chelsea is clearly not in her right mind. It seems as if she's being controlled by someone. There's no guarantee that others aren't being controlled, either—and no guarantee they're not doing the controlling. If we could have at least captured Chelsea, we could have learned some things, though."

In the end, she'd come back to that again. It made Shepherd-spie want to sigh, but he restrained it halfway up his throat. Sighing would offend Mana, and it would also make Shepherdspie unnecessarily hungry. It would bring about nothing good. If they could get back to the main building, then Shepherdspie could wield his cooking skills—there should be a little fond left—and fill their stomachs, and that would soothe Mana's heart, too. But if he was to propose such a thing, he might be the next one getting snapped at by Mana.

"It wasn't the sort of situation where I could—" Marguerite cut off halfway and froze. Shepherdspie noticed that her right hand was ready on her rapier, her eyes panicked as she stared ahead.

About ten steps ahead beyond the thick clumps of low brush was a pond. The smell of water wafted toward them, followed by the sounds of water—the sound of a splash on the surface, the sound of something sinking, and the sound of water falling. Since it was dark, he tried to capture it with his ears rather than his eyes, but he couldn't tell what was going on.

Then the surface of the water broke. Shepherdspie's eyes widened. It was a human-shaped silhouette.

From the pond? Why? Who?

The figure moved as smoothly as if there was no water resistance at all, its upper body rising from the pond.

Each of its hands held a shining object. Shepherdspie narrowed his eyes. Those objects, shining under the light of the moon, were axes, the kind a woodcutter would have.

The glow of the axes illuminated the face of the figure. It was a girl—or no, this was a goddess. Phrases like "empty-headed" or "dreamy-eyed" would be apt to describe the vacant expression on her flawlessly arranged facial features, and it wasn't even clear whether she was focused on what was in front of her. Her all-white, plain toga was floating slightly, while her lush golden locks flowed silkily in the wind. Her hair seemed light. Despite having come out of the water, she wasn't wet.

One ax shone gold, the other silver. The one who held them

looked just like the "goddess of the spring" from the stories. When Shepherdspie was little, he'd read the fairy tale about the honest woodcutter getting a golden ax in a library of the Magical Kingdom. There had been a picture book of children's tales and Aesop's from various worlds, and it had depicted the beautiful goddess carrying axes as so bewitching, it had left an intense impression on him as a child. The story itself hadn't been as impactful as the illustration. He'd just felt envious of the woodcutter for getting free stuff, rather than the lesson that honesty is a virtue.

"Is the ax you dropped the golden ax?" the goddess suddenly asked. Her voice carried through the dim forest. Her vocal quality was not only clear but transparently delicate and sweet.

The goddess raised her chin slightly, looked straight ahead at them, and said, "Or is it the silver ax?"

The look in her eyes was still vacant, like you couldn't tell where she was looking, but it was clear who she was speaking to. His heart raced.

Shepherdspie's eyes never left the goddess. He didn't even blink. But the goddess's left hand wavered slightly, and there was a sound like something being repelled. Without even time to think, Tepsekemei's upper body disappeared.

The pond surged, burst, and sprayed out. Both the goddess's arms wavered, and an instant later, Tepsekemei's lower body disappeared as well. Then Marguerite vanished, and the ground cracked open, and multiple trees broke off at the same time. Everything happened at once. Shepherdspie just stood there, unable to say anything, unable to even collapse or sink to the ground.

Something was repelled. The silver ax turned blue, and the gold ax went red. With a sound like electrical discharge, they were flowing. Another sound rang out. Something fluttered from right to left, and a whole bunch of trees were mowed down all at once. Dead leaves became shreds, and a whirlwind whipped up earth and sand as it gouged deeply into the ground. A spray of water rained down. As destroyed trees fell from above, everything was moving slowly for some reason. The goddess blocked a rapier with her left ax as she swung her right ax upward. 7753's shriek and Mana's yell grew distant.

Shepherdspie spread both arms wide. He hadn't moved because he was trying to do something about the situation. Half a beat later, he was frightened by his own actions, but it also strangely made sense. The goddess had that same vacant expression as she tilted her head and swung down her ax.

◇ **Love Me Ren-Ren**

The balance being maintained between Chelsea and Mary was even more delicate than Ren-Ren had thought. Agri had casually asked her for "another one or two, if possible," but any more people, and it would all go out of Ren-Ren's control. It wasn't that she might not be able to control them anymore; it was a certainty that she would have no control over them. Chelsea's behavior was sudden and idiosyncratic, for better or worse, and she'd been unpredictable to begin with. And on top of that, she was endowed with incredible violence. Even with the strength of all the magical girls present, they wouldn't be able to restrain Chelsea if she actually lost it.

"Well, what can you do," said Agri. "I did want a bit more numbers, but if we don't have them, that just means we do what we have to do without them."

"I'm sorry," said Ren-Ren.

"It's fine; you don't have to apologize. It's not like it's your fault. Chelsea on her own is actually worth two or three people, right? She even got..." Agri held the goggles up to face height and smirked. "...these things for us."

"They're not in a big fuss over it, are they?"

"If they are making a fuss, that's not such a bad thing, in a way."

Ren-Ren could imagine 7753, who'd had her goggles stolen, as well as the mage and magical girl who were with her, but all she could do was apologize in her heart.

"Well, you know. You don't have to look so grim about it." Agri kindly smacked her in the back, and Ren-Ren looked at her. Agri had seemed like she was enjoying herself quite a few times since coming to this island, but she'd never been smiling with as much amusement as she was now. About a step and a half behind Agri, Nephilia was snickering, even more amused. Ren-Ren was the only one grim, as Agri put it.

"But...it's a crime," Ren-Ren protested.

"This is business, okay. It's to get rich."

"But this is— Hold on a minute." Catching something moving in the corner of her vision, Ren-Ren nocked an arrow on her bow and stepped in front of Agri. A white piece of paper flew out from the deep darkness of the forest at the speed of a child casually walking. Maybe it wasn't quite flying. It was more accurate to say it wafted along unnaturally.

Standing in front of Agri, Ren-Ren gently pushed it aside, but Agri plucked the paper in her hands.

"That's dangerous," Ren-Ren warned. "It could be poisoned, or it could explode."

"No, it's just a letter." Agri opened up the piece of paper that had been folded in four and, reading the contents, smiled with just the edges of her lips. "It's an invitation. I'm going to go out for a bit. I'm counting on you to watch things."

Agri strode right off, and Ren-Ren panicked and looked behind them. Mary seemed concerned about them, but Chelsea wasn't bothered at all as she continued talking on. Ren-Ren gave Mary a restraining look to keep her from coming, while to Nephilia she said, "Please handle things here," before following after Agri without waiting for Nephilia to nod back.

"Where are you going?" Ren-Ren asked.

"You're coming, too?" Agri said. "The letter said it wanted me to come alone, though."

"Alone? No, that's too dangerous."

"I don't think it'll be an issue... Well, but...I guess maybe it'd be best to have you know about things, too. I doubt it's what he wants, but that'll probably make things easier for me." Agri nodded a bunch like that made sense to her, then headed off in the direction the letter had come from.

Ren-Ren continued to try to get her to stop many times, saying, "It's too dangerous," and "Let's talk first," but Agri did nothing but laugh and wouldn't listen or stop.

Walking through the dark forest, when Agri stumbled over a thick root that bulged up from the ground, Ren-Ren came to her side to support her. "Whoops, thanks."

"It's nothing, but more importantly—"

"It's fine, it's fine. Well, maybe I'm not very fine at walking in the dark, but it looks like we don't have to walk anymore anyway."

There was the crunch of stepping on earth from deeper in the forest, followed by the sound of kicking plants and someone cursing. Then a mage Ren-Ren also recognized—Navi Ru—plodded into view. Perhaps because the direction he'd come from had no path, thorny leaves were stuck on the hood of his robe.

He looked the same as always, and he didn't seem very tired. He moved briskly, and he actually seemed filled with energy. Only the greasy sweat and thick five-o'clock shadow on his face, plus the marks of dried blood, expressed the passage of time. Agri and Navi stood blocking either side of a narrow animal trail as they faced each other.

"You sent this letter, right?" Agri asked him.

"Yeah, I did." Navi gave Ren-Ren a look that would be difficult to call friendly, and Agri waved a hand to cut that off.

"Don't worry about Ren-Ren. She's basically like my other half."

"I'm sure that's how you see it."

"It'll make discussion harder if you won't accept her."

This time, his expression turned more clearly bitter. The way he crossed his arms and looked down on Agri, he looked like nothing other than a member of a criminal organization, and he was probably used to using his looks to pressure others.

But it didn't work on Agri at all, and she ignored Navi's look with that same amused smile. "It's fine, it's fine. It's nothing to worry about, 'kay."

Navi was the first one to look away. He muttered, "Oh well," under his breath as if to himself, then pulled a rolled-up cloth from his sleeve and flapped it open. Spread out, the cloth held floating about twenty inches over the ground, and Navi sat down on one side. It was a carpet, three feet wide and eight feet long. "Fine. Then it's talk time."

"I expected you to come faster. It causes trouble for me when you're not being very cooperative."

"You were waiting for me to come to you?"

"I knew there were things you wanted to talk about. There's no way you wouldn't come. Partly because you don't want us pulling anything to stir up trouble, and also because you want us to work with you, if possible."

"Huh, sounds like you've been thinking about this a lot. You're right; I did want to see you. You're pulling a little too much for me to let it slide."

"It was about at the point where I couldn't wait anymore; I thought maybe you couldn't find us. I was just thinking we'd do you the favor of going to you."

"Is that right? Well, have a seat." Navi patted the space beside him, and Agri nimbly hopped on. Ren-Ren never let go of her bow, watching the two mages in front of her. Though Agri couldn't have had the opportunity to groom her hair or skin, she looked about unchanged from the morning before.

"It looks like you've been gathering grayfruit," Navi said.

"We have," Agri acknowledged.

"And you made Mary your lackey?"

"Chelsea, too."

"Could you tell me why you're recklessly trying to make things worse?"

Agri pouted like that wasn't her intention, shrugging at him. "Make things worse? I'm offended. I'm trying to help you out. I said I'd make sure we'd keep each other's secrets and whatnot to keep problematic things from getting exposed to the wrong people. Isn't that right? We brought Nephy in when we first met to make a

295

contract that says just that. That contract is binding on both sides. You get that, too, don't you?"

"Yeah, I do."

"And it's not just about you and me. It counts for all your underlings as well as my friends. So then Ren-Ren and Nephy won't get hit or kicked by any of yours."

Navi touched the fingertips of his right index finger and thumb and stroked them along his jaw to pinch his beard and pluck a hair. It looked painful, but the man himself didn't seem to feel it, his attention on something else. He was staring at a tree with a look he hadn't had before, like his gaze was somewhere far away. "What're you trying to pull here, lady? Let's not do anything too outrageous. There's an old buddy of mine here on this island, as well as new friends."

"Well. I don't want to be reckless, either. You feel the same way, don't you, Ren-Ren?"

Having the discussion suddenly turned to her, Ren-Ren hurriedly nodded back. Her gesture was sudden but sincere. She didn't want Agri being reckless.

Agri smiled back like Nephilia and nodded. "I was thinking I'd give up some grayfruit to anyone who says they just have to have them. They're valuable items on this island, and there's not enough, so there'll be a lot of people like that, right? Of course, I'll receive a thank-you, too. I can make contracts, so even if they can't pay here on this island, I can just get it once we get out."

"Money?"

"Look, you're making that face."

Navi patted at his own face. The dried blood stuck on his forehead came off and sprinkled down. "What face?"

"A face that says, 'You're taking all those risks for something as petty as money?'" Just for an instant, the smile was peeled off Agri's face. She wore an expression like she was staring at something she couldn't get, and despite knowing she'd never get it, she couldn't leave. Envy, jealousy, bitterness, and frustration were all mixed together, and sprinkled on top was the determination that she was going to have it, no matter what.

"Are you in debt or something?" Navi asked her.

"No. I'm going to be rich." She said it like a child, with clear determination.

The hand over Navi's forehead closed, and he massaged away the wrinkles in his brow before shaking his head. "What you're after isn't even that great. Even if a slave saves up money bit by bit to buy the right of citizenship, they'll never become a real citizen. They're just a freed slave. All the citizens'll be whispering, *'I hear that person was originally a slave.'* They won't even think about it as malicious backbiting. They're just talking about how someone who's different from them is different. That's how they think."

"So?"

"I'm saying that even if you scraped together the money to get in with the rich, you'll be the only one who thinks you're one of them. You think you'll enjoy having them talk behind your back, like, *'She's some upstart broad with no class, the daughter of a mistress'*? I can't stand that sorta thing. Isn't it way more tasteful to be acknowledged through some clear accomplishment?" Navi gestured animatedly as he spoke. From how he talked, of course he wasn't sincerely concerned about Agri, but it seemed like he wanted her to change her mind, at the very least. After he was done saying his bit, Navi examined Agri's expression.

She was smiling. "I'll think about whether I'll enjoy it or not after I've done it."

Even Ren-Ren thought the *ksh-shh* snicker meant Nephilia was going too far, but it did suit her.

"You're too much to deal with," Navi muttered, and his expression spoke louder than his words. "Doing business when a murderer is walking around, you're out of your mind."

"A murderer?" Agri replied. "Come on—that's not what's going on. The one to kill Maiya was your magical girl, wasn't it?"

CHAPTER 9
LET'S FIGHT, LET'S STAND UP, LET'S RESIST

◇ **Nephilia**

A lot of people were interested in the words of the dead.

All people, to a greater or lesser extent, had experienced loss through death. They would live with thoughts like, *There was more I wanted to ask, more I wanted to say,* every day until the feelings faded and were eventually forgotten. When they found out about Nephilia's magic, those feelings that had been lost to memory for a time would come back, and they would beg her, "Is that true?" and "Can you really do that?" And even if they weren't that tormented, plenty of people had a curiosity about the possibility of a world after death. Some called it fantastical, and some even said, "You could solve the mysteries of history."

And then once they found out that her magic was actually just to replay the voices emitted before death, about 60 percent would shrug and tell her, "Ahhh, so that's all it was after all." About 20 percent would politely add, "I'd like to see it sometime," and 10 percent would get angry and say something aggressive to Nephilia. And though they were a minority, there were some who, knowing what her magic actually did, still wanted her to use it.

Parents who wanted to hear just one more time the voice of their dear daughter who had passed very young, an inheritance conflict between vying relatives who wanted to know if the deceased had said anything that might put themselves at even the slightest advantage, an extreme magical-girl fan who wanted the live voice of a magical girl who had recently died young so they could get an audio sample and listen to it forever—just handling clients like that got her more business than you could shake a stick at. Nephilia could make enough income to manage as a freelancer.

Since becoming a magical girl when she was little, Nephilia had completed many jobs, accumulating experience and knowledge. She liked knowing things. The world was overflowing with unknowns.

Before she was even two years old, she had pulled a picture book off the shelf and pestered her parents to read it to her, and from doing that over and over, she'd memorized the contents of the book before learning to read and write. Her parents had been surprised to see their daughter doing something so strange as reading aloud from a picture book held upside-down and had had high hopes for her. "Maybe she could be a genius." "Maybe she'll become someone great in the future." But their daughter had not lived up to those hopes—her academics were upper-middling at the most, with no literary or poetic talent to speak of. But she did grow up generally well. So her parents laughed, figuring it was their bias as her parents, and they loved their daughter who had grown up so healthily, even if she was not a genius.

But the reality was entirely different. She was not the wholesome daughter her parents imagined.

The first thing this daughter had become attached to was "the wolf." The reason she'd read those picture books over and over was to find out if the wolf in *Little Red Riding Hood*, the wolf in

The Wolf and the Seven Young Goats, and the wolf in *Three Little Pigs* were ultimately the same wolf or not. She had wanted to know more about this creature known as wolf, made of deception, stealing, and eating. It was not a dreadful villain, nor an activist who fought for the sake of their beliefs, and nor did it have a backstory as a weakling who was forced into their position through oppression—it was just vermin. That made her curious. It made her want to know more. It began with the wolves in those picture books, following which she encountered petty villains and nasty characters who appeared in all sorts of stories, and her feelings deepened. No one else shared her opinion, but nasty people were attractive. They were refreshing and somehow charming, and most of all, she could sympathize with them.

She poured her talent not into her human life but into her magical-girl activities. There was startling variation among magical girls, and they were not only fine people of character. There were also some who hid how nasty they were and those who were blatantly nasty. Nephilia actively sought more connections, using those to find even juicier work, jobs that seemed like even more fun. Work satisfied her curiosity and provided a way to meet people, and it could also get her money. Money was always important.

An acquaintance who was imprisoned after her long years of wicked deeds were exposed, only to soon escape, had said this: "Money isn't that great, but having it will make things go very smoothly." Then when she'd talked about how if you're going to make money, you might as well go for an armed robbery against the Magical Kingdom for the fun of it, Nephilia thought, *She really is kind of a hopeless idiot*, and decided that she would refrain from associating with her in the future. When the level of nastiness got too high, she'd start thinking of the faces of the victims. That type of nasty wasn't to Nephilia's tastes. In everything, moderation is key.

But there was one thing she was forced to agree with. Her remarks about the importance of money had sounded very sincere, and Nephilia had seen many people get in trouble due to a lack of money.

Money was important. Jobs that could get her money were also important, even if she had no way to use that money right now. And Nephilia would of course do her job on important missions. A fun excursion might begin when you started working, but Nephilia had already begun working before this job had started. The starting line was investigating the client's background.

Prying was always dangerous, though. Knowledge and experience were weapons and sustenance, but they could also become shackles. Those who would try to pry into other people's business weren't generally well-liked. Someone who will gloat about having learned things they were better off not knowing would most certainly not be loved. A magical girl who was not liked or loved would have a short life span.

Nephilia saw herself as a magical girl who was occasionally obnoxiously difficult to control, but she didn't at all hate herself. If an offer came, then she would look into the client, and she would also investigate those around them. When she investigated, she took the greatest care to ensure that her investigation wouldn't be exposed. She'd done as much research as possible on Agri, Sataborn, and the other relatives Sataborn might have sent that inheritance letter to, and the harvest she had gained from that was more than commensurate to her labor.

"It would be one thing if you were just coming here for a pleasure jaunt, but the kind of hard-core person who would search for cooperators as soon as he came to the island would never *not* bring the maximum number of magical girls."

No matter where Nephilia heard Agri, her voice was easy to pick up. It was nothing like her own voice.

Sitting on a rock, Nephilia pressed down her right ear, firmly pushing her earbuds with her fingers. The magical phone Agri had given her had no trouble picking up the sound. She was able to hear the whole conversation between the mages, who were face-to-face in the trees away from the rocky area to keep from being heard. It was a problem that she couldn't send a signal over to Agri or that it was too far away for her to rush over with Chelsea, but Nephilia would ignore that this once.

But what she couldn't ignore was a different problem. The audio was a little too loud. Nephilia shoved the earbuds deeper in. Mary and Chelsea were right over there flirting, so if they talked about things the two of them shouldn't hear and that sound leaked out from her earbuds, it was bound to cause a crisis.

"Well, I'm sure that's how you imagine it." Navi Ru's voice was low and a little hard to hear. It probably wasn't just because of his natural vocal quality but also the emotions coming out in his voice. Nephilia had missed Navi when doing her research. He was not only an obstinate character but a well-known and accomplished researcher. Sataborn had been working for a ridiculously long time, so many could call themselves his former pupils, but you couldn't really say Navi was high in the priority ranking. His time as a pupil had been short, and their relationship had been tenuous. Why had Navi been the one invited? Nephilia thought perhaps that he hadn't been summoned as a pupil. "The Lab" that Navi worked for referred to the nucleus of the Osk Faction. Maybe coming as a former pupil was ultimately a pretense, and they'd actually had a cooperative relationship, a power relationship within the faction. But even if she thought about looking into that, that was beyond what she could uncover in a day or two. And if she screwed up, it could get her killed.

"She was hiding in the pond, wasn't she?" Agri asked.

The place where they had met Navi had been the edge of the pond. But hadn't Agri said that Navi looking meaningfully at the pond had been a bluff?

"Oh, I assumed that had to be a bluff, too," Agri said, perhaps directed less at Navi and more at Ren-Ren, beside her. "But if you're gonna hide a magical girl you brought, I feel like there would be the best place. There are magical girls who could hide in wait underwater, right? Like a mermaid, frog, or dolphin—well, it doesn't matter what kind."

"Huh. I see," Navi commented. "So then why would she kill Maiya? There's no reason."

"That thing that made all the mages collapse and the magical girls' transformations run out. You weren't able to predict that, were you? Am I wrong?"

"C'mon, there's no way I could know that'd happen."

"Uh-huh. You passed out, too, and Clarissa's transformation came undone. It didn't look to me like you were faking being a victim who got caught in it, either. Well, things worked out for you and Clarissa 'cause the rest of us were there."

"Yeah, basically."

"But things were totally different for the magical girl A, who you ordered to hide and wait. She had no idea what was going on. And on top of that, if she was at the bottom of the pond, she'd be spewing bubbles and drowning. So she dragged herself out somehow, searched for grayfruit, and transformed again. But then look, even if she may have gotten out of the immediate trouble, it wasn't like that solved everything. If she went back to the pond and her transformation came undone again, that'd be a disaster. I think she'd wind up thinking all sorts of things, like, *Was there an attack?* or *Did something else cause this? Is it still happening or is it over?* timidly trying to probe around the area. And that's when, unfortunately, she ran into Maiya...and killed her."

There was a pause. Nephilia heard Navi clear his throat a few times, then sigh deeply. "You've got a real imagination, lady." His voice wasn't trembling or anything. But it wasn't a happy-sounding tone. Agri, on the other hand, was chatting away quite cheerily. It even seemed like she was trying to stir things up.

Agri had the tendency to play the villain sometimes and act worse than she really was more than necessary. Nephilia could understand her values, in seeing bad people as cool, but someone who was really bad wouldn't play at it. The person Agri was talking to was a mage who worked at the notorious lab.

The Osk Faction lab was said to be the final destination for magical girls. An acquaintance of Nephilia's who was versed in these matters said they dissected innocent magical girls as a matter of course. Even if he looked like just a rugged-looking middle-aged uncle, you had no idea how much nasty work he'd engaged in. Even if it was half rumors, or 99 percent rumors, she should consider him a genuine villain. The more control you had, the more you should avoid stirring things up—was what Nephilia thought, but she had no way to tell that to Agri.

"Well, you can think that if you like. That's just all what I figure is going on, after all. But I don't think I'm so far off. You got here by searching for me, didn't you, old man? Probably using Clarissa's magic."

"This is speculation—basically fantasy."

"You want to end things as peacefully as you can. That's why you had Clarissa go with that group to see Maiya's body."

"Uh-huh?"

"A is still worried she might get attacked. Now she's like a frightened mouse with crazy-powerful combat abilities, and you don't know who she might bite. Isn't that what you were thinking? So then if you or Clarissa was with the group, A would be able to tell that she shouldn't attack them. That's why you had Clarissa join the group that got sent to Maiya's body."

"That's some pretty circuitous assumptions of rationale." There was a derisive tinge in Navi's voice. "If you keep throwing accusations at me over every little thing, you can make anything sound legit."

"It was odd—odd that you made the decision to send off Clarissa so casually, when she might be the one person here who'll protect you, and we had a mysterious killer running around. That'd be different if you knew you weren't gonna get attacked, though."

"Uh-huh."

That "uh-huh" sounded completely apathetic, but that was what made it feel like she'd hit on something. Nobody could offer such an apathetic response to someone right in front of them digging at them with groundless suspicious, arguing doggedly and throwing more inferences at you no matter how much you denied them. This could basically be taken as an implicit acknowledgment that it was somewhat true, and Navi should know that as well.

"I'm not going to demand you admit it," Agri said. "I'm sure you don't want to, and I can't be sure my deductions are correct in the first place anyway. But you know, looking at the situation, I think it's not that far off… Oh, this isn't a threat. Since threatening you would be going against our contract."

What had led Nephilia to becoming a magical girl had naturally been her magic, but be that as it may, she didn't like to use it. Her reluctance to touch the dead directly with a hand went beyond disgust, and the pleasure of getting to hear the words of someone who couldn't talk aside, she felt more guilty than curious about making those words public. It was actually through seeking out the most interesting of the jobs that didn't require magic that Nephilia had learned about the Magical Kingdom, diving into study of contracts between mages, the ceremonies that came with the contracts, and the laws she had to obey with such enthusiasm that people sought her more often for those skills now. She wouldn't make mistakes when it came to contracts.

"So as long as it's in the near future, we still have an active contract between us, right?"

Their contract was what Agri was counting on most of all. No matter how crafty Navi might be, if she made the contract her shield, her safety was guaranteed. Each of the clauses had been established in detail, and if Navi violated any of them, he would lose all his assets.

In the first place, there was a difference between Navi and Agri that made it difficult to call the contract fair. It was an equal deal in the sense that they both put their assets on one side of the scales to balance them, but Agri was in destitution, and Navi was in the nucleus of the Osk Faction—their assets were on entirely different levels. It was kind of like someone with just one coin and someone with a hundred coins saying, *"Let's bet all our remaining coins on this game."*

Nephilia had mobilized all her knowledge and experience

to insert fake-outs and deception with the finest nuance, making the contract as hard to read as was legally possible. If Navi had skimmed over it or read it wrong, that was proof he was in a hurry to gain allies. Nephilia had been planning to pull out something else should he complain, but in the end, he had voiced no complaints.

"At the very least, you can't do anything to us," Agri argued. "So then we're not gonna get killed. Worst case, even if you had failed to control A completely, then you can say we're kinda safe if we can be near you."

Nephilia heard a bitter-sounding throat-clearing sound. Navi was irritated, and he wasn't trying to hide it. "Look, lady. Everything you've been saying this far has just been *admit this, give me that*, using the contract as a shield to say whatever you want. The contract we made, okay, was a win-win, fifty-fifty contract. You must have something to offer me."

"I've gathered grayfruit. I'll give you exactly half."

Meeting someone halfway also meant getting closer to them. Even if Agri was getting carried away enjoying playing the villain, she had guts. Nephilia couldn't hear Navi clearing his throat anymore.

"Huh, half…hmm. That depends on how much that is."

"You can assume the fruit that was stored in the main building has been about doubled."

"Huh?"

"Dreamy☆Chelsea and Pastel Mary are working with me, too. Chelsea is a violence specialist, and Mary's sheep can scout and search for enemies."

"God damn…you bitch. You were the one who made Pastel Mary steal those?"

Nephilia looked over at the two magical girls who were sitting side by side behind the big rock. Chelsea was pressing closer, while Mary was shaking her head with a troubled expression. The two of them were actually unstable elements: Chelsea could well direct her violence at them at any moment, and Mary couldn't completely control the sheep she made, but they had no obligation to offer up those details.

"With Nephy, Ren-Ren, Mary, and Chelsea, that's four. Add with yours, and that's six people. Clarissa and Miss A are both strong, right? So then we've basically got a hold on this island."

"Uh-huh." Compared to his earlier "uh-huh," this had some slightly more positive feeling in it.

"I'll work with you as much as possible. I'll get you what you want, too," Agri said.

"I want the positional information on this island that you guys have."

"Sure."

"And show me everything about the contracts you're planning to use on this island, format and content included. The contracts you made up were really hard to understand. I'm gonna check over them properly."

"Yeah, yeah."

"Don't lay a hand on old Grampa Ragi or Yol. You can negotiate with them, though."

"I'm not gonna be violent with anyone, okay? More importantly, if you destroyed the gate, that means you secured an escape route, right? You've got to tell me about that."

"I dunno anything about the destruction of the gates. There was probably some kind of accident... Someone did it on their own judgment. And it goes without saying, but I have no idea who."

"An accident, done on their own judgment, eh? But still, it's not like you can't escape. You don't look that desperate about it."

"I wish you wouldn't keep trying to read me."

"I'm used to worrying about what other people are thinking," Agri said. Her remark was self-deprecating, but there was nothing pitiable about it. The air between the two mages had become a few notches lighter.

"About the gates... We were talking about how they can't be repaired because they're missing parts, right. So that means whoever broke the gates has the parts. Though it's not like I know who broke 'em. If we can get the parts from them and hand those off to Rareko, we should be able to use the gates without a problem."

"I see. Thank you for the advice."

The negotiation was complete. "All right," Nephilia muttered under her breath, clenching her right fist. The reflexive reaction came out more intensely than expected, and she couldn't help but laugh—she glanced over at Chelsea and Mary, but they were flirting and not looking at her.

The negotiation moved smoothly to a discussion with a peaceful back-and-forth. In other words, it had gone well. Agri had pulled it off.

Nephilia realized belatedly that she was supporting her employer more than she'd been aware. It was easy for her to sympathize with the motive of money for the sake of money, not because she wanted money in order to do something—partially because there weren't many magical girls like that. Nephilia generally felt favorably about the mages and magical girls on this island, but she especially liked Ren-Ren, and she liked Agri second most.

Agri was trying to rise up in the world. She had a conscience and sense of ethics, but she chose to ignore them to take advantage of the weaknesses of others. Despite her own reluctance, she was acting the villain and pretending she wasn't bothered about it.

Ren-Ren would seem passive, at a glance. If Agri asked her to do something, she wouldn't be able to say no, even knowing it was wrong—or so it seemed. But Nephilia thought there was something else going on. Ren-Ren was the type who would lie to herself but still keep her eyes fixed on the prize.

Both of them were just the kind of nasty people Nephilia liked. They were a duo made up of a magical girl who didn't want to be left behind and a mage who wanted to rise up. They fit like pieces filling in each other's missing parts, but they were also precarious, like one of them would cause the death of the other. Just one would have been fun on her own, but combining the two made them twice or three times as fun.

Nephilia smothered the laugh welling up from her throat

inside her mouth and then flipped through the contract forms and content that she was about to use so she could go over them thoroughly. When she opened her palms, she found she'd left deep nail marks and felt moved in spite of herself for showing such surprisingly strong emotion.

◇ Navi Ru

Kicking leaves and stepping on broken branches, Navi lumbered along a way with no path, clicking his tongue at the sound of his own footsteps, then making sure to lift and step softly and gently.

While walking, Navi stroked his chin. The sensation of his rough, unshaven beard was even painful on his palm. His beard felt like wire, but he couldn't be living as inflexibly as his stubble. Pliant and flexible even in the face of accidents was Navi Ru's modus operandi.

He stroked his chin gently enough that it wouldn't hurt.

Of Agri, he'd just been thinking it would be enough to make good use of her. He hadn't even considered her as someone to make a deal with. But it seemed he had to revise his evaluation of her. The deductions she'd expressed to him were off the mark, but they were rational. That had made him groan, thinking, *She's got some sharp ideas.*

Her story sounding plausible meant, in other words, that he could use it. Though Navi had panicked a little back there, now he was calculating. He would revise his evaluation of Agri and use her based on that. He wasn't going to deny her deductions, leaving it up to her what to think. Doing that would enable him to predict her behavior.

It would be a great disadvantage to Agri to believe in inaccurate deductions. Navi had to keep Agri's disadvantage from becoming his own. She must have arranged for that contract to keep him from doing that. She had some sharp ideas there, too.

This may not just have been her idea, though. She must have discussed it with her magical-girl companions, and the three of them had gotten together to wring out what none of them could have done individually.

If it was a choice between Ren-Ren and Nephilia, it had to be the latter. Take knowledge of law and contracts and add wiliness and cunning, and you'd get her. And that wasn't such a bad way to use the grayfruit they'd acquired. The part that was "not bad" was how it left room for them to use the excuse "we did it for our own safety" if they were criticized for the ploy after the fact. Agri wasn't just getting herself cash—her ploy also worked as a stopper, which made it seem justified.

That said...

It was indeed a good stopper, but it wasn't strong enough to stop Navi. Worst case, he could abandon all his assets to break the contract. Agri would surely see abandoning all assets as equivalent to suicide, but there was something Navi had to do, even if it meant abandoning his wealth. Agri was still young, to base her plans on her own values. Navi had been rather like that at her age.

But that was ultimately the worst-case scenario. He wanted to avoid that if he could.

Still...

Having to do things you don't want to do where rubber meets the road is just life. Only the privileged can avoid doing things because they don't want to do them, while just about everyone else does it with a sigh because they don't have a choice.

Don't take the shirt off my back, he prayed to Agri, who was laughing in his head.

◇ **Touta Magaoka**

Touta wasn't sure how much point there was in trying to fix the cave by filling the cracks with stones. The trio's breathing echoed in the small cave, and then things went quiet after a while. Aside from the occasional droplet of water or gust of wind, everything was silent. Touta wiped his forehead with the back of his hand. The sweat he'd worked up had grown cold.

They had no more grayfruit. Whether they had any or not didn't change anything for Touta. But if they continued to wait and do nothing, then Yol would collapse. Rareko wouldn't be able to transform. If they got attacked right now, there was no magical girl who would protect Touta and Yol. There had been one until now but not anymore.

Navi had said he would come back, but they didn't know when that would be. Going outside would be dangerous, but if they stayed inside, they'd be waiting for Yol to drop. They were between a rock and a hard place.

Rareko was sitting hugging her knees in front of her. Her shoulders were slumped, and she was looking down. Yol was biting her lip and watching the cave entrance. Touta knew both of them were tired. He was tired, too. He wanted to sleep. If there had been a soft futon here, he surely would have been unable to resist.

What would Marguerite have done? Or actually, wouldn't Marguerite find them? He couldn't help but think about leaving everything to others like that. Navi had said he'd come back, but would he be able to? It was too dangerous outside. It was dangerous for Touta, for Rareko, for Yol, and for Navi, too. If having some very confident mage there would make it safe, then nobody would have run away in the first place. They had run because things had been hopeless, even with that many people and all of them mages or magical girls.

Touta wasn't any good at thinking, but that was all he could do now, so he tried his best. Marguerite would touch her finger to her chin while she pondered things, and that was very cool, but Touta's chin was more square than Marguerite's, and it probably wouldn't be cool to touch his round finger to it. So Touta hugged his legs and stared into the darkness as he thought. Maybe his head would have worked a bit better if his stomach had been full. But if he started getting greedy, there would be no end to it.

Rareko sat there in silence. Touta felt like she was gently rejecting conversation. As a magical girl, she'd been a bit more put together, even if she'd seemed timid and unreliable. Marguerite had said that when a magical girl transformed, it made not just her body but her heart stronger as well. So then did that strong heart go away once she was back in human form? Rareko didn't encourage Yol or anything, either.

It wasn't like he was blaming Rareko. This was tough, even for an adult. There were a couple of teachers at school who would lash out at the students about how they were having a tough time. This was much better than something like that. If Touta had the amazing powers of a magical girl and he suddenly couldn't use them anymore, he figured that would hit him hard, too. He really couldn't blame Rareko.

Yol was looking up at the ceiling with worry. The ceiling was covered with the magic net she'd made for them. They had repaired it, too. *Now it should be okay, if it collapsed*—this was what he had assumed, but Yol was looking rather concerned for that to be the case. Maybe it wasn't absolutely okay. No matter how secure a net you covered it with, maybe there would be no helping it if it wasn't just the ceiling but the whole cave that came down.

Going outside the cave was dangerous. But staying inside the cave might be dangerous, too. If something came flying at them like before, the cave definitely wouldn't hold a second time.

"So hey," Touta began.

Rareko and Yol turned to him. He looked between each of their faces and continued. "Maybe it's weird to say this right after we fixed the ceiling…but maybe we should leave the cave."

"Well…" Yol seemed hesitant about how to reply.

But Rareko answered without any trepidation. "We can't. It's too dangerous." She spoke crisply, punctuating every word. "You must stay in the safest place, miss."

"Yeah, I agree with that. That's why…," Touta said.

Yol was a mage. A mage could do all sorts of things. Rareko was a magical girl. If she could just transform, she would be very strong. Both of them would be needed to escape from this island. They'd also be needed to try to find the others. But Touta was a normal kid. It wasn't like there was anything special about him, compared to magical girls and mages.

"I'm thinking I'll go alone," Touta finished.

"That's even more dangerous." Yol responded immediately this time.

Rareko's mouth opened and shut, and she immediately looked down. She'd probably realized that Touta wasn't very important. Even Yol, who had hastily stopped him, probably realized that, too. When you had one rare and two commons, anyone would realize which was more important. And even if they knew it, neither Yol nor Rareko could say it out loud.

So Touta had to say it himself. That was very scary, and even thinking it made his knees knock, but he couldn't avoid this if he wanted to do what was best. He stood up. "If anyone is going, I'll go alone. I think that's the best—"

He heard something striking a rock. All three of them looked to the entrance. Rareko grabbed a tree branch and crawled in front of Yol, while Touta flinched back. Not knowing how useful it would be, he balled his hands into fists and readied himself. There was that sound again. There were two strikes, like knocking. Maybe it rang out so clearly because it was so quiet in the cave. As they waited still like that, the same *knock, knock* again.

There was no mistaking it—this wasn't a naturally occurring sound. Someone had made it. It was a person knocking.

They weren't attacking without warning, at least. Touta told himself that maybe it wasn't an enemy. What villain would announce themselves beforehand?

Clenching his teeth, he punched his knees with his balled fists to stop them shaking.

He took a step forward. Getting some momentum, he took another, two, three more steps. Once his feet started moving, they moved on their own regardless of his will. Yol called out, "Wait," but Touta ignored her and came forward. He sensed motion behind him, but he wasn't stopped. It was probably Rareko holding back Yol.

Was it Navi? Was it Marguerite? Or was it someone else? Touta cautiously and slowly poked his face out the entrance and narrowed his eyes. It was brighter than he'd expected. It seemed that more time had passed than he'd felt during their repair work. He looked side to side, and when he found someone standing right beside him, he restrained the urge to flinch away. The magical girl before him let out a smothered snicker, and Touta also smiled along with her for some reason.

"Um…you're…Nephilia…right?" he said.

The big scythe he could see in the dark felt more scary than reliable. Just seeing her bone decorations and stuff made him shiver. That was because Nephilia was smirking. She didn't look like she'd come to save them or like she was seeking their help, either. She didn't feel as friendly as the mage Marguerite knew and the magical girl with her, but she didn't immediately try to hurt him. Touta wasn't sure how to react. Still with his hand at the entrance, he kept a vague smile on as he waited to see what she would do.

Nephilia put a hand into her hat, pulled a piece of paper out of it, and handed it to Touta. It was brown and different from the notebook paper and printouts he normally used. But it seemed a lot sturdier than draft paper, with characters that weren't Japanese or the alphabet and very magical-looking figures drawn on it. He didn't know what it meant.

"What…is this thing…?" Touta asked.

"Contract…," Nephilia muttered.

"Contract?"

"Sign… Give…fruit…"

"If I sign the contract, you'll give me fruit?"

Nephilia nodded and pointed to the entrance of the cave. "Someone who can do it…come…"

She was asking for someone who could sign a contract to step forward if Touta couldn't do the job. Touta's front teeth bit his lip as he clenched the hand placed over the entrance. It wasn't that he was shocked to be called useless. Touta was, in fact, useless. But that wasn't why he was upset. He was shocked that someone was offering a contract for grayfruit—in other words, that she was basically walking around selling them.

Didn't they all have to work together? Weren't those who had some grayfruit to spare going to share with the people who had none? Touta stared at Nephilia. She was smirking back at him, not acting guilty at all.

He realized that she wasn't necessarily on their side. It wasn't okay to tell her that all their grayfruit were gone, that Rareko's transformation had come undone, or anything like that. It would be a bad idea to beg her to save them because they were in trouble. Touta thought of his aunt and Marguerite. When he was thinking about adults he could rely on, they were the number one and two people who came to mind.

"I think…we need a little time to consider. This isn't something I can decide on my own anyway…" Still smiling like he was really unsure, Touta accepted a paper from Nephilia. "That's okay, right? I have the time to think, right?"

Nephilia narrowed just one eye and, after considering a bit, nodded.

Touta put a hand to his chest and let out a *phew* before lifting his head again like he'd just remembered something. "O-oh. I'll tell them about the contract, so add in a little bonus, okay."

Nephilia cocked her head. Turning back to the cave over and over, Touta said, "It'll take some time to consider whether we're going to agree to the contract or not, right? So then we'd be stopping searching for grayfruit during that time. Rareko won't like that. Just one is enough. If you give us one grayfruit, then Rareko might try considering it."

He couldn't let her find out that Rareko couldn't transform. If someone who was trying to get something out of offering them grayfruit was to find out they had no power to resist, it might wind up like when a burglar finds out the kid is home alone. His aunt had told him that was called a home-alone incident, and they were really nasty. Touta's story, that Rareko was using her magical-girl strength to make Touta do what she wanted, also told Nephilia that Touta had no hostage value. It was actually safer to tell her that grabbing Touta now or something wouldn't keep Rareko from fighting her.

"She just told me to go out to look if there was some noise, but she'd be sure to get angry with me if I came back with just a contract and asked her to think about it. If I got a grayfruit and said it's a deposit…was it called a deposit, again? If I say that, then, um, I'm sure it would put her in a good mood."

Nephilia's smirk vanished. She gave Touta a rather serious look he'd never seen before. It felt like she saw right through him, and Touta shook violently. But he figured if he was committing to the story that he was a pitiful boy, it wasn't wrong to react with violent trembling.

Nephilia nodded deeply, and by the time she'd lifted her face again, her smirk was back. She dropped a grayfruit into his palm, and Touta accepted it with a bow. He felt less grateful to Nephilia and more thankful to the grayfruit.

"Then…see you…half hour…," she said.

"Yeah. See you then."

Holding the grayfruit he'd received politely against his chest, Touta was about to return to the cave when he felt his concerns rising more. How had Nephilia known where they were? If she'd heard about it from someone, it could only be from Navi. Was Navi safe now? When he turned back, Nephilia was already gone, and Touta sighed. He'd messed up in the end. He'd meant to keep lots of things in mind, like his aunt and Marguerite did, but he'd forgotten to ask something he should have. He didn't even know whether he'd done well in the first place. If you told him Nephilia had seen right through him and given him the fruit because she felt sorry for him, he'd just think, *Yeah, huh.* His head was on the verge of overheating, and he felt feverish. He'd heard that could happen from using your brain too much.

But still, even so, he'd been able to get one grayfruit. Clasping the piece of paper, the grayfruit, and a small sense of accomplishment to his chest, Touta rushed back into the cave.

◇ **Miss Marguerite**

The wind blew through, whipping up a cloud of dust. It was Tepsekemei's magic.

The goddess cut through the curtain of billowing sand and stepped forward with flat feet. Whether it was reflexively or deliberately, her eyes were closed.

Marguerite went through three trees to alternate like a pinball—going from facing the enemy to circling behind her with her rapier at the ready to thrust at the white flash barely visible behind her golden hair, her undefended neck—then twisted her body away the moment before she could hit to dodge the slice of an ax.

The goddess kept her feet flat on the ground, only turning her upper body the other direction to face Marguerite. It was astonishing flexibility, even for a magical girl. From that extremely unnatural stance, bent backward until she was horizontal, she swung her axes at Marguerite.

In the course of the swing, the ax blades transformed, growing one, two sizes bigger, enabling the wielder to come in range without moving her feet. Marguerite never took her eye off the enemy. She smacked the ground with her left hand, using her cape to leap, roll, and dodge the fearsome mass of destruction.

Dark clouds in the sky caught her eye, and she saw Tepsekemei up above. She was blowing air into her hands and compressing it to fire it continuously like a machine gun—you could call it bullets of air.

The goddess's ax swiped aside the continuous fire of air bullets from above as she turned at the waist in the opposite direction, keeping her left hand pointed at Tepsekemei and her right pointed at Marguerite as she slowly drew up her body. The giant axes were held still at the same angle as before her attack. There wasn't enough opening to attack even in that lazy movement. But though her stance was perfect, the way she moved was clumsy. When both attacking and defending, she avoided using her legs as much as possible; she was generally flat-footed.

Marguerite didn't wait to act. She leaped far enough away that even slices from the enlarged axes couldn't reach, hooking her fingers on tree branches and cracks in bark to clamber up a tree. The goddess stepped forward to attack, slicing at all the nearby trees, but Marguerite had already leaped branch to branch to escape behind her. While in motion, she stripped the bark from trees around, lopping off their branches with swipes of her rapier.

With wood chips raining down around her, the enemy opened her eyes. She was smiling vacantly.

"Was it the gold ax you dropped?" she asked as she repelled air bullets with her ax. She wielded the giant battle-ax with the effort of manipulating a butter knife—and with even greater speed.

Tepsekemei's bullets were made of air, so they had no color. Innumerable colorless and transparent bullets that were literally fast as the wind were flying toward the goddess. They could be detected only by their sound, but the goddess wasn't struggling at all to block them with her ax.

"Or is it the silver ax?" the goddess asked.

Tepsekemei cocked her head. She'd shrunk to one-third her size, but she still looked like her original lamp-genie form. The goddess readied her axes, the rough weapons clashing with her vacant smile. The trees that had been flung into the sky fell one after another to bound off the ground. Even as Marguerite sliced at the broken trees that descended upon her head and shoulders, she never took her eyes off the goddess.

The first attack they'd received in their encounter with her had been a response to an attack from Tepsekemei. The attack had been sudden, with no tells or preemptive motion, and completely unlike the intense lethal aura everyone had felt that time at the main building.

Marguerite could no longer hear footsteps or cries from Mana or 7753. Had they safely escaped, or were they in a state where they couldn't move or talk? There was nothing for it but to pray it was the former. As for Shepherdspie—she hadn't even had enough time to look at him, let alone protect him. She decided to leave regrets about how they could have secured his safety if they had acted first until later—she wouldn't think about it now.

A tree trunk big enough to wrap your arms around fell between Marguerite and the goddess, sending up mud. Dark-brown dirt splattered dots over the goddess's white costume.

Her right ax went red-hot, its outline turning to wavering flame. The left ax, aside from its handle, turned into a pale yellow solid covered in cracks. The blowing of the wind alone caused the substance to scatter as powder. It seemed too fragile to use as an ax. It looked like some kind of crystal, but Marguerite couldn't know for sure from a glance.

The goddess swung the yellow ax. It was too far. She wouldn't reach. But Marguerite's body reacted before her mind did, instantly leaping to the side. Intense flame blazed up from the goddess's position to lick as far away as where Marguerite had just been.

The goddess repelled the air bullets being fired at her from the opposite direction with her red-hot ax while also kicking dirt over to where Marguerite jumped. Marguerite stepped on a round tree trunk that had fallen to the ground to roll along. It was one of those that she had stripped of its bark and branches. Marguerite's magic of "bending things that are straight" had a fairly strict definition of "straight." In order to use it on natural things like trees, she had to process them somewhat. She used her magic to bend the tree that she'd processed to make "straight," using the recoil to leap upward and grab a tree branch. When she threw the rock she held in her off hand, the goddess avoided it with just a tilt of her head.

Marguerite replayed in her head the goddess's attack just then. She had changed the matter of the ax into a flammable substance, then ignited it with a flame ax and swung it at her. If Marguerite got hit by that fire, she was highly likely to become a ball of flames. The grass and broken trees all around flickered with persistent flames. Marguerite didn't know enough to say what that substance was, but it would be best to avoid touching it.

Odds are her magic is to transform her axes.

That was also how her attack had divided Tepsekemei's gaseous body. You could never do that with an ax that was just strong, no matter how you sliced at her—but if she was to attack using a material that would change the quality of a gas, then even Tepsekemei, who was literally formless, wouldn't be unscathed.

The goddess had unparalleled physical abilities, highly adaptable weapons, forceful strikes, but it was unclear if she had any intellect, and though she looked like she had to be a magical girl, she really didn't seem like one. A variety of elements came together to make up the enemy before them.

She seems imbalanced.

She used her magic with speed and accuracy. She was also highly adaptable to the situation. However, despite mastery of her magic, her use of her body was extremely rough. Chelsea also moved in a way that didn't make sense, but what was different about the goddess was that she seemed like she wasn't used to moving in the first place.

Marguerite jumped off a branch and landed, stripping off branches and bark as she wove between trees without slowing down at all to get away from the enemy. The swipe that came after her from behind sliced away all the trees around, and the earth with it. Marguerite leaped.

She jumped off the tree that came flying toward her, and the next tree she jumped to—one she'd pruned earlier—she broke with her magic to make it a launchpad that flung her in the other direction to leap toward the enemy. She read the enemy's movements from her muscle, bone, and skin. Twisting around in mid-air, Marguerite avoided a turn-around sweep from the goddess that would certainly have killed her if it hit—though it damaged the shoulder of her costume. Marguerite's surprise attack using her magic threw the enemy's movements a bit off-kilter, making them deviate slightly. It was a very small shift. Her unassailable stance had changed so minutely, you wouldn't be able to tell at a glance, but the angle of the blades had changed, with a large opening to her body.

Marguerite rolled on the ground and reached attack range on her knees. Her brain was screaming danger signals as her body's sense of time grew heavier. This feeling had once been very familiar to her. She touched the fallen tree the enemy was stepping on with her toe and cast her magic on it. The pruned log twisted toward the goddess, striking into her arm to break off and smash to splinters.

Just like a thief picking a lock, Marguerite pushed the deviation of the goddess's movements. Tepsekemei shot air bullets, and after a slight delay to time it right, Marguerite stepped forward again. The axes had opened even further. It was a chink in her defense. In a low stance with one knee on the ground and stepping in with the other, Marguerite thrust her rapier up from below. The godly quick thrust that even the fiercest of the Inspection Department had called "impossible to defend against" was easily blocked by an ax. It wasn't that the goddess had done anything with her magic. The goddess's reflexes were faster than Marguerite had anticipated, that was all.

Marguerite's body temperature shot up, while her head cooled down instead. The right ax transmuted into a sticky substance like birdlime and caught her rapier.

Now.

The sudden evasive movement had thrown the goddess even further off-kilter. Her body's axis was off-kilter, too. The deviation that had developed had been reborn as the ultimate opportunity. Marguerite let go of her weapon, matching her breathing with a leap on her knees to come closer.

For the first time, the goddess's smile faltered. It was too close for her to swing her axes. For a span that wasn't even half of a half of a half of an instant, she hesitated, and Marguerite's fingers touched the handle of the left ax.

The ax handle was a straight stick of metal. In other words, she could bend it with her magic. Like a spring mousetrap, the blade snapped up to smack the enemy's body. A very light sound struck Marguerite's ears. Without her realizing, the blade of the ax had been turned into a fluffy, cottony material that wouldn't hurt anyone.

Before she could even confirm the goddess's next move, Marguerite leaped. She just had to move, or she would die. The goddess swept up a gust with a kick that Marguerite dodged, and then she avoided the goddess's heel when she raised up her leg to slam it down. Then Marguerite got an assist. The goddess swiped away

Tepsekemei's air bullets, which Marguerite matched to try to back-step away. While blocking the air bullets, the goddess swung a sharp short hook, which Marguerite tried to push aside with the back of her right hand, but she failed to divert its full force, and the fist skimmed her shoulder. While backing away, Marguerite cart-wheeled into a tree, touched it with a hand to bend it, and with the recoil, she leaped to the right, landing on another tree to bend that as well and leap to the left.

While fleeing, Marguerite put one hand on her right shoulder and scooped thick fluid. The goddess had gouged into her flesh. There was damage to the bone, as well. It hadn't been dislocated—it had been shattered. She couldn't move her right arm.

The goddess blasted away branches and leaves as she tossed Marguerite's rapier behind her. She looked curiously at the handle of her ax, bent at a right angle, then touched her thumb to the bent part and squeezed it firmly. It left it a little warped, but it mostly returned to how it was before.

Marguerite mentally clicked her tongue. The moment the ax blade had connected, the goddess had turned the blade from metal into cotton to keep it from hurting herself at all. The bending from Marguerite's magic to "bend straight objects" couldn't be reacted to on reflex, not by any magical girls Marguerite knew. Even Marguerite, who used it herself, managed to use it by reading ahead of the magic.

Did I show her too much of my magic running up to that? No, if I hadn't used it that much, it would have been over long before then.

Marguerite focused on evasion. She emerged from the woods into a rocky area. The whole view was filled with the sound of the waves crashing and receding and the clinging smell of salt. The enemy had clumsy footwork. It would hurt to lose the trees, since Marguerite could use them as footing, but it was more worth it to force the enemy to move to a rocky area.

Marguerite turned to face the other direction, switching to running backward, facing her pursuer. She did a little hop and jumped to the side, fluttering her cape as she dodged, dodged,

dodged. It was like a full-speed sprint over a tightrope. One wrong step and she would die, but she had capable backup. Tepsekemei continued to trail them from a fixed distance behind where the enemy attacks wouldn't reach, harassing her with long-range fire. Even if she couldn't do damage, Marguerite was thankful just for the distraction that decreased the goddess's number of moves.

Marguerite jumped atop a rock, feinting occasionally to make it look like she was going to attack as she backed up along the coastline.

Stepping right to left, she crouched down and stopped. The goddess swung her ax up over her head. The goddess hadn't pulled this move before, but Marguerite wasn't rattled. Before the enemy's arm could move, Marguerite dropped to her right knee and rolled forward at a diagonal to dodge the throw. The ax whipped toward her in a rapid vertical spin, and Marguerite rose up to race toward the goddess. Perhaps out of impatience, the goddess had chosen to throw away her weapon.

The goddess shuffled her feet to move around the rocky area like she was matching Marguerite's movements, and Marguerite responded by throwing in small feints as she came closer. The goddess didn't have the defensive technique to respond instantly to Marguerite's feints when her left hand was empty. Marguerite twisted her wrist to thrust a spear hand into the slight opening in her guard. The goddess's remaining ax turned into a black, heavy, and dull-looking metal. But Marguerite would finish this before she could swing it.

Marguerite's lips twisted slightly. There was some blackish sand stuck to the ax. Though it wasn't wet, it was covering the surface of the ax in an unnatural way.

"Dodge!"

Before Marguerite could digest that call from Tepsekemei and the information she'd gained with her eyes, she rolled to the right, and a beat later came the sound of a blast of wind. It had missed her by a hair. Her feather decoration, sliced off by the shock wave of the slice, danced in pieces in the air, and Marguerite scattered shattered stones as she ungracefully rolled over the rocky ground. The sound of metal hitting metal and an impact rattled to her through the rock. The black ax had caught the iron-colored ax.

Magnetism!

The goddess had turned the iron ax into the shape of a boomerang and thrown it, then drawn it back with the magnetism of her other ax. So this was how she'd been able to wrench Maiya's magic steel stick from her grasp.

Without waiting for Marguerite to get up, the goddess bent over. It was a strange gesture that she hadn't displayed before. She made the ax in her right hand red-hot and on fire and changed the left ax to white crystal. Aside from the stance, Marguerite had seen this pattern before. It was the explosive attack that she'd used earlier. While focusing on the tells, Marguerite backstepped away. The goddess paid no mind to Marguerite, lifting her chin to look up at the sky. Tepsekemei's air bullets hit the goddess's shoulder, ripping her toga. The second and third hit her chest and head, making her hair bounce.

Marguerite readied herself in a sideways stance, right hand forward. The goddess didn't defend herself, continuing to take the air bullets. Marguerite didn't even have time to wonder why before there was an explosion. The brilliant light hit for only an instant, but it blinded her. She leaped back, but by the time she was ready to attack, the enemy was gone. Marguerite looked up. A call started leaking out from deep in her throat, and she clenched her teeth to smother it. The goddess was doing something unbelievable.

Flashes and blast sounds were generated in continuous succession, launching the goddess with each burst. She used her fuel and fire to generate continuous explosions, taking the blast wave on her body and toga to jet through the air in controlled flight. Her once-white costume was dirtied with soot, and her cheeks and forehead were similarly dirtied. But the smile remained on her face. Tepsekemei showered her with blades of air, but the ax of fire cut them in half.

Marguerite was aware she was being kept out of this fight.

The goddess was so resilient that she could fly with a blast wind. Throwing rocks at her from below didn't seem like it would do any damage. And seeing how she was taking the air bullets, they couldn't even make the enemy flinch.

Marguerite pulled out the half a grayfruit that she'd been holding on to as reserve and tossed it in her mouth. She was frustrated at herself for just refueling, but still, all she could do on the ground was yell. "Tepsekemei! Come down!"

Marguerite frowned. Something was strange. Her voice wasn't carrying well. The explosions were also weirdly muffled. Marguerite glared at the goddess racing through the sky above. This situation was familiar to her. It was the magic stone that Mana had also used. Just like that had kept whispered conversations from getting out, this was shutting out the sound of the battle, making it so she couldn't hear. Now that she was this far away, Marguerite also realized nobody outside of the battle would notice it.

The explosions kept coming in successive blasts. Smoke blocked out the night sky, blotting the fading moon entirely from view. Even if Tepsekemei was the better flier, poor visibility was the enemy's forte.

"Tepsekemei! Come here!" Marguerite yelled out. There was an intense gust of wind, and the smoke screen was scattered.

Tepsekemei was divided into two bodies, one of which took a direct hit from an ax to be scattered, while the other descended rapidly. Then the ax shone crimson. The goddess threw the shining ax at Tepsekemei, and it shone even brighter, weakening for a moment as if it were condensing, and before Marguerite could confirm the outcome, she spun around and fled. There was a burst of light more intense than any of the earlier ones, and even facing away from it, Marguerite's eyes were dazzled.

She heard what sounded like both a girl's dying scream and a gust of wind before they immediately vanished. She couldn't sense Tepsekemei anymore.

Marguerite wasn't even able to consider if Tepsekemei was okay. The racing footsteps coming after her from behind captured her ears, and when she turned around, she was shocked to see the goddess's feet were not flat-footed like they had been only moments before. She was running the way you learned in the Inspection Department, the particular way of a magical girl factoring in body weight.

She…copied me…?

She was far faster than before, when she'd been awkwardly thumping around on her feet. The goddess struck from behind, and Marguerite ducked low to evade it but never slowed in her flight. The goddess was managing to run simply from imitating her. The enemy had learned.

◇ **Nephilia**

Nephilia had heard the mage called Sataborn was an eccentric. He'd never catered to political powers or served any particular individual, continuing to maintain his childlike motivation of doing it because he wanted to and making it because he wanted to until his death, until in the end he had died in an experiment. It was probably partly because they felt like they couldn't speak ill of the dead, but when talking about Sataborn, his acquaintances had seemed somehow envious.

But Agri was the exception. She had to have suffered a lot, having a man who would prioritize research over everything else as her father.

Touta Magaoka was also a relative, but it seemed that he had no particular feelings about it, and certainly no twisted emotions like Agri. He looked like the kind of elementary schooler you might see anywhere. But nevertheless, it seemed he'd inherited the rebellious spirit. Nephilia remembered how Touta had desperately showed her his conversational skills and snickered. Maybe he would have made a good heir if he'd had magical talent, too, but things didn't work out so easily. Agri, who had no intention at all of being a researcher, had been blessed with magical talent.

Nephilia thought that relatives should get along, but it didn't seem like it would happen with those two. Agri would try to use Touta, and Marguerite wouldn't stand idly by if that happened. It might be interesting to place Shepherdspie in between them as a buffer to keep that from happening, then roll Sataborn's estate or whatever among the three relatives and watch it snowball.

Nephilia came to a stop. Even letting the wings of her imagination fly and pondering on and on about her future as she walked, she wouldn't lose focus. Keeping a watchful eye around—the treetops and above included—she crouched down, avoiding the densely crawling tree roots to put her palm to the earth.

The ground was shuddering. Not from an earthquake. Something that would make the earth shudder was happening somewhere. She felt that it wasn't far away. But if it was close, she should be able to hear it. Only the very natural sounds of the forest in early morning reached Nephilia's ears: the buzzing of insects returning to their nests, the rustling of leaves, the drip of morning dew, and the whoosh of the wind gusting past.

Was there digging going on underground? Or was someone muting the sound of a battle? Whatever it was, for Agri, this was an irregular occurrence. More surprises made things more fun, but when you were wandering around the island with contracts like Nephilia right now, it was not the time for fun.

Reporting this to Agri was more important than the contracts, so Nephilia was about to get up again when she heard a branch break. It wasn't the sound of a branch falling on its own but the sound of it being snapped under a foot. She put her hand on the ground. Walking. And slowly, too. It seemed like they were dragging a leg. Were they injured?

Combining the information they had obtained from Navi Ru with the information she had now, she had a decent grasp of what was where on the island. Even just signs of someone having been somewhere were fairly valuable. Since everyone was operating cautiously, not many of them would be moving to new positions.

Nephilia stood up and ran. She wasn't going to let them get away. After a ten-second run through the forest at magical-girl speed, she plunged through a thicket and came out to find a girl. She was different from the last time Nephilia had seen her. Her glasses and scarf were gone; her uniform was cut, ripped, and frayed here and there; she'd lost one of her shoes and walked in a dirty sock; and she was using a long, pointed branch with the end shaved like a spear to walk. Dark-red fluid freshly marked her cheek, the point of the stick, and her skirt. It spoke vividly of what an intense struggle she'd been in.

Clantail—her human form—raised the spear to her waist, and once she saw it was Nephilia, she lowered the point in relief. She had to be frightened. She possessed the skill to cover fear with something else, but she still hadn't forgotten fear.

"Where are the others…?" the girl asked.

"Right now…we're separated…" Nephilia leaned her scythe against a nearby tree and spread her hands, showing her palms.

Clantail. Even among "Cranberry's children," the group who all had combat skills and experience killing, she was a cut above. As proof, even when Keek had gathered the children to reexamine them, Clantail had not dropped out of the running and had returned alive.

The incident where a magical girl called Keek had defied the Magical Kingdom and then been purged by the Magical-Girl Hunter was fairly well-known, but the details of the incident hadn't been made public. Nobody knew that Clantail had gotten caught up in it, aside from those involved. Nephilia only knew because she'd been hired to investigate the victims during the incident. In order to find out what had happened during Keek's scandal, Nephilia had gone around to the homes of the "children"—they'd had comparatively moderate deaths of experiencing heart attacks in their homes—to stroke their bodies or their cremated remains, going all the way back to pick up their voices from the start of the game. Though it had taken an incredible amount of time and effort, it had been worth it.

Nephilia had been personally interested in the incident, too. She was so interested that in order to learn if what the magical girl Pechka had said was true—that Clantail's human and animal halves were different temperatures—she'd asked to pet Clantail's body. She'd kept the reason for that private, though.

"Why? Why would everyone split up?" the girl asked.

"Maiya's killer...attacked..."

"No way... And Ragi...?"

"...Probably...safe... No...fight..." Nephilia pulled out a contract. "Here..."

These had originally been made for mages to make contracts with other mages, but it should be more or less okay between two magical girls, too. Since it wasn't like they were outside of the knowledge of the Magical Kingdom. But this was uncommon, so if anyone found out, they might complain about it, but Clantail was worth binding in a contract, even if it meant going through those hassles. Clantail had what Agri sought: money.

She was wearing a school uniform with no accessories. Everything on her was just part of her uniform, and she also had no makeup. It didn't look like she lived a fancy life, and in fact she gave you the sense that she was scrupulous, with her feet on the ground. It didn't look like she'd thrown away all the cash she'd won in the Keek reexamination.

Nephilia remembered the final words of Nokko, the magical girl who had been made to play the role of the Evil King. She had wished for the prize to be divided into equal parts before killing herself. When Nephilia had touched the body of that little girl gone cold, had the anger she felt then been righteous indignation? She had the emotional thought that perhaps Nokko's magic had maintained its effects even after her death, and it put a strained smile on her face.

Clantail had won a large sum of money. If she hadn't wasted it, then she would have a savings account too large for her age, or personal assets, or real estate.

Nephilia explained the contract with her own sort of sincerity. Being a magical girl changed her sense of time, compared to when she was human, and made her try to talk faster, so she more often stuttered to a halt or went hoarse. She stammered in a way that was difficult to hear. It would improve a bit if she concentrated and tried to move her tongue precisely, but she was impatient right now. While restraining her tendency to race on and on, she put the utmost effort into talking. But the further along she got, the more the girl's expression grew severe, and her caution turned to hostility.

In her mind, Nephilia closed her eyes and looked up at the sky. What Agri was trying to do, what she wanted to do, her sense of values, was not compatible with good people. Touta and this girl might both see her as a tough person to negotiate with, but they would not see her as a reliable ally. It was sad, but there was nothing to be done about it. Attempting to secure profit for yourself even when it was dangerous would inevitably make people hate you. That was the same in any world. Nephilia finished her explanation for the most part and waited for the girl's response.

Unlike Touta, she took no time to answer, and neither did she demand an extra. She just asked, "Do you know where Ragi is?"

"No..." Nephilia massaged her shoulder with her right hand. While she was impressed that the girl was so dedicated as to be worried about her employer at this point, Nephilia realized this didn't please her. Maybe her answer to the question if Ragi was safe came out a bit muffled. "More importantly..."

"I understand."

If that was decided, that made things faster.

When Nephilia proposed the exchange of thirty million yen in cash for ten grayfruit, the girl acquiesced easily. Nephilia saw that as overcharging her and had assumed they would negotiate to lower the price, but it seemed the other party had no such intentions. Nephilia did a basic ceremony through the contract, then dropped the promised fruit into the girl's hands. As the girl was making to pick up the grayfruit that had spilled from her grasp, Nephilia turned away from her. Since they had made a contract, it was no longer dangerous to turn her back to her.

Once she transformed into Clantail, she would be too strong

for Nephilia to manage alone. If Clantail meant to capture her, she could do so, and if she wanted to kill her, Nephilia would die. But there was a clause in the contract that prevented that. Clantail would be unable to attack Nephilia, Agri, or Ren-Ren.

Nephilia was about to walk right off but then stopped. She couldn't articulate her feelings properly, but she felt uneasy. Something was keeping her from parting ways like this. She was going to say something. But what?

Still without having found the answer, she turned back. "Um..."

"What is it?"

"Those fruit...now...use...faster...pace...care..."

"Understood. I will use them with care."

Was this what I wanted to say? she asked herself. She heard the answer from somewhere: no. Nephilia thrust her scythe into the ground, leaned against it, and asked the girl, "You...looking?"

The girl didn't answer. She wasn't looking any less wary. She wasn't at all hiding that she was watching to see how Nephilia would act as she looked back at her. It was as if she'd already forgotten that she'd let Nephilia pet her back.

"At...building...were talking...about Keek..."

Clantail's tail swished. There was no change in her expression. But she didn't say, *"Now's not the time to be talking about that."* She was waiting for Nephilia to speak.

"Ragi...Management Department...head..." Nephilia's feelings were pulling a little too far ahead of her. She slowed down. "During Keek's reexamination...if Ragi...your employer...had given Snow White Keek's information earlier...the exam would have ended faster."

The girl's expression didn't change, but her eyelids twitched just once. It was like a spasm, but for the slightest instant, and was over in less than a second.

Nephilia turned around and left. She didn't really know what she had wanted to do in the end. It would sound plausible if she made it so that she'd tried to draw Clantail's interest, that she'd been jealous that all she was thinking about was Ragi. But Clantail wasn't a nasty person at all. She wasn't Nephilia's type.

Nephilia thought about Keek's exam one more time. Pechka's words rose in her mind, and she tried to erase them with her usual laugh, but it wouldn't come out of her throat.

◇ Ragi Zwe Nento

Ragi didn't have the time, the information, or the facilities to deepen his knowledge about the grayfruit. In other words, he had nothing, but if you were speaking about the fruit it seemed the grayfruit had been based on, he knew enough that he could snobbishly lecture a student on them. Sataborn had been a man of pleasure who lived for his hobbies, but he'd been different from the lot who would pose at sophistication through pointless modifications. The temperature of this island as well as the humidity matched the cultivation conditions of the base fruit. If the cultivation conditions were the same or close to the original, there should be thick roots growing near a water source.

It wasn't like there weren't any spells for searching for water sources. If you got yourself a couple of formal dowsing rods, then you could find water without an incantation. Ragi had to avoid using magic as much as possible right now. He had recast the camouflage spell as well as the night-vision spell since he'd begun walking. He had to avoid waste. If it was simply finding water, he should just recall the overall layout of the island. There had been a pond in the center. He remembered there was a river flowing from there.

Soon after Ragi set off, he found a little rivulet and followed it upstream. He wasn't going to go into the flow. He walked alongside the river. He managed to avoid the places where it meandered, pushing the reeds aside with his staff to proceed, but on the way, he reached a cliff three times his own height and came to a halt. It would be exaggerating to call the cliff sheer, but it was too steep for him to cross casually. A waterfall flowed over it, wetting the end of his nose with its spray, and Ragi took a step backward. Having backed up so completely automatically made him angry, and now he definitely couldn't take a detour.

He temporarily undid the camouflage and night-vision spells and crossed over the waterfall in a single bound. He waffled a bit but chose not to recast the spells. The eastern sky was already growing pale. The night-vision spell was unnecessary now, and in the light, that basic camouflage spell would have no effect at all. Any spells of dubious merit would be omitted wherever possible.

There was no maintained path along the edge of the river, and Ragi had to watch out for even the smallest pebble as he walked. This forced him to look at the ground while walking, and so he was too late to notice the shadows that approached from behind.

"Oh, that's him! There he is!"

"Um, pardon me."

Ragi turned around to see two girls scattering grass as they approached, and more bitterness welled within him. Maybe it was just indignation at his own negligence for having been frightened, thinking it was the enemy, but as Ragi saw it, anger was anger, no matter where it came from.

"What in the blazes are you two doing?" he demanded.

Dreamy☆Chelsea was one of the magical girls employed by Shepherdspie. Ragi recalled that when he'd scolded Shepherdspie for being such a good-for-nothing, she had snapped at him like a wolverine whose territory had been invaded. Ragi would never forget a magical girl who went against him.

The other one was Pastel Mary. She had also been hired by Shepherdspie. She was the one who had brought him his invitation to this island. He had the feeling she'd also pulled something outrageous, but his memories in that area were vague, and he didn't recall. Even Ragi wasn't going to scold someone based on vague memories.

It wasn't at all strange to see those two were paired up. They had to be operating under Shepherdspie's orders. Shepherdspie was more trustworthy than Navi Ru or his lackey—so Ragi would have said, but Shepherdspie wasn't reliable enough for that. At least the man had no malice. His utter lack of ambition was disappointing, but that also meant that he wouldn't set you up or betray you. A mage who was satisfied with his own circumstances would not take needless risks.

"We were looking for you, Gramps."

There was no need to criticize Chelsea for her rudeness at this point. Or rather, he'd get nowhere if he pointed out every single thing. Worst case, if she snapped at him, then she'd be more trouble than a cougar in heat. The current situation was headed straight for disaster. He would be generous about her attitude and whatnot and let that go.

"What do you mean, looking for me?" Ragi asked.

But before he could continue with, *"Was Shepherdspie also trying to find the others?"* Chelsea held a piece of paper out to him. She smiled brightly, while Mary's eyebrows descended in an expression of worry. While he felt something didn't quite make sense about their manner, he accepted the piece of paper and ran his eyes over it.

As he read along, deep wrinkles carved in his brow, the corners of his eyes rose up, and his back teeth creaked. "What…is this?"

"You don't understand?" said Chelsea. "You don't understand, huh. Chelsea doesn't understand what's written there, either. See, that's a contract."

"You're telling me this is a contract?"

"That's what I just said. It's not like you don't get what that means, right?" The way Chelsea was puffing her chest out arrogantly poured oil on Ragi's anger, making it a big, unstoppable fire that blazed inside his heart.

"You lowlife!" Ragi tried to rip it in rage, but the strength of an old mage couldn't affect the contract at all, and it ended with him stretching it out and making his arms shake. Unable to vent his anger that way, it turned to words that spilled out of his mouth. "That infernal fool Shepherdspie! What in the name is he doing at a time like this?!"

Mary was frightened and hid behind Chelsea, while Chelsea looked confused as she pouted. "Why are you angry at Mr. Pie?"

"How could I not be angry at that imbecile for showing me

a sleazy, predatory contract and displaying piss-poor judgment about the situation?! Just what is that Shepherdspie thinking?!"

"Who knows. I have no idea about him."

"...Huh?" Ragi uncrumpled the contract he'd been crushing in his fists and checked it again. The name on the contract was not Shepherdspie. It was Agri. It recognized as a payment of grayfruit, Ragi would pay in magic gems. Ragi read over it three times, and now sure he was not mistaken, Ragi's anger exploded. "What is the meaning of this?! Why are you two blithering idiots working for Sataborn's daughter?!"

"You've got it wrong; that's not what's going on at all. Dreamy☆Chelsea is working for her darling May-May. Chelsea is a magical girl who lives for love." With Chelsea shoving her forward, Mary's expression suddenly twisted in fear, and she tried to hide behind the other girl, but Chelsea's strength prevented her. Mary tried to get away from her position right in front of Ragi, but no matter how she struggled and struggled, she couldn't escape and hide.

Ragi's anger was not contained or quieted, but this baffling situation and Chelsea's odd behavior confused him. She had been a strange girl to begin with, but had she ever been the kind of wild eccentric to spew this much incomprehensible rubbish? It was also strange that she was walking around with contracts not for Shepherdspie but for Agri. None of it made sense.

Has she been controlled?

Rather than a lazy lout with plenty of funds to spare, Agri, being the daughter of a mistress, would have a reason to desire property. The fact that it was no place to be doing that in a situation where their lives were on the line, caught on an island on the brink of disaster, was no issue. The people who did that would do it anywhere.

He could use a spell to restore the balance of the mind. But Chelsea or Mary would probably subdue him before he could finish the chant. That was how magical girls were. Right now, Ragi did not have his self-made fortress, otherwise known as the head office of the Management Department.

Ragi digested his own powerlessness but was not crushed by it, instead using it to fuel his anger. Let the vulgar-minded fools do what they wanted. He didn't have the time to get mixed up with them.

Ragi was too busy to chat with two girls who were being controlled. And that contract was beyond out of the question. He took another bite of the grayfruit and turned upstream again. That was where he had to go.

When Ragi wouldn't talk to him, Chelsea dogged him. "Hey, hey, what's wrong?"

He ignored her.

"Don't you want grayfruit? They're important, you know?"

He wasn't even listening.

Chelsea must have realized that he wasn't going to engage with her, as she started using physical tactics to beg. She touched Ragi's robe and hat, squarely growing his irritation with the most obnoxious behavior possible. Ragi wasn't just on the verge of exploding; he was exploding the whole time he was walking, but he sucked it up. When she snatched away his hat, he let it go, and when she grabbed his robe and ripped it, he let that go, too, moving onward with the thought that he had to go upstream, and then he came to a halt. His feet hadn't stopped because of Chelsea's meddling. His way was blocked by tree trunks that were lying there diagonally as if they'd been cut by a sharp blade. These were firm-looking trunks about as thick as Ragi's torso, and they hadn't been sawed down but severed with one stroke. Only a magical girl could do that.

And beyond that was even worse. Trees uprooted; grass that was overturned, earth and all; fissures running through rock face; all of it the work of magical girls. Mary voiced a little shriek, and Chelsea was saying baseless nonsense: "Don't worry—I'll protect you."

Ragi hesitated a moment. While he was of two minds about it, he opened his mouth. "You two fools…weren't the ones to do this?"

"No way."

He wasn't sure if he should believe that, but there was no

reason for them to lie. Standing there, he gazed upon the aftermath of destruction and shook his head. There was no point in standing around here. Ragi started walking again, and Chelsea and Mary followed him like before.

Maybe that was actually a good thing. If the one who had destroyed the forest was ahead, it would be better to have two magical girls there with him rather than being alone. Even if they were being mind-controlled, if there was a clear enemy, the two girls would probably go to them.

The party—though it was extremely unintended on Ragi's part, they had wound up becoming a party through gradual erosion—stepped over the destruction and made their way along. Before long, they crossed over a small hill to finally look down upon the source of the river: the pond in the center of the island.

"Huh?" Ahead of where Chelsea pointed, you could see a pair of feet. There was someone lying at the edge of the pond. Everything but the feet was hidden by the thick grasses and couldn't be seen.

Ragi didn't run toward it, approaching with caution to his surroundings, but Chelsea had no such reservation or consideration as she rushed out to instantly reach the fallen someone.

"Reckless girl," Ragi cursed as he followed her, Mary trailing behind with fearful steps.

Coming to peer in from behind where Chelsea looked down, Ragi immediately turned his face away. "Horrendous…"

You could only barely tell that it was a mage in a robe. Their upper body was crushed, with nothing decent left. Blood was flowing—or it would be better to say it had splattered. Only the pitiful lower half remained. So then Maiya was not the only casualty.

"Why?" Her voice was trembling. It was Chelsea. Her shoulders were trembling, too.

"Mr. Shepherdspie!" Mary cried, and Ragi realized who it was. Ragi had been so rattled, he'd completely forgotten that only one mage on this island had a frame like his.

Chelsea's trembling gradually became more violent. Mary

tried to throw herself on the body, but on the way, she stumbled and fell in the mud. Chelsea held her head in her hands. A moan slipped from her lips. "Why...how...? Mr. Pie..."

Ragi struck the muddy earth with his right heel. His anger had now reached an utterly hopeless level.

CHAPTER 10
EVERYTHING IS A QUAGMIRE

◇ **Miss Marguerite**

There was no time for indecision. She didn't have the time to stop and think. With Tepsekemei gone, the breadth of her strategy was suddenly narrower. Holding the enemy back with a continuous fire of projectiles, circling around in the area for a pincer attack, sending a message to the others about the danger—any other such options were lost, and now Marguerite was running with no plan in mind, avoiding attacks. The enemy was chasing her at ten yards. And the goddess wasn't just in pursuit. Even from this distance, she was constantly attacking.

The goddess was swinging her axes as she ran. These were not threats or an expression of frustration. Her slices ripped open the rock face of the ground, blasting away broken rock that fired like bullets toward Marguerite. If they hit, they would break the bones and crush the flesh of even a magical girl.

Marguerite threw herself to the ground to avoid the rock

shrapnel, continuing to run without slowing. She drew herself up very gradually out of her super-low crouch, drawing the stone shards that came flying out once more toward her—this time the shrapnel came at a low trajectory—and she summoned her rapier in her palm. The rapier was part of her costume, so she could reuse it. While running, she turned back and swiped her rapier, clasped in her left hand, in every direction to redirect the shards, sharply repelling some of them to fly back toward the goddess. The goddess ignored the flying rocks, unflinchingly charging forward whether they hit her shoulders or forehead. They didn't leave any wounds on her—they didn't leave a single mark.

Even while running backward, Marguerite never slowed down. She would have liked to brag that this was the fruit of her training, but she already understood that it was dangerous to show off repeatedly to this enemy. The goddess was digging into the rock with both her axes, sending it flying into the air as she ran, but Marguerite hadn't managed to put much distance between the two of them. She'd just turned ten yards into thirteen. And the way the goddess ran was different from her earlier, awkward steps. She was running like Marguerite, shifting her body weight over and over to keep Marguerite from getting farther away. Marguerite fluttered her cape, concealing herself from the enemy for an instant to pull out two-inch-long metal skewers from the inner lining of her cape. She bent the metal skewers with her magic, processing them into hooks.

The goddess's right arm drew back.

It's coming.

Her ax shattered a rock, sending shards flying. Marguerite alternated between knocking them away with her rapier and evading them, and she repelled a few back at her opponent. She used that as cover to hold her rapier in her mouth and bend it as far as possible, hooking the bent metal skewers over the tip to flick them and send them flying. She was using it like an old-fashioned catapult. This move was born from the pain of a magical girl who had no long-range weapons—it was basically a party trick to someone who did have powerful projectiles. But even a move like a party trick could be useful. She flicked the metal hook so it flew right behind the last rock shard she'd shot back and, by shooting it faster than the rock shard, made it so they would hit at almost the same instant. The hook coming right behind the shard made it hard to see, and it was aiming right for the enemy's eyeball.

The goddess didn't dodge the rock fragments. She let them hit her, taking the impact on skin and bone. A few of the rocks shattered, the last one hitting her forehead, and then when the metal skewer made to penetrate her eyeball not even an instant later, it was swiped aside by the swinging of her golden hair, its wind alone blowing the hook away.

She avoided it, huh.

Marguerite wouldn't go so far as to say she'd already taken that into account, but considering the monster reflexes of her pursuer, it wasn't like it had been unforeseen. If she could avoid it, then it wasn't as if that evasion offered no benefit to Marguerite. It was better for the goddess to focus on distractions rather than running straight after her. This would help her get farther away.

The distance between the two of them grew to fifty feet. Marguerite gradually curved the direction of her flight to the right. To the left was the ocean, while on the right was the expanse of forest. Her plan to fight in the open rocky area had failed hopelessly, and she was at an impasse. Her enemy was a goddess of the spring who had come out from the water, so if they fought in the ocean, it was sure to be checkmate this time. It was preferable to run into the forest. Now that she'd lost Tepsekemei, the situation was worse than when they'd been running around the forest before, but there was also the plus of having experienced what the opponent was capable of and what they did. She had also learned that it would be difficult to alert others of their presence via sound. So going into the forest would leave more evidence of their fight, which would call more attention to them.

This logic was nothing but making excuses and lying to herself, but that which is magical girl, Marguerite knew, had to be positive, or everything would fall apart.

The goddess's ax shone red. Trying to end this battle before Marguerite could run into the forest was one of the possible strategies Marguerite had anticipated, but she wasn't happy her prediction was correct.

The ax propellant and the high temperature combined to make an explosion. The blast made the goddess fly along at a horizontal, jetting toward her in one burst. Marguerite thrust the rapier in her left hand into the rock.

Dodging the explosion-accelerated slash once she saw the goddess swinging would be largely a gamble. The goddess's attack range was beyond Marguerite's ability to visually estimate, her movements had hardly any tells at all, and most of all, she was insanely fast. But if Marguerite drew her sword to try to block, she would be completely crushed, blade and all. If she wasn't going to dodge or block, there was nothing for it but to move before the attack came.

Stepping up onto the rapier she'd thrust into the ground, as it bent, she jumped to the side. The ax cut through nothing and dug into the ground, making shards of rock dance in the air. Inertia pushed the goddess ten yards ahead, where she thrust her ax into the ground to bring herself to a stop. Marguerite turned away from the goddess's path at a ninety-degree angle and jumped, setting her foot at the edge of the forest. When the goddess turned back to her again, she had that same vacant smile on her face with no signs of distress, and neither could you sense any irritation about failing to capture her prey.

Marguerite fled straight into the forest, and the whole time, she never let the goddess out of her view.

After Marguerite had opened twenty yards between them, the goddess came into the forest. Marguerite kicked off a particularly large tree beside her and leaped, and the tree she'd kicked swayed wildly, making droplets of water spill out and flick everywhere from its spreading branches. The goddess paused for a moment, and Marguerite managed to get farther away.

Marguerite raced, and the goddess followed—Marguerite jumped off trees, and the goddess mowed them down. It looked as if she was just going wild, but she had no openings at all. Marguerite sidestepped a thick trunk that was flung toward her and twined her cape around a tree branch to leap upward. From there, she bounced off a branch to the ground. It felt soft under her feet. The air was filled with moisture. This was a wetland. The farther she got, the more moisture there was in the earth.

Can I use this?

Something like splashing mud in the enemy's face to get away was done to block vision. There was no point to using that move on an enemy who really didn't seem like she relied purely on sight in a battle. Marguerite could let her fall into the bog and then, when she was distracted by the poor footing, turn back to fight her at close range. But that probably wouldn't go well even one out of ten times.

Marguerite stepped on a thick root and leaped, taking care not to slip from the mud as she bounded from tree to tree, and then as she put her hand on another branch, her eyebrows furrowed. She had gotten away from the goddess—or rather, the goddess had stopped. She'd leaned her two battle-axes up against a tree and seemed to be taking a break.

Though Marguerite was confused by the enemy's behavior, her feet didn't stop. The goddess pulled out a little white box and shook out something small and round. It was too far away even for magical-girl vision, and Marguerite couldn't tell quite what it was. The goddess popped the round something on her palm into her mouth, and then she was hidden by the trees and out of view. Marguerite had never looked away from the enemy once as she ran, but since she'd stopped, Marguerite had just pulled out of visual range.

The soil in the area had finally become mud, which would slow a magical girl's running. Marguerite continued to maintain her speed by going along the trees. Though the goddess was out of sight, Marguerite replayed that scene in her brain. She had seen a gesture like that before.

A pill?

It had looked like a human pulling out some medicine and swallowing it. If she had to stop, even when nothing else had stopped her, in order to take something, it really did make the most sense for it to be medicine.

Information was firing off wildly in Marguerite's head. She wasn't organizing it or classifying it. She had drawn what seemed to click from the vast store of knowledge accumulated in her long career as a magical girl. She'd heard of a "magical girl who needs pills" described practically in those exact words before.

Prefacing it by saying that it was a rumor, one of the higher-ups of the Inspection Department had told her, "I hear there's research trying to create a new type of magical girl." They had mentioned that they would regularly require magic pills but that they were highly easy to produce. Then they'd finished off by joking, "If it goes well, then we'll be out of our jobs," but that story basically fit.

Kicking off a tree branch, Marguerite grabbed a vine to extend the distance of her leap.

A creature that had to be a magical girl, but it felt uncanny. *Was* it a magical girl?

A magical girl Sataborn created, making use of new technology?

Was it a watchman who had been stationed on the island going out of control? If not that—then had someone brought it there? Marguerite set her foot on a tree root and tensed, then slid down. She was confused. She couldn't keep her balance. She windmilled at the air and pitched forward to plunge into the swamp. Sand and muddy water got into her mouth, and she choked. She brought her muddy palm to her face. This was not the hand of Miss Marguerite, which was like an art piece. It was the hand of a human woman, with the lines appropriate to her age.

Her transformation had come undone. The effects of the grayfruit had worn off. She was bewildered. It shouldn't have run out yet. Had running continuously messed with her sense of time? She'd hit her whole body in the fall. She felt faint from the pain. Her arms had tried to come forward reflexively, but they had failed to move right. If she couldn't run, then she would be killed easily.

The words *I'm going to get killed* weighed heavily on her. Her heart raced. Her whole body hurt. Her head felt numb. What should she do? The veteran magical girl who wouldn't lose her cool, even with her death looming, was gone. She thought about what a frightened human should do.

I just have to get out of the mud, she thought, but her legs wouldn't move. They were caught on something. When she strained to pull them up, she sank farther. The mud was deep. She couldn't reach the bottom. Even when she tried to push herself up with her arms, she just sank more. She couldn't get up.

Before she could even worry about whether the goddess was coming after her, at this rate, she would sink into the mud and die. Sliding and squelching, her whole body went into the mud. There was nothing now. She couldn't even see her own body. Her chest gradually became more suffocated. She wanted to breathe, but she couldn't raise her head.

Something was rattling. She felt intense vibrations passing over the ground above. The rattling approached, then immediately vanished. She didn't have any way or basis to tell if that was the goddess or not.

Her body heat was seeping away. She wanted to breathe. She was scared. She didn't want to die. Would she have been able to die a more dignified death if she'd died a magical girl? But she really didn't know how much point there was in a dignified death. Death was death. It was the end. It wasn't like she could see people commending her with her own eyes and feel satisfied.

If she was going to die anyway, she would have wanted to die as a magical girl. She thought of Annamarie, who had managed to die as a magical girl. Marguerite didn't know if she had died satisfied. Dying as a magical girl for your own self-satisfaction was an immense burden for other people. But it still seemed somewhat better than being a human with no choice but to die trembling in fear.

◇ Love Me Ren-Ren

Chelsea and Mary didn't come back. That in itself wasn't strange. It was common for Ren-Ren's magic to cause unpredictable accidents. It was possible that Mary had carelessly spoken about her love for Ren-Ren, and then Chelsea had heard it and didn't like it, got mad, and they wound up in a fight. If that happened, they probably wouldn't be able to come straight back.

But such optimistic predictions quickly evaporated. The forest was marred by a continuous path of destruction. Trees were mowed down, dirt was dug up, and rocks were smashed into scattered shards. It stretched on and on. Ren-Ren didn't know how far it actually went, but she didn't want to check to the end. If she reached that point, that would mean running into whoever had accomplished this much devastation.

Ren-Ren turned the other way and spread her wings. She went between the trees at low altitude. Right now, it was a bad idea to fly high over the island.

Was it the other magical girl who Navi Ru had brought? It seemed like it couldn't be anyone else. The destruction that had been displayed near the main building had been basically something like this. It was similar behavior. But it wouldn't make sense for this to be Navi's companion. If what Agri said was correct, there was no need for any further violence from Navi's companion. But there were ongoing signs that she had just gone wild. What was going on? Everything was so strange.

Chelsea and Mary not coming back might be related to that. If they'd run into Navi's companion… Ren-Ren considered this, then shook her head. The wind blowing in her face played with her bangs, making them sway harder than her shake had.

Chelsea and Mary would be treated as Agri's allies. If Navi's companion was to hurt Agri's allies, that would get caught by the contract. Navi wouldn't allow that to happen. If Navi's companion was doing that of her own accord, that would mean he was failing to control her. And Navi had been calm. That hadn't seemed like acting.

So then was there something else that had kept Chelsea and Mary from coming back? What was this destruction about? She could be tearing down the forest on her own, but Ren-Ren didn't get the point of that, and it didn't make sense for her to be fighting anyone, either. There was far too much serious intent to kill here for a sudden quarrel.

Ren-Ren paused. Was Agri being deceived? Were there any holes somewhere? Something wasn't right, but she couldn't pin down what.

Ren-Ren wanted Agri to be happy. She didn't want Agri to die. She couldn't think of her as just an employer anymore. Ren-Ren cared for her. Agri was as dear to her as her own mother. She didn't want her to die like her mother.

The fluttering of Ren-Ren's wings weakened. She gradually slowed, lowering in the air, to finally land.

Ren-Ren looked up at the sky. She could see between the branches that it was bright. She could hear the cries of small birds. The brisk morning breeze was blowing. Ren-Ren clasped her head in her hands.

No. Mom isn't dead. She went away. She left me behind. She isn't dead. Why would I think she'd died? I never saw her die. And of course I could never have killed her. I would never kill her. She's my mom. I would never...

"I'd never!"

The little birds flew off, startled by her yelling. Ren-Ren drew in a big breath and blew another out, smacking herself twice in the cheeks. She was getting distracted. But she had to tell Agri as soon as possible about the strange situation going on. And that wasn't even talking about how Navi was close to Agri. That was dangerous. There was no time for Ren-Ren to be getting distracted.

Pulling herself together, Ren-Ren spread her wings.

◇ **Ragi Zwe Nento**

Ragi was going to escape this island, but he needed his magic for that. He would make an extremely basic gate and get out on his own. He would seek help. And then he would come back with help from the outside. But even a basic gate would require a ceremony for its creation, so he would gather grayfruit as a substitute for magic gems, and he would also need a mage to work with him.

He attempted to simplify matters like this to explain to the ignorant magical girls, but Dreamy☆Chelsea and Pastel Mary weren't listening to him at all.

"Mr. Pie!" Chelsea wailed. "Why?! This has to be some mistake!"

"I don't understand; I don't understand…but things I don't understand are… What were they again? Um…" Pastel Mary trailed off.

"No matter what the danger," Ragi tried to explain to them, "we need aid. Am I wrong?"

"This can't be happening; it's not right."

"What I don't understand… Oh yeah, that it's dangerous. Things I don't understand are dangerous. I mean, it's basically always been like that. I have to go save Ren-Ren, or she—"

"Where are you going, May-May?! Who cares about Ren-Ren?!"

"We must work together to overcome this," Ragi huffed. "This isn't the time to be putting your efforts into selling grayfruit."

"Wait, but—"

"You can't go roaming around when things are so dangerous!"

"But, but, but—"

"It really is Ren-Ren after all, huh, May-May, you lo—"

"Listen, you fools! This isn't the time to be fighting!" Ragi gritted his teeth. It was clear as day what was keeping them from listening at all. Both Dreamy☆Chelsea and Pastel Mary were being mind-controlled by magic. Though they were both pointed in different directions, neither was a very bright magical girl to begin with. Still, he could swear they hadn't been this bad.

The shock of Shepherdspie's death lasted only for a brief moment, and then they were going around in circles worrying about someone and being jealous. Even knowing the cause, Ragi couldn't fix it. If he tried to cast a spell on a magical girl, he would suffer for it. The best he could hope for would be being restrained— if they punched or kicked him away, that could threaten his life. The two magical girls didn't seem so villainous, but they were brainwashed. You never knew how rash they might be.

The night was already dawning. He could no longer hear the chirping of insects or see the moon. If he dawdled around, day would come. No, day might not come. Day would never come to John Shepherdspie. Ragi's bitterness showed on his face, but he nevertheless called out to the two girls. "Calm down. First, calm down and listen."

"What are you talking about?! Of course Chelsea can't be calm!"

"Ah, aw geez, I have to hurry; I have to get back right now."

"May-May! Calm down!"

They didn't even realize that what came out of their mouths was incoherent. In legal terms, they were in a state of mental incompetence. Swallowing his anger toward whoever had made them like this, Ragi considered. The two girls had less capacity for thought than normal. They also weren't properly able to shift from one idea to another. Seen from another angle, this was something he could use. There were means of deception he could use now, and they wouldn't see through his attempts.

What should he do? What did he have to do to get them to listen and do what he wanted? As he brooded over this, the two girls were continuing their meaningless argument and yelling, and it was so grating, he'd have rather covered his ears. Ragi swung his staff up and thrust it into the ground. He said the few words of a spell, made the end of his staff glow, and pointed it at Shepherdspie's body. The light left his staff to stroke over the gruesome wounds of the body to eventually fade and melt into it. The two magical girls put their argument on pause to watch, gulping. He'd succeeded in making them close their mouths and get their attention.

"I heard it!" Ragi cried.

The two magical girls looked at him as if to say, *"Is that old man okay?"* It was provoking, but this wasn't the time for anger.

"You must have heard it! Didn't you?!" he repeated.

"Heard it... Heard what?" Chelsea cocked her head.

"Shepherdspie's voice. You had to have heard it. You couldn't possibly say you weren't able to hear it."

"I think...maybe I heard it?" Pastel Mary said.

"Hmm..."

"You could hear it. You absolutely must have," Ragi insisted.

"I dunno…"

"I can say with certainty you heard it! There's no way you couldn't have!"

"Now that you mention it…I kinda get the feeling that I did hear something…" Chelsea started to give in.

"H-hmm… I'm not sure, but like, kinda…"

"You heard it, didn't you? Shepherdspie was in pain," Ragi told them.

"Well, yeah. You would be."

"Yeah, you would…"

"We must bury him. Are you going to leave Shepherdspie like this? Let us let him rest in peace at the very least."

"Um, okay."

"Yes, of course."

While the two magical girls seemed restless, Ragi somehow got them to listen. Pastel Mary created some sheep that dug a hole, while Chelsea carried Shepherdspie's mutilated body over to lay him down at the bottom of the hole. When Chelsea touched Shepherdspie, she looked terribly sorrowful as she murmured, "He's so cold," tears dripping from her cheeks. Seeing that made Ragi clench his teeth even more bitterly. Too many strange events were occurring. Shepherdspie's body was brutalized as if he'd been crushed by a large mass. Blood soaked not only his clothing but also the earth and grass all around with red, clinging to Chelsea's costume as well. Ragi blacked out his welling fear with anger and moved on to the next stage.

First, while they were working, he talked. He felt sorry for Shepherdspie, but the work itself wasn't what was important. What was important was that while they were working, they were forced to listen to Ragi talk.

"Listen to me. You two have people you want to protect, don't you? No, no. No arguing. Who those people are is not an issue. All that matters is that there are people who are dear to you. In order to protect those you care about, we need help. And for that, we need magic. Working hard on your own will not work. We need grayfruit and mages. Yes, we need to work together. I'll tell you one more time. I wouldn't normally like to repeat myself over and over, but listen well. There is an intruder on this island who is doing something very foolish. We must seek help from the outside. Do you understand? This isn't the time to be selling grayfruit. You understand, don't you?"

"Well, um." Pastel Mary looked up, then immediately dropped her head again. "Then I'll go tell Agri. Since they have grayfruit over there."

Ragi could tell his sour expression was easing and nodded. "Very good of you to understand. Oh yes, I want you to tell her this: We must make haste."

"Yes, right. I have to tell Ren-Ren, too...since I'm worried."

There was a loud splash of mud. Ragi looked over to see Chelsea stomping. "You said Ren-Ren again!"

"But I'm worried..."

"You fools are going back to talking about that again?!"

"I mean, she said Ren-Ren!"

"But I'm really worried..."

"Drop that subject! Cut this out, you fools!"

"But!"

"I mean..."

There was a rustling of leaves. The two magical girls turned toward the sound, and a beat later, Ragi looked that way, too. The thicket shook, then split open, and a magical girl emerged. Ragi narrowed his right eye. He didn't know this one. She had long, flowing golden hair, and she was wearing a toga covered in filth like mud splatter and burn marks. With a vacant smile on her face, she held a large ax raised in each hand.

The magical girl with the axes cocked her head and asked, "Is the ax you dropped a golden ax? Or is it—?"

◇ 7753

Tepsekemei stopped her flight through the air, and 7753 and Mana, following her, stopped as well.

"What's wrong?" 7753 asked.

Tepsekemei shuddered. She was only one-sixth of her original form, but nothing else was changed about her, aside from the size. She wouldn't stop for no reason.

Tepsekemei trembled twice more, then muttered, "Mei's part died."

7753 flared her nose and looked at Mana. Mana bit her lip and looked back. Her lips slowly parted, and then she turned back to Tepsekemei. "What happened to Marguerite?"

"Mei only knows that the part died."

Tepsekemei had to merge with a "part" again to learn what it had seen and heard. Their senses weren't constantly connected.

7753 examined Mana with a sidelong glance. Mana yanked her hat off her head and clasped it in both hands.

The three of them had all come to a stop. None of them suggested that they had to get going again, either. They had been running to get away from the goddess. And they hadn't simply been fleeing. It had also been to keep from getting in Tepsekemei's and Marguerite's way. 7753 and Mana weren't really fighters, and their presence would handicap Marguerite and Tepsekemei by forcing them to protect and help them. That would keep them from beating even an opponent they were capable of taking down. So the group had been actively fleeing to support the fight.

The news that Tepsekemei's part had been killed hit hard enough to reconfirm such considerations had been purely self-deception. Even if it had only been one-third of her, it was impressive to have destroyed a part of Tepsekemei. Tepsekemei was made of wind and couldn't be touched by a magical girl who only had physical attacks.

But the goddess had defeated Tepsekemei. That would mean that Marguerite was alone. 7753 and Mana didn't even know if she was alive or not.

"Um, but...," 7753 started, but Mana didn't make to move. 7753 inhaled, exhaled, and smacked a fist against her knee. "Marguerite is strong, right?"

Mana lifted her chin. An angry expression was Mana's default.

"She's strong, so she'll be okay, right?" 7753 said.

"...Of course. She was Hana's teacher." Mana smacked her hat to fix its shape, put it on her head, and let out a breath. "If you have some kind of plan, then say it."

"Mei wants fruit," Tepsekemei said.

"Here." Mana handed over one of the grayfruit that they'd found while running. Watching Tepsekemei bite into it, the wrinkles carved in Mana's brow faded just a little.

7753 put a hand to her forehead, and remembering that her goggles weren't there, she wiped the spot with the back of her hand to cover the gesture. "I think we shouldn't go back." However Marguerite was doing, they wouldn't be useful if they went back. "If Tepsekemei's sacrifice enabled her to beat the goddess, that's different, though."

"We shouldn't make decisions based on optimism."

"But there's no point in keeping going, though... It's not like we have any goal, and we don't have many grayfruit, either."

"I suppose we could just hope we run into something."

"Um...we might run into that thing, so..."

Mana drew the brim of her hat deeply over her eyes and looked around. It was nothing but trees, earth, and grass. With a little sigh, she looked up at Tepsekemei, who was still eating her grayfruit. "I have a request, Tepsekemei."

"Mei will hear your request."

"Go above the trees to look around, and tell me which way is toward the main building. Make sure not to fly too much." Tepsekemei floated up above the branches.

7753 frowned. "We're going back to the main building? Isn't that dangerous?"

"Just because that's where we were first attacked doesn't mean it's still dangerous. Or rather, anywhere on this island is equally dangerous right now. It's not really going to be safe no matter where we go."

"But what's the point in going there now...? Do you have an idea?"

"To be frank...it's just barely better than wandering around aimlessly, but..." After that timid preface, Mana blew a breath out her nose and resumed her usual angry-looking expression. "The inheritance that was going to be distributed is at the main building."

Now that she mentioned it, that was the reason they'd come to the island in the first place. The reason they'd come in the first place was long forgotten at this point.

"That should also include some tools with magical power. Since they're the sort of thing that would be in an inheritance, I assume it's items with high artistic value or academic implications, antiques or something easily resold or exceptionally rare items... basically things without much practical use. But we don't know for sure they'd have no powers useful to get us out of this."

If Mr. Shepherdspie were there, maybe he'd have gotten a look at the catalog, she added. Then after saying it, she bit her lip like she regretted it. When they'd been attacked by the goddess, 7753 had only had the presence of mind to scoop up Mana. More accurately, she hadn't even had the presence of mind to scoop up Mana, but Mana had fortunately been in her field of view. At this point, all they could do was pray for his safety—for Shepherdspie, and for Marguerite, and all the other mages and magical girls.

Mana looked at 7753, who nodded, trying to be even slightly encouraging, and then Tepsekemei came down. Whether she'd been listening or not, she looked at the two of them and nodded, and at least superficially, the three of them were nodding at one another encouragingly.

◇ Clarissa Toothedge

The morning sun filtered through the leaves above to dapple the ground below. Clarissa honestly thought it was pretty. The morning air was cold, and the humidity wasn't too aggressive. But she couldn't say that everything felt good. A couple of dropped items were bringing her down, making it no time for a pleasant morning.

In a gloomy mood that didn't suit such a brisk morning, she approached those things and picked one up. It was wet, probably from the morning dew dripping from the branches. She spun the pointed hat in a semicircle on her hand to shake off the water and found a little ding on the brim. Of course, she knew what this mark hidden in a wrinkle was. It was Clarissa's bite mark, which she'd put there while Ragi had been unconscious.

She bent over to pick up a scrap of mud-smeared cloth with grass stuck to it. It was from Ragi's cuff. This was also marked with Clarissa's bite.

Clarissa knew the position of anything she had bitten. This magic was convenient in a lot of ways. But she knew only the relative positional information of bitten objects, and she wouldn't know why Ragi had thrown away his hat and part of his clothes. Clarissa had rushed to Ragi because she'd thought he'd collapsed, but it had actually been his hat and a scrap of cloth lying there. You didn't need to be Clarissa to understand this was not a good thing at all.

She was dealing with a cunning veteran mage. Maybe he'd noticed her magic.

To excuse her magic being found out, she could just say she'd used her magic on him to secure his safety. But losing her grasp on Ragi's position was a big flub of a bonehead play. Nobody would have had any problems if he'd stayed hidden like Clarissa had told him to—him moving around was causing her trouble on top of more trouble. Silently cursing at him for being such a pointlessly active old grandpa, she looked up at the light filtering through the trees for no particular reason and narrowed her eyes.

Clarissa was to operate according to Navi Ru's wishes, while additionally being adaptable to the needs of the moment, moving free, unfettered, and with control and versatility. Put in the cool-sounding way, she was a commando unit. Now that she'd worked herself to the bone checking off the biggest hassle from her list of to-dos, Ragi's safety was a pretty high-priority ranking. She would follow Ragi's trail, find him the hard way without using magic, and secure him. She had to make sure he absolutely couldn't escape, this time for sure. Should she dislocate his joints while saying, *"I'm doing this for your sake"*? She got the feeling the old man could even get out of that. So then what should she do?

Clarissa Toothedge had been working under Navi Ru for a long time. And she did very occasionally have dangerous jobs forced on her. She was enough of a professional that even while thinking, she kept her attention sharp, and she was ready for an attack coming from anywhere.

When she heard a branch break inside the forest, she leaped backward, holding the hat and cloth scrap in her right hand. The sound of footsteps followed. They weren't human footsteps. They were also different from those of a magical girl. Clarissa's pointed, feline ears moved minutely as they captured the movements of the target. The four-legged animal was close. It was close; that wasn't what it was. They had noticed Clarissa's presence. Clarissa could basically tell what the presence was, and seeing the form that peeked out from the forest, she confirmed that her ears had been right.

It was Clantail. Her lower body was no longer a horse, now become a large feline with black stripes over gold fur. There was nothing awkward about her appearance, combined like a collage to equip her with the supple grace of the original animal.

Clarissa wet her lips with the tip of her tongue. Clantail had been trying to walk silently. She was moving like she was apt to attack somebody. Her expression seemed somehow dark. Her lips were pressed together. She had a different air to her, compared to when they'd last seen each other. Had she already fought someone? Clarissa couldn't see any wounds. She doubted she could be completely unharmed after fighting with Francesca, but maybe she'd just had some kind of squabble with Agri's lackeys.

Clarissa put on a light expression and raised her arm in a funny way as she called out brightly, "Looks like you were safe, Clantail."

Even when Clarissa tried to ease Clantail's caution, the girl didn't move. She stared right back, not even her cheeks or eyebrows twitching.

"What's the matter? Right now we're both cat-type magical girls, right? Let's help each other out."

She didn't move. The branches swayed in the wind, the morning sun angling through them. Though the sunlight annoyed Clarissa, she kept her expression the same—partly because she wanted to keep it on to make Clantail less wary and also because she didn't want to carelessly blink and offer a slight opening.

"Clarissa and Clantail, even our names sound like a good match, don'cha think?" Clarissa said.

Clantail raised her right arm and pointed ahead with her index finger. Clarissa automatically measured the distance between them. It was twenty-six feet to Clantail's front legs and twenty-four to her index finger. Maybe a little more.

She should get closer so she could chummily clap her on the shoulder and be like *hey, hey,* but she wanted to maintain enough distance so she could run if she had to. To keep Clantail from noticing that they were too far apart for just a chat, she asked in a tone that was not too loud but carried well, "So like, what's up?"

"That." Clantail's voice was low and quiet. Clarissa's sharp hearing could pick it up easily, but the remark didn't seem like a preface to conversation. "That hat."

"Oh yeah, this? I just found it. This is a mage hat, huh. If it's lying here, that means… Well, I doubt it got forgotten." It was a fact that she'd just found it now. That part wasn't a lie.

But Clantail's expression didn't relax—in fact, it tightened even more harshly. "You tried to hide it."

"Pardon?"

"You kept me from seeing that side of the hat."

Clarissa didn't drop her smile. But inside, she cursed. *Shit.*

She'd turned the hat so Clantail wouldn't be able to see the bite mark. Clarissa replayed the motion inside her mind. It wasn't like she'd moved carelessly because she'd underestimated Clantail, figuring she would never notice such a small motion. Clarissa had managed to do it in a nonchalant manner, but Clantail had noticed anyway.

Clantail wasn't only acting wary. She was observing with insight and attention. They hadn't known each other for long, but Clarissa could tell she was clearly different now. Back when she'd raced off, saying she was going to go search for grayfruit, she'd been way more careless than right now. Had something awoken her caution? Had it made her a magical girl on the battlefield?

If someone had pulled something stupid, there were plenty of idiots who could plausibly be that someone. Seeing how there were no signs of battle on her, maybe someone had given her ideas. That was really uncalled-for.

"You think I was trying to hide it? No way," said Clarissa.

The way Clantail was acting now, she'd probably figure some things out just by seeing the bite mark. If Clarissa revealed her magic honestly and explained that she'd bit it in order to know Ragi's position, would that work? Clarissa was considering what she should say next, about to open her mouth, when the sound of something whooshing through the air made her ears vibrate. She dropped the hat and scrap of cloth held at her side on the spot, rushing forward before even looking back to dodge the log that came flying at her. The log bounced high, splattering up mud, then rolled into the forest, crushing the short vegetation underneath it.

It hadn't flown at her like it had been aimed at her. There was no follow-up attack, either. Someone, somewhere, was fighting—seeing as how she hadn't heard any noise, it was probably Francesca—and it was probably just the side effects of the battle reaching Clarissa. But that wasn't what her problem was now. When she'd moved to avoid the log, she'd wound up coming closer to Clantail. There were six feet between her and Clantail, who stood with the forest at her back. They were close. Clantail raised up her front legs and glared at her. Those were the eyes of a magical girl who had killed before. Clarissa was penetrated from head to tail with the feeling that she was going to get killed. She let momentum take her forward and lifted her leg at the angle of a roundhouse kick. At the height where she'd kick, she dropped it in an attempt to swipe aside Clantail's back kick, but Clantail nimbly evaded her.

This time, she couldn't help cursing out loud. "Piece of shit." She'd thought she hadn't meant to attack. Her spinal cord had reacted on reflex to the look in Clantail's eyes, and her body had moved, thinking she had to attack first. Her penetrating, murderous intent had forced Clarissa to move. Clantail sure wouldn't listen to excuses now. Clarissa swiped like she was trying to hold Clantail off. Then right before Clantail blocked, she withdrew her hands and claws. The enemy had thicker and longer claws. What would happen if a Bengal tiger and a serval cat clashed head-on with no extra tricks? Even a child would know who would win.

And on top of that, there was Clantail's magic. What had been a horse when they'd been on a plain had become a leopard when she'd gone into the forest, and now she was a tiger. Clarissa should assume she would transform to adapt to the situation. Her magic was probably to transform her lower body into animals.

Clarissa made small steps to the left and right, keeping her opponent on her toes. Feigning a sliding tackle, she did a forward roll instead, changing the direction of force right in front of Clantail to leap to the side.

Clarissa stripped off her shoes with that leap and abandoned them to expose the claws on her feet. Leaping headfirst into the forest, taking care not to destroy the trees with the strength of her magical-girl limbs, she climbed, leaped, jumped, and evaded the attacks from behind by a paper-thin margin. Some straggling hairs of hers danced in the air. When Clarissa turned back again, Clantail's lower body was now a spotted feline. She had to be thinking that would give her all the strengths Clarissa had—feline spring, reflexes, and sharp claws.

Not so. If they were fighting in the trees, Clarissa had the advantage.

If Clantail was going to transform into a great cat, then Clarissa had to knock her down. The body weight and delicacy needed was different from when you were on the ground. If she was dealing with the lightweight to middleweight class, like a leopard or wildcat rather than a tiger, lion, or saber-toothed cat, then Clantail couldn't block her attacks with just her flesh, pelt, and bones. Clarissa had an integrated cat motif, and way more time with it than Clantail, who was not always transformed into a cat's lower half. If Clantail was to choose some other arboreal animal like a monkey or field mouse, that was fine, too. Clarissa was confident that a cat was the strongest in the trees.

Additionally, Clarissa had the advantage of her magic. This wasn't the first time she'd entered this forest. It was the second. Clarissa hadn't just been wandering around the island looking for grayfruit. If she marked a tree's bark with her bite, she'd have a hold on its position. She'd already been in this forest, so she'd already bitten the trees. Clantail hadn't realized it, but this was Clarissa's territory.

Clarissa spun around a branch and pulled the knife tucked in her sleeve out at an angle Clantail couldn't see. It didn't matter if Clantail went out of sight. When Clantail moved from tree to tree, the contact would make the trees sway. When they swayed, no matter how slightly, it would shift the position of the tree and alert Clarissa to her position. Clantail leaped from one tree to another, then leaped again, stopping diagonally and to the right above Clarissa. Without even looking at her once, Clarissa knew every move she made.

The moment Clantail leaped, Clarissa spun around and threw the knife. Her front cat paw swiped it aside, but Clarissa had anticipated that. Clantail bounded toward her viciously fast, but Clarissa jumped, too. The two magical girls watched each other in midair. They were close enough to breathe on each other. Clarissa twisted around. She avoided a frontal collision and came around to Clantail's flank. Power was one thing, but Clarissa was faster.

At zero distance, Clarissa thrust her knee into the cat torso, digging in between the ribs. Without checking to see if she'd done any damage, she drew up her shin and aimed for the upper body next. Clantail blocked Clarissa's shin with her human upper arm and tried to wrap both arms around her, and Clarissa rotated her ankle to snatch the repelled knife in her toes. She tried to scratch at

Clantail's eyes with the knife blade, but it was blocked—not by her arm but by her leg.

It was like she didn't have joints—it even seemed dubious if she was a solid body at all as she twisted her spine with the character-istic flexibility of a cat to slam down with her back leg. The knife caught in her claws was shredded to bits that bounced off branches and leaves as it fell.

Before Clarissa could even be surprised, the part that was not transformed, the human upper body, had grabbed her by the wrist. Clantail swung her up, then down. She bashed Clarissa's spine into a tree trunk, blasting the trunk into splinters, keeping a firm grip on her wrist the whole time. Her grip alone had so much force, it felt like Clarissa's bones would break. It wasn't just her lower body that was powerful. Clarissa silently cursed, *Crazy-strong bitch.*

Clantail swung her up again, higher than before. Clarissa flung out her left arm, aiming for the highest point of the swing to try to scratch at Clantail's wrist, but this time she was flung away, and her left hand swiped at the air in vain.

Even as she was breaking branches with her back, Clarissa dug her claws into tree trunks to slow her fall, then jumped downward. She crossed paths with Clantail, leaping upward, and they clashed claws. Clarissa's claws creaked as she turned aside the attack, and she pushed at Clantail's joints with her elbow to open up the inside of her front legs in an attempt to get a kick in. But before her kick could connect, Clantail fired a back kick to counter it at an absolutely absurd angle, which Clarissa evaded, and the two magical girls came apart.

Landing on a thick branch, this time Clarissa leaped upward. She tried to kick at Clantail while changing direction as well, but another back kick obstructed her. Grabbing a tree trunk with her claws, Clarissa switched to the right diagonal direction, passing by Clantail as she leaped downward, then grabbed a tree branch to come to a stop.

Clarissa looked down on the magical girl with the lower body of a spotted feline, staring up at Clarissa with frighteningly cold eyes.

Whoa...

Clantail was used to battle. She didn't show a trace of fear, even after having a blade pulled on her to target her eyes. There was no weakness in her stance or in the motion of her eyes. Not only did she possess mastery over the body of a cat, her upper body was more than just a little powerful—she was stronger than Clarissa.

This was the same magical girl who, when Ragi had collapsed, had gotten into a panic, ignoring the voices calling her to stop to race off alone. Clarissa had assumed from that display that Clantail was amateurish. However, that underestimation would embarrass anyone at this point. She was a warrior who could fight flawlessly in a potentially lethal situation. And though she had to have seen Clarissa's pretransformation form, it seemed like she wouldn't let her guard down because she was young. Had she gotten hurt against a child before?

Still...though she's giving me the eye, it doesn't look like she's planning to kill me. So is she going for a capture?

The fact that her opponent wasn't even going for the kill made Clarissa shudder. This fight was easy enough for her to consider that she could capture without killing. Clantail could already tell that she was that much stronger.

Clarissa made a branch bend and used the rebound to jump. She raced through the treetops. She could tell from the sound and sense of her presence that Clantail was following her closely.

After various considerations, Clarissa came to a conclusion: Clantail was too much for her one-on-one. Clarissa wasn't just tooth and fang. It wasn't like she had no tricks up her sleeve, but she wasn't going to use those against someone who was basically an outsider who she'd incidentally slid into fighting.

The trees gradually thinned out. The light shone through. The forest was coming to an end. Even in the forest that should have been Clarissa's home base, they were equally matched at playing tag. If Clantail transformed into the appropriate lower body wherever they went, be it fields or rocks or hills or the ocean, then Clarissa couldn't match her.

She's a real piece of shit, huh.

It was probably Navi's influence that brought these curses to mind at times like these. Thinking them meant that if she didn't watch out, they would come out of her mouth, too. No matter how much obligation and goodwill she had toward Navi, she didn't want to become like the old man, and she tried to restrain herself every time dirty words rose in her mind, but her self-restraint had never lasted very long.

Clarissa kicked off a tree with all her strength, splintering it from the impact—and scattering pieces of wood behind her, she leaped with the form of a competitive swimmer. Doing a roll, she stuck the landing and rose to her feet at a run. The sound of footsteps followed her from behind. They were not the sound of hooves. If it wasn't a horse, then it was probably a cheetah or something. This was an all-cat showdown. She should assume that her opponent wanted to get this fight over quickly.

She didn't really want to pull this move—because this wasn't a move that would actually save her. But Clarissa couldn't think of anything else. You couldn't be picky in an emergency. Organizing the positional information her magic gave her, she headed in that direction.

Clarissa inhaled a lungful of air, then blasted it out in a yell. "Help! Rareko!"

The footsteps behind her slowed. A magical girl in a robe popped out from the long rocky stretch fifty yards ahead, staff in hand. She moved faster than expected. Clarissa was thankful.

Clarissa knew the positional information of anything she had bitten. And if they were a human or mage—or an unobservant magical girl like 7753 or Pastel Mary—then it was easy enough to leave a bite mark without being noticed. Aside from exceptions like Yol, who constantly had Rareko beside her, or Agri, who always had either Ren-Ren or Nephilia glued to her, Clarissa had sneakily bitten a spot on the clothing of all the mages on this island.

She knew where Touta was, and if she ran toward him, Rareko would obviously be there as well. Clarissa would have been able to request backup a little more easily if it had been Agri, but Touta was the closest, so she was okay with that. She wasn't in a position to be picky.

"Go eat the grayfruit I shared with you! You'll be in trouble if you detransform while fighting!" Clarissa yelled, more directed at Clantail than Rareko. If Clantail understood that Clarissa and Rareko had a relationship where they would lend each other grayfruit, that should narrow Clantail's options. Though Clarissa had concluded that she couldn't beat Clantail one-on-one, it was different if she had a reliable ally to fight with her. Clantail was aware of that, too. Clarissa believed in Clantail's strength, since she'd evaluated Clarissa's abilities in such a brief time. She'd make the right decision.

The footsteps behind her came to a stop, then raced off in the other direction. Clarissa cursed silently, *Get lost already, shithead*, as she breathed a sigh of relief.

◇ Touta Magaoka

After dashing out, Rareko came back. Clarissa was with her, too. Yol stood up and asked, "What was that?"

Touta followed. "What happened?"

Rareko looked at Clarissa as if she was suffering from the bottom of her heart.

Clarissa sighed in disappointment. "I got attacked—by Clantail."

"Clantail?" Yol said. "You mean that magical girl who was half-animal? Why?"

"I don't think it's 'cause Clantail is a bad guy or that she's scheming or something, mm-hmm." Clarissa, who was telling them that she'd been attacked, was defending her attacker for some reason as she folded her arms and nodded. "Situations like these, like extreme circumstances, everyone gets on edge. Some people do wind up thinking they can use violence to make you do what they want."

It was true there were sometimes characters like that in manga.

But manga was manga. Did this come up in fiction a lot because it happened often in real life? Touta tried to remember about Clantail. He recalled what she'd looked like when she'd raced off before the main building had been attacked. That had been kinda cool, but he thought someone had said she wasn't very cooperative. Would someone who was uncooperative attack others in an emergency?

"But that's…very scary…isn't it?" Yol said, sounding concerned.

"I mean, um," said Clarissa, "I'm sure that means there are other dangerous characters out there besides the scary person who attacked us. When the grayfruit were already starting to run out, too."

"Oh yeah, that's right. I'd forgotten about the grayfruit," Touta said. That wasn't something he should be forgetting about. Touta told Clarissa about how there were no more grayfruit and how the pace they used them seemed to be accelerating—and about how Nephilia was going around selling them.

Hearing that, Clarissa put her hand on her forehead. "No matter where you go, there are people who'll cause trouble, huh."

"It's just, so, honestly… I thought we said we have to work together," Yol said.

"Yeah, man, this is a pickle for real." Clarissa nodded. "For now, I'll leave the fruit I can share with you here. Sorry, but I can't give you all the fruit I got, so that'll mean leaving out the ones I need for myself, but forgive me. Do what you can to hold out with this."

She dropped a total of five grayfruit into Yol's palms. All five of them had loose skins, which had to mean some time had passed since they'd been picked. That wasn't a lot, either, but they couldn't complain. Even if they were starting to go bad, even if it was just one, it was a lot better than slowly nibbling away at the one fruit Touta had wrangled from Nephilia.

When Yol, Touta, and Rareko all said their thanks in turn, Clarissa waved her right hand back shyly. Her catlike ears swayed side to side along with her hand. "It's fine, it's fine; don't thank me. Look, times like these, you've gotta help each other out, y'know; I just did the obvious thing." Saying things like "aww" and "c'mon," Clarissa walked off to the exit. At one step before the opening, she turned back to say, "Well then, I'll be back later. Old Man Navi might come round, too, but, well, one of us'll show up. Promise I won't bring extra trouble next time. You all sit tight, 'kay? It's dangerous outside, so you can't go out."

Yol cocked her head. The swaying of her rolled curls just about made her hat fall off. Touta supported the hat from the side sneakily so that it wouldn't be noticed.

"Aren't you staying here, too, Clarissa?" Yol asked.

"Nah, I'm heading out."

"You can't. It's dangerous."

"Alas, I must brave the danger to do what must be done."

Yol reached out an arm, but Clarissa left before she could touch her. Clarissa raced into the morning light, and before long, her footsteps were out of earshot. Yol timidly retracted her extended arm and gave Touta a look that said, *"Honestly, this is so troubling."* "But it really is…dangerous, isn't it?"

"Yeah, um, I do think it's dangerous," Touta agreed.

"Yes, you're quite right, miss."

"Since we were only just attacked, weren't we?" Yol said.

"Yeah, um, that's true."

"Yes, of course."

After that, Yol continued to repeat, "I wonder if it will be all right." Though she seemed worried the whole time, since they couldn't go after Clarissa, and in the end, she gave up, saying, "I do hope she'll be safe…," sitting down in her original spot with an expression of sincere concern. Rareko said, "Yes, yes," agreeing with Yol as she also went to sit back down in her old spot.

Only Touta didn't sit down. Still standing with his back to the entrance, he turned to Rareko and Yol. "Hey."

"What is it?" Yol answered.

"I really do still think…"

"Yes?"

"I think I should go out."

"Didn't we just talk about how that was dangerous?"

"That's right," Rareko said, "we should keep hidden here for now."

With the both of them against him, Touta closed his mouth for the moment. It wasn't that he was withdrawing his argument about going outside. He felt that something strange had happened, and he was wondering if he should talk about it.

The other two seemed to assume that Touta going silent meant he'd given up on going outside. They started talking about what they should do when Nephilia came. He did think that was also important to think about, but he didn't join in, working on his own thoughts instead.

There was something he'd felt was strange. And not just one thing.

The skins of the fruit they'd gotten from Clarissa were sagging. That meant that some time had passed since they'd been picked. Normally, wouldn't you eat the old ones first? You wouldn't keep the old ones when you didn't know when they would go bad. But Clarissa had been holding on to fruit that had been harvested some time ago. When had she harvested them? If it had been before everyone had gotten split up, that was odd—since the fruit picked back then had been gathered in one place and then stolen. They'd said Pastel Mary had been the one to steal them, and there was no way Clarissa could have those fruit, but the fruit Clarissa had given them were old.

A few other things were odd, too. Clarissa had told them to wait there. But Clantail had to have pursued her until she was very close to this place—so wouldn't that mean she also knew that Rareko had been around here? If someone who attacked others knew where they were, that would make it so they should at least move to a new spot.

If it were just that, then Touta could have talked about it normally. But one last weird thing kept him from bringing it up.

When Rareko had heard Clarissa's call, she had zoomed off with incredible speed. Despite being so against going outside, she hadn't even hesitated. She had abandoned her mistress, who should have been more important than anything else, and raced off so fast, you couldn't even see her. Yol was the type to say, *"If there's someone in trouble, then we have to help them out,"* so she wouldn't tell Rareko off for that. But to Touta, watching it from the outside, it had felt very odd. It was strange.

Rareko had been insisting this *whole* time that they not go outside. Touta had assumed that was because she wanted to protect her mistress, and she was probably a coward, things like that. But when Rareko had heard Clarissa's voice, she'd taken her weapon and boldly leaped out—abandoning her mistress.

Touta hated himself for doubting Rareko. He'd only just listened to them talking about how they had to help one another, and he was already thinking things like this. But the more he thought about it, the more nasty ideas kept sticking in his head and wouldn't go away.

The one adult and magical girl who he should have been able to rely on, Rareko, he couldn't trust. He couldn't talk with Yol without Rareko there, either. Saying, *"It's dangerous to be here; let's go outside,"* wasn't going to convince Rareko, but now he didn't even know if she would listen if he tried to convince her with a proper reason.

What would Miss Marguerite do? he wondered but got no answers. It seemed that he had to think about not what Marguerite would do but what Touta would do.

◇ **Rareko**

Maiya had been killed. She was gone now. Rareko had kept thinking about that all day. She would surely continue to think about it and consider it in the future as well. It was a world-shaking disaster to her. Maiya was dead.

Clarissa and Navi Ru were both operating proactively. Were they just responding to the emergency, or had they anticipated this situation? With Navi Ru, either was possible. The scary thing about the man was that it wouldn't be surprising for him to pull anything.

He was a scary man, even to Rareko. If Maiya had been there, she would have been the more frightening one, but Maiya being gone changed things. Navi Ru was more frightening right now than Yol, who was here with her.

Yol was naive. She was privileged. That kept her from recognizing the true nature of frightening people. Though there was no way Navi was just some gentle and jolly uncle. She didn't get it.

Yol was the master Rareko should be serving now. Rareko had known her since she was a baby, so she was fairly attached to her. She did think she was cute. When Yol had given her a robe for her birthday, Rareko had been moved and cried, and then when she'd found out how much it cost, she'd wondered if she could somehow sell it to a pawnshop.

But even so, Rareko wouldn't place Yol before herself.

Yol was worth protecting because she was connected to Rareko's social position and because Navi Ru clearly needed her. Of course, he was counting on her power on this island. He would need her in the future. That was exactly why Maiya had despised Navi Ru like vermin, not letting him get close to the miss. Maiya's plan had also been Rareko's plan, but Maiya was gone. She had been killed.

So then what plan should Rareko follow? Yol or the family? The answer was neither. Rareko should only follow Rareko. She had to follow this path of thought.

There was something else that Maiya had said that Rareko liked: "Always be adaptable." Maiya had used those words as justification to make unreasonable demands of Rareko, and when she hadn't been able to meet those demands, Maiya had yelled at her and knocked her down. Even though that behavior was unreasonable, Rareko thought it was okay.

You could say of all the lessons Maiya had given her, the thing Rareko liked most was the one that was most convenient to her—of making the optimal choice in each given situation.

Never letting her expression of concern falter, Rareko looked at Yol.

Yol was weak enough that it looked like she would fall over from a push. It stirred up protective instincts. However, it was just enough protective instinct that Rareko would like to protect her if she had anything to spare, and she had none to spare anymore. She had her hands entirely full protecting herself. While she prioritized herself over everything, she had to pose for the moment like she was protecting Yol.

Touta, who had been talking with Yol, glanced over at Rareko, then immediately looked away. She didn't care about that one. If not for Yol, she would've abandoned him long ago. It wasn't even her responsibility to protect him in the first place. This was Marguerite's fault for not being there, since she'd originally been his guard.

But though it was true she didn't care whether he lived or died, it seemed like he wasn't worth absolutely nothing, as someone to use. It wasn't bad that he'd wrangled one grayfruit, instead of just bringing in the contract. Rareko hadn't had that much good sense when she'd been around his age. Just going to inform the one in charge would've been the most she could have done.

Maiya had often been angry with her because she would panic when she was pressured, but now that she thought about it, *Yeah, of course you wouldn't like having someone around who does nothing but panic when pressured, huh?* Touta not being just a burden made him useful, in more ways than one.

It did seem like if she was going to sacrifice this kid somewhere along the line, it would be a waste to have him die without doing anything. And he'd want to die a meaningful death, if he was going to die anyway.

But of course, Rareko wasn't going to throw him to the wolves herself. Yol would stop her if she tried, and then she'd consider Rareko a nasty person who would try to sacrifice a child. She still intended to incidentally protect Touta for now despite having no formal responsibility to do so.

So that brought her back to the question of what to do. Maiya might have come up with some good idea and announced it arrogantly with an equally obnoxious expression on her face. She'd do it successfully and with insolence. But Maiya had been killed. Rareko had come back to this same point again. She would surely continue to think about Maiya's death over and over, to digest it. Rareko adjusted her glasses with her index finger.

HAVE YOU BEEN TURNED ON TO LIGHT NOVELS YET?

86—EIGHTY-SIX, VOL. 1-10

In truth, there is no such thing as a bloodless war. Beyond the fortified walls protecting the eighty-five Republic Sectors lies the "nonexistent" Eighty-Sixth Sector. The young men and women of this forsaken land are branded the Eighty-Six and, stripped of their humanity, pilot "unmanned" weapons into battle...

Manga adaptation available now!

WOLF & PARCHMENT, VOL. 1-6

The young man Col dreams of one day joining the holy clergy and departs on a journey from the bathhouse, Spice and Wolf. Winfiel Kingdom's prince has invited him to help correct the sins of the Church. But as his travels begin, Col discovers in his luggage a young girl with a wolf's ears and tail named Myuri who stowed away for the ride!

Manga adaptation available now!

SOLO LEVELING, VOL. 1-5

E-rank hunter Jinwoo Sung has no money, no talent, and no prospects to speak of—and apparently, no luck, either! When he enters a hidden double dungeon one fateful day, he's abandoned by his party and left to die at the hands of some of the most horrific monsters he's ever encountered.

Comic adaptation available now!

Dreamy ☆ Chelsea (Part I)

At what age did you become a magical girl?

"Chelsea thinks she was born destined to become a magical girl. Actually, you can just say Chelsea was already a magical girl at birth."

Do you have any role models?

"Chelsea's mom! …Wait, you're gonna put this interview in an article somewhere, right? So then Mom'll see that and be like, *'Goodness, she actually does respect me.'* Oh, but cut out that part, please. Just keep the 'Chelsea's mom!' part."

Are you scared of your mom?

"Maybe not scared, but… Okay, yeah, scared."

She's quite famous.

"Why do you wanna ask about Chelsea's mom when this is Chelsea's interview?"

Because you keep bringing it up.

"Show more interest in Chelsea! Just look at how cute she is. See, here goes… Leave it to Dreamy☆Chelsea! Haaah!"

(Continued in Part II)

Magical-Girl
Interview No. 1

Magical-Girl Interview No. 2

Nephilia (Part I)

Celebrating the
novelization!
Breakdown
Magical-Girl
Interview

②

**At what age did you become
a magical girl?**

"Preschool… This clown was…
handing out candy…"

**Sounds like the opening of a
horror story.**

"Got a candy… Licked it… Became a
magical girl…"

That…really is like a horror story.

"Looking back…it's basically
terrorism…"

Do you have any special skills?

"Memorization…"

Memorization?

"Laws…curses…textbooks…
documents…faces… I'll memorize
everything… Super useful…"

**So your memory is that good
because you pick up the
memories of the dead?**

"Overthinking it…"

Ah, of course. Sorry.

"Ksh-sh-sh."

(Continued in Part II)

Pastel Mary (Part I)

It seems like you fall down quite often.

"I've really given it a lot of thought, but I just don't quite know why it happens."

Is your clumsiness part of an act to look cute or something?

"No, it's not! Please, why would I fall on my face and get a bloody nose while I'm working just to make myself look good?"

At what age did you become a magical girl?

"I guess when I was in the ninth grade. By the way, what's with this format? This isn't, like, one of those sexy things, is it? Ah, um, sorry. I shouldn't have said that."

Do you typically see those sorts of things?

"Why are you trying to dig into that? It's common knowledge."

Has something like that happened to you before?

"Once when I was handing out flyers for a Magical Girl Resources event. My sheep got all red like a scene out of a horror movie. I don't even want to remember it… Wait, can we not talk about nosebleeds anymore? The things you're probing into are honestly kind of weird."

(Continued in Part II)

Magical-Girl
Interview No. 3

At what age did you become a magical girl?

"In elementary school. There was a showing of an anime film, and before I knew it, a number of us had become magical girls ourselves. We were then taken straight to the exam. I heard the rest of the students had their memories altered. Rough methods, compared to these days… Oh, not that I'm criticizing it."

Apparently, you were a member of the Inspection Department. You must really hate crime.

"No, it's merely that teaching has always suited me. That's why I spent some time in Magical Girl Resources, but it wasn't quite the right fit, so I transferred to Inspection."

So you started in Magical Girl Resources. I hear they pay better than Inspection.

"You can say this of any job, but ultimately, a sufficient income is what matters most. As for Inspection, well, I eventually quit that job, but I still believe it

Magical-Girl Interview No. 4

was fine."

Is this a difficult topic for you to talk about?

"Quite."

Then let's change the subject. What kind of animal would you compare yourself to?

"A dog. People often called me one on the job. The people I was supervising, that is."

(Continued in Part II)

Miss Marguerite (Part I)

Love Me Ren-Ren (Part I)

At what age did you become a magical girl?

"I was still very small. As for exactly how old I was… Hmm… It's all so jumbled; I can't remember. Anyway, I was very small."

What do you think of your magical-girl form?

"Oh, I just love it. Look, these are dove wings. Don't you think the messenger of peace fits perfectly for my work?"

And not just the wings— the horns and tail are also wonderful.

"Those parts? You don't have to pay attention to them."

Then I won't. So what do you think of your magical-girl name?

"I like my name, too, although that should be obvious since I came up with it myself. I truly believe that love is the most important thing of all."

And that's also related to your magic, isn't it?

"It is. I have a lot of feelings about family… I'm honestly so, so glad I was able to get this job."

(Continued in Part II)

Rough Sketch Collection

From **Marui-no**, who brings the world of *Magical Girl Raising Project* to life! We're showcasing **a bunch of the rough sketches** for *Breakdown*!

※ Please be aware that some designs are not in the final manuscript.

Candy-like staff

Robe looks like a traditional bridal kimono

Klimt-inspired

Her pose vis-à-vis Marguerit

Front

...vi's stubble:
...lue→black?

Fabric like velour

Dignified. High-class robe, pricey fabric

Expensive decorations, picky about each item

Two on the back as well

Underlayer of her hair is paler
(Same as underlayer of her bangs)

Hard to see, but more visible when mussed

ORIGIN WORK

Rough Sketch

Kaoruko Rokugou
Miss Marguerite

Rei Koimizu
Love Me Ren-Ren

Iria Funada
Nephilia

Yoh Tanada
Pastel Mary

Chie Yumeno
Dreamy☆Chelsea

Kotori Nanaya
7753

Nene Ono
Clantail

Maiya

Rareko

Rough Sketch

Gold   Silver

• Blond hair
• White clothes
• Fabric scattered with ☆
• The same

Hatchet Size

Rough Sketch

HAVE YOU BEEN TURNED ON TO LIGHT NOVELS YET?

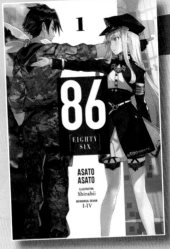

86—EIGHTY-SIX, VOL. 1-10

In truth, there is no such thing as a bloodless war. Beyond the fortified walls protecting the eighty-five Republic Sectors lies the "nonexistent" Eighty-Sixth Sector. The young men and women of this forsaken land are branded the Eighty-Six and, stripped of their humanity, pilot "unmanned" weapons into battle...

Manga adaptation available now!

WOLF & PARCHMENT, VOL. 1-6

The young man Col dreams of one day joining the holy clergy and departs on a journey from the bathhouse, Spice and Wolf. Winfiel Kingdom's prince has invited him to help correct the sins of the Church. But as his travels begin, Col discovers in his luggage a young girl with a wolf's ears and tail named Myuri who stowed away for the ride!

Manga adaptation available now!

SOLO LEVELING, VOL. 1-5

E-rank hunter Jinwoo Sung has no money, no talent, and no prospects to speak of—and apparently, no luck, either! When he enters a hidden double dungeon one fateful day, he's abandoned by his party and left to die at the hands of some of the most horrific monsters he's ever encountered.

Comic adaptation available now!

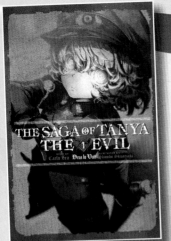